## Praise for *Stand Your Ground*

"Murray has written a tension-packed novel around the hot-buzz national topic of an unarmed black youth shot by a white male, an act then subjected to the Stand Your Ground rule as a legal defense tactic . . . Murray's writing admirably shows the often overlooked human emotions following racial violence . . . The pulled-from-the-headlines story line will captivate readers."

—*Library Journal* (starred review)

"Murray, winner of several African American Literary Awards for fiction, powerfully captures the nuances and tragedies engendered by stand-your-ground laws. A must-read."

—*Booklist* (starred review)

"Using a vivid, realistic premise, she takes a 360-degree view to bring all sides to the forefront for us to enjoy, learn from, judge, and celebrate. *Stand Your Ground* has great literary relevance for our time."

—*USA Today*

## Praise for *Forever an Ex*

"Murray spices up her story line with plenty of juicy scandals . . . Readers seeking an inspirational tale with broad themes of trust, betrayal, and forgiveness will do well by choosing Murray's latest effort."

—*Library Journal*

## Praise for *Fortune & Fame*

"The scandalous characters unite again in *Fortune & Fame*, Murray and Billingsley's third and best collaboration. This time brazen Jasmine and Rachel, who has zero shame, have been cast on *First Ladies*, a reality TV show that builds one's brand and threatens to break another's marriage. Sorry, buttered popcorn is not included."

—*Essence*

"Priceless trash talk marks this story about betrayal, greed, and stepping on anyone in your way. A great choice for folks who spend Sunday mornings in the front pew."

—*Library Journal*

## Praise for *Never Say Never*

"Readers, be on the lookout for Victoria Christopher Murray's *Never Say Never*. You'll definitely need to have a buddy-reader in place for the lengthy discussion that is bound to occur."

—*USA Today*

## Praise for *The Ex Files*

"The engrossing transitions the women go through make compelling reading . . . Murray's vivid portrait of how faith can move mountains and heal relationships should inspire."

—*Publishers Weekly*

"Reminds you of things that women will do if their hearts are broken . . . Once you pick this book up, you will not put it down."

—UrbanReviews.com

## Praise for *Destiny's Divas*

"With *Destiny's Divas*, author Victoria Christopher Murray triumphs again. The depth and storytelling mastery in her latest novel demonstrate why she is the grande dame of urban Christian fiction."

—FreshFiction.com

## Praise for *Sinners & Saints*

"Murray and Billingsley keep things lively and fun."

—*Juicy* magazine

"Double the fun, with a message of faith, *Sinners & Saints* will delight readers with two of their favorite characters from two of their favorite authors. It's a match made in heaven!"

—*Grace Magazine*

## Praise for *The Deal, the Dance, and the Devil*

"Murray's story has the kind of momentum that prompts you to elbow disbelief aside and flip the pages in horrified enjoyment."

—*The Washington Post*

## Praise for *Sins of the Mother*

"*Sins of the Mother* shows that when the going gets tough, it's best to make an effort and rely on God's strength. It gives the message that there is hope no matter what, and that people must have faith."

—FictionAddict.com

"Final word: Christian fiction with a powerful kick."

—Afro.com

## Praise for *Lady Jasmine*

"She's back! Jasmine has wreaked havoc in three VCM novels, including last year's *Too Little, Too Late*. In *Lady Jasmine* the schemer everyone loves to loathe breaks several commandments by the third chapter."

—*Essence*

"Jasmine is the kind of character who doesn't sit comfortably on a page. She's the kind who jumps inside a reader's head, runs around, and stirs up trouble—the kind who stays with the reader long after the last page is turned."

—*The Huntsville Times* (Alabama)

## Praise for *Too Little, Too Late*

"[In this book] there are so many hidden messages about love, life, faith, and forgiveness. Murray's vividness of faith is inspirational."

—*The Clarion-Ledger* (Jackson, Mississippi)

"An excellent entry in the Jasmine Larson Bush Christian Lit saga; perhaps the best so far . . . Fans will appreciate this fine tale . . . a well written intense drama."

—*Midwest Book Review*

## Praise for *A Sin and a Shame*

"Riveting, emotionally charged and spiritually deep . . . What is admirable is the author's ability to hold the reader in suspense until the very last paragraph of the novel! *A Sin and a Shame* is a must read . . . Truly a story to be enjoyed and pondered upon!"

—RomanceInColor.com

"*A Sin and a Shame* is Victoria Christopher Murray at her best . . . A page-turner that I couldn't put down as I was too eager to see what scandalous thing Jasmine would do next. And to watch Jasmine's spiritual growth was a testament to Victoria's talents. An engrossing tale of how God's grace covers us all. I absolutely loved this book!"

—ReShonda Tate Billingsley, *Essence* bestselling author of
*I Know I've Been Changed*

## Also by Victoria Christopher Murray

# LUST

*A Seven Deadly Sins Novel*

VICTORIA
CHRISTOPHER
MURRAY

TOUCHSTONE

New York   London   Toronto   Sydney   New Delhi

Touchstone
An Imprint of Simon & Schuster, Inc.
1230 Avenue of the Americas
New York, NY 10020

This book is a work of fiction. Any references to
historical events, real people, or real places are used fictitiously.
Other names, characters, places, and events are products of the author's
imagination, and any resemblance to actual events or places or
persons, living or dead, is entirely coincidental.

First Touchstone trade paperback edition February 2017

TOUCHSTONE and colophon are registered
trademarks of Simon & Schuster, Inc.

For information about special discounts for bulk purchases,
please contact Simon & Schuster Special Sales at 1-866-506-1949
or business@simonandschuster.com.

The Simon & Schuster Speakers Bureau can bring authors
to your live event. For more information or to book an event, contact
the Simon & Schuster Speakers Bureau at 1-866-248-3049 or
visit our website at www.simonspeakers.com.

Manufactured in the United States of America

10  9  8  7  6  5  4  3  2  1

Library of Congress Cataloging-in-Publication Data is available.

ISBN 978-1-5011-3410-4
ISBN 978-1-5011-3411-1 (ebook)

# LUST

# Tiffanie Cooper

It felt like we were in the middle of an earthquake, the way the bed trembled beneath me and Damon.

This was the christening of our brand-new mahogany sleigh bed—the designer piece that I saw in a magazine and just had to have for our new house. Even though it cost almost ten grand, Damon, my boo, hadn't even blinked when he saw the price.

Last night, the bed had been delivered and assembled, and although I had wanted to wait and share this bed for the first time on our wedding night, not even an hour had passed after the delivery men were gone before Damon and I were hitting the satin sheets.

Now, as the first rays of the new day seeped through the windows, bringing along the fragrance of the azaleas on the balcony, I was being treated to Damon's early-morning "good good."

"You like that, don't you?" Damon leaned over and whispered in my ear.

"Yes," I breathed with as much enthusiasm as I could push

into my voice. A second later, he cried out, and a moment after that, I mimicked him.

Damon was breathless as he fell on top of me and all I did was glance at the clock. Thank goodness that hadn't taken too long. Damon rolled away, still trying to steady his breathing. "Thank you, bae."

"What are you thanking me for?" I did my best to sound as out of breath as he was.

"For everything."

I twisted until I was on my back and glanced up at the ceiling, wanting to reach my hands to the heavens. Damon was thanking me? I was the one who needed to be thanking him . . . and God . . . for all that I'd been given.

There wasn't room, not in time or space, for me to count all my blessings. First, I'd just made love to my fiancé, a man who'd given me love when I'd never wanted this kind of love in my life, a man whose business filled his bank accounts with money but a man who made it his business to please me always. From the fifty-year-old Victorian-style home in the center of DC's gold coast, to the Harry Winston ring that I rocked on the second finger of my left hand, I was living a life that I'd never believed would be possible.

When I heard Damon's soft snores, I rolled onto my side. I just wanted to watch him for a moment before I had to shake him awake.

My Damon was such a beautiful, scrumptious dark brown man with full lips and a square and strong jawline. I often teased him about having a little Indian in his family because his closely cropped beard was a soft, smooth, jet-black layer of satin. His eyes were close to being catlike, and then there were the two, yes, two dimples that deepened in his right cheek whenever he smiled. All of that, all of him made me shake my head with pleasure every time I set my eyes on him.

I never thought it could be like this. Never thought I'd know a love like this. I sighed as I thought about all the years that I'd let pass by with Damon, but then I shook that thought away. I was here now, we were engaged now, five days away from being husband and wife. No more time wasted.

Slowly, his eyelids fluttered and when they opened and he looked at me, I saw nothing but lust in his eyes.

"Oh, no." I shook my head and giggled. "We have to get ready for church."

"Come on, Tiff." He pulled me close. "One last time before you cut me off," he said, referring to the fact that I told him I was going back to my place right after church.

"Don't be so dramatic." I scooted out of the bed, then strutted across the Berber carpet. Not that I wanted to trouble the waters—no, I'd had enough sex with my fiancé to last me more than awhile. But I was still a girl and I wanted my guy to want me. "I'm not cutting you off," I said, when I got halfway across the room. "I'm just trying to make our wedding night more special."

He propped himself up on his elbow and drank me in with his eyes. "Every night, every morning, every noon is special when I'm with you."

Dang! That was just another reason to love him. Because not only did he show me how much he loved me, he told me all the time.

"Why can't we just keep this going?" Damon said with a tinge of begging in his tone. "Why can't I make love to you every day and every night until we say 'I do'?"

I stared into his bedroom eyes and almost wanted to run back. Because he'd done so much for me, I always wanted to satisfy him. But I wasn't going to give in.

I'd already broken the promise I'd made when I was fourteen to remain chaste until marriage, even though, at the time, it was really my pledge to remain a virgin for life. But I'd told Damon that I was going to stay at my place because I was hoping that maybe with a few days of celibacy between now and "I do," not only would I feel like I'd done something right, but I was praying that these few days of abstention would make our wedding night special . . . for both of us.

Eyes glazed with lust, Damon reached his hands toward me. "Please!"

Inside this moment, all of his gangster was gone. There were no important people to meet, no celebrities to impress, no paychecks to sign, no Glock on his hip.

He was just a man who loved a woman.

"Tiffanie, please," he begged again.

My eyebrows rose just a bit hearing him call me Tiffanie. Though everyone else in the world addressed me by my full name (my grandfather demanded it, since Tiffanie meant Manifestation from God and he was the one who'd given that name to me), Damon was the only person who called me Tiff. And he only did that when my grandfather wasn't around.

So, using my full name right now meant that Damon was in full pleading mode, and I shouldn't have, but I laughed.

He tossed a pillow across the room, hitting me in the calf.

"Ouch!" I hopped, pretending to be wounded. Turning, I rushed back to the bed and jumped on top of him. He wrestled until he was on top, pinning my hands above my head. Then, with the gentleness of a gentle man, he kissed my forehead. Then my eyelids. Then my neck. "I love you," he said, his tone thick with a desire that I knew was only for me.

It was an instant fever, the way his words heated my skin.

"I need you to do me a favor," he whispered.

With the way he had me pressed beneath him, I could only imagine what Damon wanted me to do.

"Can you pick up Trey at the airport tomorrow?"

I blinked. "Trey?" I couldn't believe that in this moment, he was talking about the man he still called his best friend. "I thought he was coming in on Thursday."

"Change of plans. He's coming in early to see his grand-mother. This will be the first time he's seen her in seven years, you know what I'm sayin', and he wants to spend some time with her."

I'd met Ms. Irene and visited with her a few times over the years whenever I went with Damon, so I didn't want to begrudge that sweet woman a visit from her grandson. But still, I just couldn't make myself happy about Trey coming to town. And now, he was coming days early?

It was weird 'cause I'd never met Trey; but on the real, even sight unseen, I did not like this man. Yes, he was my man's best friend, but he was part of my man's past, an underground past that had landed Trey in federal prison with a sentence of twenty years for possession of drugs. And I just had a feeling, because of Damon's and his history, that he could interfere with Da-mon's and my future.

But how could I fight their connection? Damon King and Trey Taylor had lots of times gone by. They were childhood friends who'd met in kindergarten in one of DC's Southeast schools. Then two years after Damon graduated (but Trey didn't) from high school, they'd moved to Atlanta to celebrate the new millennium and to wreak major havoc in the streets and make major money in the game.

Damon's kiss pulled me back to his request. "So, can you do that?" It must've been because I didn't give him a quick response that he added, "I'd do it, but I have that call with Jaleesa Stone and her people; she wants to make sure I have everything in place for her red-carpet event. Remember, that'll be just a little more than a week after we get back, so I need to set it up as much as I can before we leave on Saturday." A pause. "So, please?"

My first response: No! Why can't you send one of your drivers or have him take Uber? My second response: I have so much to do for the wedding; I don't have that kind of time. My actual response: "Sure," because what else was I going to say to the man who would do anything for me?

Then he asked, "Can you do something else for me?"

Lust, once again, glazed his eyes and thickened the sound of his words. I almost wanted to do it again to see if *this* would be *the* time when Damon would finally satisfy me, but I had to shut this down.

He still had my hands pinned above my head when I said, "No, we have to get ready for church. You know how my grandfather is."

Damon chuckled. "And, I don't want to tangle with Reverend CJ Cooper."

"Then, you need to get your fine . . . naked . . . behind up off of me."

Damon leaned his face closer to mine. "What would your grandfather say if he heard you talking like that?"

"Probably the same thing he'd say to you if he found out that I won't be a virgin on my wedding night."

My words made Damon release me. "Hey, hey, hey! You can't blame that on me alone; you were there, too."

I laughed. "I'm just sayin', my grandfather would kill you if he knew about the things that you did to his innocent grand-daughter!" I paused, tilted my head, and gave Damon one of what I called my not-so-innocent glances. "So, do you still wanna . . ."

Damon didn't even let me finish. "Nah, you ruined it; I'm good." He pouted as he twisted completely off me, though he pulled me into his arms. "Let's just get ready for church."

"Great idea," I said.

"But after church . . ."

"Mr. King, you are a mess!" I shook my head as I pushed him away. "Remember . . . our wedding night. Special."

Damon poked his lips out even more.

"Please don't be mad." I leaned over and kissed him the way he'd kissed me: On his forehead, his neck, and I finally settled my lips on his. And right beneath me, I felt this man melting.

That's when I started melting, too. How could I not? This man showed me that I, Tiffanie Cooper, had his heart and would have it forever. And for the rest of our lives, Damon King would have my heart, too.

# 2

# Damon King

Y ou're not there yet?" I tried my best to keep my voice calm, but I couldn't hide my agitation. Really, I had more than a little attitude, I was pissed. I mean, I had called Tiffanie early enough to get her up, figuring if she got out of bed at seven, she could make it to DCA by nine. But she'd used my first call like I was a snooze button and when I'd called back at almost 8:30, my woman was still asleep.

"Well, how much farther?" I asked. "His plane probably landed already."

"I'm pulling into the airport now," she said, then hung up without saying good-bye, letting me know that now she had an attitude, too.

Glancing at the clock, I was a little impressed. It was 9:27; in less than an hour, Tiffanie had dressed and made her way to the airport, even at the tail end of the morning rush hour. I'd told her Trey's plane was landing at 8:45 'cause I knew my girl. By the time she parked and got inside the terminal, she'd be right on time, since his plane wasn't landing until 9:45.

Leaning back in my seat, I sighed. Maybe I shouldn't have

been so hard on Tiffanie, but if I were being honest, her going back to sleep this morning wasn't the issue. It was the fact that she had kept her word and gone back to her place yesterday after church, leaving me to sleep in that big ole new bed by myself. Yeah, I was in a funky mood because no matter what I did last night—and I ain't too proud to admit that I had begged—Tiffanie still hadn't come home to me.

The problem was, though, I didn't have to look that deep to know that Tiffanie was right. I mean, there wasn't a lot that was right about our sexual situation; Tiffanie and I had been holding it down in bed for the last couple of years, though it had been work to get to even that point. At first, I'd been all about hittin' that, but that hit had made a quick left to love. That was my bottom line—I loved that woman and couldn't get enough of her.

But I guess after our long three-year engagement, what was a little more time? If having four sexless days were important to her before we stood in front of God and her grandfather, then I was going to do it. On Friday she'd be mine—all alone and all the time.

"I promise, I won't hassle you about this anymore." I made that promise as if she were standing in front of me.

But on Friday night? On our honeymoon? Forget about touring Dubai; the most I planned to see of that city were the sights I could take in from the hotel window.

I swung my chair around, needing to get my mind right. I had to stop thinking about Tiffanie and our honeymoon or I wasn't going to be ready for this call with Jaleesa.

I opened the folder that my assistant, Hillary, had laid out on my desk, but now, instead of thinking about my girl, my thoughts shifted to my boy.

Just thinking about seeing Trey in an hour or so made me lean back, take in the moment, and smile. It had been too many years. We'd hooked up a couple of times after I'd left him in Atlanta, but once he got locked down, I'd locked him out.

It wasn't that I wanted to leave my boy out there like that. It was just something that my father had taught me:

*Don't associate your name with or on anything that's connected to someone on the inside. Because what folks don't know is that they watch those on the inside and their connections on the outside.*

It was a lesson from my father, Jerome King, who was the truth—at least when it came to matters of the street. He'd raised me, or should I say he *mostly* raised me. The amount of time we spent together was limited by the amount of time he spent in jail. My childhood memories were filled with him being on the inside way more than he was ever on the outside. But he was still my teacher, passing on to me a perspective that I needed. He didn't want me in prison. Period. That was the extent of his dreams for me, but he was serious about his responsibility to make that happen.

So even though the only opportunities I ever saw came to me from the streets, I wasn't gonna be *that* cat. I had the same dream for my life as my father. That's why I had no choice but to handle Trey the way I had when he went to prison.

Four ounces.

Twenty years.

I never thought I'd see my boy again. But the thing was, I hadn't left Trey out there alone. He just didn't know that I had his back the entire time he was locked up.

Slamming the folder shut, I pushed back from my desk. I needed to get my mind into my business. I hadn't gotten to this level without strict discipline, but right now, it was hard to concentrate. Standing in front of the window that covered the whole wall, I took in this grand view of U Street. Trey and I weren't even teenagers when we worked this block, first as runners for Smooth Luke, one of my father's connects, then for ourselves after we started buying our own bricks. At fifteen, sixteen, and seventeen, we had more money in our pockets than most people who lived in this neighborhood then earned in five years.

But U Street was a different place now. No longer was it the pulse of the ghetto. Now, the U Street Corridor was a bustling section of this metropolis with hardly a black face in sight. Chocolate City had turned from dark to white in the seven years that Trey had actually served.

Seven years.

In prison.

The guilt I had to push away every few weeks passed over me like a shadow. And with that old guilt came that old thought: Maybe if I'd been down there in Atlanta with Trey, I could have controlled him and he wouldn't have done that time. But like I always did, I pushed that thought aside. No matter where I was or wasn't, no matter what I said or didn't, this story would have had the same ending—because of Trey Taylor.

*"You know we don't need to be getting in any beefs with those boys over in Northeast."*

*"You should have let me handle him," Trey said as he slammed his fist against the dashboard of my first car.*

*I kept the car moving because I wasn't trying to catch any kind of Five-O attention. But if Trey put any marks on my Mustang, he and I were gonna have a situation.*

*I kept my calm, kept my voice steady as I tried to school my boy. "This is business, Trey. You need to stop taking things so personally."*

*He looked at me as if fingers were growing out of my ears. "It was business that he made personal. Don't no white boy call me boy."*

*I sighed. How many times was I going to have to check this cat? He was my boy and everything, but there was always something; we were always on the verge of some kind of blowup.*

*"We're seventeen; to most people we are still boys. Plus, what difference does it make what he calls you as long as you got his money?"*

*"Yeah, well, that may be how you handle it, but I need more than his money, he better give me his respect, too. He's lucky that I didn't have my piece on me."*

*"And what would that have done? Suppose he had a piece?"*

*"You think that matters to me? I fear no man."*

Just like back then, my head started to throb. Over the years of our brotherhood, I'd had to check Trey too many times. I'd had to talk us out of too many beefs. My boy was wild with a spirit that listened to no one, especially not me. He'd head left just because I said go right. He hated that I was the decision maker.

But that's how it had to be because no one wanted to deal with Trey and his hot head; I'd tried to tell him that a cool head always claimed victory. But Trey believed that rolling up on someone defined him as a man.

Trey'd been the reason why I'd finally quit the game. Between his mouth and his temper, I felt the tick of the clock. Someone was going to come for us—either another player or Five-O.

So when it was time to leave, I left. But I couldn't convince Trey to get out with me because he lived on adrenaline and the edge and he wasn't afraid to serve time.

That right there was his problem. He liked the fact that he'd had a few short stays; that added to his street-cred résumé. As long as a shorty came to hit him up once in a while, he had money on his books, and he had access to his Mary Jane, he was straight.

Until.

Four ounces.

Twenty years.

Moving away from the window, I hoped that by the time I got to my desk, my mind would be back to business. But when I sat down, it was still all about Trey. What I wanted to believe was that this hard time had been a good thing. Maybe in a twisted kind of way, this bid had changed him, had helped him to get some sense.

And if he had changed, then I was ready to do all that I could to help. While he was here, I was gonna talk to him, feel him out, and if I liked what I saw, I'd set him up, have him work with me.

The thought of that made me smile, 'cause as rough as the bad times were, it really was all about good times. Trey was my brother and I could imagine us standing shoulder to shoulder again.

But the wild card—had Trey changed? And that question brought along a bunch of others—if Trey hadn't changed, could I work with him again? Could I trust him? Would he (knowingly or unknowingly) ever bring me down?

So many questions.

The vibration from my cell phone broke my thoughts.

**Are you ready for your call with Jaleesa? She and her agent are on the line and I will connect you.**

I texted back: **Y**

That was all Hillary needed, and by the time my cell phone rang, I had flipped from personal to professional.

"What's up, Jaleesa?" I said to the former model, former talk show host, now minister, who was the breakout star of a reality show and would, in the fall, be starring in her own series.

Right now, my head was back into my business. I'd handle this and in about an hour, it would be all about my friend; then I'd have all the answers I'd need.

# 3

# Tiffanie

He was just a man. This was just an airport. But both that man and this airport had my blood pressure rising.

I jumped from the car and sprinted across the lot, even though I didn't feel stable running in these four-inch-heel red bottoms. Really, I shouldn't have been running—I shouldn't have even been walking. Trey's behind should have met me at curbside, but Damon wanted Trey's homecoming to be more personal.

I slowed my steps and tried to pull back all the negativity that was rolling through my mind. The only reason I was upset was because this was Trey. I would've met any of my friends right at the gate if I could get past TSA.

It was crazy that I had these feelings for a man I'd never met. It was just that I had heard too many stories about him that I just didn't like. Now, of course, Damon had told me all about his role and the things he'd done. But a person only had to spend two seconds with my boo to know that he'd changed. It wasn't hard to see Damon's heart. He'd been changed from the inside.

But Trey? He hadn't changed. I knew that because when

Damon and I first met, I would hear him on the phone trying to school his friend, but Trey didn't want to learn. And so what happened? Prison! And he was probably harder now than before. That's why I felt he didn't need to be anywhere near my man.

But on some ole program for nonviolent criminals, Trey had been released, just in time for our wedding, and Damon wanted him to be there. It didn't make a lot of sense to me; seven years was a long time not to see someone and still call him your best friend. But Damon explained to me that just because you hadn't seen your brother, no amount of time passing would ever take away the fact that you were brothers.

I tried to understand that, though if I had to explain it to anyone, it felt like Damon was trying to make up for the lost time to Trey, especially since it was Trey's idea to stand up for Damon.

All I could do was pray that Trey would stand next to Damon on Friday night, and then be on the first thing heading back to Atlanta on Saturday morning.

I rushed into the terminal, peeped at the screen, and released a deep breath when I saw that Trey's plane had just hit the tarmac.

I strolled over to the carousel where his bags would be and took a moment to calm down and focus my thoughts. There were so many things I had to do this week, and I pulled out my phone to review my personal to-do list. Today alone, I had to meet our wedding planner at the Willard to review the seating arrangements, and then run over to check on my grandmother's dress. As I scanned the checklist, my mind kept wandering back to my favorite subject, Damon King, and right away, I smiled.

Yeah, he had an attitude this morning, but how could I be mad at my baby? All I had to do was think about all that he'd done for me, from the fabulous gifts that he gave me—usually wrapped in one of those little blue boxes from a store that shared my name—to the credit cards I had for all the top designer stores. And then there were the gifts that really mattered—the thousands of dollars he'd given me so that I could finish my last two years at Howard, the opportunities he'd provided to help me polish my social skills in a Jack and Jill sort of way, the events he took me to: legacy banquets with Oprah, political fund-raisers where I'd even met Michelle Obama.

His goodness rained down on me, yet one of the best gifts was still a month away—because of this man, I was about to have my own business.

My grandparents always told me that my blessings began the day I was born; not that I ever believed them. How could I, once I became old enough to understand why I was living with them and not my mother?

But then, one day back in 2008, I began to feel that maybe God hadn't forgotten about me. I leaned back on the post where I stood, closed my eyes, and remembered . . .


May 27, 2008

HOWARD UNIVERSITY. THE Blackburn Center. Waiting to speak to my financial adviser and praying that he could help me. I shook as I waited—not out of fear, just anticipation. Two years of college and every bill had been paid. But now there were two years in front of me, and even though I had walked by the faith that my grandparents had taught me, I couldn't figure out how faith was going to get me to graduation.

My grandparents had already scraped together what little they had, and without their sacrifices, I wouldn't have made it this far. Howard had done its part, too, with a partial scholarship that covered what my grandparents couldn't.

But now, facing my junior year, expenses were going to be higher by a third. Everything, from textbooks to housing, cost more. My grandparents told me to come back home to save money on room and board, but now that I'd tasted this morsel of freedom, there was no way I was going back to living under my grandfather's roof and rules. The lock he kept me under didn't even have a key. I knew it was because he loved me, I knew it was because he didn't want me to end up like my mother. But his love didn't let me breathe and I had come to love all the inhales and exhales of my life.

So, if I wanted to graduate, if I wanted to stay on campus, if I wanted to continue living this life . . . I needed cash money.

I picked up the current issue of *The Hilltop* and flipped through the pages, hoping one of the articles would keep my attention until Mr. York called me into his office. But then, something caught my eye, and it wasn't anything in the school newspaper. Actually, it wasn't just my eyes that were distracted. It was more like—all of me; like a feeling swept over, then hovered above me. I looked up to search for what had upset my equilibrium and at the front door, there stood this brother.

Even though he was feet away, I could tell that he wasn't a student. He was way too distinguished-looking in that tailored suit, looking like a model in an ad for life after graduation. As he strolled closer, I saw the diamond earring that glittered from his lobe and the gold diamond-laced watch that peeked from under the hem of his sleeve.

But what really gave him away, besides all of his sophistication and apparent money, the real reason why I knew he was a full-fledged man, was because of the way he moved. He strutted like he knew all about life.

My lips parted as I watched him, and I hoped that he didn't think I was gawking. It was just that I couldn't take my eyes off what looked like power personified. I was impressed with his importance.

As he turned toward the information desk, his eyes met mine. He stopped. He stared. He pivoted. And then, without speaking to anyone else, he came straight toward me.

He stood just a few inches outside of my personal space and said, "I can fix it."

I blinked and even turned to my right and left because I couldn't figure out a couple of things: number one, was he speaking to me? And number two, if he was, what did he mean? "What?" I asked.

"Whatever you need, whatever you want," he said, with his catlike eyes laser-focused on mine, "I'll give it to you."

Then he sat down next to me. At any other time, I might have gotten up and moved, just because I didn't want to be pulled into a conversation, but with the man who'd introduced himself as Damon King, I wanted to stay.

"And your name?" he asked.

"Tiffanie Cooper."

He held his hand out and I shook it, remembering all the things I'd learned about being professional: keep your handshake as strong as your eye contact.

"So, what is it that you need?" he asked. "How can I help you?"

I hesitated, because for a second I wondered if he were some kind of pervert. But then, if he were, why would he be so dressed up and hanging out in the financial aid office of a college?

"I don't think you can help me; I'm here to talk to my adviser."

"So, you're a student here?"

I resisted the urge to say, 'Duh,' and just nodded. "I'm a rising junior, and it's time for me to get a job."

He grinned. "See? I told you I could help you. I'm looking for an intern to expand my company and you're the woman to help me."

The word *pervert* came back to my mind because his response was a little too convenient. "What kind of company do you have?"

"Oh, I do a little of this and a little of that."

What in the world?

"I really have several small companies all rolled into one," he said, explaining further. "Entertainment, real estate, anything that can make money in this new millennium."

"So you're looking for an intern?"

He nodded. "And like I said, you're the woman who can help me make this happen."

I tossed the magazine I'd been holding back onto the table and shook my head. "I'm not looking for an internship; I need a paying job."

He frowned. "What do you mean?"

"Internships. They give you experience, but no money."

"Who would work for no money?"

"Exactly!" I said.

"Well, my internship pays."

Once again, this man had my attention. "How much?"

"How much do you need?"

I laughed out loud and he grinned. But he didn't get it because he asked, "What's so funny?"

"You . . . asking me . . . how much money I want to make."

"What's wrong with that?"

When I'd first laid my eyes on this brother, I thought he was the sophisticated, intelligent type. Now, I didn't know if he was playing me or had just gotten off some kind of boat. But if he were playing, I was gonna play him. I decided to give him a number—around the minimum wage and then increase it by two dollars. "I'm looking to earn about eight dollars an hour."

Not a beat passed before he said, "I'll give you twenty."

I had to look stupid with the way my mouth opened as wide as my eyes. "An hour?"

"What? That's not enough?" he asked, though I could tell he was amused. "Do you want twenty-five?"

"No, no . . . I mean, yes, yes. I mean, I'll take twenty or twenty-five. Either one. That's more than enough!" But then I pushed pause and rewound my excitement.

I leaned back a little to get a clearer view of this joker. Now that he was sitting down, I noticed the diamond studs in *both* of his ears, big and bright. A quick glance at his watch gave me the same impression. Who was this guy and what did he do to be able to offer me that kind of money? And . . . what did he want *me* to do for twenty or twenty-five dollars an hour?

"I'm not looking to get caught up in anything that's not legal," I told him, thinking that he was just some drug dealer. But I told him this with attitude so he'd understand I wasn't some naive little girl.

"Do you think I'd be here—at Howard—looking for an intern if I wasn't legit? If I wanted just anybody to do just anything, I could find that girl anywhere."

Okay, he had a point. But still, some kind of catch had to come with that kind of offer. "And, I'm not interested in . . . you know . . ."

"What?" he said. When I didn't respond, he added, "You're not interested in . . . something sexual?"

The way he said it made heat rise to my cheeks, but I said, "Yeah," as boldly as I could.

He laughed. "Sweetheart, if I were looking for sex, there are easier ways for me to find it instead of coming down to the Student Office. I'd just head straight to the dorms."

Okay, he had another point. But, I needed to make my points, too. My voice was still strong and solid when I told him, "I'm just sayin', I do everything on the up-and-up. I'm straight."

"That you are."

It was more than just needing the money that made me say, "So, if you are, too, then you got yourself a new intern." I felt like I could trust him.

I never saw my financial adviser that afternoon; no need, since I started my new position as Damon King's personal assistant the next day . . .

The sound of people—their chatter and their movement made me open my eyes. I must've had one of those "Damon grins" on my face because folks were giving me those what's-got-you-so-happy stares. Whew! They just didn't even know.

There was just one blip in my wonderful life.

Our lovemaking.

I wanted to slap myself for thinking about that. Everything

else was beyond good—why couldn't I just be satisfied? And it wasn't like I was an expert on good or bad sex, since I'd had no experience before Damon.

With a deep sigh, I looked up and my eyes settled on a man. And my glance got stuck right there. He strutted toward me, wearing a smile—no, it was more of a smirk that said, *I can make you happy.*

I inhaled a quick breath. And then another when he walked right up to me.

Now, it wasn't that I didn't know who he was. Damon's description had been spot-on: six-three, 220 or 230 pounds.

"He's about my complexion," Damon had told me. "And the last time I saw Trey, he was sporting a bald head."

Damon was right on every single count, though there had been no need to give that complete description. He could have just told me to find the finest, swaggiest man in the airport.

Because that's what Trey was. It was more than his looks, it was the way he moved, with a little dip in his strut. With confidence so cool it made me weak, and I'm not talking about in a laughing kind of way.

Without any real conscious thought, I crossed my legs and squeezed my thighs together. I had never done that before—not even while reading the sexiest scenes in a book. But something was going on south of the border and I had to get it under control.

As Trey came closer, my focus shifted from his swagger to his eyes. His golden-brown eyes were piercing, as if he could see right through . . . my clothes. That scared me—could he see my yearning?

"You must be Tiffanie," he said in a deep, melodic voice that tore straight through to my center.

He wrapped one arm around my waist, pulled me into his chest as if he knew me, and pressed his lips against my cheek.

His lips lingered and lingered and lingered.

And after about the third second, I shuddered.

And shuddered.

And shuddered.

Then I wilted.

After that long, slow, earth-shaking moment, he released me and I prayed that he hadn't felt the way I trembled. But he must have because he stepped back, searched my eyes like he was one of DC's finest, and then broke into a little chuckle.

"Let me go get my bags," he said as if he'd just done his job and now he was on to the next task.

My eyes followed him as he strutted away and I tried to wrap my mind around what had just happened. A man I didn't know said my name, kissed my cheek, and a tremor went through my body like that?

I inhaled a couple of deep, quick breaths, but I never took my eyes off him.

"What just happened?" I whispered.

And then, as if he'd heard me, he twisted around. And winked.

And right there, I shuddered and wilted again.

# 4

# Tiffanie

This was nothing but pure torture.

Being inside the car with Trey tested every single fiber of my will. There wasn't enough space. His presence felt dangerous, perilous . . . and gave me a thrill that I didn't understand.

"It sure is hotter here than I expected it to be," he said.

I looked down at my dashboard, where the digital thermometer showed 46 degrees.

He just had to add, "Yeah, hot and sticky."

My heart raced and the little hairs on my arms stood all the way up.

I stayed silent and he kept on talking. "I don't know what it is," he began, "but something's got me all fired up."

The car's brakes squealed as I slammed them hard. "Oh, my God," I screeched, staring at the back of the Lexus SUV that was just millimeters from the front of my BMW. At the speed I was traveling, we would've been dead for sure.

But though my heart was beating hard for a different reason

now, Trey didn't seem fazed. He just looked at me and chuckled. As if a close call with death was a regular, everyday occurrence for him.

"Sorry," I said and turned my eyes back to the road. I gripped the steering wheel, determined to concentrate, no matter what Trey said. No matter what was going on between my legs. "I'd better slow down."

"That's cool, 'cause I like it fast, but I can certainly handle it slow, too."

I couldn't believe this—Trey was flirting with me! But in the next instant, I talked myself out of that madness. This was Damon's boy, his man, a hundred grand. A dude didn't play with his boy's main woman. Since I was Damon's main—and only— woman, this had to be all in my head.

"What about you, Tiffanie? You're driving slow, but when you ride, do you like to go fast or slow?"

Okay, I wasn't imagining it. And this wasn't even flirting. This was almost like—he was making me an offer!

I gripped the steering wheel even tighter, but this time, it was as much to control myself as the car. I needed to keep my hands wrapped around that wheel before I reached over and touched him.

Because that's what I wanted to do. To steal a little touch of his hands or maybe his head. I paused, took a quick glance, and my gaze landed right between his legs.

What was wrong with me? Shake it off, I told myself. Just shake this devil off!

I couldn't pull up to the Georgian—an exclusive office building located in the heart of DC's U Street Corridor—fast enough. When I turned over the keys to the valet, I wanted to do a happy dance. But I couldn't do anything except walk and focus on keeping my knees from knocking.

"Damn! Take a look at this," Trey said. Hoisting his garment bag onto his shoulder, he looked first down one end of the block and then in the opposite direction.

I knew what Trey was talking about. He hadn't lived in DC since 2000, and this wasn't the same city.

And the city wasn't the only thing that had changed. I wondered what Trey really knew about Damon's success. Did he know that Damon had taken advantage of gentrification and not only purchased real estate in the area but also made this the center of his business, King Commotions?

"Yeah, things have changed," I said as Trey followed me into the building.

I felt his eyes behind me. As we waited for the elevator, the heat of his stare burned me. This man was setting me on fire, but I refused to turn around. When the elevator doors opened, I wanted to cheer; I'd made it. But once we'd stepped into the small chamber, Trey stood way too close.

I felt his breath on my neck and then, with a deep breath of my own, I took in his scent, a blend of sandalwood and cedar and leather. He smelled like pure man.

Inside the car, I'd wanted to touch him; now I wanted to lean back, fall into his chest, and feel his lips on my cheek just once more. Maybe this time, I'd turn my head so that our lips could meet and our tongues could dance.

I could feel that kiss.

Dang! I was dreaming with my eyes open!

"Can you feel that?" he whispered into my ear.

My mouth opened wide. Had he heard what I was thinking? Before I could turn around and ask him, the elevator doors parted.

And there was Damon!

Waiting for me.

# 5

# Tiffanie

I had no choice but to fall into my man's open arms.

"Hey, bae," Damon said, frowning just a bit. With the tips of his fingers, he wiped the perspiration from my forehead. "Are you all right?"

Oh. My. God. How was I supposed to explain sweating when it wasn't even 50 degrees outside? I was twenty-eight, not forty-eight, so I couldn't claim menopause.

"Tiff?"

I shrugged because I wasn't sure what my voice would sound like. Plus, what would I say? *Hey, your friend is so fine that I just want him to stroke me from one end of the earth to the other?*

"You good?" he asked me.

This time I nodded.

I guess that was enough, because he looked at me for only a moment longer and turned to Trey. Damon's grin was big and welcoming when he said, "What's up, son?"

The two greeted each other with the universal black man's handshake and hug, and I used that moment to make my getaway. I tore into the bathroom and almost broke down the door the way I barged inside. Stumbling like a drunkard, I made it to the sink and gripped the edge, using it to hold myself steady.

A minute passed. Then another. And another.

I was still wobbly when I turned on the faucet, then used my palms to toss cold water onto my face.

*Can you feel that?*

What had Trey meant when he said that? Had he been thinking what I'd been feeling?

"Get it together, Tiffanie." I shook off my leather jacket and laid it on the counter. "There is nothing for him to think because there's nothing for you to feel. Damon. Remember? Your fiancé. Remember?"

I moaned at the thought of the man I loved. Bringing Damon to my mind at this moment wasn't exactly the solution; there was nothing in my memory that I could grasp about Damon that would help to stop the foolishness going on inside of me. The only thing thinking about Damon did was make me want Trey even more.

I pulled the turtleneck of my sweater away from my neck and waved my hand, trying to push cool air inside. But I was still thinking about that kiss. Dang, it was only on my cheek. With that, Trey had done what I'd been yearning to feel with Damon.

I leaned back against the tiled wall and closed my eyes. In less than two hours, Trey Taylor had changed my life. Well, maybe not my whole life, but my consciousness . . . my sexual awareness. Just thinking about it filled me with an urge to shudder again, filled me with a want to have another . . . orgasm. My eyes popped open. Was that an orgasm?

No! It couldn't be.

It was a doggone shame that at my age, I just didn't know. I'd been that girl, a twenty-three-year-old virgin when Damon and I did it for the first time. I wasn't untouched because I had to be, though it would have been difficult to be living that life under my grandfather's heavy thumb. But even when I got to Howard, I just wasn't interested. Actually, that's not even right—I just didn't want it. I didn't want sex; I didn't want that thing that had destroyed my mother.

But enter Damon King. He'd had to fight to get me, but once we'd made it official, I was ready to experience all that my girlfriends were telling me sex could be. And I was sure that this man, seven years my senior, would bring it. But the first time we lay together—nothing; the second time, even less. Weeks turned into five years of nada, naught, zilch.

In the beginning, I'd talked to my best friend about it, but Sonia had been no help.

"Oh, my goodness! *¡Por fin lo hizo!*"

I looked around Busboys and Poets, hoping that no one else in the restaurant understood her. "Sssshhh," I admonished my Latina friend, who always blurted out Spanish here and there in our conversations, even though I couldn't speak a bit of that language. But I'd been hanging out with her since seventh grade, so I understood enough when she reverted to her native tongue.

With my hand, I motioned for her to bring it down a level. Then I whispered, "Yes, we finally did it, but can you just focus?"

"*Bueno.*" Pushing her veggie burger to the side, she leaned across the table. "I'm sorry. It's just that you finally let yourself go. I didn't think that you ever would." She reached across the table and covered my hand with hers. "*Estoy tan feliz,*" she said, telling me she was so happy. And were those real tears in her eyes?

It was a bit dramatic for me, but I understood my friend's

theatrics. She knew why I'd kept myself chaste all these years; she knew that it was because I'd been afraid of being cursed.

"So," Sonia finally breathed, "was it just amazing?"

I paused. "That's not quite the word I'd use." I let another moment pass before I added, "We made love but, I didn't feel . . . anything."

After a "Hmmmm" and a couple of pensive moments, she asked, "Are you holding back?"

I shook my head. "No, I don't think so. And why would I?" When she gave me a long look as her answer, I said, "No. Once I decided to do it, I was all in. I love Damon, you know that. So I wanted to love him in every way. But I don't"—I slowed my words down—"*feel . . . anything* when I'm with him."

She gave me a couple of slow nods and waved her hand. "That's just because he doesn't know your body yet. And you don't know him." She paused. "Be patient. It will get better, I promise." Then she gave me another one of those proud mama looks.

I was glad that she was happy, because I wasn't. Once I'd decided to finally have sex with Damon, I'd expected my eyes to cross and my toes to tingle. I'd expected to be shouting "Hallelujah" while falling backward into that abyss of ecstasy that *everyone* talked about.

But now, as I faced my reflection in this bathroom mirror, I spoke the truth out loud. "Damon wasn't hitting it." In fact, I was being generous, because in the five years since we'd been together, he hadn't hit it once.

I'd convinced myself that maybe this was the way sex was for *the real people* and I just needed to give it up. Not literally, but give it up in my mind.

I'd done that.

Until now.

I never thought I'd be turned out.

Turned out. By Trey.

And then . . . another thought. If Trey could do that with his lips, I wondered what he could do with . . .

Really, Tiffanie? I sighed and shook my head. Is this how it had been for my mother? Is this feeling that I'd been yearning to have with Damon what had ruined her? Is this what had her, the good Christian girl, the pastor's daughter, turned out when she was only seventeen? All I'd had was a little taste and now I felt almost . . . obsessed.

Maybe the curse that I believed I'd had all these years had been real. And maybe that was why, after all this time, Damon couldn't satisfy me. Maybe God had really been keeping me. Maybe this was why He'd chosen Damon for me. So that I would never *feel* this, never get consumed with something that could lead to death.

"Get it together, Tiffanie," I whispered to my reflection, now understanding the true blessing of Damon. He was a good man and it was a good thing that he didn't turn me on and hadn't turned me out.

Reaching for the faucet once again, I splashed lots more water on my face, ruining my makeup, but that was fine. Then I paced, taking the moments to silence my thoughts. I didn't want to think about Trey, I just needed to remember what happened to my mother.

When my mind was back to the place where it needed to be, I reapplied my makeup, finger-combed my hair, and set my game face in place.

I was ready to go back to the girl I'd been when I awakened this morning.

But then I took one last look at my eyes and they told a different story. And the fluttering in my stomach did, too.

I'd experienced that feeling and now, I just knew that I would never be the same.

# 6

# Damon

**M**an, I knew you were doing good, but I didn't know you had it like this!" Trey said as he settled into one of the oversize leather chairs in front of my desk.

Even though he'd said this before while I gave him a tour of my operation that took up the entire seventh floor, I still grinned. It felt good to show my boy how I'd flipped my game.

"So, Damon, you like this square life?" he asked.

I noticed that as he asked that question, he was peeping the framed photo of Tiffanie on the corner of my desk.

I couldn't help the little bit of a frown that squeezed between my eyebrows. "Yeah." I readjusted the photo so that Trey would look at me.

When his eyes finally drew back to mine, he said, "Looks like leaving the Big A was wise. And coming home, even wiser. You did good, bruh."

He was right, but I wasn't the braggadocios type. I do all right," I said, maintaining my humble. "You know me, though. I'd always tried to have a mind for business. But I didn't do anything special . . . just put my ducks in a row, got to work, and made a little something happen."

Trey's eyes swept around my office again. "Looks like you did more than a little somethin'."

I watched as his glance took in every part of the room that I'd paid a top designer top dollar to decorate. His eyes focused on it all: the marble bar with the wrought-iron stools, the original wall paintings by a young street artist whom I'd set up in his own gallery just a few blocks away, the crystal chandelier that hung right over his head. I could tell that all he saw was wreaking havoc on his senses and all I'd accomplished was messing with his mind.

Was that why his eyes kept wandering back to the photo of my lady?

Every time Trey glanced at her picture, he sank deeper into the leather Empire chair as if he were getting more comfortable. But I got distracted for a moment because Trey was getting cozy in the place where Tiffanie and I got our freak on from time to time.

I chuckled as I thought about the last time Tiffanie had sat on my lap in that chair and Trey gave me one of those what's-so-funny looks.

Clearing my throat and my mind, I said, "Yeah, yeah, I guess I did do more than a little something. But this ain't no different from what we were doing. I'm taking care of business; the only difference is I don't have to keep looking over my shoulder. But I've worked hard and now, I'm just reaping what I've been sowing."

Now it was his eyebrows that bunched into a frown, though his eyes were filled with laughter. "Reaping? Sowing?" He buckled over like that was one of the funniest things he'd ever heard.

"Seems like you came home and got more than a little money; you got a little religion, too."

I laughed with him because I didn't mind being the punch line of this kind of joke. I had changed—a lot—and it was good that Trey was seeing and understanding.

I wanted him to understand something else.

"My only regret," I began, "my only wish is that you had come back here with me. You and I . . . us . . . together, we could have taken this city to a whole 'nother level."

He paused as if he were contemplating my words, as if he were remembering all the times that he'd turned me down. I wondered if he was thinking about all the lessons I'd tried to pass on to him. And I wondered if any of those lessons, along with the time he'd done—had any of that made him ready to listen to me?

"So you turned in your G-card," Trey said.

I shook my head. "You know I still know how to handle mines." I wasn't like Trey; no one in or out of the game considered me a hothead, but my name was known and respected. I never went after anybody, just handled those who came for me. I did what I had to do to show the rest that I was that onetime gangsta, never to be messed with, no matter how straight my game had become.

I'd been tested. When I first came back to DC, I'd had to handle a couple of situations, but it had been a few years now since I'd been challenged or disrespected. 'Cause the word was out—disrespecting Damon King still came with a price tag.

"Yeah, I'm sure you still do handle yours," Trey said. "But it doesn't seem like there's much to handle up here." He looked around my office again. "You seem more Wall Street than U Street."

I laughed. "Son, these days, U Street ain't nothing but Wall Street."

He laughed with me and I took that moment to really study my boy. He looked the same, really not even a year older. I was glad to see that doing some time hadn't turned him hard, at least not visibly. But my other questions were still skating through my head. Had he changed and could he be trusted?

His glance returned once again to Tiffanie's picture. "So what's the major arm of King Commotions?" It seemed like he had to struggle to bring his eyes back to me. "What's your major business?"

"Setting it out for the rich and famous," I told him. "Any happenin' DC red-carpet events go through me. One weekend I'm doing an event for some rappers, and the next weekend I'm in black tie with some politicians."

Trey chuckled. "That's what's up. You hanging with the Obamas or the Trumps?"

"Both! They all got money."

"I hear you."

Then his eyes did that roving thing again and I kinda felt like I was gonna have to damn near lay the picture frame flat for him to stop staring at Tiffanie like that. Finally, he glanced at me, but only for a second before he went right back to the photo. With a nod, he said, "Your girl . . ."

"Yeah?"

"She's phat as a motherf—"

I leaned forward just a little, stopping him before he cursed my woman. "Yo, son, slow your roll. That's my wife." Even though I had somehow put a smile on my face, I was straight up serious. Trey knew me well enough to know that what I had with Tiffanie was real. I was getting ready to wife this girl and life didn't get any realer than that.

"Ah, let me step back," Trey said, holding up his hands like he was surrendering to the police. "You know I didn't mean nothing; Tiffanie seems like . . . a nice girl."

As if that were her cue, Tiffanie pushed the door open and strutted into the office. My woman looked good; her makeup was fresh and that leather bomber hugged her, making her look like one of those magazine models.

But it was the look in her eyes that knocked me a little off-center. She had this mischievous glint and as she strolled closer, she never took her eyes off me. Once she was in my personal space, she leaned down and kissed me with the kind of passion that she usually saved for our bedroom.

Now, Trey was my boy, but thoughts of entertaining him went right out the window. 'Cause all I could think about was how last night I hadn't gotten mines. Maybe that's what Tiffanie was thinking about, too.

I kissed my woman back, though I was surprised by Tiffanie's public display of affection. This wasn't anything like my girl. But whatever had her like this, I savored our kiss, hating it when she finally pulled back.

I loved this woman.

Even though all I wanted to do was kick Trey out so that Tiffanie and I could handle our business right there in that chair, I couldn't do that. Because after all of these years, today had to be about Trey since he'd made this trip up here just for me . . . well, and his grandmother, too. But his offering to stand up for me was a brother-brother thing that I would never forget.

Glancing over at him, he just sat there, looking like he wasn't even a little uncomfortable. His hands were folded in his lap and he nodded as if he was enjoying and approved of our little love show.

Standing up, I put my arms around Tiffanie. "You ready to go to lunch?"

She nodded, but when she wrapped her arms around my waist, her eyes narrowed. She didn't have to speak a word . . . she felt my Glock. My girl wasn't green and she knew not to mention it in front of anyone. Trust me, though, I'd hear about it later. It would be just another disagreement, because Tiffanie hated guns. But she didn't understand the streets. I may have been legit, but I stayed loaded. I was still Damon King, a man with a name, a few skeletons, and a lot of connections.

"Hey . . . well, then, don't let me hold you two," Trey piped in.

"Nah, nah," I said, turning my attention back to him. "This is all about you. Tiff and I are gonna take you to an early lunch; one of the most famous places in DC."

Trey grinned, knowing right away that I was talking about our spot from back in the day. "That's what's up!"

I frowned just a little 'cause Trey was supposed to be talking to me. So why were his eyes on my woman?

I shook my head. My thoughts were stupid. He was being friendly since he and Tiffanie had just met. And he probably sensed her apprehension about him. He wanted her to be comfortable.

"Let's roll." I took Tiffanie's hand as we strolled toward the door.

And I heard Trey's footsteps on my hardwood floor very close behind us.

# 7

# Tiffanie

Sitting across from Trey made it hard for me to breathe. My prayer had been that since I'd had that little talk with myself, it was going to be different. My prayer was that with Damon right next to me, Trey wouldn't be able to get to me in any kind of way.

But that wasn't true. Even with Damon so close to me in the booth that our shoulders touched, Trey still taunted me. I wasn't sure if it was conscious or unconscious on his part, not that it mattered. Because whichever it was, it was the purest form of torture. His lips. The way he put his lips on his glass, the way he'd lick them after every single sip.

Damon and Trey were talking and joking it up as if they'd never been apart.

But all I could do was watch the man's lips.

"Man, Tiff," Damon said, "Mr. Ali would give us free hot dogs to make us go away."

I forced myself to giggle, though I didn't find any of this funny. Torture was never funny.

I glanced around Ben's Chili Bowl, hoping that checking

out the people in the long line that stretched onto the sidewalk would be enough to keep my eyes and my mind away from Trey. It was still a little less than an hour before noon, and the famous eatery was already crowded. There was enough activity—with the people and the chaos, the chatter and the clanging—to hold my attention for at least a few minutes.

But I didn't stay away very long. The surprise in Trey's voice brought me right back to him.

"Get out of here with that, D!"

Damon nodded. "I'm telling you, they're my biggest clients."

"Churches?" Trey asked, as if he couldn't believe it.

Damon shrugged, nodded again. "I've put together some of the baddest church conventions, and those pastors have the biggest budgets. I'm telling you, forget about the fountain of youth; those reverends have discovered the fountain of money!"

Not even a second had passed, when Trey added, "They have, it's called their congregations!"

When they laughed, I frowned. How could Damon be joking like this? Yes, churches were some of his best clients, but many of those pastors had been introduced to him by the man who'd raised me. Was he making fun of my granddaddy?

I said, "Well, if you're the best, babe, why wouldn't churches want to use you?"

There was a silent moment after I'd spoken my mind, and I wanted to slide right under the table. Not because of what I'd said. The problem was, I'd drawn Trey's eyes right back to me.

"True dat," Damon said. "When you want it big, you gotta go through the King!"

Trey's sign of agreement was to lick his lips. From left to right, then right to left.

I couldn't breathe.

Finally, God gave me a reprieve when Trey turned his glance once again to Damon. "I'm not surprised you're doing it big here. We did it big in the ATL, too. Don't forget that, bruh. When you and I were together, nobody could do it better."

"Yeah, man," Damon said, "we had some good days down there."

Trey nodded. "But the best thing, what I will always remember, is that you always had my back."

It seemed like a normal enough statement, until the air shifted, and Damon shifted, and I twisted so that I could get a good look at my man. The way that muscle in his jaw jerked, something about Trey's words had touched him the wrong way.

"Yo," Damon began, "you know . . ."

But Trey held up his hand. "No issues, I'm just sayin' you had my back."

Damon squinted.

Trey said, "And I gotta thank you from the bottom"—with his fist he pounded his chest—"for taking care of my grandmother. I've got nothin' but love for you, bruh."

That fast, the air shifted back to the way it had been seconds before. Fists bumped again and then Trey's eyes came back to me.

Didn't Damon notice how Trey kept looking at me? Or maybe there was nothing to notice. Maybe this was all about me. And my imagination. Forget about my prayers, this was all about what I wished and wanted.

"My grandma's my heart," Trey said. He rested his arms on the edge of the table and leaned forward. It felt like he was trying to push his face toward mine.

The booths at Ben's were not wide enough. There was not

enough space between us, so I looked down into my iced tea to stop my body from going into overload. Because that's what happened when I looked at and listened to Trey at the same time. Too much at once.

"Ah, bruh," Damon said, "it was nothing. Like you said, it's all about having each other's back."

"But man, you put her in the Arlington House . . . that's serious. You went above and beyond and I owe you big-time. Just so you know, I'm gonna pay you back every dime."

"Negro, please! I love Ms. Irene like I would've loved my own grandma if I'd known either one of them. Ain't no way I would've put her anyplace but the best, so you don't owe me a thing."

I shifted to keep my eyes and my mind on my man, but my thoughts were on Trey. They were new thoughts, though, about him and his grandmother. It sounded like his connection with Ms. Irene was strong. I knew how she felt about him; when we went to visit her, all she'd talked about was Trey, but I thought that love had been one-way. It seemed, though, that he really cared about her, which was nice . . . but did that mean that he might be thinking about moving back to DC?

That could not happen.

"So, while Damon's holding all of this down, Tiffanie, what are you up to?"

I almost choked and I didn't even have anything in my mouth. The very last thing I wanted to do was get into any kind of direct conversation with Trey, especially with Damon sitting next to me. Because if I talked to Trey, I'd have to look at him. And if I looked at him, I'd see his eyes. And if I saw his eyes, I'd wonder what was behind his eyes. And if I wondered, I'd wonder and wonder and wonder. And wonder what it would be like to feel his lips again.

Before I had one of those shuddering feelings again, Damon saved me. "Ah, man, Tiff is what's up. She helped me build my business, and now she's leaving me to do her own thing."

While I sat silently, Damon told Trey about the day spa that we would be opening in a few weeks, though he made it sound like I'd done everything myself. Damon finished my litany of accomplishments with, "That's why I have to hold down King Commotions so hard, 'cause my baby is about to outdo me." He took my hand and squeezed it.

That was what gave me courage. I could look at Trey as long as Damon was holding my hand. So, I let my eyes rise back up, and this time, I held his gaze. Looking at him, I couldn't tell if he was impressed with what Damon had told him, but before I could figure it out, he stuck his tongue out at me!

Well, it wasn't that way exactly. Trey locked his eyes on me, took a sip of his tea, and then he did that lip-licking thing again. With the tip of his tongue, he grazed his lips, crawling over the terrain of his skin, slowly, milli-inch by milli-inch, from right to left, then left to right.

And my mind did that wonder thing again. Wondered whether his lips would feel as good on the other parts of me as they'd felt against my cheek.

Then my glance dropped down to his hands and the way his long fingers wrapped around his glass. And I wondered again . . . what could he do with his fingers?

I released Damon's hand to grab a napkin. My eyes were still on Trey's fingers as I dabbed at the perspiration on my fore-head, my hairline, my neck. If I could have reached under the table without Damon noticing, I would have dabbed at my inner thighs, too.

"Tiff!"

"Huh?" It took work for me to break my gaze away from Trey's fingers.

"You didn't hear me?" my man asked.

I shook my head and Damon and Trey laughed. As if I was the punch line of some joke.

"Babe," I began, "I've got to go."

"What?" Damon frowned and seemed confused. "They haven't even called our order yet."

"I know"—I glanced down at my watch—"but I just remembered . . ."

I hoped that was going to be good enough, because I didn't have anything else to add to my lie. But then my man did what he always did—he made me feel better when his frown turned upside down and his lazy smile spread across his face.

That was my cue. I could leave—no drama.

We both scooted out of the booth, and as Damon hugged me, I closed my eyes, held him tight, and remembered all the reasons why I loved him. Then I opened my eyes, and while still holding my man, I looked at Trey, watching us. Well, he wasn't exactly watching *us*. His eyes were on me, though it felt like he was looking at more than just my face. It felt as if he were looking at every part of me.

Trey blinked, and I felt naked. He blinked again. And I wanted to be naked.

Oh. My. God. I would combust if I didn't get away fast.

"Make sure you get something to eat," Damon said when he let me go.

"I will." It was only because I had on stilettos that I walked and didn't run like I was trying to place first in the 100-yard dash in the Olympics. I didn't even look back to throw Damon a kiss like I normally did, because my kiss might've missed—and landed on Trey.

The March air provided a cool breeze, but I was dripping with perspiration as I walked the block and a half to Damon's building. It didn't take the valet long to bring my car, but even then, I sat in my BMW for five minutes before I could even start the ignition. I didn't want to drive when I had no control and my palms kept slipping down the leather steering wheel.

Over and over, I whispered, "I love my man. I love my man. I love my man."

All I had to do was keep saying it, keep remembering it, and everything would be okay. But even though I sang that mantra like it was giving me life, I couldn't say it enough to make me stop thinking about Trey.

I needed to do something, because clearly my solution of thinking about my mother was not working.

And then I realized: I could go home.

# 8

# Tiffanie

This is where I came for peace. To this house that had always been my home. I turned off the ignition, but I didn't budge. Neither of my grandparents' cars were in the carport, not that I expected them to be. It wasn't even one in the afternoon, although my grandmother would be home soon.

I leaned back and closed my eyes, waiting for the peace that always enveloped me, even before I stepped through the front door. But the calm that accompanied me every other time I came home didn't cover me today. Instead, my mind was filled with thoughts of Trey. And once again I asked myself, was this what it had been like for my mother?

She had been lured into a love affair by a married man. To this day, my grandfather never talked about what happened, though I knew his sternness came from a place of his love for me and the loss of her. My grandmother was more open, telling me when she was sure that I was ready. I guess it was all my questions that made her think that I'd been ready for the whole story when I was just eleven. But what was the proper age to tell a child that her mother lost her life over love?

The tap on the window startled me, dragging me away from my history before I could delve too deep. "What are you doing sitting out here, honey? You okay?" My grandmother's voice came through my closed window.

I lowered it just a bit to say, "Hi, Gram. I just came to check on you and hang out for a little bit."

That made her smile. "You not working today?"

"No, ma'am," I said as I slid out of the car. "I had some things I wanted to take care of for the wedding."

"Well, come on inside. You got your keys, don't you?" She didn't give me a chance to answer. "I can't stand up too much longer. You know my feet are killing me."

I slid out of the car and watched my grandmother trudge up the walkway, then waddle up the five steps that led to the front door. Her sixty-four-year-old stride showed just how weary she was.

That made my heart hurt. I hated that my grandmother had taken all kinds of jobs since her retirement as a clerk from the Department of Social Services a few years ago. Her most recent position was as a Walmart greeter at the new Superstore in Northwest.

My grandmother didn't have to work this way. For all the years that Damon had been in my life, he had tried to take care of my grandparents. From the condo he wanted to buy them in downtown, to the positions he created just for them with his company, his desire was to do for them what he never got the chance to do for his own grandparents. But they'd said no to it all.

Trotting behind her, I got to the front door before she did. With my own keys, I opened the security gate first, then the door, and stepped aside so that my grandmother could go in first.

She dropped her purse and keys on the entry table and I paused at the door, giving myself a moment to bathe in the sight and the smell. Like always, the house wrapped itself around me, welcoming me home.

Seconds later, my grandmother did the same to me, and even though I towered over her five-foot-two-inch frame, I melted into her arms. She didn't hold me for long. Instead, she stepped back and looked up and into my eyes. When I was a little girl, I not only believed that my grandmother had eyes behind her head but also often wondered if she had some kind of telephone line to God. Because my grandmother knew everything. She knew when I wasn't feeling well, when I was tired, when I'd done something wrong, or when something was wrong.

"What's bothering you, honey?" she asked.

"Nothing," I said, even though I dang sure knew she'd know I was lying.

"How you gonna tell me that when I already know something is up?" She took my hand and led me to the couch. "Come on, you sit down right here, and I'll make us a cup of tea."

"No," I told her.

My grandmother went into eyebrow-raising mode, and before words could come out that matched the look she was giving me, I continued, "I mean, you sit down and I'll get the tea for us."

Her gaze stayed with me for a couple of moments before she nodded. "You trying to change the subject?"

I shook my head. "When the tea is ready, we'll talk."

My words must've been good enough, and my grandmother

sat down in the leather recliner that she did accept as a Christmas present from me and Damon. Before I was even all the way in the kitchen, I heard her moan with the pleasure that came with rest.

I had that hurt-heart feeling again and wondered if I should use this time to talk to my grandmother once again about letting me and Damon help. Maybe she would take a job with me at the spa.

Inside the kitchen, I eyed the Keurig that I'd purchased for my grandmother, but then turned to the kettle sitting on the stove, remembering that she had never bought any more K-Cups after she used up the ones that came with the machine.

"The tea just don't taste the same," she'd told me.

After I set the teakettle down, grabbed two mugs from the cabinet, and prepared both cups with the store-brand tea bags that Gram insisted tasted best, I leaned against the sink and thought about what exactly I would tell my grandmother.

While my grandfather had been been strict and forbidding, my grandmother was the flip side, open about everything, and her show of love was all about letting me know the real story, schooling me so that I could make the right decisions. Though I'm not sure it was my grandmother's intent, she was the reason I'd stayed far away from the love that destroyed the woman I couldn't even remember.

The kettle whistled, I filled our cups and carried them into the living room. Setting them down on the table in between the recliner and the sofa, I took my place on the corner of the couch and then patted my hands on my lap.

The sound made my grandmother open her eyes and she gave me that smile. "You don't have to do this, honey. I just want us to talk."

Not listening to her protest, I lifted one of her legs onto my lap. By the time I'd tugged off the slip-ons that she wore for comfort, my grandmother's head was back and her eyes were once again closed.

With my thumbs, it only took two presses and the room filled with her groans of pleasure.

"That . . . feels . . . so . . . good."

I thought about all the times I'd done this for my grandmother, after seeing it on one of the soap operas that she loved. Even as a five- and six-year-old, I knew that this was something I could give back to her for all that she was giving to me.

"Did you have a tough day, Gram?"

She hummed her reply.

I kept kneading, she kept humming, and I glanced around the room, slowly taking in the pictorial story of my life that surrounded us. Covering three walls were dozens of photos that were starting to fade inside twenty-year-old frames that were beginning to rust. So many pictures of so many moments and so many achievements.

Just pictures of me. With my grandparents. Not one of my mother. As if I were their child; as if my mother never existed.

And then, in the center of the mantel, there was the largest picture of all—Damon's and my engagement picture, the photo that had appeared in the *Washington Post*. We were in profile, me looking up, him looking down. Nothing but love.

"Gram?"

Another hum.

My eyes were still on that picture when I asked, "How did you know you were really in love with Granddaddy?"

It was a rapid flutter, the same way butterflies flap their wings, and then her eyes opened.

My thumbs and fingers kept moving, but I had a feeling that her attention had shifted from her pleasure to my anguish, which she sensed. She didn't say a word, just studied me.

So, I rephrased the question. "How did you know? Like really, really know he was the man for you?"

She slid her foot from my lap, planted both feet on the floor, and leaned so close to me that our noses almost touched.

"Where is this question coming from?" she asked.

"No place." It was my second time knowing that she knew I was lying. But what was I supposed to tell her? That today I'd met a man who made me want to forget about Damon?

She nodded a little, then said, "It was a feeling, or rather, I should say, it was a knowing because of the way your granddaddy made me feel. Every time I saw him, I'd smile. No matter what I was going through that day, or how I'd been feeling, he made me smile. And I'm not talking about on the outside. I'm talking about right here." She pressed her hand over her heart. "And in other places, too." She laughed a little, and so did I.

Shaking her head, she continued, "All I can say is that it's a feeling that led to a knowing." She paused. "Why are you asking me that?"

I sighed and picked up my cup of tea that was cool enough now for me to sip. It was my way of stalling, but my grandmother let me sip and sip until I'd swallowed half the cup. I put it down and faced her, but before I could say anything, she said, "This is not about your mother, is it?"

I shook my head, only giving her a half-lie this time, because this was about Trey as much as it was about my mom. "I just want to be sure," I said.

After a moment, she chuckled.

"I want to be married like you and Granddaddy. I want to be married forever."

Another chuckle and a shake of her head. "God has given us so much, but one thing that He hasn't given us is guarantees. But He's given us discernment and that spirit when you know that you know that you know."

How many times had I heard my grandfather say that?

"If this isn't about your mother . . ." She paused, giving me time to speak, but I sat stone-still. She continued, "Are you having doubts about Damon?"

I shook my head and inside said, *I'm having doubts about me.* "It's not really doubts. It's just like I said . . . I want to be sure."

"Do you love Damon?"

I couldn't get the word out fast enough. "Yes."

Leaning all the way forward now, she pressed her hand against my chest. "Right here?"

"Absolutely."

She gave me another one of those stares right into my soul. After a few moments, she spoke. "That's what I'm talking 'bout," she said in a way that made me think if she'd had a mic in her hand, she would've dropped it.

"It's just that in a few days, I'm gonna be married, Gram."

"Yeah." She grinned. "And I'm so happy."

I chuckled at that. "It wasn't always that way." Shaking my head, I remembered the time I first brought Damon home and they'd grilled him like a Sunday steak.

"That's true." She nodded a little as she sipped her own tea. "We had to make sure that he wasn't just some street hustler. We had to know that he'd changed his ways."

"He has changed," I said.

She put her cup down to take my hands into hers. "You changed him. That man had already started, but you helped him to finish it. That's why I'm sure he's the one God chose for you. Because while Damon loves you, you're his covering. Your prayers, your presence will just continue to help that man grow as a man after God's own heart." She paused. "Baby, there are no guarantees, but you and Damon are as close as it gets for me."

I sat there, holding her hands, letting her words settle in my ears, and settle in my heart.

She added, "These doubts, these questions are all normal; now, I don't want you to go forward with anything that you don't believe in."

I shook my head. "No, I believe in us."

She nodded. "Good. Then just stay right there and keep God in the mix . . ."

I laughed at her choice of words, but she didn't crack a smile.

"And you and Damon will be fine."

She squeezed my hands as if that was the period on this conversation, then she leaned back in the chair, and this time, she was the one to put her other foot in my lap. She didn't say another thing, just closed her eyes.

It had only been a few words, a short chat, and my grandmother had filled me with peace. I didn't have to be concerned about what happened today with Trey. He was just one of those bad boys who'd made me curious for a moment. This had nothing to do with my mother; this was natural and I was fine.

Looking at my grandmother sitting back, so peaceful, I didn't want to disturb her. So I mouthed "Thank you," then thought about all that she'd said. She'd been so sure, and I chuckled about that telephone line I thought she had to God—maybe

He'd told her something, too. "Oh, one more thing," my grandmother started.

Glancing up, I didn't even notice that she'd opened her eyes. She kept her foot in my lap, though she did lean forward just a little bit. "I have no doubt that God chose you for Damon and Damon for you for a great purpose. He wants this union."

See? God had spoken. That made my smile wider.

"That means that the devil will come and try to kill, steal, and destroy."

The corners of my lips drooped in an instant.

"You cannot let that devil in."

My heart stopped beating.

"Don't give him any kind of foothold into your life or into your marriage. Because I'm telling you, if you do . . ." Then, just like that, she leaned back and closed her eyes.

It took me a moment to catch my breath so that I could continue her foot massage, but my heart, which had stopped for a moment, was beating like it was making up for lost time. And that peace that my grandmother had given me was stolen. It was what she'd said about the devil that took my peace away. The devil that made an image flash through my mind. Trey Taylor.

# 9

# Damon

Yu know you didn't have to do this, bruh," Trey said right
before he slid into the booth facing me. "I thought I was
just gonna stay at your place with you and Tiffanie."

Even though I smiled, that was never gonna happen. Trey
was my boy and everything, but I'd learned a long time ago never
to house your dog too close to your cat.

I said, "Nah, son. You needed your own space, and since
you're my best man, getting you a room for this week is my way
of saying thank you for offering to stand with me."

He nodded his appreciation.

"Everything okay with your room?" I asked.

He shook his head, but I knew that gesture wasn't negative.
There wasn't anything bad anyone could say about the rooms at
the Willard Hotel. "Bruh, I'm telling you, after where I've been
for the past seven years? This is great."

"Cool." I gave Trey some silent space to glance around. That
would give me a moment to figure out how to approach him
about leaving Atlanta and coming on board with me.

"Bruh, this place . . ." He paused as his eyes took in the

sights and the sounds of the bar in the hotel's lobby. "This place is thick with money." He inhaled like he was taking a long hit.

"That's because this is where money lives," I told him.

He gave the place another glance, like he was trying to soak up the lounge that was packed to the perimeter with the movers who shook DC. Even though I was no longer affected by this place, which has been around so long that Abraham Lincoln had sipped a libation or two here, I remained conscious of its impressiveness. That's why this was my go-to spot whenever I needed to make my own grand impression. Many deals had been closed standing at that bar.

"Mr. King!"

I grinned before I even looked up. "What's up, Walter?" I greeted one of the bartenders who served me often.

He shook my hand, I introduced him to Trey, and he took our orders: a Budweiser for Trey and a Ramos Pinto for me. I added a couple of orders of the Angus burger sliders and cala-mari for us to snack on.

When the waiter turned away, Trey said, "So it's like that?"

"What do you mean?"

"They know you by name?"

His tone was filled with disbelief, but I didn't know why. Trey knew that whatever I was involved with was always top-shelf.

I nodded. "I do a lot of business here."

He paused, did another one-eighty glance. "This is a long way from the spots on the block."

"Truth. But when you're asking for the big money . . ." My shrug finished my sentence. "They need to know my name with the amount of money *I be* droppin'." I laughed.

"Makes sense now . . . that you're having your wedding here. Did they give you the spot for free?"

"No, son, nothing's really free at this level, at least not the way you're thinking. But they always give me enough incentives to encourage me to keep coming back."

He nodded and at that moment, Walter slipped in, placed our drinks on the table, then slipped out, the way he always did, never hovering like the waitstaff at other restaurants.

Trey held up his beer and I did the same with my port. "To my man, and his bride, may she bring you all that you deserve."

There was nothing close to a smile on his face when Trey spoke those words, then took a long swig of his beer. I hesitated, watching him before I brought my glass to my lips.

*May she bring you all that you deserve.*

Odd words for a toast.

When Trey placed his glass onto the table and looked up, half his face was covered with his grin. Okay! He was back and I breathed, then took a sip of my wine and pushed away my hesitation.

I felt like I was trippin'. I was analyzing and scrutinizing his words. I was acting like I needed to keep my guard up with my boy, but what I needed to do was chill and remember that no matter what, Trey had always been down with me. No one had been closer or knew me better. I needed to keep that top of mind and get back to the discussion of us working together that I'd planned.

So, pushing my paranoia all the way back, I said, "Thanks," to his toast and brought my glass to my lips once again.

The moment my glass hit the table, Trey asked, "So, Tiff must be some kind of girl to make you turn in your card."

That made me toss aside all thoughts that I had of talking to my boy, because he wanted to talk about my girl. But there was one place where I had to set him straight. The thing about my soon-to-be bride was that everyone called her by her full name—Tiffanie. No one shortened it, except for me. But how would Trey know that?

"So," Trey began, "you ain't got nothin' to say about that?"

I was trying to get a measure . . .

"Nothin' to say about Tiff?" he said as if I needed a reminder of who he was talking about. "Where'd you two meet?"

I couldn't quite explain the suspicion that rose inside me, making me once again scrutinize, analyze, and hesitate. But after a moment, I just slid right into the story. "At Howard. I needed some help, so I went down to the campus looking for an intern and found my wife. When I walked into that building, she was sitting there waiting just for me."

"Just sitting there, huh?" he questioned with a smirk. "A young one."

I nodded. "That's the way it happened." I left out the part about how long the struggle had been that had taken us from that day at Howard eight years ago today.

He laughed. "You always did have major game. What line did you give her?"

He wasn't lying. Both Trey and I had lots of game when it came to females. We used to entertain each other with stories of our conquests. But what Trey didn't understand was that this right here with Tiffanie was no joke. She had earned my heart and I needed to set Trey straight about that.

"I didn't give her any kind of line."

His glance was filled with doubt. "So what're saying? That you . . ."

"Felt her from the beginning," I finished for him. "From the moment I saw her, my heart knew, even if my head didn't."

He nodded, kinda slow, like he was finally coming to an understanding. "Cool."

I nodded, too, ready to change the subject back to my purpose for getting together tonight, when Trey asked, "So it was like that? Love at first sight?"

It was another one of those perfect Walter moments—the bartender stepping up to the table with a tray covered with three plates. As he arranged our snacks in front of us, it gave me a moment to do a little more studying. Now I asked myself straight out—why did Trey want to talk about Tiffanie? I'd already explained that she wasn't like the females in my past. She was my wife already in my heart; it had been that way for a long time for me. So, Trey needed to understand that I didn't want to nor was I going to talk about her in the same way we'd talked about chicks before.

But then, in the next moment, I saw it. While Trey chatted with Walter, asking him how long he'd worked here and how he liked it, I saw the curiosity on Trey's face. My boy just wanted information so that he could connect.

I was forgetting that he'd just paid seven years. He wasn't around when Whitney died or when Alicia Keys's and Swizz Beatz's baby was born. He'd missed the rise of iPads and the fall of BlackBerry. He didn't get to celebrate the Redskins choosing RG3 or mourn the disaster that followed after.

And he certainly missed most of Barack Obama's presidency and how white folks had lost their damn minds.

Yeah, I needed to give my boy some space to acclimate. That's why he wanted access to my life. Maybe, if I gave him that, Trey would see how I lived and loved and would want a piece of my peace.

When Walter walked away, I blessed the food, and when I looked up, Trey had already taken two bites of his slider as if he didn't even notice that I'd bowed my head. That was one of the things I couldn't wait to do—take Trey to church with me and Tiffanie. He would be suspicious about the whole preacher thing since we'd dissed pastors, calling them pulpit pimps, back in the day. But I was pretty sure that Tiffanie's gramps would help Trey see the light. My hope was that God would change him like He'd changed me.

"So," Trey began, ready to take us back into the conversation, "you fell in love with her"—he shook his head as he said those words—"just like that?"

I grabbed one of my sliders. "I can't say that it was love at first sight. I just knew when I saw her that she was special."

"So, she wore you down all the way to marriage?"

I paused, wondering if I should share more—like how I'd been the one to do the wearing down and how it had taken a year for her to even go out with me. "Something like that," I said, thinking that was all the access he needed.

Food filled his mouth, so he only chuckled and nodded. After a couple of swallows, he said, "So back then, you were just hittin' it?"

Even though I didn't want to let him too far in, I needed to correct him on this fact real fast. "I told you, it was never like that."

He shook his head as if my words couldn't be believed. "So

what caught you? Why her?" He didn't give me a chance to answer when he continued, "'Cause I've got to say that when you told me you were getting married . . ."

"I know. I wasn't looking for love, but love found me."

His face creased like he'd just seen a horror show. "Ah, bruh, you're not going out like that, are you? You're not gonna start quoting love songs and Shakespeare?"

"Nah." I laughed, but then I got serious. "All I can say is that Tiff is nothing like the others; she wasn't into me for my game, she never cared about what I was stackin', she never asked me to buy her a thing. Hell, it took me . . ." I hit the brakes and pulled back my words. "So what about you? What you got going in Atlanta?"

My thought was that this would get me and Trey back to the track that I wanted to take.

But I was on one track and he was on another, because he said, "I just cannot believe it. I cannot believe you got caught. I can't believe she's that special to you."

I reminded myself that he was just feeling himself around my world. "She's that special. Made just for me. She's not sitting at home waiting to live off my dollars; she's focused on her own dreams in her own world. But then when she comes home, she makes it all about me. That girl loves me, loves every part of me. And that's what makes her different from the others." I slowed down my words. "She loves me."

The size of the smile on Trey's face told me that it was amusement not agreement with my sincerity.

"You believe her when she says that to you?"

His skepticism didn't bother me because we'd always dealt with the same kinds of females; we'd never trusted any of them, both of us knowing they were there for just one thing. Seeing me with my heart wide open had to be a concept that was hard for him to grasp. "I don't have to take her word." I began to break it down for him. "When you're loved like that, words aren't needed. It's in here." I pounded my chest. "This is real, for her and for me. And I'm never gonna do anything to mess this up."

He sat back in the booth, looking like he was about to bust out laughing. "So what are you sayin'? You gonna turn down the strippers at your bachelor party? Gonna give up your last chance until the first jump-off comes along?"

Now he couldn't hold back his laughter. He cracked up, and I just smiled, letting him have his laugh. I put my burger down, crossed my arms in front of me on the table, and leaned forward. I waited till he got all of his chuckles out of his system before I said, "I'm not gonna turn down the strippers."

"That's what I'm sayin'." He lifted his fist like he wanted to give me dap, but I left him hanging.

"Because there ain't gonna be no strippers."

His hand dropped to his lap.

"I don't roll like that no more. No strippers, no jump-offs, from this day forward"—I tapped my forefinger on the table— "Tiffanie Cooper is the only woman for me."

Trey didn't say a word, but he didn't have to; his expression said it all—wow!

I leaned back and sealed what I'd just told him. "Trust that."

He looked at me now as if I was the one who needed to be studied. But then he began to nod. And a smile came with it.

"Any more questions?" I asked, feeling pretty good about what I'd just broken down for my boy.

"Nah." He chuckled. "You just dropped some knowledge *and* the mic."

I laughed.

"Well, maybe I do have one more. Since you're going all the way, taking this step and everything . . . you gonna have kids?"

With that question, I couldn't even stop the left-to-right grin that spread across my face. "Of course. I want dozens. That's why I got me a young one."

His head fell back and he howled. "You're right. Tiffanie's a pretty young thang. But dozens? She's agreed to that?"

"Not quite. I haven't been able to convince her that the world needs dozens of little Kings. But I'm good with what she's talking about . . . one, maybe two." I paused. "For now."

His smile was as wide as mine when he said, "Seems like you got it all worked out. Your life is set."

"You know how I do. It's all about planning your work and then working your plan. My life has always been that way. I knew what I wanted and I got it." This time, I was the one to raise my glass. Trey raised his, too, and clicked it against mine. Then, without another word, we finished up our sliders, with Trey probably reflecting on the education I'd just served him. The conversation had left me thinking, though, that this wasn't the right time to talk about bringing him on. I'd just let him get settled tonight and circle back to this. We had plenty more days to discuss it.

# 10

# Tiffanie

When I left my grandparents' house, my plan was to come home and go straight to bed. Because surely it had to be some kind of exhaustion that had me acting like some kind of fool.

I just wanted this day to end so that I could wake up tomorrow with a new beginning. All fresh, without thoughts of Trey.

But what was that cliché about the best-laid plans? Because now, here I was, an hour after midnight, sitting in my darkened apartment, with a half-filled glass of wine. I hadn't had one minute of sleep . . . the new day was here . . . and Trey was still all up in my head.

I'd only been in his presence for . . . how long was it? The ride from the airport, then in the booth at Ben's. I hadn't spent a full hour with Trey, yet, I had to turn to make sure he wasn't sitting right here on this sofa with me.

His face, I could see.

His hands, I could feel.

His lips . . . oh . . . those . . . lips.

I closed my eyes and inhaled, and when I opened them

they were damp as if tears were coming. I was so afraid. How had I fallen into this abyss of ridiculousness? How could I be a grown woman and not have control of my thoughts or my feelings?

I sighed. Why was I asking myself that? I knew the answer before I asked the question.

I took another sip, leaned back on my sofa, stretched my legs onto the coffee table, and in the darkness forced my mind to focus on Damon. It was so easy to do because every memory of him was filled with fairness and goodness and kindness. That's who he was to me. Even after I began to reveal my secret to him.

May 1, 2009

IT WAS THE rain, at least that's what I was going to tell Damon, even though the clouds hadn't fully released their wrath yet. After working together for a year, of course Damon knew that I was time-challenged, but still, every time I promised myself that *this time*, I'd be *on time*.

That thought made me groan and with a hard swing to the right, I swung my car in front of a taxi that hadn't even come to a stop. The cab's horn blared, but I ignored the sound and rolled my car to the curb. Stopping in front of the valet stand, I jumped out the moment I turned off the ignition. I didn't wait for the valet to come to the car; I tossed the keys to the first one I saw and dashed through the doors.

Old Ebbitt Grill was packed as usual, but I caught Anita's eye. She nodded, stepped from behind the hostess's station, and led me through the restaurant. Speaking above the din, I said,

"I got caught in the rain," as if I were practicing the line on her before she took me to wherever Damon had been waiting, probably for close to thirty minutes.

Anita chuckled, nodded, and then, to my surprise, we exited the main section of the restaurant and stepped into the area with more private tables and even some private dining rooms. But then I just figured that this was Friday night and all of the main section's tables were probably occupied.

Damon and I had never had our weekly review meetings on a Friday before, but he'd had to cancel last night and reschedule it for today.

My thoughts were on that and all the items I wanted to go over with Damon as I followed Anita: I had the fully executed purchase agreement for the art gallery he'd just bought; I needed his review on that. Then there was the budget that Delta Sigma Theta had given for their scholarship ball; Damon needed to approve that. Then there were all the people who'd come to us to sponsor their events—everything from 10K charity runs to charter school sporting events. And then finally, I would give him the good news about . . .

Anita stepped aside and I stepped inside, to a dimly lit room, the flicker from the flames of the three candles that sat in the center of the single round table the only light.

I frowned and blinked, then blinked and frowned. "Damon?"

Damon sat facing the door, and when I entered, he pushed back his chair, stood, picked up a single rose from the table, then took a few steps and handed me the flower.

I did a little bit more blinking, a little bit more frowning. "Damon?"

He said nothing, just took my hand and led me to the other

chair. The only reason I sat down was because I didn't know what else to do. My brain wasn't computing any of this. "What's going on?"

Still there were no words from him, at least not until he finally sat in the chair that was more next to me than across from me.

"What does it look like?"

"We were supposed to be having our weekly review."

He took the portfolio from me and laid it on the table beside him. "We're having dinner."

"We always have dinner. But, what's this . . . candlelight?"

"You've never heard of a candlelight dinner?"

I placed the flower down on the table. "Damon." My eyes were lowered when I sighed his name.

"Tiffanie," he sighed back.

I didn't even look up, just shook my head. In the last year, Damon had made a couple of little comments about how we should go out together. But every clue that he tossed to me I let drop right there. And it wasn't just because of the women who passed through the revolving door of his life. I just wasn't interested in any kind of relationship.

So it came as a shock to me when he'd asked me to go out with him the week before. I told him no and this time, the shock was his. When his eyes widened and his mouth opened, I knew it was because he was Damon King. He was the owner of one of the top event-planning companies in the DMV area . . . and that was just the beginning of the conglomerate he was building throughout DC, Maryland, and Virginia. But, no matter how fine or on-his-way-to-rich this man was, me and him . . . it was never going to happen.

With that thought, I finally lifted my eyes and met his. "I told you last week, I wasn't interested in going out with you."

"It's too late now. We're already out."

Looking at the candles, I shook my head. "No. We're not."

He gave me a long glance before he shrugged. "I don't get it. We get along so well, Tiffanie. I love talking to you, being with you, and unless my gut is wrong, I think you enjoy being around me, too." He paused, then lifted his arm and sniffed. "Do I stink or something?"

I laughed because it was funny, and one of the things I loved about this man was that he always made me laugh. But our laughter would have to stay in the workplace. The smile was still on my face when I said, "No, of course you don't stink. But I told you, I don't mix business with pleasure. It's not a good idea to date the boss."

He let a couple of beats go by as if he was pondering my words. And just when I was sure that he got it, he said with the straightest of faces, "Then, you're fired."

"What!" It took me a second to realize that he couldn't mean it. But just in case, I crossed my arms and said, "If you fire me, that's sexual harassment." My tone told him that if he wasn't playing, I would sue.

But he was as cool as a beach breeze, the way he gave me one of his sideways two-dimple grins. "No, it's not. Not sexual harassment if I continue to pay you."

Was he kidding me? "That's prostitution."

He grinned. "I'll take that. I'm the pimp and you're the . . ."

He looked so serious that I had to crack up. "Damon! Come on. I love working with you. I love everything about it, all that you've taught me, all that we've done together. But I want it to stay this way. Heck, if you want to do something, promote me. But I don't want to go out with you."

Even with only the candlelight, I saw the shine leave his eyes and his smile dim. "I guess it's just that everything else is there." He shook his head as if he couldn't believe that a woman wouldn't go out with him, and I would've been mad at his arrogance if he didn't look so sad.

He said, "I don't get it. I mean, all the other girls . . ." He cleared his throat as if he didn't mean to say that out loud.

But even if he hadn't spoken those words, I knew all about him and the women. In the year since we'd met, the women—from politicians to party girls—hadn't stopped. "You're just different from anyone I've ever dated. I like you."

I needed to just tell this man so that he would understand, and then we'd never have to do this dance again. "It's not you, Damon," I said, trying to put a softness into my voice that would ease him into this rejection. "I'm just not interested in dating. Not you, not anyone. I just don't want to go out with any guy."

"Oh." He stared at me for a long moment. "Oh! Okay!" He nodded. "That's cool." Now he shook his head. "Wow."

I breathed, relieved. Because I loved working with this man and he'd been such a great friend; I didn't want to lose that relationship.

He said, "I didn't know you were gay."

"What?" I slapped my hands on my lap. "I'm not gay," I said, glad that we were in a private room, because the volume of my voice probably made the walls shake. "I didn't say that. Because I don't want to go out with you, you think I'm gay?"

"No." His volume matched mine. "You just said you didn't want to go out with a guy."

"Not because I'm gay," I shouted. "It's because I don't want to end up dead like my mother!"

My words stunned him but not as much as they stunned me. Because that was not what I'd meant to say; it just slipped out. It wasn't until his hand covered mine that I realized I was trembling. When I looked up at him again, questions filled his eyes and inside I sighed.

I'd gone back to my inside voice when I said, "I don't want to date because of where it could lead me in my life."

"Your mother died because . . ."

I could tell he wanted to finish the sentence, but he couldn't because he didn't know, and even if he did, he wouldn't understand. All he knew was that my mother had passed away. But now the door had been opened. It was just that I wasn't sure how much I wanted to tell him.

"My mother died . . . of a broken heart."

He blinked, but then his shoulders relaxed. As if my words were just a cliché. As if a broken heart wasn't a real cause of death. Well, it may not have been medical, but it was the truth. "Do you want to talk about it?" he asked me.

I didn't, but I didn't know any other way to get Damon to accept the fact that I would never date him. "My mother fell in love with a married man."

"Oh."

"She was only seventeen when that happened."

"Oh."

"She got pregnant. With me. She was only eighteen when I was born."

"Oh."

"And he left her. Alone to handle being so young, to handle being a pastor's daughter, to handle it all by herself."

"Oh."

"He denied that he ever loved her and in the end . . ." It was hard to finish my sentence. "In the end, it killed her."

He nodded and squeezed my hand. "I'm really sorry that happened to your mom. But Tiffanie, what does that have to do with you?"

Now he wanted me to go into the specifics of how I was damaged, how my DNA was so screwed up that I couldn't take the chance on love.

"I just want my life to go another way" was all I told him.

He stared at me for a moment, then stood up. Was he really going to just walk out? Was he going to leave me here because I wouldn't go out with him? Was he going to fire me for real?

He paused by the door, flipped the light switch, and illuminated the room so brightly that I had to squint for a little while before my eyes adjusted. Back at the table, Damon blew out the candles, then sat next to me once again.

"Okay. I hear you and I'm glad about two things."

I released a long breath of relief.

He continued, "First, I'm glad that it's not me and I don't stink."

I smiled.

"And second, I don't have anything against gay people, but I'm glad you're not gay."

I grinned.

"Because I know I do have a chance."

The ends of my lips turned downward.

He held up his hand as if he wanted to stop any protests coming from me. "Just kidding, okay?"

I wasn't sure if he was or wasn't, but I prayed that either way, he heard me . . . and he believed me. I hadn't told him that I would remain single and loveless until the end of my time on earth. I hadn't told him that I knew any kind of love in my life would kill me. It was a fact that would sound crazy to other people, but something that I believed down to my bones. Because it had to be something in my mom's DNA that would let her leave me, something inside of her that she couldn't help and I was so afraid that she'd passed that on to me.

But because I didn't want to talk about this anymore, I simply nodded, reached across his place setting, and retrieved the portfolio. "So, can we get back to business?"

He nodded, took off his jacket, and loosened his tie as I opened first to the Delta Sigma Theta event.

In between, a waiter entered and took our orders, and we continued to work, doing our review the way we'd done each week for the past eleven months. Through sips of our drinks (water for me and ginger ale for him) and forks filled with crab cakes and Caesar salad, we went right back to being Damon King and Tiffanie Cooper, the pulse of King Commotions. I was grateful that Damon understood, at least he seemed to, at least for tonight.

OPENING MY EYES, I reached for my wine before I pushed myself from the sofa. I took in the darkness of the city from my twelfth-floor window, the blackness broken only by the white dome of the Capitol that sat in the center of my view as if my window was its frame.

But this view that had always been able to capture my attention did nothing for me tonight. Instead, my thoughts were on how Damon never gave up on me. Even after I'd given him that solid no, he continued. His pursuit was slow and respectful, but he kept at it until I couldn't do anything else except give in to his love. With that history, how could I even think about another man now?

Placing my glass on the window's ledge, I closed my eyes and with my fingertips massaged away a headache that wasn't there physically but certainly was emotionally. It was clear that Trey did something to me—I'd be a fool if I didn't accept that fact. And wasn't acceptance the first step?

My second step was to make a plan and that plan was to stay away from Trey. I only had to see him two times this week—at the dinner Thursday night and then at our wedding on Friday. All the hours between now and then, I wouldn't let him into my sight. I would decline any lunches or dinners that Damon arranged; I wouldn't even go by Damon's house (my new home), since Trey might very well be hanging out there.

Then, once the wedding was over, once Trey returned to Atlanta, it would be all Damon, all the time.

Damon.

Picking up my wine, I leaned my head back, turned my glass upside down, and swallowed the last drop.

Damon.

I left the glass on the living room table, then headed straight to my bedroom.

Damon.

Snuggling under the covers, I closed my eyes, and with gratitude in my heart, I whispered a prayer, "Lord, thank you for this man that you made just for me. Thank you for Damon and every blessing that you've given to me through him and this life. My heart is filled with so much gratefulness, Lord. Thank you."

I said a silent Amen and then stayed in that spiritual space for a little while, wanting the prayer to not only reach God but to settle into my heart. When I opened my eyes and rolled over, Damon was still on my mind. When I closed my eyes, Damon was there, too.

But then I drifted and I dreamed. And in my dreams, there was only one man. And it was not Damon King.

# 11

# Tiffanie

Without even looking, I knew my eyes were red; they had to be, since I had tossed to the left and turned to the right all night.

I hadn't slept anywhere near two hours, but before my cell phone alarm even started with Sam Smith singing "Stay with Me," I jumped up and out of my bed. Even though I was my own boss and never rolled away from my mattress before nine o'clock, there was no need for me to remain in bed having these eyes-wide-open dreams.

I moved with purpose, glad that I had so much on my to-do list today, since I'd accomplished nothing yesterday. In the shower (I'd kept the water on chill), I tried to tick off the tasks in my head, but I couldn't maintain any kind of focus.

I may have been naked, but I felt like there were ants in my pants—I could feel them. And there were still thoughts in my head—I could see them.

I adjusted the showerhead and turned the flow to pulse. The stream felt like pellets striking my skin, but I welcomed the attack. By the time I stepped out of this shower, every ant, every thought would be dead.

I could almost feel my blood pulsing when I turned off the water. There was no need for my usual dash, since it wasn't even seven when I slipped into my jeans and white tailored shirt. I even had time to bump my hair instead of pulling it back into a ponytail.

Then I did something I hadn't done in months—I made breakfast. Well, if you could call dumping two slices of wheat bread into the toaster and pouring a glass of orange juice making breakfast.

The sun pushed through my windows when I sat at the counter, took a bite of toast, and logged onto my iPad. I pulled up the *Washington Post*.

*If you want to guarantee never getting ahead in life, watch TV. The most successful people turn that off and find out what's going on in the world.*

Those had been some of Damon's first words to me, the morning of my second day with him. He'd taken me into a conference room where the table was stacked with newspapers. Not just the *Post* and *Wall Street Journal* but the *Times* (both New York and Los Angeles), the *Chicago Tribune*, and the *Dallas Morning News*.

That was just one stack—I was shocked to find international papers from London, Paris, Frankfurt, and Milan in the other pile.

I'd felt like I was being tested every day for those first two weeks. But checking out the papers became a part of me, and after I stopped working for him, reading the newspapers was my habit.

But not even the circus of the upcoming election was enough to keep my thoughts in line.

I slammed my iPad shut, jumped up from the table, and

went into my normal dashing mode. The way I moved, there was no space for Trey as I slipped on a navy blazer, gathered my tote, stuffed my purse, and rushed out of the door and down into the underground garage. But the moment I slid behind the steering wheel of my car, I moaned. Trey was there; he'd left his scent behind. I inhaled, and remembered yesterday.

I couldn't get to the office fast enough. There would be plenty there to distract me from these thoughts and memories that I didn't understand. As I wheeled my car out of the garage, I rolled down the window (even though it wasn't even fifty degrees) and turned on the air conditioner (to high!), hoping to circulate Trey's scent right out of my car.

The streets were filled with rush-hour traffic, and I had to dodge so many cabs and Uber cars I couldn't focus on anything more than not getting into an accident. And when I pulled into the parking lot right next door to my new spa, Utopia, there were new thoughts to take up the space. Just a couple of dozen feet away, my best friend was standing in front of two contractors, her finger pointing, her head snaking, and her lips moving fast. She was going off on someone about something.

This was why Sonia Rios Matthews was part of my team. As the project manager for the renovation of Utopia, she worked directly with the contractors who'd been hired to refurbish this sixty-year-old building that had once housed an old department store.

I grabbed my purse and tote, and by the time I slipped out of the car and was within a few feet of Sonia and the men, I was shaking my head. She may have had a problem, but the two workers didn't seem to notice. They watched her like they were about to devour their favorite meal.

Their reaction to my bestie was typical. That's just the way it was with Sonia. My Latina sister had been a looker from way back in the seventh grade when we met. Back then, Sonia looked like a teenage model rather than a twelve-year-old. The high school boys were all over her, so much so that there were times when I didn't want to walk down the street with her.

Don't get me wrong, I turned a head or three wherever I went. But my girl was what the guys called a true dime. She was fine in the only way that mattered to men, she was nothing but curves. And the arches and bends that made her a woman gave her measurements that demanded men's attention. When she walked by, every man had to stop, every eye had to stare, and it came dang near to every knee had to bow.

The thing that was funny, though, was that Sonia never seemed to notice. Like right now; her 38 Gs (we'd just been measured at Victoria's Secret and who knew you could be a G?) jiggled with every syllable, making those men pant.

Stepping up, I played Good Samaritan, rescuing the men. "Good morning." Giving my brightest Colgate smile, I asked, "Is there a problem?"

The men turned their big grins to me, while Sonia's glare stayed on them.

"No, no problem." Sonia spoke in her no-nonsense tone. "Everything's under control, right?" she asked, with one hand planted on brickhouse hips like that old-head group, the Commodores, sang about back in the day.

The men's heads bobbed up and down, but then with a final (and what looked like reluctant) nod, they stepped away.

Sonia didn't even look at me when she said, "We're opening on time. No matter what." But then her gaze came to me. *"De acuerdo; no te preocupes."*

"I'm not worried," I said, as always surprising myself, even after all these years, whenever I understood Sonia.

"I just want to make sure that your focus stays on your wedding," she continued. She entered the building and marched across the bare concrete floor as if she were on a mission.

I followed, but right before we stepped over the threshold and into the office that we shared until mine was completed, Sonia paused, turned around, and frowned as if she had a sudden thought. "What are you doing here?"

"I work here."

"But it's"—she glanced at her watch—"not even nine, no where near your normal arriving time of ten, eleven, noon."

Pushing past her, I said, "I don't come in that late."

"Yes, you do. So, *qué pasa?*"

"Nothing." As I sat at my desk, she leaned against the edge, staring down at me. But I didn't look up at her; I grabbed the budget folder and opened it. She waited, saying nothing as I shuffled through papers, trying to ignore her so that she would ignore me.

It felt like minutes, though it was probably no more than just a few seconds, but she was the one who blinked first when she asked, "What's really going on, *chica?*"

Tossing a page back into the folder, I sighed. "I told you. Nothing."

My words didn't deter her. "So why aren't you out taking care of last-minute stuff for the wedding?"

"Because getting married isn't the only thing I'm doing. I have a business to run, too."

She placed her hand across her chest and pouted. "My feelings are hurt. You don't trust me. I told you to take this week off. I told you I'd handle everything while you were away."

"Well, I'm not away yet," I snapped.

I guess it was my tone that made her raise one eyebrow.

"And since Utopia is my life, I need to be here to make sure that everything happens the way I want."

This time, I didn't know if it was my words or my tone that made both of her eyebrows rise high. But she stayed quiet, as if waiting for my rant to continue.

After a couple silent moments, she shrugged. "Okay," she said, and walked to her desk on the other side of the room.

She hadn't even sat down when I got that tug in my heart. It wasn't her fault that I was exhausted because I hadn't slept, nor was it her fault that even though I'd been staring at the budget for the last three minutes, it wasn't numbers that filled my mind.

"Sonia . . ." I began.

She interrupted and finished my statement for me. "You're sorry."

I pushed myself up from my chair, then took steps toward her, that probably looked like I was walking the last mile.

She waited until I sat and settled into the seat in front of her before she asked, "So, do you want to talk about it or am I going to have to play twenty questions when you know we don't have that kind of time?"

I hadn't come to the office to talk to Sonia, but since working *wasn't* working, maybe my best friend would have some wisdom to share. Not only was she the (five years) married one among us, but she knew me best.

I bit the corner of my lip, trying to come up with the right words. What did I want to say? What did I want her to know? Did I really want to tell her that I'd met a man just yesterday, who, if I'd been given a chance, I would've taken into my bed last night?

"So . . ." Sonia paused to pick up a half-eaten glazed dough-nut in front of her. She took a bite, closed her eyes, moaned, then got right back to my business. "Are you going to talk to me?"

My eyes darted from one corner of the room to the other; I gnawed on my tongue, I folded then unfolded my hands in my lap. The entire time, Sonia sat, stared, and waited. Finally, all I could get out was, "Like I said, there's nothing to talk about."

After a moment of a you're-kidding-me stare, she shrugged again and shoved another piece of doughnut into her mouth. It was one of those reverse psychology moves, because right as her hand hovered over her doughnut again, I added, "Except for Trey."

She squinted and cocked her head a bit, as if trying to recall that name and put it together with a face, but she blanked out. "Who?"

"Trey, Damon's best friend." It was my pause and then the way I exhaled his name once again, "Trey," that made Sonia nar-row her eyes.

She pushed her plate aside and leaned forward. "You better start talkin'."

So I did—the gates opened and the (almost complete) truth flooded out. I reminded her of the history of Damon and his best friend and how I never wanted Trey to come back to DC, but how Trey had told Damon he wanted to stand up for him when he found out we were getting married, and Damon happily agreed. Then I went into yesterday: the airport, the kiss, and how he'd taken me straight to heaven's door. By the time I got to the end of my story, I had to unfasten another button on my blouse to allow cool air to brush against my skin.

Sonia just stared at me in silence that felt like it went on forever until, "Damn!" She leaned back in her chair. "Damn, " she said again. Then she looked at me like she was seeing me for the first time. "Damn!"

"Maybe this would be a good time for you to switch to Spanish." I hoped that she heard how annoyed I was.

She nodded. "Okay." Then she thought for a moment and said, "Damn!"

I blew out a long breath and Sonia laughed. "I'm sorry, *chica*. I was just kidding with that last one. But, is he that fine? That sexy?"

My lips parted, but then I shut my mouth. How could I explain what I didn't understand?

Sonia said, "So tell me, what is it about this man?"

I paused before I said, "I'm not sure *this man* is the problem."

"What do you mean?" she asked without thinking, because once a moment passed, she added, "No!"

I shrugged.

"No, Tiffanie. This has nothing to do with your mother."

"How else can you explain it then? I meet a guy and . . ."

She shook her head, even as I spoke. "It's not that. It has to be . . . him. He's one of those bad boys, and you're a good girl. That's why you're attracted to him. Everyone in your life treats you like a porcelain doll and you wanna know what it would be like to take a trip on the wild side."

She was right about the bad boy part. I did find everything from his strut to his swagger sexy and intriguing. And it seemed like he just didn't care—about anything. But still, there had to be more to it than that. "But it's not like I've ever been attracted to bad boys before."

"You never allowed yourself to be open to *any* guys. But now that you've opened your heart to Damon, of course you're noticing other men."

I paused, pondering her words. No, that couldn't be it. I'd been with Damon for six years. Why hadn't any other man ever turned my head?

Then she said, "Wait, has he made some kind of move on you?" Her eyes got wider than before. "Is he trying to hit it?"

This time, I was the one shaking my head before she even got the last word out. "He hasn't done anything" was what I told her, though that wasn't quite true. Trey had done everything.

He looked at me.

He talked to me.

He kissed me.

He got to me.

I continued, "He's not trying to make any kind of move. He's Damon's boy."

Sonia squinted. "Hmph. Sounds like he's got something on his mind."

"No, really," I said, needing to convince Sonia, because my girl was so protective, she'd walk right up to Trey, get in his face, and tell him to stay away from me. Then he'd laugh in *her* face and tell her the truth—that he wasn't interested in me at all and that everything had been my imagination.

Sonia leaned back in her chair. "So it's not him, and"— she paused and spoke with an emphasis on each of her next words—"it's not you or your mother." She waved her hand in the air. "Then, you don't have anything to worry about." That was her prognosis. "What's happening is normal. Think about it: it's just days before your wedding and your mind just needs a distraction."

"Really?" I was desperate to believe her.

"*Absolutamente.*" She nodded. "I went through the same thing right before Allen and I got married."

I didn't remember anything like that. So I said, "Really?" again.

"You must've forgotten. I was like a dog in heat. Remember I kept telling you how every man who walked by me wanted to sleep with me?"

When she laughed, I did, too, only because I knew she was trying to make me feel better.

"I had pre-wedding jitters, and now you do, too."

If I wasn't in crisis mode, I would have told Sonia to give up her chairside therapy, because if I'd been paying her, I would've asked for my money back. Every man wanting to sleep with her? That was an everyday occurrence. But since I realized that my confiding in her hadn't helped, I just nodded so that we could move on.

"Don't worry," she said. "Just be happy," she sang. "A few more days around Trey, and you'll get used to him."

That's what I was afraid of.

She said, "This will all go away."

That wouldn't happen.

"You'll be back to your old self on Friday night; right after you and Damon say, 'I do.'"

That's what I prayed.

"So, you're good now?" she asked.

"*¡Absolutamente!*"

She laughed the way she always did when I tried to speak in Spanish. Coming from around her desk, she gave me a hug, then leaned back. *"De acuerdo; no te preocupes."*

"I won't worry."

She pulled me into another hug, I was glad, because it gave me a few moments to blink back my tears. The only thing this conversation had done was make me sure that I was in trouble. I wanted Sonia to be right, but I knew she was so wrong.

That meant that there was only one solution—the one I'd come up with last night. I'd stay away from Trey. Never laying eyes on him until I had to. And I just prayed that would be enough.

# 12

# Damon

Man, this tux is like that!" Trey grinned as he twisted and turned, looking at himself in the full-length mirror. "You know you doing the damn thing when you have your best man fitted in Armani."

Watching this dude acting like he'd never had on designer clothes was blowing me. Come on, now. Trey was acting brand new, like he expected something less. He couldn't have forgotten. This was me, the King, getting ready for my royal day. How else was this gonna play?

But instead of breaking it down for Trey, I just sat back in the leather chair inside the private fitting room of Mr. Spangler's Gallery—a high-end clothier whose clientele were the who's who of DMV ballers.

Trey nodded at his image as if he approved. "Yo, bruh, I'm liking this." He paused and, through the mirror, looked back at me. "But I guess this is how you have to roll when you got a dime like Tiff on your arm."

I stiffened, then straightened my shoulders. "Yo, I meant to tell you." He caught my stare through the reflection in the mirror. He didn't turn around and I didn't crack a smile. "My girl likes to be called Tiffanie."

He didn't even hesitate when he said, "Really? You call her Tiff."

The muscle in my jaw jumped. This was how it had always been. Trey just couldn't accept what I told him. There were always shots fired, though some shots were friendlier than others.

I leaned forward and pressed my hands against my knees. "That's me, son. I call *my* wife Tiff. No one else."

We kept our stare, eye-to-eye. I waited for his comeback. One beat went by, then another. And Trey blinked first.

Then he shrugged. "Tiffanie."

I nodded.

"Well"—his hands slid against the satin of his lapels—"*Tiffanie* is fine for real."

I frowned. He may have blinked, but he was talking like he was still challenging me. Hadn't I told this boy to keep it respectful? He knew I didn't play, didn't have much of a sense of humor. He had to know this was especially true about Tiffanie.

But I made the mistake of not saying anything, and he continued, "Yeah, Tiffanie's fine as hell." Now he wasn't even looking at me. His eyes were on his reflection like he was talking to himself. "Fine." His voice was lower, but still loud enough for me to hear. "And phatter than a second-grade pencil."

He laughed, and that was the only reason why he didn't hear my growl. There was no way, though, that I was gonna let him see that he'd broken my cool.

I leaned back in my chair like I was a king holding court. "Hey, blood," I said. He brought his glance back to mine. Still looking at him through the mirror, I said, "I promise you, you gonna have to keep it respectful when you're talking about my lady."

We had another one of those staring matches and just like before, Trey blinked, but this time, it came with a chuckle. I joined him just to throw him off. But truth—he was getting to me. Yeah, we used to talk like this, but I'd already told him that she was different and I didn't like repeating myself.

"My bad." Trey turned all the way around and faced me. "You know I didn't mean nothin', right?"

I nodded and kept my smile. But I knew that Trey could see in my eyes that he'd reached me. I expected him to step up, give me some dap, let me know that it was all good. But he didn't do none of that. He just kinda grinned and turned back to his image in the mirror.

Then he said, "Yeah, I didn't mean nothin'." He was looking me straight in my eyes, when he said, "Just like you didn't mean nothin' when you cut out on me in Atlanta."

Now I was the one who blinked—a couple of times. That was a quick left, but I nodded, letting him know that while it had been a sharp turn, I approved of his message. We didn't need to talk about Tiffanie anymore, but this talk right here—this was one that was waiting to be had.

I told him what he already knew. "Son, the block was hot, it was time to get out. I never wanted a lifetime membership in the game, you know that. You know what my pops always said." I repeated the words my father spoke whenever he was out and had the chance to sit me *and* Trey down. "The game ain't meant to be permanent. Anybody who plans to stay deserves to go down."

It was like a heavy cloud had slid into the room, darkening

everything. His eyes narrowed as he studied me, trying to figure out if I was clownin' him. Not that I was; I was just stating a fact.

But, since Trey looked like now he was the one about to growl, I changed directions. "You know why I got started." I didn't wait for him to answer. "We were kids trying to find our way." The only reason I was taking him on this memory-lane stroll was because he was acting like he'd forgotten what he needed to remember. Maybe breaking it down would help to get rid of whatever animosity he was holding. I continued, "But you knew when we were what? Fourteen? Fifteen? You knew we were gonna make that turn one day from the left to the right." I paused to give him another moment to remember. "We were supposed to get out."

"That was *your* plan."

"I thought *my* plan was *our* plan."

He was still, except for that little vein right above his left eyebrow. I recognized that—Trey was heating up. His next words told me I'd assessed the situation correctly. "That was one of the problems. That's what *you* thought, that's not how it was."

Just like I had to do all the time back in the day, I told him, "That's how it should have been. That was our agreement."

That vein above his eye still pulsed, more visible now, and I hoped he wasn't about to bust that thing. "No!" He shook his head and his voice got a little louder. "Our agreement, the real deal was that we'd have each other's backs always no matter what went down."

He'd shot from zero to sixty, but I kept my calm like I'd always done with him. Nodding, I said, "And I've always abided by that."

He took two quick steps and I thought he was gonna come for me. I stiffened and it took all kinds of mental strength to hold back my reflex and not reach for my piece.

"You abided by that?"

If his tone had been a knife, I would've bled out already.

With a move that was meant to put him on ice, I just nodded, thinking he'd see that he needed to bring it down.

His volume may have been lower, but his tone was still murderous. "When did you ever have my back when I was inside?"

The way to get him to really chill was just to blurt it all out; I could've told him that the only reason he ate in prison was because of me and the money I'd put on his books. I'd put the money there anonymously, not only following my pop's rules, but because Trey didn't need to know. He was filled with too much pride to take a dollar from me; he would've rather starved.

And that was why he would never know about my major contribution. For the last seven years, I'd been paying Hank Morris, a renowned attorney who founded an organization to get reduced time for nonviolent offenders. From the beginning, Hank had been optimistic about Trey, so I footed the bill for more than eighty months, and each of those months, Hank kept me up to date. It was because of Hank and my checks that Trey stood in front of me right now.

But again, because of my pop's lessons, because of who Trey was, I wouldn't say a word. I could, though, remind him of what he did know, and the reason why I'd made sure this news had made it to him.

"Ms. Irene," I reminded him. "I'm not looking for gratitude, but I had your back with your grandmother 'cause I didn't want that on your mind when you were dealing with that time."

His eyes, his tone were still dark. But at least his eyebrow stopped doing that little dance. "Like I told you, I will always be grateful," he said.

"And like I told you, I'm not looking for gratitude. I was just giving you a little reminder of how I had you."

"But I'm talking about when I reached out, when I was first picked up."

It was like he'd ignored what I said; he just wanted to make his point.

Shaking my head just a little, I said, "I don't know how many times we got to go over this."

He chuckled, though there was no smile in the sound. "Yeah, your pops told you . . ."

"He told you, too."

With his fist, he pounded his chest. "But I wasn't just ordinary people; we were fam."

Trey knew that didn't matter, that didn't make a difference to my father. If he didn't want me, his son, communicating with him when he was inside, I certainly wasn't gonna put myself out there like that with Trey. I kept my tone flatline. "We will always be fam. But . . ."

"I knew the rules," he finished for me.

I nodded. "And don't act like I didn't try to get you out the game before *and* after I left." I paused and let the room sit in silence, giving him space to remember some more. Even if he couldn't remember the couple of dozen conversations we'd had with my pops through the years, he had to remember the last talk he and I had a couple of nights before he was picked up.

The conversation hadn't started with Trey. The call had come in from my major connect . . .

June 13, 2009

"YO, THANKS FOR the heads-up," I told G-Money. Even though I had left Atlanta about four years before, my partner's news had me grasping the telephone tight.

"I had to make this call, son. You my boy and I just wanted to make sure you weren't coming back down here."

That's how G-Money had always been. He may have been one of my connects, all business when it came time for that. But when it came to lookin' out, we were like fam. "Nah, I'm out. I put a period on the ATL."

"I hear you. This has been where I laid my head for a long time, but it's time to bounce. They got a stranglehold on the streets."

"So where you headed?" I asked him.

"To parts unknown as of right now," he said, though before he got the third word out of his mouth good, I knew he was lying. G-Money always had a plan, he knew where he was going. But even though I was one of his most trusted soldiers, he wasn't gonna tell me. No one knew when tables could turn. And if anyone ever came to me, I couldn't give information that I didn't have.

He said, "All I know is that I'm not gonna get caught up in no setup. You need to tell your boy to either go home or lay low. There's a spotlight on him."

I told G-Money that I would make that call to Trey, though he could have done it himself. But most folks at the top didn't want to deal with Trey. He was too volatile and no one wanted to get into a beef with him over a simple conversation.

So I hung up and made the call to my fam. But Trey had no brotherly love for me that day.

I told Trey what I'd heard, and his response confirmed the reason why G-Money hadn't reached out to him.

"Bruh, you need to miss me with all this bull. My pockets are phat 'cause I know what none of these cats down here seem to know—no risk, no reward."

"There isn't a reward on the end of this risk," I told him. "The police are taking down everyone, getting promotions on cats' backs. Come home, and I'll set you up here and—"

He howled so loud I had to pull the receiver away from my ear.

"You're gonna set me up?" He was laughing so hard, he could hardly get the next words out. "Bruh, don't insult me and my intelligence. I'm making so much money right now, I can buy you and yours."

I wanted to be done. But that wasn't how you treated fam, not even your crazy relatives. So I changed course and rang the warning bell.

"If anything happens to you down there, you know you can't call me. We agreed that . . ."

"Bruh, you the last person I would need to call."

Then a second later, there was nothing, except the dead air that came from having the phone hung up in your face . . .

◆

I WAITED A couple more seconds, hoping Trey remembered that call, before I said, "And you know, if it had gone down the other way around, I wouldn't have expected anything more from you."

He didn't let a moment pass, like he had his answer ready. "But that's the difference between you and me. I wouldn't have treated you the way you treated me."

I shook my head, but there was no need for me to say anything more, no need to continue or to justify. I'd made righteous moves, and no matter what Trey said, he knew that.

That twitch in his brow came back and made me once again consider telling him all that I'd done. But that would serve no purpose and could hinder my hope. If I told him about what I'd done in the past, he wouldn't let me help him in the present. And the present was most important. The only way to really help Trey was to get him out of Atlanta and up here with me.

Then he did something I didn't expect. He stepped back, pivoted, and once again faced the mirror. Looking at me in the reflection, he said, "I get it. You had rules, you had a plan."

"What I had was a desire to live the kind of life that I couldn't behind bars."

Even in the mirror, his stare was hard, cold . . . and sad. I could take the hardness, the coldness; it was the sadness that filled me with guilt.

"I'm sorry I left you down there; I'm sorry you did that time." I owed him at least those words. "And I'm really glad that you're here now."

It took a few seconds, but his smile and his swagger were back. "Well, thank you for saying that. That's all I wanted to hear."

I nodded.

"It's cool, bruh. I had some good times and made some good money."

He sounded like he was trying hard to put some positivity into his spin. But he couldn't hide the sadness I saw and the hurt I heard. That's why I said, "Not this time, not this place, but we need to talk. I got some plans for you and me."

He popped the collar of the tuxedo and with a look that was more of a smirk than a smile, he said, "I got some plans, too, bruh."

Before I could ask a question, an Asian man stepped through the curtain and into our space. "Mr. Taylor," he said, "we're ready to do your measurements." He motioned for Trey to follow him, and my man grinned as he readjusted the lapels of the tuxedo.

"Okay, let me go back here so that this man can do what he do. 'Cause I'm gonna be the freshest one standing at the altar on Friday." He paused. "Besides you, of course."

"Of course," I repeated.

He reached out and gave me dap, but before he leaned back, I asked, "We straight?"

He hesitated for a moment that was a second too long.

But then he said, "Oh, yeah, man. Definitely. We're good. We're cool. We're straight." He strutted away as if we hadn't had this hard talk. Right before he stepped out of the space, he turned back and pointed at me. "'Cause you the man." He laughed.

I waited for a couple of moments before I asked myself what he meant. But then I settled back and told myself that Trey and I were fine; we'd said those things that needed to be spoken. The situation had been handled and now we could focus on being brothers again.

The only thing was . . . I had this feeling. Because nothing in life was ever simple when it came to Trey Taylor.

# 13

# Damon

My hands were stuffed in my pocket as Trey and I strolled up the walk. The Arlington House was a haven in the middle of the city, which is exactly why I'd set Ms. Irene up in this place. Right across from DC's natural gem that could rival New York's Central Park every day, the grounds of Arlington House, with all its majestic trees and thick greenery, made it feel like we weren't even in the US of A anymore.

"This place," Trey said just as he strode to the right at the fork in the path, veering toward the sign that read, "All Visitors This Way."

"Yo." I paused and motioned with my head for Trey to follow me to the left.

He frowned. "We don't need to check in?"

Pulling the key from my pocket, I tossed it and he snatched it from the air. "Nah, man. Those rules ain't for me," I told him.

He chuckled and shook his head. "I guess some things haven't changed."

I gave him a slow nod before we turned up the walkway that led to Ms. Irene's building. She lived in one of the apartments on the lower level, and even though I had a key, I was always respectful. I always called her when I was on my way and I always knocked when I got to her place.

"Damon? Is that you?" she called out, her voice strong from inside her apartment.

Trey stood behind me, and even though I couldn't see him, I could feel his smile. We'd decided that we wouldn't tell his grandmother he was home. It had taken a long time for her to get over the fact that her only grandchild had been given a sentence that ensured she wouldn't live long enough to see him as a free man.

When she pulled the door open, I marveled, as I always did, at how spry this eighty-four-years-young woman looked. She really could have lived on her own, but it was that one fall and the twelve hours that passed before her neighbor found her that had me move her to this assisted living facility. She had her privacy, but she had support all around her and our minds were at peace.

Her dentured smile was wide when she saw me. "But as for me and my house . . ." She paused the way she always did, waiting for me to finish the scripture.

I knew the rest, of course. Had been knowing it since I'd known Ms. Irene and Trey. The same way my pops schooled me and Trey on the streets, Ms. Irene tried to get into our heads with scripture. My pops had the greater impact; for years, all I knew about God was from Joshua 24:15 and the words Ms. Irene made me say every time I entered her home. But today I wasn't going to say anything.

Behind me, Trey finished the verse, "We shall serve the Lord."

She tilted her head and squinted.

Then that eighty-four-year-old, no-more-than-one-hundred-pounds, silver-haired woman reached out and with one hand shoved me to the side so hard I hit the brick column at the side of her door.

"Dang, Ms. Irene!"

But neither the old lady nor her grandson heard me because they were tucked in each other's arms, Ms. Irene looking like a dwarf being swallowed up.

They made no sounds—well, except for Ms. Irene's "Jesus. Jesus. Jesus."

Now, I wasn't the sentimental type. I mean, I could get my romance on with my girl, but you weren't never gonna see any kind of weakness in me in any kind of way. But this right here; man, this could have made an OG cry. And as she called out to Jesus at least seventeen dozen more times, I pounded my chest and raised my fist to the sky, expressing my own gratitude to the Lord.

I don't know how many minutes they stood there, but I waited until Ms. Irene stepped back and finally spoke new words. "I never thought I'd see this day."

"Grandma." Trey's voice kinda shook and now I understood why he'd said he needed a day or two before he visited her. She was the only person walking this earth who got to him, and he knew that one of the reasons her health had deteriorated so quickly was because of her constant worry about him.

"Are you home?" she asked, but before he could answer, her eyes got small. "Wait a minute." Her voice was lower. "Are you supposed to be here? You didn't escape, did you?"

I laughed, but Trey answered seriously, "No, Grandma. I'm cool. I'm out. It's all legal."

She blew out a long breath before she grabbed his hand. "Well, why we standing out here? Come on, let me show you this nice place that Damon got for me." She paused where I stood and she reached out her other hand to me, but I shook my head.

She frowned.

"Ms. Irene, I'm gonna let you and Trey have a little time together."

Her smile told me she really appreciated that, but her words said, "No, you come on in too, baby. I can't believe this. I have both my grandsons with me."

Leaning over, I gave her a kiss on her cheek. "I gotta make a run."

She looked like she was about to ask me again but changed her mind.

I said to Trey, "Text me when you're done and I'll . . ."

Before I could finish, he said, "I know my way around this city. Where you want to meet up?"

I told him that I'd be in my office, then I gave Ms. Irene another kiss, trotted down the long path past the Administration Building and into my car. There were parking spaces on the grounds, but I'd parked on the street so that Trey and I could take that walk. I'd wanted Trey to have the full effect of the atmosphere where his grandmother lived.

Now that Trey and Ms. Irene had been united, I had to take care of business. But before I could get focused on all that I had to do, my cell phone binged and when I glanced at the screen, there wasn't a single thought of business in my mind.

Tiffanie's photo popped up on my screen with her text beneath:

**What are you wearing?**

That made me laugh out loud. Just days before our wedding, Tiffanie was turning into a freak! Not that I'd ever been unhappy with who she was and how she took care of me between the sheets. But since yesterday, my girl was out of control.

First there was the way she kissed me in front of Trey. Like if I hadn't stopped her, she would have been willing to put on a show right there in my office. And then there were the texts that had started coming, with all kinds of innuendos.

I texted back:

**You first. What you got on?**

A couple of seconds later:

**Nothing.**

I smiled.

**Wanna see?** she texted back to me.

I started up the car and hit the engine.

**OMW!**

I'd barely typed the last letter when my cell vibrated. Thank God there was no one (not even Trey) in this car, because if anyone saw the look on my face, I would have lost my gangsta card for sure.

"What's up, bae?" I said.

"Just you. Are you up . . ."

I groaned and shifted in the seat.

She finished with, "For our wedding in just two days?"

"You know you need to stop playin', right? Where you at? I wanna see you now, woman!"

She laughed, but it wasn't just a chuckle or a giggle. This was a sound that came from her throat, the sound of a woman, a woman in need.

And every part of me that made me a man wanted to go and help out my damsel who was in distress.

I asked, "Are you home? I'm on my way."

"No, Damon."

Had she just *purred* my name?

"We have to wait," she said. "Just two more days. You can hold on for two more days, can't you?"

And then she moaned and groaned the way she did when I was handling my business with her.

"Tiff!"

"Good-bye," she whispered. And then, nothing.

I stared at the phone for a second or two, hoping that she would call back and demand that I be at her place in fifteen minutes.

I would have made it there in ten.

But she didn't call, and after a few more moments, I tossed my cell onto the passenger's seat, shifted my pants again, and pushed the accelerator.

My girl.

She'd been right about shutting down the sex until our wedding night, because it had done something to her. And now there was all this anticipation.

My wife.

I couldn't wait.

Friday night, April 1, was going to be epic.

◆

THIS WAS RIDICULOUS. With all the work I had to do, I was just sitting here, looking at the texts that Tiffanie had sent to me.

These photos weren't off the chain, they'd broken the chain. I stared at the picture of her bare leg that stopped high on her thigh. Just her leg. Then the one where she wore what looked like one of my shirts or maybe her grandfather's, though I hoped not because she had it completely unbuttoned and had nothing on underneath.

There was no way I was going to survive forty-eight more hours.

My phone binged again, and I was almost afraid to open the new text. But I did. And I jumped up. Because she was lying on her bed in her birthday glory, surrounded by bills. Lots and lots of dollars.

**Your two loves.**

That was all the text said.
I laughed. Then moaned. And laughed again.

**If you don't stop,** I began my text, **I'm on my way.**

**Okay. Sorry. I have to get back to work. Call me to-night. Love you.**

I sent her ten hearts back, once again glad that I was alone because if anyone saw me sending texts with emojis . . .

"What's up, bruh?"

I jumped two inches off my chair.

"Whoa!" Trey held up his hands as he walked into my office. "What's got you acting like you running from the police?"

"I'm cool, just didn't hear you come in."

"Yeah, I knocked 'cause Hillary wasn't at her desk, but you seemed a bit preoccupied." He kinda craned his neck, trying to get a glance at my cell, but I slid it off my desk and into my top drawer. In case Tiffanie checked back in with me, I didn't want Trey to see my girl like that. "So, how're things with Ms. Irene?"

Trey leaned forward and shook his head. "I'll never be able to thank you."

"We already said these words. No gratitude necessary. This is what we do. We have each other's backs."

It was only a millisecond, but I'd been trained to notice every little twitch of a man's body. And I saw that little fade of his smile, though since I was looking straight at him, he kept his front.

*We're good, we're cool, we're straight.*

That's what he said to me yesterday.

"So, Ms. Irene's good?" I repeated.

He nodded.

"She got everything she needs?"

Again he gave me a nod, but this time he added, "Anything she needs from now on, I can take care of."

I wanted to tell him that he didn't have to worry about all of that, but I remembered who I was dealing with, so I just sat back and nodded. "So, Ms. Irene didn't try to get you to move back here? Get you to move in with her?"

He laughed, and the tension that had been between us, eased. "You know my grandma."

I shrugged and tried to keep my tone nonchalant. "Maybe you should give that some thought."

"That's what she said." He paused and his eyes scanned my office the way he'd been doing every day since he'd been home. If I didn't know my boy, I would've thought that he was casing the joint, checking out everything to do a hit on me. His eyes rested on Tiffanie's photo once again when he asked, "You use all that money that you were stackin'?"

"Damn, son!" Since I'd been hangin' with Tiffanie and her grandparents, I'd kept my mouth clean. But Trey had surprised me with that question. "Get your hands outta my pocket."

Even though I said that with a grin, Trey knew I wasn't playing. I never talked about my money with anyone, especially not Trey, since I didn't trust him that way. He wasn't the only one, though. No one needed to know more about my finances than I was willing to tell. Only Tiffanie could ask, and she was the first person to get close to me like that.

"Why you blow like that? I'm just askin'. We boys, right? Fam, right?"

I paused and reeled myself in.

*We're good, we're cool, we're straight.*

I told him, "Yeah, I used some, saved some, spent some to make some more." I gave myself another moment to pause and try to figure out these nagging thoughts I had about why Trey kept checking out my space, why he always had his eyes on Tiffanie's picture, and why now he wanted to know about my money. So I decided to just ask him, "Why you wanna know?"

The only answer he gave me was a shrug. But then, in the silence, it hit me. Trey *was* worried about money. First, he had Ms. Irene, and he had to be concerned about how he would pay that bill at Arlington House. And then, I didn't know his situation in Atlanta, though it couldn't have been stable, since he'd been out for just a little more than a month. No matter where he finally settled, he needed finances, since I was sure he didn't have any money stacked. I couldn't go at it from the angle of his grandmother, nor could I say that I just wanted to help, but I could make an offer from another place. "You're doing me a real solid by standing next to me when I do this thing on Friday," I began. "So just know that I got you. I got the hotel and all the expenses there, but anything else you need, I got you. You don't come out of pocket for anything while you're here."

I hadn't even finished before Trey was shaking his head. "No, I'm good. No need for charity."

I wanted to make one of those old-school moves on him, where my aunties and uncles in the neighborhood used to slap me upside my head when I said something stupid. Who'd said anything about charity?

But I had to let him have his respect. I'd figure out another way.

He said, "Yeah, I'm no charity case. No need for that. I'm stackin' like never before." He stood and began to move back and forth behind the chair he'd been sitting in. "I've been rolling in it for a minute now. You know how it was for me before I went in; I was able to set some of that aside, the government didn't get it all." His words flowed like a river. "So you ain't got to worry about me." He shook his head the entire time he talked and walked.

I wasn't going to call him a liar, so I just sat back and let him rant about all the things I was sure he *didn't* have.

When he'd tired himself out and sat down, I said, "I'm glad to hear that. 'Cause if you're good, then I am, too. Just know—"

He held up his hand and I didn't continue. "So, bruh, what we gonna do now? Wanna go out? They still got some good strip clubs up here?"

I kept my eyes right on him, not even blinking when I said, "No strip clubs for me. I was thinking about heading out to the Congressional Country Club. Hit a few balls."

At first he frowned.

I clarified. "Golf balls. I was gonna head out to the driving range."

He shook his head. "You can't be serious."

I stood behind my desk. "As serious as Donald Trump's hair stylist."

He laughed. "Bruh, I may have been locked up for a while, but I know that cat ain't serious."

"He is; I've met him. So get up, let's go."

He slapped his hands on his legs, shrugged, then said, "All right . . ." He gave me a look from the corner of his eye. "You sure you don't wanna go out and meet some females?"

I didn't even let a moment go by. "No need for me to do that, son. I got the one I want."

He grinned. "Yeah, you do." After a moment's pause, he added, "That's what I'm looking for. A female exactly like the one you got."

Now that made me smile. "That's what I'm talking 'bout. That's what I want for you. The right female can settle you down, help you get in the right place."

"That's what I'm saying. That's why I want one like the one you got. I want her to be so much like Tiff, that maybe we won't even be able to tell them apart."

He laughed and I frowned. I had told him about her name.

"Yeah, Tiffanie is the truth," he said.

I took a breath and calmed myself down. That Tiff he'd just spoken was just a slip. Truly, I needed to stop taking myself down this lane where I constantly doubted Trey.

"Well then, good thing we're heading out to Bethesda, 'cause you ain't gonna find one like the one I got at no strip club."

He laughed. "What you got against strippers? I remember

the days when you put out so many dollar bills, by yourself you paid some of those girls' college tuition."

"Yeah well, those days are gone," I said walking toward the door.

He paused as he passed my desk, glancing down at Tiffanie's picture once again. "Yeah, bruh, I guess those days are gone."

He walked past me out the door, leaving me wondering for the millionth time, why he kept peeping my girl's picture.

# 14

# Tiffanie

I was so ready to be Mrs. Damon King.

But I wasn't going to be Mrs. King until tomorrow. Tonight, I had to settle for just being Damon's princess.

That's how I felt as the valet opened the door to Damon's Bentley and then my man came around to take my arm.

Damon told the valet, "Take her bag and that garment bag up to the bridal suite."

The man nodded and took the fifty-dollar bill from Damon's hand, and then my man and I stepped together into what was known as the Crown Jewel of Pennsylvania Avenue.

Inside the Willard Hotel, I felt like I was entering a castle, with the lobby that exuded elegance from every inch of the massive space. From the marble floors, twenty-foot columns, and tropical plants—this hotel made the same grand statement it had been making since the mid-1800s.

This was where my man had decided that we would celebrate our union. From the friends and family gathering tonight to the reception tomorrow, this was also where I was going to spend my last night as a single woman.

My head was high as Damon and I walked past the other patrons, who'd paid hundreds, even thousands, for these five-star hotel rooms. While I always felt a little stiff and a bit too formal whenever I was in a place like this, Damon was the opposite—always relaxed as if he were at home, which he was, since he did so much business here.

As we took the elevator to the second floor, where our dinner was being held in one of the private rooms, I wanted to close my eyes, pinch myself, do something, anything, to make sure that this life, my life was real. And then I wanted to do something, anything to make sure that it would always be this way.

I had to take another deep breath when we stepped off the elevator and into the space that was ours. The grandeur of the hotel had followed us up from the lobby and into this taupe- and bronze-colored room. The ten tables, which sat ten people each, circled the perimeter and were swathed with taupe and bronze satin cloths that matched the draping on every wall. Inhaling, I took in the wonderful fragrance of the fresh-cut lilac tulips and pink roses that I'd ordered, my only contribution to this night.

The room was already filled with most of our guests and as we stepped over the threshold, our friends and family applauded.

The first to catch my eye were my grandparents—standing in front, beaming as if they were proud of my accomplishment. I hadn't done anything—except chosen a good man. But that had to be huge for them—I was the success they could tout that allowed them to forget the failure.

"Baby girl, you look beautiful." The voice of my grandfather, the Reverend CJ Jackson, boomed through the room, even though I'm sure to him, he spoke barely louder than a whisper.

But that's what happens when you're almost six foot five, almost three hundred pounds, and sure 'nuff one of the most renowned reverends in DC. He had to lean down a ways to kiss my cheek.

"You do, too," I said. Then I laughed. "I mean, not beautiful, but you look so handsome, Granddaddy."

That was the truth. My grandparents often dressed up for events they had to attend, mostly religious affairs, but tonight they'd taken dressing to a level where few of their friends would recognize them.

My grandmother wore a rose-colored, tea-length silk dress that didn't look like it had come off any rack. My grandfather, who had to shop at those Big Men stores, was in a suit that for sure had been tailored. Knowing Damon, it had been designed by one of his people. My grandparents looked hooked up and happy.

At least they'd looked happy when I'd first walked in, but now there were tears in my grandmother's eyes. And when she reached for me, her tears flowed.

"Gram." I hugged her, pulling her into my chest. "What's wrong?"

"This is just a prelude," my grandfather answered for his wife as she sniffed over and over. "Trust me, she'll be crying all weekend."

"Oh, I hope not," I told my grandmother as I wiped her tears with my thumbs.

But that was the end of my private time with the people who were the king and queen of my life. Damon and I were surrounded by our friends in a rush that swept us in different directions.

"Girl, you look so beautiful," Sonia said.

I grinned. We had picked out this lilac, raw-silk two-piece together. The outfit looked like a regular, tailored suit—until I turned around and the bare back made my girlfriends moan with envy.

"Oh yeah," said Dana, one of our classmates from Howard. "That suit is first-class fly!" She snapped her fingers with each word she spoke.

On the other side of the room, I heard Damon receiving the same accolades about how good he looked. But he got extra commentary about this being his last night of freedom.

I rolled my eyes. Whatever! His boys knew that Damon had won the prize!

Within minutes, our party was poppin'. This was supposed to be just a dinner, a small gathering to do an unconventional rehearsal and then to thank our family and friends for their current and future prayers.

"This is the reception before the reception," Damon had told me as he'd planned this event. I had wanted to help, but he told me to focus on the wedding 'cause these kinds of parties were what he did best. So I'd let him handle it, and handle it he did.

The waitstaff was plentiful though discreet and the men maneuvered through the maze of our guests, balancing crystal flutes on sterling silver platters filled with nonalcoholic champagne—a bow to my grandfather. Behind them were the women, offering an abundance of imported caviar and lime-crusted scallops and jumbo shrimp wrapped in barbecued bacon.

In the corner, a harpist sat on a golden stool and filled the air with music that sounded like melodies from heaven. We chatted, we laughed, we joked, we reminisced. Good times passed, and it wasn't until we prepared to take our seats for dinner that I noticed that Trey wasn't there.

He wasn't there.

And it took all this time for me to notice.

How great was that?

I'd kept to my plan, not seeing Trey at all. I'd be lying if I said that because he was out of my sight, everything else was easy. It had been a battle to keep thoughts of him out of my head and longing feelings from between my legs. But I'd fought one heck of a good fight by keeping my focus on Damon. All that attention on him and all my texts to him had my man ready for our wedding night.

Even I was anticipating the consummation of our marriage. Looking back, Trey walking into my life had been good; it made me change it up and make it spicy-hot for Damon. It had been thrilling to have my man moaning and groaning without him laying a single finger on me.

Maybe one day I would thank Trey, but right now, my prayer was that since he hadn't yet arrived, maybe he'd stay away. Maybe God had done something to make him change his mind about standing up for Damon. Maybe Trey was already at the airport waiting on the next thing smokin' back to Atlanta.

As Damon held out my chair for me at the head table, I prayed that all of my maybes would become actuallys. Then, right as I scooted my chair under the table, I looked up.

And there was Trey.

Standing at the door with the bright light from the hall shining on him like a spotlight.

Every bit of the calm I'd felt since the last time I saw Trey fled. My breathing almost stopped, and without even thinking about it, I grabbed Damon's hand.

"You all right, bae?" he whispered.

"Yes," I gasped. "I just wanted to . . . needed to hold you."

He grinned. "After all you've been doing to me this week, I'm telling you, tomorrow night"—he lowered his voice some more and brought his lips right to my ear—"you'll be able to hold me all day and all night." He moaned and for a moment, my thoughts were only on him.

Then Trey's voice came between us.

"Hey, sorry I'm late," he said, leaning a little too close to me.

Damon scooted his chair back. "No prob. How's Ms. Irene?" he asked as he stood.

"She's good. You know, once I saw her yesterday, I had to go back today."

I looked up at Trey. "Is your grandmother all right?"

He nodded. "Yeah, it's just been years since we spent any time together and I'm trying to make up for that." He put his hand on my shoulder and squeezed. "Thanks for asking, Tiffanie."

I wondered if anyone else felt that sudden surge of electricity that charged through the room. I pressed my lips and my legs together, nodded, and turned my attention back to the table, grateful for the salad that had been placed in front of me. Now I had something to do with the energy that rolled like waves through me.

Thank God Damon sat on one side and my grandfather was on the other. Between the two men who gave me life, their presence would keep my eyes and mind away from the man who had no business in my life at all.

Through the three-course dinner of chilled lobster salad, then filet mignon and stir-fried spinach, and a seven-layer double-chocolate cake for dessert, I was able to chat and pretend that Trey Taylor wasn't there.

I gushed at every word that Damon said. I laughed at every joke my grandfather told. But it was all an act because with every gush and every chuckle, I was more aware of Trey than I was of Damon or my grandfather. I was aware of every breath that man took, even though he was on the other side of Damon.

It seemed that these days away from him had done me no good. With his absence, I'd grown more sensitive to him. He was too far away for me to hear his words, but when I cocked my head a certain way, I could see his lips as he talked. His lips that made me moan.

Then I watched his hands. He spoke with grand gestures, flamboyant, almost, but still masculine. Definitely masculine. I wondered, for what had to be the millionth time, what he could do with those fingers.

I was so focused on Trey that I didn't even notice Damon stand up. It wasn't until he tapped his glass with his fork that I broke my Trey-trance.

When the room quieted, Damon spoke. "First, I'd like to thank you for coming to celebrate our final night as an engaged couple." He paused and looked down at me. "I just want to make sure that everyone in this room knows how much I love this woman."

Ooohs and ahhhs took the space of the silence and I smiled up at Damon. "Before we really get this party started, we've got to get a little bit of business out of the way."

He went on to explain why we weren't having the traditional

rehearsal and dinner, since we were all grown folks who'd attended plenty of weddings.

"So, since we're just having my best man"—he turned to Trey and patted his shoulder—"and Tiffanie's best girl"—he paused and raised his glass to Sonia—"we didn't need to waste a couple of hours practicing when we could be partying!"

Laughter and cheers came from everyone.

"I know everybody will be able to handle their business tomorrow night," Damon said. "So now I can get to what I really want to say." He paused, and when he looked down at me, all joking was gone. "Tomorrow will be the first day of the rest of my life, and no one in this room knows how much I cannot wait to make this woman my wife."

"Dang, you're a poet," one of Damon's boys yelled out.

Another shouted, "Nah, he's a rapper."

Everyone laughed.

"Seriously, though," Damon continued, "anyone who's here who's known me for more than ten years knows that this is not a place where I'd ever expected to be. I didn't live that Huxtable life; heck, Florida and James and 'em lived better than me."

There were lots of chuckles in the room.

"I had no examples of how good life could be, but then I walked into Howard University . . ."

"There he go," someone shouted, "rhyming again."

I was grateful for the laughter because it gave me a moment to blink back my tears.

He lowered his eyes to mine once again. "I'm not complaining about my past, God blessed me in lots of ways, but this blessing He's given me in you, Tiffanie, is the ultimate. If He stopped right now, it would be enough."

"Dang, dawg!"

More laughter.

Damon cleared his throat and looked up as if he'd forgotten that we weren't alone. He took my hand, helped me to stand, and with his glass raised again in the air, said, "To the woman that I will love forever."

Cheers filled the room and we kissed, just a peck on the lips, then we all took sips of the sparkling cider. When Damon placed his glass down, so did I.

"And now, I'd like to do something that isn't usually done at rehearsal dinners or rehearsal parties, or whatever you want to call this; what I want to do right now is dance with this woman for the last time as my fiancée, because the next time I hold her in my arms, she'll be my wife."

The aaahhhs filled the room and the tears came back to my eyes. If this was how it was tonight, would I make it through everything tomorrow? Everyone clapped as Damon led me to the middle of the room. I hadn't even noticed that the harpist had been replaced by a young man whom I recognized as one of Damon's employees. Jay Johnson was Damon's best DJ and he was going to be working our wedding tomorrow during the times when the live band took breaks.

We were the center of all attention when I heard the first three chords of Luther Vandross's "Here and Now." All I could do was melt into Damon's arms and let him hold me as we swayed together.

"I promise to love faithfully," he sang into my ear.

I closed my eyes and just listened to my man sing to me. Inside his arms, the world faded to the wonderful color of serenity.

I knew every word, every stanza of the song, so when it was

close to being over, I wanted to shout for the DJ to let it replay the way I did whenever it came on one of my playlists.

As if he knew that he needed to wake me up from this dream, my Prince Charming kissed my forehead, then my eyelids, my nose, and finally, his lips made their way to mine.

With the last note, our guests clapped and I reluctantly backed away.

He held my hand as he spoke again to everyone, "Okay, now. We got this room for a couple more hours. But before we get this party really started, I'd like the maid of honor and my best man to join me and Tiffanie."

My heart started pounding right then and I did everything that I could to keep my eyes away from Trey's. When Sonia and Trey stood in the center of the floor with us, Damon said, "All right—one more dance, for tradition's sake—and then, everyone else can join in."

Before I could protest, Damon handed me off to Trey.

What?

"The best man will dance with Tiffanie," Damon explained, "and I'm gonna hit the floor with this beautiful lady."

"All right now," Allen, Sonia's husband, yelled out.

Everyone laughed—except for me and Trey. If Damon had any idea what he'd just done . . .

Just shoot me now! Because there was no way I was going to make it through this dance.

Damon made a motion to the DJ, then grinned at me. "I did this for you, bae. Your favorite old-school song," he said before the keyboard chords of The Gap Band's "Yearning for Your Love" bounced off the walls of the room.

Oh. My. God!

What was Damon thinking? This was just plain stupid. If he'd wanted to go old school, he should've gone all the way back to my favorite song when I was four. "If You're Happy and You Know It" would have been more appropriate.

Trey chuckled, as if he was entertained by my pain. He wrapped his arms around me, pulling me close. It didn't take but a couple of seconds for my blood to pump harder. I just prayed that I didn't . . . shudder the way I'd done before.

Then Trey's hands started moving. From around my waist he edged them, almost imperceptibly, up my back.

Keep breathing, I told myself. In and out. Out and in.

Then I stopped that thought. Not exactly the right words to be thinking. It was too late, though. Those words stayed, now with new meaning—in and out and out and in.

His hands set a fire against my bare skin, but I had no time to focus on that because he leaned in closer and his lips grazed the top of my forehead.

"Back off," I hissed.

He bent a bit back with surprise in his eyes. "You okay, Tiff?"

"My name is Tiffanie and I want to keep this dance respectful," I said, using one of Damon's favorite words.

"Oh . . . kay." The way he spoke, the way his forehead wrinkled into a frown made it seem like he had no idea what I was talking about.

I took a breath and tried to lower my anxiety a few notches. Was it just me? Everything I was feeling . . . was this just my imagination, just what I wanted him to do to me?

Damon and Sonia were just a few feet away, and over Trey's shoulder, I watched Damon hold my best friend close. Then he whispered something, they laughed together, and Sonia rested her chin on Damon's shoulder.

Okay, they weren't dancing like strangers and as I looked at the folks who surrounded us, no one thought anything was up with their dance. Sonia's husband was even capturing the moment with his cell phone.

I needed to chill.

So I went back to concentrating on my . . . breathing. In and out. Out and in.

"Relax, Tiff." His voice broke through my focus and ignored what I'd just told him about my name. "There's no need for you to be nervous."

I was looking at my husband-to-be, but to Trey I said, "I'm not."

"Really?" A pause. "Then why are you shaking?" Another pause before he had the audacity to chuckle.

I backed away, just enough so that when I looked up, I would be able to see right into his eyes. I wanted him to see that I was in no way afraid of him.

I lifted my eyes and his were waiting for me. His dark, seductive eyes that said all the things that I'd been dreaming about.

And then it happened.

Again!

I closed my eyes and squeezed my legs together. It was a small shudder, and Trey grasped me, holding me up like he knew what happened.

Damn!

I was mad. I was embarrassed. And thirty seconds later, when the song ended, I was relieved. Pressing my hands against his chest, I gave him a shove that was way too gentle for what

I really wanted to do to him. With my eyes down, I passed by Damon and Sonia, and my grandparents, who had joined us on the dance floor, I guess. I hadn't even noticed.

I moved past all of them into the hallway and dashed right into the ladies' room, taking refuge in the last stall. Without pulling my dress up or my panties down, I sat my butt on the toilet.

What on God's earth was going on? In all the times I'd been with Damon, he had never made me feel this way . . . or made me feel . . . that thing. And now this man . . . Trey had done it by just looking at me, by just talking to me, and now, just by holding me. Three times.

The bathroom door creaked open and I groaned.

Please, God. Don't let this be anyone I know.

Whoever it was, I just wanted the lady to come in, do her business, and then leave without getting into mine.

But then a whisper. "Tiffanie?"

There was no hiding from Sonia, so I swung the stall door back. She frowned when she saw me just sitting there.

"¿Qué está pasando?"

I sighed and kept my voice low, too. "Are we alone?"

She bent down and looked at the floor of the other stalls. "Unless someone is standing on the toilet, we're cool." Turning back to me, she asked, "Are you all right?"

I shook my head, then pushed myself up. "It's Trey."

It took a moment for my words to register and make sense, and then she waved her hand at my words. "Oh, goodness." Sonia turned to the mirror as if problem solved! She flicked the curls from her face. "Really, Tiffanie? That again?"

I closed my eyes and wondered if I had the guts to tell Sonia what had just happened. All I could come up with was, "I think Trey's the devil."

Sonia faced me with a straight face, but then busted out laughing. "Girl, I've never known you to be so dramatic." Then she turned right back to that mirror as if she didn't care.

But she was my bestie and I knew that she did, so this was on me. I had to find a way to convince her.

"You're right," I spoke to her reflection. "I'm not the dramatic type, so doesn't that tell you something?"

"Yeah, it does." She faced me again. "It simply means that your behind needs to get married so that you can stop all this mess."

"It's not me," I insisted. "It's him."

"No, it's you. It's because you've only been with one man and now you're fantasizing about what it would be like to be with one more, except your time is just about up. Tomorrow, it'll be just one man for the rest of your life. Touching my arm, she added, "But it's all right." Her words were soft and soothing as if she was giving lessons on the birds and the bees to a child. "It's normal."

"It's not normal and it's not that. It's him."

She released a long breath and gave me another wave like she was tired of talking about this. "Well, whatever it is, it'll be over tomorrow. You and Damon will be married and Saturday, Trey will be back where he belongs. In somebody's hood, slinging somebody's dope." She laughed and patted my face with one of the lavender-scented cloths that rested on silver trays on each sink. "It's just your imagination."

"Just my imagination," I repeated.

"And you and your imagination don't have anything to

worry about, because Trey told Damon he had to get going right after you left the room."

Her words let me breathe.

"Now, come on. Because with the way you ran past me and Damon, he'll be coming in here any second if I don't get you out there and show your man that you're all right."

She grabbed my hand like she was my keeper, and I stumbled out behind her. Just like she said, Damon was waiting a few feet from the restroom door, his forehead creased with worry. "Bae, please tell me that you're not sick."

"I'm not sick."

His shoulders relaxed, but then he stiffened again. "Then what happened?"

"I felt a little dizzy."

He took my hand. "Maybe you didn't eat enough," he said as if it was his job to figure out my problem and find a solution.

"Don't worry about her," Sonia butted in. "It's just love. Nothing that a few wedding vows won't cure," she added before she sauntered away.

"I'm fine. Really," I told Damon once we were alone.

Damon kissed me with one of his signature kisses, the kind that had made me fall in love with him in the first place. The one that was gentle and made me feel so loved, so special and safe.

"Well, if you're sure. But maybe if you're not feeling well, I should go ahead and walk you to your suite now."

"No, I told you, I'm fine. Plus, I thought we had this room for a few more hours."

"We do, but some of the fellas . . ." He paused, giving me a couple of moments to figure it out. "Well, you know . . ."

I did know. Without him saying another word, I knew that

Damon's friends wanted to blow this joint and get some kind of bachelor party started.

I couldn't say that I was all that excited about *that* party, but there was one thing that I could say—I trusted my man and I knew no kind of cheating would be going down tonight or any night.

He said, "Half of the fellas are gone already."

"You go on," I said. "I guess we'll just have an all-girls party here."

"Not quite all girls. Your grandfather will still be here."

Not even a second passed before I suggested, "Why don't you take him with you?"

Damon's eyes bucked so wide, there was no way I could hold back my laugh. This time I was the one who pulled him into my arms.

"Go on. Have a good time," I said. "But not too good."

"Thanks, bae. And don't you stay too long. I want you to look beautiful tomorrow, though I don't know how you're going to improve upon perfection."

I smiled before we gently pressed our lips together.

When he leaned back, he said, "Whew, I better get out of here or I might never leave."

Laughing, I said, "Go on." When he turned around, I tapped him on his butt. "Behave yourself; I don't want to have to bail you out of jail tonight."

"Bae," he began, looking at me over his shoulder, "because of you, I can't do anything but behave. I don't know any other way." Then suddenly, he turned around and ran back to me. Grabbing me, he whispered, "Do you realize this is our last good-bye?"

"I know. Next time I see you . . ."

"We'll be ready to be man and wife. The day is finally here."

"Finally," I said. "I love you, Damon King."

He sighed. "Are you sure I can't spend the night with you?"

"Come on, babe. We've made it this far. Tomorrow . . ." I finished my sentence with a kiss.

He moaned. "Okay, well, I may not be able to see you, but will you . . . text me?"

He leered, I laughed.

"I'll text you."

"Okay, and at midnight, I'll call you. Our final 'good night'."

"You better."

"Hey, King," one of his friends shouted from down the hall, "you riding with us?"

"Go on," I told him again. He backed away, slowly at first, then with a laugh, he turned and strutted the rest of the way. As I watched him, I whispered, "Please, God. Help me!"

That made me smile. I wanted that man in every way. I really, really wanted Damon King and couldn't wait until tomorrow.

# 15

# Damon

can't believe you're really gonna do this," one of my boys said.

Another added, "What I can't believe is that *Tiffanie* is really gonna do this. Does she know your history, D?"

Before I could respond, another one of my friends said, "Maybe we should tell her."

Their laughter bounced off the walls of the Martini Lounge, one of the classiest spots in DC, a private men's club that not many in the city knew about, which is why I often came here whenever I wanted to chill.

I joined in the laughter, knowing that what my boys said was in fun, understanding that this was all part of the night-before-the-wedding ritual.

As we sat around the octagonal mahogany table, it seemed that everyone was having a good time, even though I hadn't been sure how they would take this gathering. I hadn't told any of them how this bachelor party was gonna go down. Of course, they'd offered to plan it weeks ago, but I knew that I would be in for some kinda trouble if I'd turned this over to the hands of one of these cats. We would've been at a strip joint somewhere, with a woman named Delicious hanging all over me.

Through the corner of my eye, I saw activity at the front. Someone was coming through the door. My man.

Trey whispered something to the attendant, probably giving his name. When the man nodded, giving him permission to enter, I watched as he peered into the dimly lit, cigar-smoke-filled room. He didn't spot me until I raised my glass above my head.

In just a couple of long strides, he was at our table. "Yo, what's up?" he said, slapping my shoulder.

"I was worried you weren't gonna make it." I slid to the side a bit so that he could pull up a chair. But he didn't make any moves to sit down.

He stood over me as he said, "Wouldn't miss this. My boy going out like a straight . . ."

"Hold your roll." I held up my hand. "No talk like that tonight. I know you've probably never been in a place like this, but this is a true gentleman's club."

Not even an instant passed before I realized what I'd done. When every part of Trey stiffened, I knew I'd insulted my boy. That's not what I meant to do; I just didn't want any problems with the members who always looked at me and my boys like we didn't belong.

"No, problem, bruh. I'll keep my hood to myself." His tone dripped with sarcasm.

Pushing my chair back, I excused myself, though no one seemed to notice, and I motioned for Trey to follow me. On the other side of the room, I stood at the bar and held up my hand to the bartender.

But Trey said, "Unless you're ordering something, don't call him over for me."

I frowned.

He said, "I've gotta keep a clear head for tomorrow. I'm the best man, remember?"

I grinned and had to admit I was relieved that he wasn't holding that misstep a moment ago against me. "Okay, no drink for you." I downed the rest of my martini, then held up the glass to Ed, the bartender I knew best.

As I waited for my drink, I said to Trey, "I'm really glad to have you here."

"I wouldn't want to be anywhere else, trust me. I'm so glad to be here in DC, so glad to be staying at the Willard, so glad to be in your wedding, so glad to have met Tiffanie."

That made me smile inside, though I kept my stance serious. "All week I've been trying to find the right time to talk to you. Wanted to discuss, where do we go from here?"

He squinted as if he didn't understand.

So I explained, "I'd really like you with me, the way it used to be. You and me. Side by side."

He didn't even let a beat go by before he said, "With you telling me how high to jump and then me jumping?"

His tone made me take a couple of mental steps back, though physically, I didn't even flinch. "Is that how you really saw things?"

For too many seconds, not a single word passed between us. Then Trey grinned. "Just messing with you since I have to watch my language and everything in this place." He slapped me on my shoulder again, this time a bit harder.

Or maybe I was just imagining it.

"Seriously, I want to talk about bringing you on."

"What? As a charity case?"

Even if he was being sarcastic again, I didn't like his words. I shook my head. "You're no charity. I just want us to be working together again."

He waited a moment like he was really giving it thought. Then, as his eyes scanned the room, he said, "This isn't the time or the place to talk about it."

I nodded. "Agreed. Will you still be here when I get back from my honeymoon?"

"Honeymoon?" He laughed as if that concept was the most hilarious thing he'd heard, but I couldn't figure out what was the joke.

"What's funny?"

He shrugged and released a few more chuckles. "I dunno. I guess there are a few words that I never imagined you saying. *Marriage* and *honeymoon* are two of them."

I nodded, realizing that he wasn't being facetious.

He asked, "So where are you going? On your *honeymoon*?"

The way he said it made me take back what I was thinking. He was being flippant and I didn't like it. "Dubai," I told him. "We'll spend the night here tomorrow, then leave on Saturday."

His head moved up and down as if he approved, but his eyes seemed to still be laughing at me.

I tried to ignore that and took us back to my question. "So, will you be here when I get back?"

He gave me a half-shrug. "Depends."

"On what?"

He let another long moment pass. "I got something in the

works here tonight and if it goes down the way I expect, I might be long gone by the time you get back."

It was my turn to pause and think. Trey was really making noise like he was going back to that life. "Sounds like something big. Something serious." I gave him another pause, more space, so that he could bring clarity to his words. When he didn't, I asked, "Business?"

He gave me a slow nod. "You might say that. Something that I should have taken care of a long time ago. Some payback."

My eyes got even thinner. "Trey, it's been a long time since you were in DC. You can't be holding on to any kind of beef."

He didn't say a word.

I continued, "Don't get mixed up in anything. It's not worth it."

He held up his hands. "It's not what you think. It's not conflict. Just some business I gotta handle. In fact . . ." He glanced down at his watch. "I need to get going, need to put my plays into motion."

He was being so cryptic, and I knew what that meant—whatever he had to handle wasn't something that would meet my approval. Or maybe he had some kind of deal going on and he thought that I might try to take it from him.

Now I was feeling annoyed, but with myself, not Trey. He'd been here four days and maybe if I'd had this talk with him already, he wouldn't be about to get caught up in something. I just couldn't seem to find the right time, and now time may have run out.

"Well, go do what you have to do." And only because I really cared about my boy, I asked, "Just one question . . . is this play you're about to run . . . is it legit?"

With a smirk, he said, "More legit than you will ever know."

My head started to do that pounding thing, but I pulled my anxiety back. I wasn't Trey's daddy. "Then go handle yours and I'll see you in the morning."

"Maybe."

I leaned back.

"Just kidding." He laughed. "Man, this wedding has you all kinds of serious."

That was true; I was more serious now than I had ever been. But that wasn't my issue. It was my gut that had me on edge. My gut that told me that something tight was about to go down with Trey. Maybe he needed me.

He gave me dap, then turned around and strolled away, without saying a word to me and without giving a nod to my boys.

But once he disappeared through the door, I grabbed my glass from the bartender. Whatever Trey was going to do, I couldn't tell him not to go, I couldn't tell him to stop. That was the thing about grown folks, you had to let them handle their business. I just hoped that Trey's business wasn't something that would bring him down.

By the time I sat back down with my boys, my thoughts of Trey were on ice. Tonight it was about the celebration of my future life with my future wife and I wasn't going to let anything from the past get in the way of that.

# 16

# Tiffanie

I didn't have the energy to stay at the party too much longer. It was a fusion of exhaustion and excitement that made me eager to get to the bridal suite.

My grandparents had left right after Damon and the guys, so it was really just us girls dancing and talking about the good old days when we were nineteen, twenty, and twenty-one.

But pretty soon, I'd had enough and after saying all of my good-byes, Sonia walked me to the front desk to retrieve the room key. Even though I'd been trying to talk her into staying with me, I couldn't convince her.

"Isn't this the major responsibility of the maid of honor?" I asked making one last effort. "To stay with the bride?"

"A maid, but not the matron. Matrons go home to their husbands *every* night." She kissed my cheek. "Trust me, you'll be glad you had this last night of solitude."

With that, she handed me off to one of the hotel staff, who escorted me to my room.

"There are several restaurants on the premises," said the

man—Mr. Blunt, I read from his brass nameplate—"and our room service is twenty-four hours as well."

"Okay," I said, though I wasn't going to eat another thing, not if I wanted to fit into my Vera Wang tomorrow.

As we moved toward the elevator banks, Mr. Blunt said, "Our gift shop is also open twenty-four hours." He pointed to the store to our right.

"Really?" I said, eyeing the space that looked more like a small mall than a hotel gift shop.

"Yes, our goal is to supply our guests with the ultimate in convenience."

Inside the elevator, Mr. Blunt continued chatting, filling me in on the never-ending list of amenities.

All night long, I had been marveling at the beauty of the Willard, but when Mr. Blunt unlocked the door to my suite and then stepped aside so that I could walk in first, all I could say was, "Wow!"

The room was pure white—everything. From the carpet, to the furniture—it looked like a chamber in heaven.

"Here," Mr. Blunt said, after we walked through the marble-floored foyer, "is the first powder room."

"First?"

He nodded. "There's another one off the dining room."

Dining room? This time I didn't say it aloud. But dang! A dining room in a hotel room? Yes, this was the Willard, but still.

It wasn't until I was closing the door behind the concierge that I took notice of the card atop the dozens of roses set in the middle of the coffee table.

Smiling, I read the first words, and tears sprang to my eyes.

*I will always love you and I look forward to a lifetime of days showing you how much.*

I clutched the note card to my heart, loving his words, loving these flowers. Roses were so traditional, but they meant so much to me. Because whenever Damon and I had done anything romantic, he surrounded us with red roses.

With a sigh and a shake of my head, I wondered how I could ever have had thoughts of another man.

Inside the bathroom, more gifts from Damon were waiting. On the side of the Jacuzzi was a basket filled with scented bath beads and imported oils—in my favorite scent, jasmine—and beside it an array of chocolate-dipped fruit. I turned on the faucet full blast, stripped right there, and made full use of my gifts, relaxing in the tub and enjoying a couple of strawberries.

An hour later, I had dried off, and with nothing to do (and nothing on), I strutted around the suite, reveling in the opulence of the place, while I enjoyed one of the chocolate-dipped bananas from Damon's basket.

Back inside the bedroom, I pulled my wedding dress from the closet. Carefully unzipping the garment bag, I slipped out the satin halter gown that made me feel like a princess every time I tried it on. When I held it in front of me, all I could do was sigh and smile. The full tulle skirt was a bow to all the wedding dresses I'd dreamed about as a little girl. The fitted bodice was the grown-folks part of the design, and the plunging V neckline . . . well, that was all for Damon, who loved my boobs as much as he loved my butt. I'd been going for a royal yet sexy look, and I think I got it right.

Gathering the dress, I returned it to the hanger but left it outside of the garment bag, letting it hang from the closet door frame. I stepped back and imagined myself and Damon tomorrow, taking this pledge in front of God that would forever change our lives.

And then there would be our honeymoon, the time together that I anticipated the most. Pulling open my suitcase, I unwrapped the lingerie that I'd purchased for my wedding night. As I held up the baby-girl-pink La Perla sheer camisole and matching thong, I wondered if it was bad luck to put it on.

Shrugging that thought away, I slid the camisole over my head, slipped into the thong, and then grabbed my pink stilettos from my suitcase. When I pranced back and forth in front of the mirror, I couldn't believe how I looked. I'd never been into this kind of thing; I'd only purchased this lingerie because Sonia told me I should.

But now, looking at my image, this was what had been missing from our relationship. If I'd been wearing outfits like this, maybe Damon would have been hitting me the way I dreamed that Trey would.

Trey.

Why in the world was I thinking about that man?

I rushed into the bedroom, grabbed my cell from my purse, then ran back into the bathroom. Squaring my shoulders, lifting my chest, and tossing my head back, I snapped that picture, then sat on the edge of the tub.

Opening my Messenger, I typed:

**Tomorrow**

and sent that along with the photo to Damon.

Even though he was with his boys, I still did a countdown the way I'd been doing this week whenever I sent the other texts:

Five, four, three, two . . . and before I got to one, Damon hit me back with **Oh, yeah!**

I laughed.

As carefully as I could, I slipped out of the lingerie, returned it to my suitcase, and then, still naked, I climbed into the bed that was fit for two kings. Even before my head had melded into the pillow, I felt exhaustion overtake me. Of course I should be tired after the week I'd had: my wedding, my spa, my Trey.

Trey.

My Trey.

What the hell was I thinking?

It was like all Trey, all the time. I just kept thinking and thinking. Imagining and imagining. Wanting to feel that feeling that he'd given to me again.

I squeezed my eyes shut, but whether my eyes were open or closed, Trey was *in* my mind.

"I'm just tired," I whispered, knowing temptation came when one was drained of energy and didn't have the strength to fight back. At least that's what my grandfather told me.

Rolling onto my other side, I stared at my wedding dress, and that helped to shift my thoughts. I imagined Damon when he first saw me, then our exchanging vows, and the celebration at our reception.

Then the best part—tomorrow night, when Damon would take my dress off. I relaxed even more as my eyelids became heavy with sleep. But as soon as I closed my eyes, all that waited for me in the darkness was Trey.

Sitting up, I glanced at the clock and it had just ticked beyond eleven. I prayed that time would rush to midnight, because if there was ever a time when I needed to speak to Damon, it was now. But until then, I had to find something that would relax and exhaust me, something that would keep my mind occupied.

The all-night gift shop.

Jumping into a pair of yoga pants, a sports bra, and a tank top, I headed down to the lobby. Now, I'd stayed in lots of upscale hotels, but I'd never seen a shop this large. I took my time and browsed through, hanging out a little longer in the handbag section.

Just as I was turning to the jewelry section, a tiny red-and-white beaded clutch made me pause. Slipping the bag from the shelf, right away I knew I'd found a treasure.

It had only been about thirty minutes, but that little browsing and shopping had done me good; I'd be able to fall asleep with the right thoughts on my mind.

At the elevators, one of the doors opened right away. Just as I stepped inside and pushed the button to the penthouse, someone yelled out, "Hold it!"

It was instinct that made me press the button to keep the doors open.

It was dread that made me sorry when Trey stepped in with me.

# 17

# Tiffanie

B y the time my brain caught up to what I'd done, it was too late. The elevator's doors had closed and now I held my breath, and didn't say a word.

"Well, hello, to you too," Trey said, stepping behind me.

"Hi," I finally managed to say, though I kept my eyes on the steel doors. What was he doing here? And then I remembered, this was where he was staying too.

"Hi? Is that all you have for me?"

I nodded and wondered why this elevator was crawling. It hadn't moved this slowly when I came down.

"Damn, baby. It's almost midnight. Does Damon know you're up and hanging out?"

Still, I said nothing. Just pressed my legs together. Just looked at the numbers above my head—second floor . . . third floor . . .

Trey laughed. "You might be mute, but you're still looking good."

The days I'd spent this week doing everything I could to stay away from Trey hadn't helped at all. Now, as I stood in his presence, I realized that his absence had only made me yearn for him more. I'd hidden it beneath texts to Damon, beneath focusing on our wedding, beneath working long hours at the spa. I'd done the best I could to shift my thoughts and pretend that Trey didn't exist. But I couldn't pretend now. There was no way that I could pretend he wasn't standing here because of all the things his presence was doing to me.

I was remembering and wanting to feel it . . . again.

Fourth floor . . . fifth floor . . . sixth floor . . .

That was when I noticed that Trey hadn't hit a number. I wanted to press the seventh floor, then push him out when the door opened and hope that the earth would swallow him whole.

But I didn't ask him what floor he was on because I didn't trust myself. There was no telling what words might come out of me.

Eighth floor . . . ninth floor . . . tenth floor . . .

Trey stood behind me, so close I could feel his heat. I closed my eyes and prayed. And counted the floors, this time without looking up.

Eleventh floor. Please God. Twelfth floor. Please God.

He had moved even closer because now I could feel him *and* smell him. His fragrance was so familiar; it was the one that he'd left behind in my car. The one I was sure was part animal, part man, all him.

And then.

He touched my shoulder and I moaned. If I were being completely honest, I'd admit that I moaned a couple of milliseconds before his hand made contact. As if my body had anticipated his skin on my skin. With his fingers he pressed, then squeezed. It was only a press, only a squeeze. But it was so sensual. Because of the time and space. Approaching the midnight hour, in an elevator.

Alone.

He pressed and squeezed—a one-hand massage on one shoulder. But it was the sexiest massage I'd ever had, and his caress caused all kinds of sensations within me. I was heading back to that place where he'd led me before.

I wanted to tell him to stop. I really did. I wanted to pull myself away from him in righteous indignation. But I couldn't do that because I had to be sane to take those actions and I couldn't find my sanity. I was tumbling, tumbling, tumbling.

My knees could no longer hold me. My brain could no longer control me.

Then.

His lips sought and found one of my weaknesses—the soft space at my lower ear. He blew his hot breath against skin that was already aflame. "You okay, baby?" His voice was strong and sure. Like he was confident and comfortable with what was happening. That was my first thought. And my second—I needed to tell him that I wasn't his baby.

But I didn't answer him because I wasn't okay and he knew it. I was burning, I was panting.

Why couldn't I just turn around and face him?

No! Because if I did that, if I stole even a single glance, something terrible—even more terrible than what was happening now—was going to happen. So what was I going to do? Just let him continue to ignite these fires within me?

I mustered up fortitude and turned. And there were his eyes, waiting for me. Dark. Seductive. They told me all the things I wanted to hear, and this time, his eyes told me that they weren't going to let me go.

"No," I said aloud.

"No, what?" he asked, holding me hostage with his stare. "I didn't say anything for you to say no to."

"But . . ."

"No buts, baby."

There were so many things I should have said, so many things I should have done. But all I could think about was how much I wanted to touch him. Just a single touch. If I could have just a little feel, it would be enough, and then this infatuation or whatever I had with this man would be over and it would all stop here.

That's what I told myself—in those seconds between lust and lunacy. Lust won . . . or was it lunacy? Because I did something that I never thought I'd do, something I'd never done before. I reached for a man who wasn't mine; I reached for *that* part and grabbed him as if he were Damon.

His gift was waiting for me and I gasped. I'd been right all along.

This. Was. Not. My. Imagination.

This man wanted me as much as I wanted him.

It had been a mistake to touch him, though. Because that touch had *not* been enough. Now my hands were drawn to his chest, and when I pressed my palm against him, he moaned. Or maybe that sound had come from me.

Then he made his move, though he didn't touch me. He pressed something on the elevator's panel behind me. The elevator jerked, then stopped. He'd pressed the Emergency Stop button, I supposed, but I didn't have time to figure that out because right after that, his lips were on mine. And my lips, then my tongue welcomed him.

Our tongues waltzed, a slow dance, and I sighed, savoring each second. His lips were exactly what I'd dreamed. Thick and juicy. Sweet and wet.

The elevator filled with sounds of our pleasure and his excitement made me want more of him. So, I moved my lips to his neck, a treat worth tasting, and he thanked me by slipping his hand inside my pants.

"Oh!" I cried out.

I pressed myself against him, realizing now that I might never be satisfied, not until I had every bit of this man. I pulled away for just a moment, just so that I could pant, "Please."

He smiled, but it was audible. His smile was really a snicker, a victorious sneer as if he'd just won a prize.

"Please," I panted again.

This time he laughed.

Shame filled me, it really did. But I couldn't walk away. It was as if I couldn't control my feet or my hands or my thoughts or my words. For the third time, I just begged, "Please!"

I half expected, half hoped that he would deny me. That he would speak sense and tell me that I was Damon's woman and he was Damon's boy.

Instead he taunted me. "Tell me what you want, Tiff."

"Please," I cried because there was no way I was going to say it. Didn't I have to keep just a bit of my dignity?

But he shook his head. "Tell me. Say it."

Wasn't it enough that I was in his arms? Why did he want me to speak my desire aloud?

He said, "Say it . . . or . . ."

Or what? Was he going to deny me? He couldn't.

With his eyes still on mine, he reached over my shoulder and pushed in the Emergency Stop button, setting the elevator back in motion. My heart pounded with anticipation.

Seconds later, the elevator stopped again on the seventeenth floor and I stumbled out, leaving behind the fragrance of our desire that filled the space. Trey didn't follow me, though; he stayed in place. "Say it," he demanded from inside the elevator.

I swallowed, trying to get air, trying to keep the words he wanted to hear inside of me.

The door began to close, separating us.

No!

"Say it," he ordered again as he began to disappear from my view.

"I want you!" I exclaimed, in full panic. "I want you!"

With his foot he stopped the door from closing completely, then jumped into the hall, where I stood heaving for what felt like my final breath.

"I want you," I said again, grabbing him and pulling him to me.

He laughed as he lifted me into his arms and I pressed my face into his neck. As he carried me, I kissed him. On every spot I could find. But even that wasn't enough; I ached for so much more.

At the door, I handed him the key. He jiggled the lock with one hand and held me in his opposite arm. My eyes roamed to the gold plate on the door—Bridal Suite.

I tore my glance away and pressed my face into the curve of his neck. He kicked the door open, then kicked it closed as if he was a madman. I waited for him to carry me across the massive suite into the bedroom. But just four steps into the living room, he stopped and gently laid me onto the soft carpet.

On the floor?

I looked up and into his eyes—dark, seductive.

It didn't matter where he took me, just as long as he did.

"Tell me again," he said as he brought his body above me and his lips close to mine. "What do you want?"

Wrapping my arms around him, I whispered, "You. I want you."

He laughed and rewarded me, by pulling my top and then my bra over my head. My breasts tumbled into his hands and together, we moaned as he did that pressing and that squeezing thing again.

After an eternity of making love to me that way, he shimmied my pants over my hips and away from my body.

His eyes never left mine and once I was completely naked, he stood and stared down at me. His eyes were filled with all the lust that was inside me and I wondered what he was waiting for. Through his pants, I could see that he was as ready as I was.

I reached up for him, but he backed away.

I frowned, wondering if he planned to make love to me with his clothes on. He reached for my hand and pulled me up. Again, he lifted me into his arms, and as he swung me around, my legs hit the vase, and the roses that Damon bought for me spilled across the floor.

But there was nothing I could do about it. Because right now, I had to focus on breathing alone. Anticipation had me shaking and unsteady. When Trey laid me on the bed, then parted my legs wide, an unspoken promise of something wonderful to come, I gasped.

He lowered himself over me once again and my breath quickened even more. He whispered in my ear, "Tomorrow night when Damon brings you in here, remember this, remember me."

Every bit of desire drained from me when Trey said Damon's name.

I blinked.

He pushed himself up and away, then strutted toward the bedroom door. The trembles I felt were different now.

He glanced over his shoulder and with a smirk, said, "I told Damon that his woman was fine." His eyes swept over my nakedness again. "See you tomorrow . . . at your wedding." Then he laughed, a depraved sound that bounced from wall to wall to wall.

Seconds later, the front door to the suite opened and then closed.

For at least a minute, I stayed on that bed, still spread-eagle, still waiting, still anticipating. I didn't move until my cell phone sang and my eyes roved to the clock. It was midnight.

Sam Smith sang, *"Won't you stay with me . . . 'Cause you're all I need . . ."*

I moved, but not toward the phone. I curled into a ball and the first tear fell.

> *Won't you stay with me . . .*
> *'Cause you're all I need . . .*

I cried until my phone stopped singing.

And in the silence that followed, I began to think and I began to sob.

I thought and I sobbed because I had become my mother.

# 18

# Damon

This is Tiffanie. I can't believe that I'm missing you . . ."

I clicked off the call without leaving a message and started to hit Tiff's picture again, but then I paused. There was only one reason why she wouldn't have answered—my baby was asleep. I wasn't gonna even call it beauty rest, because she didn't have to do anything to be beautiful.

But the rest part? She needed that. Because after the way she'd been teasing me these past few days, I planned to keep her in bed for a week. When I finished with my baby, it would take her a month to walk straight.

I laughed out loud as I turned onto Sixteenth Street. "Yeah, rest up, woman," I said out loud.

But right away, my chuckles kinda died down. I really wanted to speak to her. Just to say good night on this, our last night before we'd be united forever. But I needed to chill because number one, she was asleep and no doubt, dreaming about me, and number two, I was about to enter into a lifetime of good nights with my wife.

My wife.

I repeated that thought in my head.

My wife. My wife? My wife!

As much as I couldn't wait, I couldn't believe it either. I was still Damon King, hardcore in every way, whether I had to handle my business in the streets or in the suites. I was cool until I was crossed, and more times than I cared to remember, I'd left a bloody mark behind, complete with the yellow tape.

But Tiff had taken my hardened heart, held it, melted it, and now she owned it. It was not only her innocence that had gotten to me but her vulnerability. She needed me to take care of her and that made me want her even more. The good thing was that she was one of the good girls and wanted only the best for me. I could trust her; I loved that about her. After life on the streets, trust was what I needed most.

That's why I knew—she was my first and she'd be my last love.

At the red light right at Rock Creek Park, I picked up my phone again and clicked on the picture in the text that she'd sent me just a couple of hours ago.

"Damn, bae," I whispered. With the tips of my fingers, I made the photo a little bigger so that I could get a good look at that see-through number she wore. It wasn't until a car blared its horn behind me that I tossed my phone onto the seat. I needed to put that thing down, or I was gonna have an accident.

But for real, though, that girl was the truth and I couldn't imagine my blessing coming in a better package. We would be Team King forever. Just the two of us, no one else wanted, no one else needed—except for our dozens of children, of course.

That thought made me laugh out loud, but at the same time, I looked up to the heavens and thanked God for this. Because there was a point where I'd been sure Tiffanie and I would never get together. A point where I never could've seen where we were today . . .

September 7, 2010

I'D ONLY BEEN back in DC and legit for five years, yet here I was making a seven-figure investment. That old five-story building on U Street would house the conglomerate I was building: my event-planning business, my real estate investment companies, the art gallery I'd just purchased, and the college prep center that Tiffanie had started for my business, right when she graduated from Howard.

As I shook hands with the banker and then escorted him to the door, I thought about how much I'd changed, how much I'd grown, and I had to wonder, for at least the thousandth time, if any of this would have happened without Tiffanie.

When I returned to my desk, I folded my hands behind my head, and reflected on the discussions Tiffanie and I had that led me to this place. It had only been two years and she'd already had such an impact as my strategic planner of operations. Now that she was a Howard graduate, she'd be working for me full-time, trying to find businesses that would expand my brand. With her at that helm, I couldn't imagine where the two of us would go— professionally.

But personally—I had given up that ghost. I'd moved on, though I hadn't made any progress. There were lots of different females in my life, but I couldn't get into any of them, because each made me feel like I was settling. It was because of the comparisons I'd made to Tiffanie. None were as beautiful, as smart, or as ambitious—unless you counted the great efforts they'd made to spend my money and try to get me to attach their names to mine.

That thought made me sigh. I was twenty-nine and ready to become that one-woman man I always said I'd never be. I'd made it this far without baby mamas, but I wanted children. I wanted a woman, I wanted a wife, I wanted Tiffanie.

My ringing cell phone took me away from that dark hole that I was about to enter. I didn't recognize the 202 number, but that wasn't unusual these days; my growing reputation as one of DC's top event planners had all kinds of people reaching out to me.

"Damon?" the female voice asked after I said hello. "This is Sonia."

It took me another moment to put together the name and the voice. "Oh, hey, Sonia." I'd met Tiffanie's best friend a couple of times and, about a month ago, I'd taken the two of them out to eat. It was a spontaneous lunch, though if I were being honest, it was a bit of a ruse. When Sonia had dropped by to see if Tiffanie could have lunch, I'd finagled an invitation under the guise that a man had to eat, too. The truth was, I thought it might be a good idea to get to know Sonia. I was thinking that maybe she could give me some tips on how I just might get to Tiffanie, though I'd left that lunch with no more hope than I had going in.

"Hey," Sonia said. "Listen, I tried to call Tiffanie and I didn't get an answer. Is she there? At work?"

Even though she couldn't see me, I shook my head. "Nah."

"Crap!" she said before I could say anything else.

I continued, "She told me yesterday that she wouldn't be

in today, but I didn't ask her why." I paused. "Is there anything wrong?"

"*Espero que no.*"

Her words made me frown. "Excuse me?"

"I'm sorry. I said that I hope nothing's wrong. It's just that today's Tiffanie's birthday, and I'm worried . . ." Now she paused. "Never mind. I'm sure she'll call me back . . . later."

She said good-bye and hung up before I could ask any questions. I was still holding my phone as I tossed Sonia's words over in my mind. Tiffanie's birthday? She hadn't mentioned that, but lots of people took off from work for their birthday. So why would that make Sonia worry?

I scrolled to Tiffanie's name in my BlackBerry and clicked on her number. After a couple of rings and no answer, I hung up and called back. Again, no answer. I wouldn't have thought much about it, especially now that I knew it was her birthday. But it was Sonia's words—*I'm worried*—that made me grab my keys and wallet from my desk.

"I'm gonna make a quick run," I said to my assistant. "Hit me on my cell if you need me."

Before Hillary was able to nod, I was out the door, in the parking lot and heading over to the new apartment that I'd talked Tiffanie into renting just a few months ago. Gentrification was happening all over DC, but it had hit this area of Southeast like a powerful locomotive. The area that had been known for its high crime and gay clubs was the center of the new ball park and shops that catered to the young Capitol Hill crowd. It was the perfect spot for Tiffanie, though that wasn't on my mind as I pulled into a spot across the street from her building.

Inside, I slipped past the concierge, blending in with residents, then took the elevator to the twelfth floor. I knocked on her door with authority, as if I were supposed to be there and after just a couple of seconds, she opened it.

"Damon?"

For a moment, I paused, just to take in this woman. She always looked good to me in her tailored dresses and suits. But now, wearing nothing more than a pair of navy sweat pants rolled to her knees and a white T-shirt, she'd never looked better to me.

"Damon?"

It wasn't until she repeated my name that I realized I had to say something. "I wanted to come by and say happy birthday." That was the first thing that came to my mind. I didn't want to tell her that Sonia had called me. I didn't want to tell her that Sonia was worried and then I got worried.

She tilted her head.

I repeated, "I found out that today was your birthday and—" I stepped by her, even though she hadn't quite invited me inside—"I wanted to come by and say I hope you're having a good one."

Even though I had walked all the way into her living room, she stood at the door, her arms still folded, making me feel like I was intruding. I had to talk myself into standing there in place until she realized I was gonna stay for a moment and finally closed the door.

With a slight shake of her head, she said, "What's going on? Why are you here?"

"I told you," I said as she walked by me. "It's your birthday."

She lowered herself onto the sofa. "I thought something was going on with work."

"Nope, all's good there." I continued to stand, thinking that I'd already stepped inside without an invitation.

She picked up the remote and took the TV off mute, bringing the CNN anchor's voice into her living room. When she kept her eyes on the TV and said nothing else to me, I repeated, "Happy birthday."

"Thanks," she said.

I was trying to hold my grin in place, but the way she looked, the way she sounded—

"Tiffanie, what's wrong?"

She still didn't look at me when she shook her head.

Now I didn't care if she invited me to sit down or not. I sat next to her. "It seems like something's wrong."

She didn't respond and I didn't know what to do next. I was used to seeing Tiffanie strong, confident, decisive. I'd never seen her like this. Never fragile, never broken. It was reflex that made me put my hand over the one that was in her lap. She didn't move away and I squeezed her hand a little. "I wish you would talk to me."

When the tear pooled at the corner of her eye, then trickled down her cheek, I knew this was serious.

"Please, I wanna help."

She shook her head. "You can't help me. No one can."

I scooted closer, really just so that I could hear her better. "I can't help you with what?" I let a few seconds go by and when she didn't say anything, I added, "Remember when we met? I told you that I would fix it and I did, right?"

For the first time, she turned to me. I smiled but couldn't pull a smile from her.

"There's nothing that you can do with this, Damon. You can't fix everything."

"How do you know?"

Her eyes were back on the television when she said, "Because this is something that I have to work through by myself."

"What is it? And why do you have to do this on your birthday?"

She gave me a shrug.

"Okay," I said after a few moments. "I know what we can do. I'll take you to lunch . . . for your birthday. That may help."

She faced me once again, when she said, "You're not going to stop, are you?"

Even though she'd spoken those words with a leave-me-alone attitude, I said, "Nope, " and grinned, trying with everything inside of me to lighten this up.

But a heavy darkness hovered over her. And now her eyes were filled with tears that threatened to gush right out of her. "I don't want to go out, Damon. I don't want to celebrate. I don't have anything to celebrate. Because what's bigger than my birthday is that today is the day my mother died!"

"Oh!" I said, wishing that I hadn't pushed her to this but then thinking it was best. She probably needed to talk about it.

"I'm really sorry, Tiffanie. I didn't know. And now, I get it. I wouldn't want to celebrate either, I guess. But I have a feeling that your mom would want you to celebrate. It's not like she wanted to die on your birthday."

She gave me a long stare before she laughed, and that startled me. Because she laughed so hard that it took her a while to be able to talk. "Oh, yes, she did. She wanted to die today. Because my mother, in all of the love she was supposed to have for me, she chose my birthday to die." She paused. "She committed suicide. On. My. Birthday."

I was sure that there had never been a time when my mouth was open wider than now.

Tiffanie continued, "She made sure that I would never be able to celebrate my birthday."

Now I'd always been quick, having to think while I stared down guys holding guns and while running from bullets that flew over my head. But nothing had prepared me for this.

The only response I could come up with was, "Maybe it wasn't that she didn't want you to celebrate your birthday, Tiffanie. Maybe it was her way of making sure you always remembered her. She was hurting and she didn't want you to forget her."

It seemed like I'd said the right thing because after a couple of moments, Tiffanie wrapped her arms around my neck. I closed my eyes and held her as she sobbed and sobbed and sobbed . . .

✦

EVEN NOW, AS I remembered, water kinda filled up my eyes. Tiffanie been so broken for all of those years, since she'd discovered that when she was only two, her mother had taken a boatload of pills: sleeping pills mixed with aspirin, then she held Tiffanie in her arms as she left this world. It was a neighbor who'd heard Tiffanie wailing and called the police.

For the rest of that birthday, I held Tiffanie as she explained how she couldn't get into a relationship because down to her soul, she believed the obsession that her mother had with her father was a mental illness.

*"No one would commit suicide over love unless they were mentally ill"* was what she told me.

That was why she felt that she could never take the chance in a relationship.

*"Mental illness is hereditary."*

It had taken so much time to convince her otherwise. So much time to convince her that she could and deserved to be with someone who loved her. So much time to convince her that she needed to give herself a chance . . . and that she could take that chance with me.

MY CELL BUZZED as I had that thought and I smiled. Tiff and I were so connected; all I had to do was think about her and she'd call. But then when the number popped up on the screen, I frowned.

"What's up, son?" I asked the moment I clicked on the Bluetooth in the car. "Everything okay?" If Trey was calling me now, that business he needed to handle had probably turned into some kind of beef.

"Just checking on you," Trey said.

I didn't hear trouble in his voice and I breathed, relieved that nothing was going down the night before my wedding.

He said, "I just got to my room and I was thinking, I'm your best man. Shouldn't I be hanging out with you? Isn't that one of my duties?"

He laughed and I chuckled with him.

"I'm on my way," he said.

"Nah, man. I just left the lounge."

"For real? So where you at? On your way to see Tiffanie?"

He didn't give me room to respond. "Yeah, come on over here, check on her, and then I can meet you down in the bar."

"Nah, I'm not gonna see her tonight."

There was a moment's pause. "Seriously? Don't tell me you believe in that superstitious stuff about not seeing the bride before the wedding? I think you should go see your lady."

"It's not superstition. I just wanna give her a little space tonight. Plus, it won't hurt me to get home 'cause you know I have to hold it down. I have to get my rest so I can be my best tomorrow."

"No doubt. 'Cause you gonna be hittin' that like free throws all tomorrow night!"

I didn't like his overly excited, overly expressive tone as he talked about Tiffanie like she was an ordinary girl. "Yo, son, I keep trying to get you to understand."

"Whoa. Wait. I'm sorry." He paused for just a moment. "You gonna have to give me a minute to catch up to where you're at."

His words were righteous, but that wasn't enough. "Get used to it." My tone was straight, no chaser.

"I guess I better," Trey said, sounding like he took no offense. "I apologize again and I promise, I will give you all the respect you deserve."

There was that word again. *Deserve.* Why did he keep saying that?

Trey said, "But, bruh, on the real, you did good with Tiff . . ."

I inhaled.

"I mean, Tiffanie," he corrected himself before I could do it for him.

I exhaled. It was clear that Trey was trying, so I reeled in my attitude.

But then he had to mess it up with, "It's just that every time I see Tiffanie and I think about you tappin' that all day and all night . . ." It wasn't a complete thought, but Trey stopped as if it were.

This was exactly why, for all the years we rolled together, I was the one in charge. Because Trey didn't know how to listen. If I were anyone else, Trey would have major beef right now just 'cause he didn't know how to show respect.

I had turned into my driveway when he added, "'Cause if she were my woman, I wouldn't let her up out of the bed."

I pressed the button to turn off the ignition and my Bentley purred before it settled into silence. And I sat in that front seat just as quiet as my car. Trey was pushing me over and again and I couldn't figure out why. It seemed, though, that my closed mouth said more than any spoken words could.

"My bad," Trey said. "This is real for you, huh?"

"As real as that heart that's beatin' and keepin' you alive."

"Okay, I promise you from the bottom . . ."

Even through the phone, I heard the way he pounded on his chest.

"From this point forward," he continued, "you'll have nothin' but respect from me for you and Tiffanie."

It was my turn to say, "Cool."

"So now that that's settled, why don't I meet you at your place; we can reminisce about the good ole days when we owned these streets together."

For a moment, I thought about having him come over. We could have a couple of beers and maybe I could talk to him about what I hoped would be our future. But being on the phone with him for even just this little—I'd had enough, at least for tonight. "Yo, I think what I wanna do is rest up, you know what I'm sayin'?"

"I get that. Just know that I'm here for you. No matter what has gone down, you're my brother."

Words from his heart that made me blow out a long breath. Maybe he wasn't trying to get to me. Maybe he was just being who he was.

"Thanks, bruh," I said. "And thanks again for having my back."

He laughed. "Oh, I always got that. I got you, like you got me." He hung up.

His laugh felt out of place and his ending felt abrupt. But we weren't the kind of cats who spent time saying a long good-bye.

As I stepped into my home and replayed our conversation in my mind, I began to think that I was doing too much analyzing. If I had any doubts about Trey, all I had to do was think about where he was right now. This was his idea to be here with me, even though he'd been a bit pressed by our lack of communication. And now even tonight, after he'd taken care of whatever business he had, he'd called to check on me.

I needed to keep my focus on Trey's actions and not his words. And not this gut feeling I had that had to be residue from the old days.

That's what I kept telling myself, even for the hours when I just couldn't fall asleep.

# 19

# Tiffanie

I had a list of lies ready.

"I was at the gym . . . and left my phone in the room."

"I took a stroll through the hotel . . . and left my phone in the room."

"I fell asleep in the Jacuzzi . . . and left my phone in the room."

That was what I was going to say to anybody who asked me why I hadn't answered my phone. Not that it had started ringing yet, since there were still a few minutes before the sun even began its rise.

But I had to be ready with my lies, because it was going to take me hours before I'd be able to face anyone, even on the phone. Of course, through my cell, they wouldn't be able to see my red-rimmed eyes or the bags that had to be forming beneath them. Surely, though, they'd hear my tears and through our connection, feel my shame.

The only lie I didn't have was the one for Damon.

Just the thought of him made me curl up even more. I'd been in bed this way, wallowing in my humiliation, trying to forget last night so that I could make it through today. But my mind couldn't get into the space of forgetting.

*When Damon brings you in here, remember this, remember me.*

After almost six hours of steady crying, I had no more tears. But there were still plenty of sobs within me.

How could I have done this? Was it really because I was just like my mother? I felt that way. I felt the way my grandmother had described my mother, with an obsession that had pushed her into madness. An obsession that had her making calls to my father's wife, showing up at their home until they obtained a restraining order, and even, one day, leaving me on top of my father's car while it was parked in front of his house. It was an obsession that had forced my grandparents to send my mother (and me) away, to live in a vacant apartment that one of their past church members owned in Los Angeles. It was my mother's obsession that made her take her life just a little more than a year after we arrived there.

But my mother's obsession had made her the stalker, and that wasn't what happened with me. I'd done everything to stay away; it was Trey who came into my space, he was the one who came after me. He was the stalker and far more dangerous than my mother, because he'd come into my space and he'd never left my mind.

And because of that, last night happened.

How in the world was I ever going to face Damon? Or look at my grandfather? Or walk up to that altar and stand before the God Who I prayed still loved me.

God.

Still loved me.

My mind stayed there for a couple of minutes, repeating that. I rolled from my bed and as I fell to my knees and folded my hands, I felt so unworthy. Isn't this where I should have started? If I'd prayed last night, maybe I would've been able to resist that temptation. But I hadn't and I was here. And praying was the only way I would be able to face today.

The only thing was—what was I supposed to say to God? Was I supposed to ask for forgiveness for being a tramp? Ask Him to take away the pain of my shame? Ask Him to shift the molecules of my DNA so that I could be sure this would never happen again?

I had no answers, so I just raised my hands and cried out the way I'd been taught by my grandfather. I prayed over and over for God to forgive me. Even when my knees began to ache, I stayed there, talking to God, ignoring the ache in my knees, so that I could ease the ache in my heart.

When I was empty, I opened my eyes. I couldn't say that I felt complete peace, but I could say that I didn't feel the war that had been raging inside me. As I pushed myself up, my glance rose to the closet door. My wedding dress made me pause. I waited for the anguish that I'd felt minutes ago to rush over me once again.

But, when I felt nothing, I stood and walked to the closet, focusing on what I wanted today to be. Pulling the dress down, I gathered the mounds of fabric and held it in front of me, then opened the closet door wider so that I could see my reflection in the mirror.

For the first time in hours, I felt an emotion that didn't leave me crying. I couldn't quite smile yet, but I did feel some kind of happiness as I imagined Damon seeing me for the first time. I could see him giving me that love-filled smile that always reached inside and crossed my heart.

I imagined him taking my hand when I got to the end of the

aisle, and when I got to the part where we faced my grandfather, I closed my eyes, wanting to imagine the rest of the day.

It was like I was really standing right there, hearing my grandfather's Barry White kind of singsong voice as he began:

*Dearly beloved, we are gathered here to witness the marriage of this man and this woman . . . if there is anyone here . . .*

My eyes sprang open and I repeated that line in my head: If there is anyone here . . .

Oh, my God!

I pressed my hands against my lips to keep my sobs inside. I hadn't thought about that part. I hadn't considered the line where everyone would be asked if they knew of a reason why Damon and I shouldn't be married.

Trey.

He had a reason!

Oh, my God!

Falling back onto the bed, my wedding dress slipped from my hands and slid down my lap, spilling onto the floor in a mass of silk and satin. If this were a different time (yesterday), if this were a different place (not this hotel room), I would've been on my knees almost in tears trying to gather up my gown. Because surely a wedding gown on the floor the morning of the wedding had to signify something.

But this was *this* time and *this* place, and my thoughts weren't on my dress. All that was in my mind was . . . is there anyone here . . .

What would Trey say?

All kinds of scenarios played in my mind, all of them disastrous. I heard Trey laughing, Damon asking him what was so funny, Trey telling him that he was about to marry a whore.

I heard Trey laughing and me begging, though all Damon did was glare at me, the loathing seeping from his eyes before he left me at that altar.

I heard Trey laughing as I turned to my grandfather, who lowered his Bible with more than disappointment in his eyes. And my grandmother crying, no, wailing was the better word.

And all the time, Trey laughed.

The way he laughed last night.

There was no way. No way I was going to do this, no way I was going to set up Damon or my grandparents or even my friends to play roles in Trey's sadistic game.

I wasn't going to the church. I wasn't going to get married today.

The singing telephone froze my thoughts and every other part of me.

*Won't you stay with me . . .*

*'Cause you're all I need . . .*

I had to answer, because I hadn't answered last night and Damon would never let two calls go without speaking to me. If I didn't answer, at best, he'd have hotel security checking on me or, at worst, he'd speed over here himself, the way he always came to me whenever he thought I was in trouble.

I grabbed my cell, accepted the call, took a deep breath, but then paused. What if Trey had already gone to Damon? What if Damon already knew?

"Tiff?" Damon's voice came through the speaker.

I raised the phone to my ear, squeezed my eyes, prayed that my heart didn't stop, and croaked out a hello.

"Hey, beautiful," Damon said. "I missed you last night."

I released the breath I'd been holding and pressed my fingers against my lips to stop their trembling.

He kept on, "I called you, but I guess you were asleep already."

"I was," I managed to say, even though I was sure that my lie had been muffled because now I was using my fingers to push my sobs back inside.

"So, did you have a good night? Did you rest well?" he asked.

How was I supposed to talk to this man?

"Tiff?"

I took a deep breath. "Yeah, I did." I closed my eyes and wondered what I could do to travel back in time. What could I do to get a do-over?

"I'm happy to hear that." He paused. "Aren't you going to ask me?"

I blinked. Was there something that I'd forgotten? Something that had left my mind because of Trey? "Ask you what?"

"About my night and whether I cheated on you with some bimbo who jumped out of some cake."

He laughed.

I cried.

When no words came from me, he said, "That was a joke, Tiff. You were supposed to laugh, because I would never do that to you. You know that, right?" He didn't give me a chance to respond. "You know what? I shouldn't have even joked like that. I'm sorry, bae. That is something you will never have to worry about with me."

I didn't even try to wipe my tears away. I just needed to sit and take my punishment.

"Tiff?"

"Yeah?"

"I can't wait to make you completely mine."

*If anyone here . . .*

He said, "I'll always love you. You know that, right?"

Even though he couldn't see me (thank God!), I nodded. "Yeah."

There was a longer pause this time, then, "Tiff, are you okay?"

"Yeah."

"Oh . . . kay." I could tell he heard my tears, though he wasn't sure what to make of my despair. "You just sound funny."

"It's just that . . . I love you, Damon. I love you so much." I couldn't stop my voice from cracking.

"Awww, bae, don't go getting all sentimental on me. You can't cry now; we have all day to do that, right?"

"Yeah." All day. Except I didn't have all day. I couldn't show up at that church and have my daydream turn into a nightmare.

"So, I'm gonna let you go so that you can get yourself together and get more beautiful—though that's not even possible."

I didn't deserve this man.

He said, "The next time I'll see you, you'll be minutes away from being Mrs. King."

"Yeah." I cried, but now that he had a reason for my tears, he ignored it.

"I love you, Tiffanie. I'll see you tonight."

I hung up without saying good-bye because the sob that I'd been holding back exploded through my lips, and I was so grateful that Damon hadn't heard my full-out wail.

Leaning back against the satin headboard, I did nothing to stop my tears. I just had to come up with a plan, some way to tell Damon that I couldn't become his wife.

Should I just call him back? No, Damon at least deserved

a face-to-face explanation of my betrayal. But as I imagined the words I'd say, all I could see was Damon's face and his pain that was beyond anything that man deserved.

My only choice was the coward's way. I could pack my bags and get on the first plane to anywhere.

The room was bright now with the sun that had fully risen above the horizon, but before it set today, my life would be completely changed. And so would Damon's.

Glancing at the clock, I saw it was just a little before seven. I had some time to rest and figure out where I was going. I'd never lived anywhere besides DC, and the thought of leaving all of this behind made my heart ache. What would my grandparents do? And Damon? My heart contracted at that thought.

I slipped under the duvet and closed my eyes. If I could just have a little bit of rest, just a few minutes, maybe an hour. Then I'd get up and do what I had to do.

I'd disappear.

And with that thought, I slept.

# 20

# Tiffanie

I was running.

Running faster than I'd ever run before.

The darkness was darker than any dark I'd ever seen, but still I kept running. The ends of what felt like bare tree branches scratched me and I felt blood oozing from my arms. But I couldn't stop to check. I had to get away.

And then I stopped.

I had no more inside of me to go on. All that was left was for me to turn around and face the one who'd been chasing me.

He came closer and the moon rose higher with each step he took. Until the moonlight shined so bright that the night turned into day. And I saw his face.

"No," I cried. "Damon. Please. No."

The tears in his eyes matched the ones flowing from mine.

"I'm so sorry, Damon. Please. I'm sorry."

My words did nothing. He still raised his Glock.

He readied.

"No!" I screamed.

He aimed.

I squeezed my eyes shut.

He fired.

But the air didn't explode. It . . . rang.

Like a bell . . . it rang and rang and rang.

I was too scared, but I had to open my eyes.

I did. I blinked. Where was I?

More ringing.

I was in DC.

The bell again.

In the Willard.

I shot up in the bed and a quick glance around the room brought back all the memories.

Another ring of the bell; I jumped up and grabbed the hotel's plush bathrobe that hung in the closet. As I scrambled to the front of the suite, I pushed my arms into the robe, then tightened the belt.

My hand was on the knob and I was already pulling the door open when I thought about slamming it shut. Supposed it was Trey? Or Damon . . . with the gun. Had Trey gone to Damon while I slept? Is that why I had that dream?

It was momentum that opened the door and then, with "Happy Wedding Day!" Sonia greeted me as if this were a national holiday.

When she stepped into the room and dropped her bag, I grabbed her into a hug, so grateful that she was the one on the other side of the door. I had to tell her what happened, what was going on, and then she'd help get me out of DC.

When she stepped back, her face was bright, with her smile and her expression the same as my grandparents' last night—like she was so proud of me.

That was when I knew I couldn't say a word to her. There was no way I could share my shame.

"How are you feeling?" she asked when she stepped back from our embrace. It was a question, but she continued as if I'd answered. "Are you ready? Are you excited? Oh, I know, you're just so happy, aren't you?" she sang, clapping her hands.

If she only knew.

But then her applause slowed and she frowned. *"¿Qué pasa?"*

I was about to cry, I could feel it. She was going to find out that I was a woman with no honor. Then something (it had to be God!) took her attention away.

My glance followed hers to the sixty roses that were sprawled on the floor.

"Dang, girl. What happened?" She lifted the vase, saving the few still inside. "Must've been some party last night," she said as if that were a joke and not the truth.

My lips were about to quiver, but with a strength I never had, I held the tremors back. "I must've knocked them over and didn't realize it."

Her frown deepened as she squinted at me. As if I'd just told a story she could not believe. But then, like a moment before, there was a new distraction. Where she stood, she had a view into the bedroom.

"Oh, my God, Tiffanie! Is that your dress on the floor?" She barreled into the bedroom, making all kinds of groaning sounds. "What is it doing down here?" She sounded like she was about to cry as she gathered my dress in her arms. *"Oh, Dios mio."*

I just stood there as she laid the dress on the bed, then smoothed it out and turned, like she was searching for where it should have been hanging. But her glance instead found me, and while she was the one who sounded like she would cry, I actually did.

Now there was more than a frown on her face. "Tiffanie, what's wrong?"

I didn't want to tell her, I never wanted anyone to know what kind of woman I really was, but before she grabbed my hand and led me to the bed, I was spilling the story.

She was careful to sit us on the edge of the bed, away from the dress. Even as I talked, she still held my hand (a great sign!) as I told her about last night, from finding that purse to finding Trey. And then, how I grabbed him, and kissed him, and begged him.

She only released me when I got to the part where he had me on the bed with my legs spread from east to west.

"And then, and then . . . he left." I finished telling the story, and I had finished crying, too, because I had no more tears left.

Sonia let moments go by. Then, "Wait. What?" She sounded as if she thought I was leaving out the most important part.

"He left," I repeated. "He left me on the bed and told me to remember him when I was with Damon tonight."

"Damn!"

My chin tapped my chest when she said that. "Please don't start that again."

"Okay." She took a breath. "*¡Eso es una locura!*"

"I know. It was crazy to me, too. The whole night."

"So . . . nothing happened?"

Even though I'd just told her that, I understood her need for clarity. "If you're asking me if we had sex, no. But something happened. Which is why I can't marry Damon."

"Huh? *¿De qué estás hablando?*"

"I can't marry Damon," I told her when she asked what was I talking about. "How can I marry him when . . ."

"Don't say it," she warned.

I finished anyway. "I've become my mother."

"That's not what happened."

"It is. Something is clearly wrong with me if I was so willing to jump into bed with Trey."

"But you didn't."

"Not because of me, because of Trey."

"Minor technicality."

I stared at her.

"Okay, major technicality. But here are the facts: nothing happened and you love Damon." She paused. "You do love Damon?"

"Are you kidding me?"

"Then, case closed."

I jumped up from the bed. With my arms crossed, I paced in front of her. "It's because I love him that I can't marry him. He deserves better than what I almost did."

"It was one mistake, *niña*. You've known this man for eight years and you've made one mistake." She glanced at me sideways. "It's just one, *correcto?*"

I gave her one of my really-you're-asking-me-that looks.

"Well, I don't know. I mean, from what you just told me, I don't know you at all. I would've never pegged my best friend as a freak."

A second passed, and then I discovered that I'd been wrong. I did have some tears left, and they rolled out of me.

"Oh, come on, Tiffanie. I was playing and you've got to stop crying, because we only have eight hours and it's going to take at least nine to get all of that puffiness to go away." She pulled me back down onto the bed. "Here's what I know. You love Damon and you are not defined by one mistake. And from the moment you met him until last night, you've been good to Damon."

I let her words settle and it only took a couple of moments to agree with her. I'd made a single mistake. But there was the other question, the real reason why I couldn't show up at that church this evening. "What if Trey tells Damon?"

She shook her head so hard, her long hair swung from her right shoulder to the left and back again. "That ain't gonna happen. Damon may be walking the straight and narrow now, but he's still from the streets, still carrying his gun. That's to let everyone, even his boy, know that he doesn't play. So, not only does Trey not want to mess up his friendship, but I'm pretty sure he ain't trying to get shot either."

I had my question ready. "Then why did Trey do all this?"

She leaned back so that she could get a better look at me. "'Cause he thinks you're fine," she said as if that answer was so clear. "And his heart was filled with lust, too."

It made sense enough for me to nod, but I still wasn't sure. The lust part, that was me. But with Trey, it felt like something more.

"So, can you stop all this so that we can start getting ready for your wedding?"

I only nodded because I didn't know what else to do.

"Okay." She jumped up and clapped her hands in a chop-chop fashion. "First thing we have to do is get some nutrients into you. I'll order breakfast while you go take a long bath," she commanded.

When I didn't move, she took my hand, pulled me up, and

then shoved me into the bathroom. "Take your time, but not too long. You only have three hours before Candy and Ebony get here," she said referring to my hairstylist and makeup artist.

She closed the door and I staggered to the sink. My thoughts were like shooting stars, exploding inside my mind, but I couldn't capture a single one.

I turned to the shower instead of the Jacuzzi, thinking that inside there, I could scrub, not soak; I'd scrub Trey right off.

I stepped out of the bathrobe and then, under the hottest water my skin could take, I scoured every inch of my body. As the water beat against me, I wanted to cry again, but I pushed the tears back.

Sonia was right, this was one mistake. And one mistake shouldn't stop me from experiencing the lifetime that I truly wanted with Damon. I needed to suck it up and shrug it off. Last night had happened . . . period. Last night would never happen again . . . fact.

The first thing I saw when I stepped back into the bedroom was the bed. Sonia had made a bit of an effort to make it up, but still the image flashed:

Me.

Naked.

Spread-eagle.

Waiting.

Wanting.

His laughter.

I squeezed my eyes and pushed those thoughts away.

One mistake.

I was forgiven.

I had to believe that.

# 21

# Damon

I stared at my reflection, wondering why I couldn't get this bow tie straight. Dropping my hands to my side, I just stood there. Was I nervous? Was that why my fingers were fumbling? Being nervous wasn't a state I was familiar with, but I couldn't knock myself too much. This . . . this was about to really go down. I, Damon King, the Chocolate City playa, real-time gangsta was about to get married.

Taking a quick glance at the ceiling, I pointed my finger toward the heavens, my way of once again giving God thanks. And with my eyes still raised, I said, "You blessed me with the girl, now can I get some help with this tie?"

I chuckled, then squared my arms, ready to conquer what I'd done thousands of times. That was when the door behind me opened and through the mirror, I watched Trey stroll in. His eyes settled on me, then just a couple of seconds after that, he shook his head.

He didn't say a word as he strutted toward me, already decked out in his tux. His tie was perfect, but why shouldn't it be? He had no reason for clumsy fingers.

Standing in front of me, he took the ends of the tie from my hands, and in one, two, no more than five swift folds and tucks, he had me looking like I could step right into the role of some kind of James Bond.

With a final glance, and then a nod, Trey said, "You're set, bruh."

As he moved away, I stood straight, checking out my look in the mirror. "Thanks. Always there. Always having my back or this time, should I say, my front."

I chuckled, but Trey did not as he sat down in the middle of the brown velveteen sofa that I was sure had been in this room that Reverend Cooper used for counseling since the beginning of this church, sometime in the early 1900s.

With a shrug, he said, "We're fam, damn near blood. That's what I'm supposed to do."

I nodded, liking the way he said that. Taking a glance at my watch, we still had almost an hour before Reverend Cooper would come for me. Until then, it would be just me and Trey. So, this was the perfect time, and in all the world was there a better place?

I said, "I wanna finish what I started to talk to you about last night."

He looked at me but didn't say a word.

"You know, about us partnering up."

Again he had no words, there was hardly an expression on his face.

So I kept on. "I want to make a place for you in my business." And before he could come back at me the way he did last night, I said, "No charity, straight business, side by side."

Now he spoke. "Let's not talk about this."

I frowned and let a moment pass to see if he would expound on what he'd said. When he said nothing more, I asked, "What're you saying? You don't want to do it? You don't want us to be partners again?"

"I'm just saying that I don't want to talk about this right now." He spoke in a tone like his decision was made and there was no need for further discussion. "I told you last night, I got some things in the works, some things I'm trying to handle."

"What does that have to do with what I'm offering?"

"Nothing." He paused and added, "Everything."

"Look," I began, "why're you being so cryptic? Just come out and tell me what's going on. Are you back in the game?"

He shook his head. "Not that I owe you any kind of explanation." He paused. "I just have some things I have to take care of before I can talk to you or anyone about my next steps."

I stood there, staring down at him, trying to get what he was saying to make sense. Because I knew that he couldn't have much going on in Atlanta. I was offering him an opportunity to stand up again.

He added, "I'm not saying that I don't want to do it, I'm saying that I can't do anything right now, so there's no need to talk about it until I'm free to make decisions and moves."

I still couldn't tell if he was trying to tell me something, or if he was just keeping secrets. I wanted him to talk to me the way he used to, because then, maybe I could offer him some direction. Not that he would take it, but I really didn't want him getting another bid. If he got back in the game, if he got caught up, then locked up again, he'd be down for the count.

But when he said nothing more, I didn't push, out of respect. Because if the tables were flipped, I'd want that kind of respect given to me.

"So, we good?" he asked.

I gave him a slow nod, still trying to read between his lines. What was up and why couldn't he share?

"Yeah." I finally gave him an answer. "We're straight. Maybe you'll have your business handled by the time I get back from Dubai."

He took more time than I thought he needed to answer that question, like he was calculating his situation in his mind.

He said, "Yeah, maybe. Maybe it will be done." Then, as if he were throwing me a bone, he added, "Yeah, it'll probably be done and you and I . . . we'll sit down and talk."

"Okay. Good. So, you're gonna hang out here till I get back?" Before he could give me an answer, I told him, "'Cause I got you covered at the Willard."

His face brightened with his grin. "That's the spot. I had something go down there last night."

I grinned with him. "You hooked up with somebody?" It wasn't that I was surprised. He'd been on lockdown for all of these years; there wasn't a female within thirty feet of him who would be safe.

He shrugged a bit. "Kind of. I just set the wheels in motion for the big hookup."

I had to give my man dap. "That's what I'm talking about. Is she visiting DC?"

"Nah, she lives here. She was at the hotel for some kind of special function."

"Well, see, son, that's another reason for you to stay now. Maybe something will come of this." And I laughed.

But Trey's face stayed as hard as stone.

I said, "Wouldn't it be something if you came up here for my wedding and you ended up getting married yourself?" I was still laughing 'cause that was a joke. Trey settling down? Not happening.

But he didn't find anything funny with what I said, because at first, he just stared as if my words sounded foreign. Then he said, "You know what? It wasn't until you said that at this moment that I realize that's what I'm hoping."

That stopped my chuckles. "Really? You ready to jump the broom?"

Before Trey could answer, the door opened and Reverend Cooper stepped inside the room that he'd set aside for the grooms of any weddings he performed. He was already donned in his purple robe trimmed in gold, looking like some kind of African king. "Just checking on you, son."

I smoothed the lapels on my tux. "I'm fine, Rev. I'm ready to do this."

He smiled, nodded, as if my words pleased him. "We're going to have to do something about you calling me that." He held up his hand before I could protest. "I'm giving you my granddaughter's hand in marriage, and that means everything, including that you're family now."

I dipped my head a little, wanting to give him respect for his words, wanting to show him that I was grateful, because the road to acceptance from him and Mrs. Cooper had been rough. "Thank you, sir. I think you know this already, but I promise to take care of Tiffanie."

My words were meant to give him life, though that's not what happened. Instead of him shaking my hand and giving me one of those brother-to-brother slaps on the back, his whole countenance went left; his smile dimmed and his eyes looked like they'd gone black when he looked through me.

I was relieved when he finally spoke. "You do that, son. You take care of my granddaughter." He stopped, stared, made me shift from one leg to the other. "And don't you ever do anything to hurt her. Or I promise, I'll hurt you."

Now, I'd met many boys and men in the streets and there was not one that I feared. That's how I got my rep, that's how I'd made my money in the past. But standing here, in this church, in front of this man of God, who'd just made a promise to me that was similar to ones I'd made, all I could think was that it was a good thing my pants covered my knocking knees. My voice was still strong, though, when I said, "I'll never hurt her," because I was still Damon King. And . . . Trey was watching.

But when Reverend Cooper turned around and walked out of that room without giving me another word nor another smile, I blew out a long breath of relief.

"Man," I said with my eyes still on that door, "I have the feeling that if I ever did anything to Tiffanie, there would be a price to pay."

I expected Trey to laugh, but all he did was shrug, then turn and follow the reverend's footsteps. Right as he put his hand on the knob, he said, "You're straight up now. You won't hurt her."

I grinned and nodded. Trey was finally coming to an understanding of how much I'd changed and how much Tiffanie meant to me.

He added, "I just hope you'll be able to handle it . . . *when* she hurts you." Before I could ask him what the hell he meant by that, he walked out of the room.

# 22

# Tiffanie

'd been fine. Especially because of Sonia. The entire time as I prepared for the wedding, she stayed by my side. While my makeup was applied and my hair was styled, she kept chatting, making sure that her voice was louder than the doubts in my head. Even when the photographer arrived, Sonia stayed close, whispering, even when I was being photographed alone.

Now, in the limo, she kept talking.

"You love Damon."

"Forget about last night."

"It doesn't matter because nothing happened."

"You love Damon."

It all started and ended with how much I loved Damon King. And since that was the truth, it became easy to make peace with my conscience.

But then the car stopped in front of Greater First AME. It must've been seeing that house of God that turned me into a woman about to become undone.

"Oh, come on, Tiffanie."

I hadn't said a word, but Sonia knew that I was about to lose it again.

"*¿Qué quieres que te diga?*"

It took a moment for me to push back my tears and I shook my head at her question. "No, you don't have to say anything else. I'm just . . ."

"Ready to get married," she finished for me.

After a very deep inhale, I nodded.

As the driver opened the door for us, Sonia stepped out first, and then instead of letting Damon's driver do it, she reached for my hand. When I grabbed hers, she squeezed mine, sharing her courage.

It was enough to get me up the steps and inside the vestibule. But it wasn't enough to help me face my grandmother.

"Here she is, Mama Cooper." Sonia passed me off and then with a final squeeze and a nod, she stepped away and into the main foyer of the church.

Standing in front of me, my grandmother looked up. And she gave me that stare, which let me know that God was telling her something.

I stiffened, trying to stop myself from shaking as my grandmother peered into my eyes. She squinted and her expression was stern as she scrutinized me. That look was so familiar and made me tremble more. This was the expression she wore right before she gave me a scolding or a spanking.

The seconds ticked by, one by one, and I knew, just knew, that she knew.

But then her lips curved into a smile and now her eyes shined with tears that had not yet fallen.

"You are my beautiful little baby." She stood on her toes to kiss my cheek. "I have dreamed of this day for a long time, and I am so pleased because God chose the perfect man for you. I'm so proud of you."

When she wrapped me inside her arms, I wanted to fall to the floor and cry. She wouldn't be pleased or proud if her radar had been working.

Stepping back, she said, "With the Lord's help and guidance, you're going to be a great wife."

There was so much wisdom in her eyes and such surety in her tone, I had to believe her. I was going to be a great wife.

"Thank you so much, Gram," I said, knowing that she had no clue how much her words meant to me.

My grandmother gave a nod to Ms. Erlene, one of the church mothers who'd known me since I'd first toddled into this church. Ms. Erlene opened the double doors that led to the sanctuary so that Sonia could step inside. The moment she took her first step forward, Ms. Erlene secured the doors so that no one would see me and my grandmother as we took our places.

From the side table, Ms. Erlene handed me the spray of golden-yellow lilies and purple-blue irises. As I took my bouquet, she burst into an ugly cry.

"Stop that, Erlene," my grandmother scolded her friend. "Before you have me and Tiffanie doing the same thing."

Ms. Erlene nodded, though neither her tears nor her sobs stopped as the music seeped through the sanctuary doors.

Brenda Rae was a rising R&B star whom Damon had chosen to sing, while I'd chosen the song . . . *Lying safe within your arms, I'm born again . . .*

Closing my eyes, I imagined myself in Damon's arms. I

imagined how it would be from this day forward. And I asked God to please help me become the great wife that my grandmother thought I would be.

My grandmother squeezed my hand. "Baby, are you ready?" Her voice was softer than a whisper.

"I am. Just a little nervous."

The tears she'd been trying to hold back now pooled in the corners of her eyes. "Don't worry, I'll be right by your side until I give your hand to Damon. You're just moving from one safe place to the next," she told me.

She'd said those words just in time, because the doors to the church swung open and the opening of the Bridal Chorus vibrated through the space.

I saw the people rise as my grandmother held my hand a little tighter and I took that first step into the sanctuary. I sucked in my stomach and some more courage, too.

We took slow steps down the aisle, and the whole time, I spoke inside my head: *It was a mistake.*

*With Trey.*

*People make mistakes.*

And I reminded myself of the most important thing: *I love Damon King with every beat of my heart.*

As I had that little talk with myself, I kept my eyes steady, not looking left, not looking right. I stayed focused on my grandfather and the golden cross that hung high on the wall behind the altar. And I prayed and prayed and prayed, keeping my eyes straight ahead.

The closer I got to the altar, the more I felt Damon and his eyes on me. Everything inside of me yearned to shift my glance. But I couldn't because I knew who stood next to him.

Just a few steps after I had that thought, it became impossible to keep my eyes away, and when I saw Damon's dimpled smile, my heart did one of those butterfly flutters before everything inside me settled down.

But then, a little movement to the right, and just like I knew he would be, there was Trey.

That flash in my mind:

Me.

Naked.

Spread-eagle.

Waiting.

Wanting.

His laughter.

I blinked as my body heated with my embarrassment. My eyes were still on Damon, though, which meant that I could see Trey, too.

He grinned as if he was remembering last night. Then his tongue traveled across his lips . . . slowly . . . from the right to the left.

And I stumbled.

"Oh," my grandmother cried out, gripping my arm so that I didn't hit the floor.

The sanctuary filled with gasps and in an instant and three giant steps, Damon was by my side, helping me to stand straight and steady on my feet.

"You okay, bae?"

"I'm fine," I whispered, though I was so far away from fine. I was shaking with fear and embarrassment. "The hem of my dress . . ."

Even though I was upright, Damon moved to my other side,

and both he and my grandmother escorted me the rest of the way to the altar. Then Damon took his place once again, next to Trey.

There was concern in my grandfather's eyes when he looked down at me. I nodded, then gave him a smile before he finally did the same.

Then, from nowhere: *When Damon brings you in here, remember this, remember me.*

I squeezed my eyes shut, forcing that thought away. But in its place was the other one: *Was Trey just waiting for this moment at our wedding to make my mortification complete?*

"I'm supposed to begin this ceremony with 'We are gathered here today,'" my grandfather started, giving me a reprieve from the meltdown I was about to have. "But since this young lady who stands before me is so special, I want to say a few words that are not in here." He raised the leather-bound book that held all of his ministerial rituals.

"I have loved this little girl, and yes, she's still a little girl to me, since before she was born," my grandfather announced to the guests in the sanctuary. "And she is as special to me today as she was back on that day." He turned just a little so that now his eyes were on Damon. "You're getting a special gift from God. You already know the meaning of her name."

"Yes, sir," Damon's bass filled the sanctuary.

My grandfather said, "Always remember that, always treat her that way."

"Yes, sir."

My grandfather took a couple of extra moments to stare, as if he was giving Damon a warning in front of everyone. He stared long enough for Damon to shift just a bit. And I did, too.

Because Damon wasn't the one who needed this admonishment right now.

"I've said my part, so we can begin." My grandfather and I were the only ones who didn't laugh. After the laughter, "Dearly beloved, we are gathered here . . ."

Like too many other times today, I wanted to cry. These words, this moment had been in my mind since I finally agreed to marry Damon and now, I couldn't bask in the wonder of it. I couldn't, because each word my grandfather spoke got me closer to the moment when Trey would blow up my world.

My heart raced, my knees weakened, my hands trembled, and my bouquet shook so much that it stirred up a breeze. I was going to faint if I didn't switch mental lanes. I had to take my mind back to what Sonia had said: Trey wouldn't say a word. He didn't want to get shot.

My grandfather kept talking about the sanctity of marriage, the seriousness of this decision, but also the wonder that would come from the union of two who really loved each other.

And all I could think about was last night.

*Please, God.*

I felt the tick of the clock.

*Please, God.*

Seconds . . . passing . . . time . . . moving . . . closer . . . to . . .

"If anyone here has any reason why these two should not be married, speak now or forever hold your peace."

I bowed my head.

I closed my eyes.

I held my breath.

The silence went on forever.

I prayed. *Please, God.*

I prayed harder. *Please. God.*

Then, "Nobody better say anything."

I opened only one eye and saw Damon looking over his left shoulder and then his right.

The congregation laughed and I used the moment to start breathing again. Until my eyes betrayed me and moved to Trey. Still wearing that smirk. But I didn't care; his chance to ruin my life, at least at this moment, had passed.

"Well, you all heard my grandson," my grandfather boomed. "So let's get to the good part. Let's get these two young people married."

There was light applause before my grandfather kept on.

"This is a covenant you are about to declare before God."

A covenant. A pledge. A bond that was meant never to be broken.

My grandfather said, "Do you both understand that?"

"Yes," Damon and I said together, though his voice was stronger and louder than mine.

"All right, then." My grandfather looked down at my grandmother and smiled through his next words. "Who gives this woman to be married to this man?"

My grandmother turned to me and said, "I do." Then she looked at my grandfather. "Well, you, too. I guess I should've included you."

There was more laughter as my grandmother gave my hand to Damon and placed a feather-soft kiss on my cheek.

As my grandmother sat, I handed my bouquet to Sonia. She gave me a smile that made me brave. Because now I had to face Damon. And behind Damon, Trey. Turning to the man I was minutes away from calling my husband, I kept my eyes planted on him, even though I could see half of Trey's face over Damon's shoulder.

That's all I could see. Only Trey's left eye, his left cheek, the left side of him. I could only see half of him; half a man stood behind Damon.

That was a message.

Our ceremony continued, through our declaration to be with one another till only death parted us, through the vows that we'd written, and finally through the blessing of our rings.

"Forasmuch as Damon and Tiffanie . . ."

I breathed in.

"I now pronounce you man and wife."

Damon's lips were on mine before I could fully comprehend that it had happened.

I relaxed into his embrace and was so happy to kiss him that I didn't realize that we were all the way into it.

"All right now!" my grandfather said.

To laughter, we pulled apart and I stared at the man that I loved so much. I couldn't help it . . . I kissed him again. The sanctuary filled with chortles and applause and when I stepped back, I laughed, too.

"Ladies and gentleman, I present to you for the first time Mr. and Mrs. Damon King."

I could've jumped ten, fifteen, twenty feet into the air. Damon took my hand and we stroll-dapped down the aisle as Prince's voice filled the sanctuary.

*Could you be the most beautiful girl in the world*
*It's plain to see you're the reason that God made a girl . . .*

My grandfather had raised his eyebrows when Damon told

him we wanted to dance out to a Prince song. But once he'd listened to the words, he approved the song and then only asked, "What's this dap dance you want to do?"

I laughed now as I remembered that, and my laughter became louder when I looked over at my husband.

My husband.

He grinned and when we got to the end of the aisle, he pulled me close and kissed me again, to the applause and the approval of all who'd come to share this day with us.

Then I heard "Hey, can I get one of those hugs?"

Beside us stood Trey, with Sonia on his arm. I'd forgotten that she had to walk down the aisle with him, and I was surprised that Trey was still alive.

But then, it was like my girl had forgotten everything I'd been through. Because all she did was grin, nod, hug me, and then turn to Damon.

Leaving me there alone to hug Trey!

I wanted to kill her.

I wanted to kill him.

My plan was to give Trey one of those Sunday church hugs, where I stand about two feet away, give him two taps on his back, and then walk away without even another glance, never to talk to or touch him again.

But as Sonia turned to Damon, Trey wrapped his arms around me, pulled me close, and whispered, "That was some show you gave me last night. Can't wait to do it again."

He leaned back, stood there, and grinned. I wanted to slap him with everything in me, but I was smart enough to hold back, since that act would be hard to explain.

So I had to just stand there. And glare. And watch his smirk, then hear his laughter as *he* was the one to turn and walk away from me.

"Bae."

I had to blink away my anger before I looked at Damon. "Huh?"

"You okay?"

"Of course," I said, kissing him before he took my hand. "I'm married to you, right? So, of course I'm okay."

But as Damon led me out of the sanctuary, I had doubts that I would ever be okay again—at least not as long as Trey was in DC.

I was going to have to do something. I wasn't sure what, but the same way I'd just taken this vow to love and honor Damon, I was making another vow. No matter what I had to do, Trey Taylor was going to be out of my life. And out of Damon's life, too.

# 23

# Tiffanie

O ur reception felt like a repeat of last night's dinner, only grander. Today we were in the Skyline Terrace, the ballroom on the top floor of the Willard. The windows, which completely encircled the room, had a Western view and our wedding had been timed so that we'd have a sunset reception.

The fifty tables, each with seating for ten, were draped with white silk and chiffon and displayed identical centerpieces—two black angels with their hands raised to the heavens.

That's exactly how I felt—as if I were in heaven. Even with Trey on the other side of Damon as we sat at the head table, it didn't matter, because God had already answered my prayers. He'd assuaged my guilt, He'd kept Trey silent during the ceremony, and so I knew that He would give me what I needed to make Trey go poof! once all this was over.

But for now, I was able to bask in this evening that had seemed only possible in a dream. My husband led me to the floor for our first dance and we swayed to the band, who did a hella rendition of "Adore." And then, as our guests enjoyed the first course of the five that would be their dinner, we angled through the tables, greeting each of our guests and thanking them for coming.

And we thanked them for their contributions to the United Negro College Fund. It had been my idea to do that in lieu of gifts that we didn't need, and I was so proud because we'd raised more than $75,000.

By the time Damon and I returned to our table, the third course was being served, but I pushed the arugula salad aside to enjoy the grilled shrimp cocktail that had been placed on the table first. I laughed as Damon decided that he *needed* to feed me, and when he lifted the shrimp to my lips, I played with it with my tongue.

He moaned and I licked.

"Uh . . . I think you two need to get a room." Sonia laughed from her seat next to me.

"Oh, we have a room," Damon said, as he brushed another piece of shrimp across my lips. "As a matter of fact, I think we need to get to that room right now."

"We can't leave!" I protested like I was astonished, even though I knew Damon was kidding. "We still have the cake."

"And don't you have to dance with the best man?"

I hated the way I shivered a little, just at the sound of his voice. For the hours that we'd been here, I'd acted like Trey was not. I did my best to keep my voice light, but my eyes . . . I glared at him. "I'm only dancing with my husband tonight."

He just laughed: that laugh that was a reminder. Of last night. I had to fight to keep the humiliation from rising within me as I turned back to Damon, making it my turn to feed him.

When it was time for the toasts, tears filled my eyes when

Sonia stood and took us all on a stroll down her memory lane, from the days when we met in seventh grade to how we'd worn purple everything to our first Prince concert at the MCI Center in 2004, to our roommate days at Howard. When she closed with *"Deseo tu felicidad,"* I wiped away a tear, tapped my hand over my heart, then blew her a kiss, before Damon and I raised our glasses to her good wishes for our happiness.

Then Trey stood, though I hardly listened to his memories. I wasn't interested in his history with Damon. So, I sat there, not cracking a single smile at his jokes, but when he got to his closing, I had to raise my glass with everyone else.

He said, "And, like Sonia, I wish you two all the happiness that you deserve."

I leaned forward to click my glass against Damon's and was a little surprised at the way my husband hesitated. I followed his glance, which was on Trey, a hard stare, as if Trey had said something wrong. But before I could question him, Damon turned to me with a grin and we clicked our glasses together.

Damon only gave me time for a quick sip of champagne (which my grandfather had approved for the wedding reception) before grabbing my hand and pulling me to the dance floor, right in front of the band.

We never did get to enjoy the fourth course of steak and lobster, though we did pause to do that traditional cake cutting/ feeding/photography thing. But then we were back on the dance floor and partying like it was 1999.

"I've got to take a break!" I laughed at Damon when we'd danced for what I was sure had to be more than an hour straight. "I'm gonna run to the restroom."

Damon nodded, but instead of releasing my hand, he pulled

me closer. "Okay, but when you come back, get ready to leave, Mrs. King."

"What time is it? I thought we had this room until two."

He nodded, but said, "It's just a little after eleven, but I plan to have you upstairs naked and in that bed before the clock strikes midnight."

His words brought that flash:

Me.

Naked.

Spread-eagle.

Waiting.

Wanting.

The laughter.

"Do you know how much I love you?"

I blinked myself back from that misery, and when I looked into Damon's eyes, all I saw was his pure love. He pressed his lips against my forehead and I warmed with expectation. The days of abstinence before our wedding had been the right thing. I knew for sure that tonight would be the night with him.

When Damon leaned back, I leaned forward and kissed him, all tongue, all grinding, making promises of what was to come.

He moaned when I stepped away. "I'll be right back."

"Hurry," he whispered.

I held up my dress, and then through the crowd of friends and family, I maneuvered, smiling, stopping, speaking a few words. I spotted my grandparents on the dance floor, and just as I turned toward them, Trey brushed past me. I stood still, though my eyes followed him, and when he got to one of the exits, he paused, turned, stared, then smiled. He held my gaze for too many seconds before he strutted out of the ballroom.

It only took me a moment to do a three-sixty scan of the room to make sure that no one noticed that little exchange. I lifted my dress higher, lowered my head, and pressed through the rest of the guests until I was in the hallway.

Looking to the left, I saw just a glimpse of Trey before he disappeared around a corner.

I followed, walking for the first few feet, then, I put some pep in my step and almost trotted, making that same turn that Trey did. And I bumped right into him. Hard. He caught me before I fell.

"What are you doing?" I hissed, pulling away from his hold.

"Making sure that you don't fall and make a fool of yourself."

"I've already done that."

Even though I'd snapped at him, he chuckled as if my words pleased him.

I straightened my dress, then looked around to guarantee that we were alone. When I turned back to him, his eyes were waiting for me. Still dark. Still seductive.

I sighed. "I need to talk to you."

"Talk." He smiled and took my breath away.

I was so mad at myself.

He said, "So . . ."

That simple word captured me. After all the tears I'd shed and all the promises I'd made, all I wanted to do was to have that feeling again. All I wanted to know was what it would be like to be with him. In every single way.

I hated myself.

"Tiffanie?"

It was everything about this man, down to the way he said my name.

"Are you going to say something?"

I leaned in closer so that no one would hear our words. "I just want to make sure that you're not going to say anything to Damon."

Then he did that thing. Licking his lips. From the left . . . to the right. So slowly. And I watched every milli-inch of his movement.

I had to get away, but I had to know his intentions, too. So, I took a couple of steps back, then crossed my arms as an extra barrier, and waited for his answer.

It seemed to take him forever to formulate his thoughts, but finally, he said, "Do you want me to tell him?"

I wished my glare were filled with heat—the same kind of heat that warmed me whenever I was near him. Then, with just my eyes, I could set him on fire and make him burn in that place that was thousands of millions of miles south of heaven. "Of course not. I don't want you to ever say anything to Damon. This isn't a game, Trey, and this isn't a joke."

"Do you see me laughing?" He did that licking-lips thing.

And I had that waiting . . . wanting memory again. Only this time, in my mind, he finished what he'd started. This time he took off his clothes and lay on top of me. He licked his lips. And then . . . he licked me.

Oh. My. God.

What was happening?

"I just need"—I had to take my eyes off of his lips to continue—"for you to give it to me straight."

"Okay." He stepped closer, breaking the space barrier that I'd built between us. But I kept my arms folded. "You want it straight? Here it is—straight, no chaser, as your *husband* would say: I'm not saying a word to Damon."

I breathed or at least I tried to, but it was difficult with him all up in my space this way.

He said, "Why would I do that and mess up this good thing?"

"What?" I folded my arms tighter. "You don't have a good thing with me."

"Oh, yes, I do. I have a very good thing. Because this is what I know—I can have you at any time and in any way that I want." His glance started at my feet and strolled up my body, at the same speed that he used his tongue. He paused on certain places, as if he were imagining what I looked like beneath this wedding gown. Only he didn't have to do much imagining.

When his eyes met mine, my breath caught in my throat. Then he stepped even closer, if that was possible. So close that I almost felt his lips; I wanted to taste his lips.

With the tips of his fingers, he lifted my chin. "I want you, Tiff." He didn't even lower his voice.

My hands dropped to my sides.

He said, "I'm just waiting for the right time."

He held me in place, with his fingers and with his stare. When he'd made his point, he dropped his hand and walked away.

All I heard was the beating of my heart, pounding so loud I was sure that the sound filled the entire hotel. I felt sick, but not in my stomach. My pain was in my head and my heart. Because of the throbbing between my legs. The throbbing that was for the wrong man.

"I have lost my mind," I whispered as I leaned back against the wall and closed my eyes.

Just a moment later, I felt him and my heart quickened again. I opened my eyes.

But it wasn't him.

I looked into Sonia's eyes.

She held the same stance that I had just minutes before. Arms folded. Eyes glaring.

For a while, we stood there, her eyes filled with disapproval and mine filled with tears. I heard the faint sound of music coming from the ballroom and . . . my heart, doing that pounding thing again.

Without a word, she whipped around and marched away and I followed her, knowing where she was going, knowing that she wanted an explanation. What I didn't know was how much she'd seen, how much she'd heard.

Inside the restroom, Sonia led me to the left, to the lounge away from the stalls. She closed the door, and when she turned back to me, she looked like she wanted to fight.

"Do you want to tell me what's going on?"

I was standing in front of the person who knew me best. She was way more than a friend; this woman was my sister. Which meant that any lie I wanted to tell would only prolong the misery.

"I don't know what to say."

My countenance, my shame didn't deter her. "Why don't you start with why you're having secret meetings with Trey."

"It wasn't like that." I shook my head. "I just wanted to talk to him to find out what he was going to do. I had to know if he was going to tell Damon."

Her arms fell to her side. "I already told you that he wasn't going to say a word."

"I know that's what *you* said, I just wanted to know what *he* had to say."

"*Maldición,* Tiffanie." She stomped her foot in temper-tantrum mode. "Don't you see that you're playing his game? I heard what he said to you."

"Oh, God," I moaned and fell back onto the wicker love seat.

"So, are you trying to play this game with him? Are you trying to have an affair? Did you hope to set up your rendezvous? On your wedding day?"

"No! Of course not." I couldn't believe that I was in this restroom, just hours after I'd said 'I do,' about to burst into tears because my best friend was making this accusation. "Why would you say that to me?"

"And why would you be hunched up in some corner with your *marido*'s best friend? After last night?"

I squeezed my eyes together, fighting to keep that flash (that came whenever I thought about or heard the words *last night*) out of my mind.

"Well?" she said, sounding just like my grandmother when I was little and she was waiting for an explanation for my bad behavior.

"I already told you why I was talking to him."

"Well, this is what I have to tell you." Her tone was still harsh, still stern, still like my grandmother's. "Stay away from Trey."

"How can I do that? He's in the ballroom, should I ask him to leave?"

I thought that was a dumb question, but I thought I was making a point until she said, "If you have to do that, do it. Or, if you and Damon have to leave, do that. *Lo que sea,* stay away from him for the rest of the night. Is he heading back to Atlanta?"

I shrugged. "I think so."

"You better hope so."

"Do you think I want any of this?" I held my hands out, palms up, and my voice trembled with my tears. "I can't even explain why I'm drawn to him. It's like an unnatural pull that I can't control. Like something inside of me just has to do this, even with the risks. And I hate myself for feeling that way every single time."

She stood there for a moment, just looking, and then I felt her softening. "Oh, *chica*." When she sat down next to me, she wrapped her arm around my shoulders.

At least that brought me a little bit of relief. My friend was back and she'd console and convince me that everything was going to be all right. But then she asked, "What do you mean every single time? How many times . . ." She stopped, thought, and added, "I thought you said it was just last night."

I sighed. "I'm talking about just being around him. Every time I see him." I paused, wondering if I should say the words aloud, and then I reasoned that I should. Because if I did, I'd take away the power he had over me. So I said, "Every time I see him, I want him."

She gave me a long, sideways glance. Then "Damn!"

"Please don't start that again!"

"*Lo siento.* But really, it's like that?"

I nodded and I cried. "Every time. I hate him, but I want him. I want him to make love to me."

She shook her head. Said, "Damn," then held up her hand before I could protest. "This is just lust. Pure, unadulterated lust. And that means that it's something you can fight."

"I want to do that, but how?"

"By staying away from Trey. Just until the end of the reception, and then when you and Damon hit it tonight . . ." She stopped like that was the explanation and the solution. "Damon will knock that lust for another man right out of you."

Sonia thought that she and I were the kind of close that had no secrets. And we were. That close. Except for this one secret. I'd never told her again that Damon couldn't satisfy me. Because after I told her the first time and she'd been so sure that it would be fine, I didn't know how to tell her that even after knowing me, nothing good happened. And I'd never been sure if the problem was with me or with Damon.

But clearly, that question was gone. Trey proved that my body could feel . . . things. And that feeling? I wanted to have it again and again and again and again.

This would have been the time to tell her, but Sonia stood up, grabbed one of the scented cloths on the counter, and wiped away my tears. Then she returned to my side, took my hands in hers, squeezed them, and assured me, "After tonight, all of the desire that you have for Trey will be gone. I promise you it's different physically and mentally when the man you're with is your husband. When the sex is between your ears *and* between your legs . . ." She paused and waved her hand, cooling herself. "Damon'll make sure that you'll never want another man."

I nodded, though I didn't believe a word of her promise. And I hugged her, though all I wanted to do was sit here and cry alone.

When she pulled me up from the sofa, I went with her. I followed her from the restroom to the ballroom, and I stayed with her as she led me straight to Damon. And then she gave my husband my hand in the same fashion that my grandmother had during our ceremony.

"I've been looking all over for my wife," he said. He gave Sonia a grateful grin, but then he whispered just to me, "It's time for us to go upstairs, bae. Time for us to really be man and wife."

He sealed his words with a kiss.

24

# Damon

Women just don't know their power.

Not at all. Because right now, inside this bedroom that glowed with its all-white everything and the flicker of the candlelight that surrounded us, my wife had complete and total control over me.

My wife.

She hadn't done anything. Was just sitting there on the edge of the bed. But it was the way she sat, so demure, almost pure, completely perfect.

And she was all mine.

Her eyes raised to look at me and I'm telling you, at that moment, I would have given her anything, given her everything. But she already had what I held close; she already had my heart.

Taking her hand, I lifted her from the bed and as she rose, her eyes never left mine. I kissed her, keeping my desire at bay, just wanting her to feel how much I loved her.

When she leaned away, her eyes glistened in the candlelight, and the way she looked at me . . . this was love.

I turned her around and she lowered her head as I reached

for the zipper on the back of her dress. My fingers trembled, though of course, it didn't come from fear. It was just that this was the first time I'd have this woman as my wife. I wanted it to be a time that she'd always remember.

As I let the zipper go down, down, down, I took a deep inhale of air at her lower back when I saw the top of her thong.

She turned and faced me, letting me slip the straps from her shoulders. When the dress fell to her waist, she did the rest, doing a little shimmy to slide it over her hips. I took a couple of big steps back so that I could really take in this vision. She stood before me in nothing but her bra, thong, and those stilettos. And I'm telling you, I didn't know how I was going to hold it. Then she challenged me as a man when she did a little striptease—first her bra, then her thong. Gone. All she wore were those shoes.

It wasn't like I hadn't seen my girl naked, but there was something different, now that I could call her completely mine.

All I wanted to do was toss her onto the bed and go at it, but these moments before our consummation we'd remember for the rest of our lives. There would only be this first time, so I wanted to stay right here for a while.

Her hips swayed as she placed one leg in front of the other. One of those sexy model strolls. But I couldn't really enjoy it because I was nervous about what would come next. If she touched me . . .

And then she did. With just one hand behind my head, she pulled me to her for another kiss.

*Hold on. Hold on. Hold on.*

I was glad when she leaned away, just so I could breathe. But it was still hard because of her eyes. The way she looked at me as she undid my bow tie made me want to holla. I needed to help her, to move this along, but when I reached for the buttons on my shirt, she slapped my hands away. I grinned, but that was only to hold back my moan. My girl, I mean, my wife was letting me know that this was her show.

It was painful the way she undressed me, so slowly, as if she could wait and she wasn't aware that I couldn't. First my shirt, then she ripped the belt from my waist before she lowered my pants. When she knelt down before me, I was on my way to heaven, but she only helped me to step out of my pants.

Then she stood back up as she once again kissed me, her hands sliding down my briefs. I stepped back to step out of them, then looked down and laughed.

She laughed, too. The two of us, naked except for our shoes. She looked so much better than I did.

I kicked off my shoes, but told her, "Keep yours on." And then I stood, just holding her hands. That's all I wanted for the moment.

The way her fingers curled around mine made me almost lose my gangsta. The tears were coming to my eyes, but I held them. There was no way I would cry. It's just that I never knew that this was what love could do.

Raising her hand, I kissed each of her fingers before I turned my lips back to hers. I was trying, really trying to make this last forever, but forever was about to come to an end.

Leading her to the bed, I laid her down. I still wanted to take this slowly; I knew she'd bought something special to wear tonight. But there just wasn't any more patience in me. I connected with her with more than our lips, and I made love to my wife.

I squeezed my eyes shut, feeling the warmth of her beneath me, around me, throughout me, and there were all kinds of thoughts in my mind. But they were all broken up because with the way my body was set up, I couldn't think. All I could do was breathe and hold on, breathe and hold on, breathe and . . . I couldn't hold on anymore.

When I cried out, a moment later, Tiffanie did, too. It took a few minutes for that pounding in my heart to lighten up and then, I lifted my head and kissed her. That's when I felt the moisture on her cheeks.

Dang! Had I gone so hard that I hurt my girl? "What's wrong?" I whispered.

Beneath me, she shook her head.

Slowly, I rolled off of her, but kept my arms around her. "You're crying."

After a moment, she said, "I'm happy."

I let out a long breath and then smiled. Leaning over, I gave her another kiss and pulled her into me. I couldn't get my body close enough to hers. I wanted to be one again.

*I'm happy.*

I'd never made a woman cry, and I have to say, it felt kinda good to satisfy my wife in this way. Even as my breathing steadied, I kept my mind in this place, this time.

*I'm happy.*

For the rest of my life, this was how I wanted it to be. I wanted to fill Tiffanie's days and nights with everything that she wanted. So that when she laid her head on her pillow every night, she'd cry from all the happiness that our life together gave her.

Then, while she cried, I'd smile, just like I was smiling now. Because I'd achieved the most important goal in my life.

Leaning over, I kissed her cheeks, over and over, until I'd kissed her tears away. Then I closed my eyes. And I'm sure that I slept with the smile of all smiles on my face.

# 25

# Tiffanie

Flight attendants prepare for landing."

Over the console between us, Damon took my hand, and my fingers curled naturally around his. I didn't turn toward him, though; instead my eyes were on the sweeping skyline below.

If we hadn't spent thirteen hours in the air, someone would have easily convinced me that we were flying into Chicago, or any other metropolitan city in the US. But then I saw the Dubai City Tower, stretching so high the top pierced the clouds.

"It's beautiful, bae, isn't it?"

"It is," I breathed. Then I felt his lips on my neck. I leaned back so that I could receive him more and when I opened my eyes, I blinked over and over, making sure that my tears stayed behind my lids. But it felt like the water was about to overflow, so I closed my eyes because I just couldn't cry.

Hadn't I done that enough?

First last night, when I lay with my husband and all I heard were Trey's words: *When Damon brings you in here, remember this, remember me.*

I'd done just that—remembered how I'd lain beneath him, if only for a moment. Remembered how I wanted him and how I thought he wanted me.

Trey was all I could think about as I'd lain with my husband on our wedding night. Trey was all I could think about because, without ever having been intimate with me, he could make me feel what my husband couldn't.

Not even on our wedding night.

When I'd thought about that this morning, I'd cried, releasing my tears inside the shower where they mixed with the water. I didn't want Damon to have any questions, but he hadn't joined me. Our flight had been too early for an encore from last night, thank God.

But now I had to face today. I had to find a way to respond to my husband, because I couldn't face a lifetime of never being satisfied. So I told myself that the only reason Damon couldn't satisfy me last night was because of me—and what had been in my head. The next time would be better because Sonia was right. Sex had to be wonderful with your husband.

The jet's tires skidded along the runway, and one of the flight attendants spoke over the loudspeaker. "Welcome to Dubai, where the local time is eight twenty a.m."

I glanced at my watch and wondered if I should reset it. I usually didn't when we took continental or Caribbean trips, but thinking about the eight-hour difference between Dubai and Washington made me slip the gold watch off my wrist and change the time.

We didn't stand like everyone else on the plane when the jet came to a stop. There was no need, since we'd be the first ones off anyway.

Only a few minutes passed before the door opened and we exited. My first thought when I stepped onto the jet bridge was what would this humidity do to my hair? And the next one— even though I truly wanted to honor their culture—how was I going to survive in this heat wearing long sleeves and long dresses the whole time we were here?

But the moment we left the jet bridge, my focus was on the sights, or rather the people. In the bustle of the airport, I couldn't discern the natives from the tourists. The nationalities: Asian, East Indian, and many who looked American, though they could just as easily have been European. And, of course, there were the women dressed in abayas and the men in long white robes and ghutras. I was fascinated by the internationalism of it all and we were still in the airport.

At the baggage area, Damon got a cart, then loaded the luggage and his golf clubs onto it before we went through Customs. We showed our passports and after a couple of questions about the purpose for our visit (the agent almost smiled when Damon told him we were on our honeymoon) and where we were staying (he definitely smiled when Damon told him the Burj Al Arab), we were waved through.

Right outside Customs, a man walked up as if he knew us. "Mr. King?" The tanned man, who wore a very long white kandura and a white ghutra, greeted us. "I'm Khalid and one of our drivers will be taking you to the hotel."

He grabbed the luggage cart from Damon, then passed us over to another man (whom he didn't introduce), who was wearing a similar robe, only much shorter. We were led to a white Rolls-Royce and once we settled inside, the man rolled the car from the curb.

As I peered through the window, Damon tapped me on my shoulder. "I am so looking forward to this. Our honeymoon."

I gave him a smile . . . and a kiss . . . and I prayed.

I almost pressed my nose against the window, wanting to see everything in the most expensive city in the Middle East. But the beauty of the scenery didn't stop me from yawning.

"Tired, huh?" Damon glanced at his watch. "It's almost one in the morning for us."

"I know, but it still doesn't make sense that I'm tired. All we did was fly."

He chuckled. "It's hard being an international traveler."

I smiled and this time, I was the one to take his hand and squeeze it. All I wanted to do was enjoy this beautiful time, in this beautiful place, with this man and his beautiful heart.

Leaning over, I kissed my husband, then told him, "I love you so much."

His dimples were carved deep in his cheek when he grinned. "I bet you I love you more."

"If you do, I'm going to spend the rest of my days trying to beat you."

"We'll spend the days together." He pulled me over and laid my head on his shoulder.

Even though he'd taken me away from the window, I could still see the sights that made this faraway place feel like another cosmopolitan city, especially with the traffic that crowded the streets. We traveled slow enough for me to take in the buildings and the shops with signs in Arabic, though just as many were in English. And the people. Even though it was morning, the streets were filled, just like at the airport, with a medley of nationalities.

It couldn't have been more than twenty minutes before we rolled over a bridge and then came to a stop. The driver turned off the ignition but didn't say a word as he got out and opened the door. Damon stepped out, then reached for my hand.

I had one leg out of the car, then stopped . . . and took in the massive skyscraper that was the symbol of Dubai. I'd seen pictures, of course, of this structure with the silhouette of a sail. But up close, the world's most luxurious hotel was stunning. It didn't even look like a building.

Gathering myself, I slid out of the car, then held Damon's hand as we entered the Burj Al Arab. Like whenever I walked into the Willard, I tried not to appear too impressed by all of the grandeur, though it didn't work. I probably looked like Dorothy right after she touched down in the Land of Oz, but what was I supposed to do? It was the fountains that filled the foyer and the six-hundred-foot-high atrium rising to the heavens that made me stop and stare.

We were whisked through the lobby, straight up to our suite, where we were met at the door by one of the hotel staff.

"Mr. and Mrs. King." The young woman spoke English with a western accent and I wondered if she'd attended school somewhere in the United States or maybe in Great Britain. "Welcome to the Burj Al Arab. I'll be checking you in."

I nodded, and glanced at Damon with a smirk. Really? Private check-ins inside your suite? He gave me a little shrug and a what-else-did-you-expect-from-me look and then took the paperwork from the young lady.

As Damon handled that business, I gazed around. The first word that came to my mind was—*vibrant*. I was used to a more understated décor, but I guessed the people of Dubai believed in opulence through colors. From the heavy burgundy drapes that hung at the twentieth-floor windows to the green brocade sectional sofa with overstuffed pillows and the forty-two-inch flat panel television that hung on the wall inside a golden frame, it was clear that this hotel was all about overstated luxury.

When the young lady began to speak, I turned to face her. "We are here to make sure your stay is all that you want it to be. This is the living room with the lounge and your bar." She pointed across the room. "Your bedroom and the master bath are upstairs." Then she listed the amenities: from someone to unpack our bags (I declined that) to the twenty-one-inch Mac in the bedroom (I couldn't wait to take a look at that.) "There is also a printer, copier, and scanner there. Our concierge is available twenty-four hours and your personal butler is as well."

*Personal butler?*

Damon thanked her and I nodded as if I were used to all of this extravagance. I didn't exhale until she left us alone.

"Oh, my God." I pressed my hand over my mouth like I was twelve years old again. "This place . . ." I dashed up the stairs to the bedroom so that I could see the rest of our suite.

Yup, there was a computer all set up inside the purple room. While the purple was a really deep, deep purple, at least the bedroom was monochromatic. From the draping that hung across the top of our bed to the plush carpet—all purple. Even the desk that held the computer blended into the room.

I walked to the wall that was nothing but three floor-to-ceiling window panels, just like the ones in the living room below, and I sighed, taking in the panoramic view of the Persian Gulf.

Damon came up behind me and when he wrapped me in his arms, I sank into his embrace. "That water out there? That gulf isn't deep enough or wide enough to hold the love that I have for you."

This man. His love. How could I not love him?

"You see what I got here for you, baby?"

What more was he going to say? What more could he do? I turned around with a wide smile until . . .

"Six dozen roses," he said, pointing to the vase on the table in front of the small sofa in our bedroom.

Just like the roses he'd left for me in the Bridal Suite.

Flash:

Spread-eagle.

Naked.

"Your favorites," he added.

Waiting.

Wanting.

I swallowed the big lump of guilt in my throat.

"What? Are you tired of getting flowers?" He laughed a little. "Sorry, you can't get tired of getting something that I love giving you."

In my mind—that flash—again.

"What's wrong?" There was a frown on his face and in his tone.

I shook my head.

"You're acting like you saw a ghost or something."

"No, it's not that." Finally, some semblance of my voice squeaked out. "It's just that they're so beautiful."

"Oh . . . kay," he said. He moved toward me and I tried to hold my breath to stop my shaking. He took my hand. "Maybe you'll like this better."

He led me into the bathroom and as soon as I stepped

over the threshold, I stopped, and this time it wasn't because of the lavishness around me. I didn't really notice the mosaic on the walls or the orange marble around the Jacuzzi tub that was sized for at least four or the storm shower with six showerheads. No, this time, my eyes stayed on the edge of the tub and the basket . . . just another reminder of that night.

All I could do was turn around, leaving Damon standing alone, trying to figure this out. It took him a few moments to follow me, but not enough moments. I'd needed more time because I had some explaining to do.

Sitting next to me on the bed, we were both silent until he asked, "Do you want to tell me what's going on?"

How was I supposed to explain this? How was I supposed to make him understand that I might never want to see roses again? I tried, but my effort was not enough; there was nothing I could do to stop the slow trek of tears down my cheeks.

"What's wrong?" His voice had concern and confusion, but I could hear his hurt, and that hurt me.

There was nothing I could do but lie. "I guess . . . it's just . . . all of this," I whispered. "I want to love you back that same way."

With his fingertips, he lifted my chin. I had no choice; I had to look at him. "You don't have to do anything more than just be you."

When he held me, I didn't think it was possible to love him more than yesterday. But I did. When he laid me back on the bed and ripped my clothes from me, tossing everything to the floor, I welcomed him, I wanted him.

And I prayed that this time would be it.

# 26

# Tiffanie

stared at the purple wall, the same way I'd been doing for what felt like a day's worth of hours. But a quick glance at my watch showed that only four hours had passed since we'd landed, which meant that it had only been two hours since we'd been in this bed.

But those two hours? Torturous. Because. Nothing. Happened. Why couldn't my husband satisfy me?

The chirp on my phone made me frown. Damon had added the international plan for our trip, but that was only to stay in touch with my grandparents. And even they'd told me that they would only call or text in case of an emergency.

Picking up my iPhone, the text message was right there on the screen.

**Thinking about me yet?**

At first, those words confused me. Then those words shocked me. My eyes widened and I glanced over my shoulder, staying still for a moment. After watching Damon's chest rise and fall a few times in the steady rhythm of his sleep, I scooted out of bed, moving as few muscles as possible. I stepped over the jeans and the blouse that I'd worn on the plane and, without a stitch of clothing on, I tiptoed down to the living room.

Once down there, I breathed. I read the text again.

**Thinking about me yet?**

There was no name, no signature. But I didn't need either to know who'd sent this message. How had he gotten my number? But then right away I answered my own question. He was Damon's boy.

I read the text and paced and my heart sped up. Read the text and paced and my heart sped up more. And in between, I tried to breathe.

"Tiff?"

Now, my heart stopped.

"What's going on?" Damon was as naked as I was, but I hardly noticed. "I heard your phone go off."

I stood frozen, my eyes wide, my mouth stuck. I'm sure looking stupid. Then stupid words came out of me. "Ummm . . . ummm . . . it's nothing," I said, trying to figure out how I would delete the text in the two seconds it would take Damon to reach me.

"Who texted you?"

I wanted to cry all over again. "Sonia," I said in a confident tone that could only come from the most proficient of liars.

He frowned as he moved to me. "Everything okay?"

"Yeah, she just wanted me to know something about the spa."

That frown of his deepened. "On our honeymoon? I thought she was gonna handle everything."

I wasn't sure if it was confusion or annoyance that I heard in his voice.

"She is." I spoke as fast as I could without a beating heart. "She's handling everything and she won't text again and I don't think she really had a problem and she just wanted to know that we'd arrived safely and I told her that we had and she said she wouldn't text again."

He craned his neck to take a look at my cell, but I hit the button to return my phone to the home screen, the whole time keeping it from Damon's view.

I couldn't believe how calm my voice was when I said, "I don't want to think about this. I want to just think about you." For emphasis, I took a couple of steps back. With my eyes, I took a slow stroll up his body; starting at his size elevens, I crept up (pausing only once) until my eyes were on his.

For a moment, he looked like the emperor who'd just discovered that neither he (nor I) wore any clothes. That fast, he forgot about my cell, forgot about my lie. "You want to think about me?" His voice was thick with lust.

I nodded. But I only gave him a quick kiss before I stepped away from him again. "I want to think about you and this wonderful city. Let's go out, let's see the sights." It was the look of disappointment that made me add, "We have plenty of time for that. Our whole lives. Let's go out." Adding a little pout to my voice, I said, "I want to because the world's biggest mall is here, remember?"

That was enough for him because actually my man loved shopping even more than I did. "Okay, let's take a shower and then get out of here."

"Together?" I said, wanting to give him something.

"Is there any other way?" he said. "I'll race you." Then he dashed, taking the stairs two steps at a time.

I was in no rush. So, I let my husband win, hoping that my win would come tonight.

◆

THE WORLD'S LARGEST mall had everything. It felt like we'd walked fifty football fields going through every luxury store that I loved: Christian Louboutin, St. John, Versace . . . those shops were for me. We stopped by a few for Damon, too, though he wasn't much for buying clothes off the rack. His retail drug of choice had us browsing through Harry Winston, Montblanc, and Cartier.

After an early dinner (though it was really brunch, since our bodies were still on DC time) at P.F. Chang's (which was better than where Damon wanted to go—California Pizza Kitchen), we continued our exploration through the mall, which even had an indoor skating rink (Really! Even though it was almost ninety degrees outside!). But though we walked like we had no particular destination, I had one last stop in mind.

La Perla.

This was by *my* design. I'd spotted the store earlier and steered Damon away, already forming a plan. Now, as we walked by, I paused and he did, too.

He grinned. "You want something from in here?"

"The question is, do you want something?" When he frowned, I added, "Pick out something, whatever you want." Getting closer to him, I added, "And I'll model it back in our room since you didn't give me a chance to model on our wedding night."

I was surprised at his control—he didn't rush in and pick out the first thing. Rather, we sauntered through, checking out all the merchandise—the bodysuits and the bustiers, the bras and the panties—and settled in the baby-doll section. I was surprised when he picked out a whisper slip with a matching thong.

"This" was all he said before he asked the store attendant if she had that in my size.

I'd expected something a bit more risqué, but I went with it. Because if this was what it took . . .

I was giddy with anticipation as we were driven back to the hotel. The day had been exhausting and I was tired down to my jet-lagged bones, yet I was filled with exhilaration. I couldn't wait to be in bed with this man that I loved and finally . . .

When we stepped into the hotel, I would have taken the stairs if we weren't on the twentieth floor, and when we walked into our suite, I told Damon, "Let me change into something more comfortable. You put on some music."

I couldn't slide into that slip fast enough, and in my mind, I imagined what I would do. Maybe I'd pretend that I didn't know Damon, and that I was a stripper. Or maybe I was a young woman who'd just come to the big city and I was lost.

Laughing out loud, I made a note to tell Damon that we needed to buy some stock in La Perla. Because when this worked, I might want to buy the entire company.

Strolling out of the bathroom, I was a little disappointed to find Damon in the bed. As if he didn't really want a show, as if he just wanted to get right to it.

"Hello, there." I tried to speak from my throat, though in my ears, I sounded like a frog.

Not that it mattered; the way Damon looked at me, I doubted that his ears were working. I did my supermodel stroll across the room and I was sure I could see Damon's heart beating.

I said, "My name is . . ." I paused, wanting to think of some-thing really good. "Cyclone. 'Cause you 'bout to get caught up."

It was a corny line, I knew that. But it was the best I could come up with when my heart was beating with such expectation.

He reached for me, as if that name meant nothing. As if the slip meant nothing. As if my show meant nothing.

"I love you, Tiff," he said, as he laid me on my back.

"I love you, too," I told him. "Let's take this slow."

He followed my instructions—kind of. His kisses were slow. And his caresses were slower. This time, I was ready . . . and wanting . . . and waiting. When we connected, I was more expectant than I had ever been.

And then . . .

And then . . .

And then . . .

Nothing.

# 27

# Damon

There wasn't a lot that I could see in the dark, but the dim light from the digital clock gave me enough light to see that smile on my wife's face. A smile that was, even in her sleep, wider and brighter than her smiles had been since we arrived in Dubai.

Pushing myself up, I leaned against the bed's headboard and, with my eyes still on Tiffanie, I took myself on a trip over the last days. It had been a whirlwind of a honeymoon, exactly the way I'd wanted and expected it to be. Every day we explored the city. From the mall on Sunday to the walk through the village of Dubai on Monday, and then hanging out at the beach on Tuesday. Wednesday we'd toured the desert in dune buggies and then yesterday we'd gone to the Miracle Garden, which had been my idea. I'd been sure that would have been one of Tiffanie's favorite stops. What woman wouldn't want to see over one hundred million blooming flowers? If someone had asked me that question, I would've said, my wife, who just loved flowers.

But she was unimpressed and had rushed us out of there and

back here to the hotel, where we'd made love the way we'd done every single day.

That was the best part of this honeymoon. Making love to my wife.

At least it was—until tonight.

Our last day.

Over the last few years of traveling together, it had become our vacation custom to separate on our last day. She did the spa thing in preparation for going home and I did what relaxed me—I played golf.

At first, I hadn't really wanted to do it. I mean, this was our honeymoon, and would be the first time I was away from my Tiffanie since we'd said, "I do." But she'd insisted and since I'd brought my clubs . . .

Being out on those links at the Emirates Golf Club was all that the brochures said it would be. I'd played golf in a couple of wonderful places around the world—in Kauai, Cabo, London; but I'd never played anyplace where the skyline was right there in front of us . . . that view was the truth and I could have just stayed on the driving range all day. But I'd put my name in and ended up one of a foursome. I'd been partnered up with a couple of guys from the UK and one from Germany. All were here on business, mostly real estate development, and the talk was as beneficial for me as the game had been. I'd told them what I did back in DC, exchanged cards with all, and promised that if their business ever brought them to America, I would roll out a golden carpet for them.

But even though the day had turned out great, tonight would be greater. Tiffanie and I were going to have a celebration of our last night, our one-week anniversary. We wouldn't have a full night since we had to be at the airport at midnight for our 2 a.m. flight back, but we'd get in a few hours of room service . . . and so much more. It was the so-much-more that I'd been looking forward to.

But when I got back from the course, I found her in bed. My guess was that all those spa treatments had lulled my baby to sleep, although I was sure some of it was that her body clock was still jacked up, like mine.

I should have left her alone. I should have just waited until she awakened. But she'd looked so beautiful, sleeping. And so happy, with that smile.

At first, I'd touched her kinda tentatively, not really sure that I wanted to wake her. But my fingers had hardly made contact when she rolled over and grabbed me!

From there it was on. With a force that I'd never seen, she pushed me down, straddled my lap, and she rode me like she was a jockey on a championship stallion. It was a little shocking— the way she'd taken over . . . and the way she never opened her eyes. It seemed to me like she may have kinda still been asleep, kinda still been dreaming. I'd heard of sleepwalking, but I'd never heard of . . . this. She just kept going and going and it was because of the surprise of it all that I guess I held on a little longer. In fact, I held on so long that she released first—something else that had never happened before.

She screamed a scream that filled every inch of the suite, upstairs and down. The way she shuddered and trembled made me wonder if she was having a seizure. She convulsed so much, I couldn't even move.

Then in the middle of all of that, she opened her eyes. And looked at me. And looked as if she were confused. As if it wasn't me that she'd expected to see beneath her. As if I hadn't been the one in her dream.

Bringing myself back from that moment, I shook my head because that couldn't have been true. But it seemed, just for a moment, that Tiffanie thought I was another man. It had only been a second, because she was still mid-scream, still mid-shudder. But then she fell back and off me. She lay there for just another moment before she closed her eyes . . . and went right back to sleep. With that smile.

And I wondered again . . . had she ever really been awake?

I blew out a long breath. That was some good sex right there . . . so why did I feel confused?

In my mind, I heard her screams again. In my soul, I felt her tremors again.

That was what every man wanted to do to his woman. It was what I did to my wife every night.

Except tonight was really different.

My eyes drifted down once again to Tiffanie and, as if on cue, she snuggled deeper into her pillow. With that smile. Was she dreaming? About me?

My ego told me that she was. But then, there was this thing that my father had taught me:

*Many a man has fallen because of ego, Son. Never listen to your ego. Trust only your gut. Ego will have you emotional, but your gut is your intelligence. Trust only your gut.*

My father had been right. All these years, my gut had been my life raft. It was the number-one tool in my survival kit. It was how I'd endured the streets, and endured with lots of paper stacked.

So right now, I listened to that part that never lied to me— and my gut said something was going on.

All kinds of questions shot through my head. Then all kinds of memories came to me with answers.

The first thing—that text Tiffanie received our first morning here. I'd be a fool to think it was Sonia texting her about the spa. Not on the first day of our honeymoon and not at four in the morning. Yeah, it was noon in Dubai, but Tiffanie had forgotten about the time change. Sonia wasn't up in the middle of the night asking her any kinds of questions.

So, of course I'd known that she was lying, but I gave her a pass because, with the way she'd tried to hide her phone, I was thinking she was working some kind of surprise for me, but now I wasn't for sure.

And then Trey. Looking back, he'd been giving me little hints, especially when he said that he hoped Tiffanie didn't hurt me. I'd never gotten the chance to ask him why he'd say something like that just a couple of hours before I was getting married. Did he know something? Had he seen something?

I shook my head. First of all, it was just a text and I was sure it was just like I surmised. Tiffanie was planning some kind of surprise for me, probably back in DC. As for Trey, he'd always been pretentious like that, pretending that he knew something that other people didn't. And if he did know something about Tiffanie, he would definitely tell me. He would never let some female take me down.

"Whoa!" I whispered. I couldn't believe I'd had that thought. Tiffanie wasn't *some female.* She was my wife, and what I was thinking about her was just ridiculous; we were on our honeymoon.

This was nothing but the devil. Trying to put his foot in my good thing.

I needed to get all this out of my mind and just accept what happened tonight—I'd just hit it with Tiffanie like that.

But my gut: *Something's going on.*

Slowly, I inhaled a lot of air, and then released it. Just like I always did when I needed to calm myself so that my mind was clear—something else that my father had taught me.

The thing was, whatever situation I was in, I always figured it out, I always got it right. Because I never rushed. I always watched, always waited. The truth always ended up shining bright when you watched and waited.

It was already seven. I set the alarm for ten, giving us time to dress before heading to the airport. Then I slipped back down in the bed and pulled the covers over me. My stomach growled, but I didn't want anything to eat; I'd lost my appetite.

It was probably best that Tiffanie and I rested anyway, because when we got back home, that time change was gonna be a beast.

Turning toward Tiffanie, I stared at her smiling face. She did another one of those snuggle things into the pillow, and I didn't think it was possible, but her smile widened. I kept my eyes on her for just a little longer.

Then I rolled over. And slept with my back to my wife.

# 28

# Tiffanie

We were back, there was no doubt about that. Damon and I sat in the back of the car, both of us, tapping the screens of our phones, reading emails and returning messages. Damon had a lot more to catch up on than I did; he'd hardly taken his phone with him anywhere or checked it while we were in Dubai.

I, on the other hand, took my phone everywhere, even when I went into the bathroom. Not only because I checked it every fifteen minutes, wanting/not wanting another text from Trey, but because I couldn't take the chance of Trey's text coming in and Damon being on the receiving end.

And there was a chance of that, because the first text was not Trey's last. He'd sent six, one each day since Sunday. I should've just sent him a text back telling him to lose my number. But I'd said nothing, thinking ignoring him was best.

"So, do you want to go home or over to the spa?"

I looked up and tilted my head. It had taken one hour longer flying home than going—fourteen hours instead of thirteen.

That was the only difference with the flight. But with my husband, everything seemed different.

He wasn't himself, not laughing, hardly chatting. When I'd asked him on the plane if he was all right, he said that he was and I believed him, because we'd done a lot on our honeymoon; we were both exhausted. Plus, he had that red-carpet event for Jaleesa Stone coming up. With over five hundred guests expected, plus all the celebrity looky-loos, that had to be what was filling every space in his mind right now.

I said, "Would you mind if I went to check in at the spa?"

He shook his head. "Of course not. I know you have to get over there. To take care of that problem, right?"

I frowned. "What problem?"

Now he tilted his head. "You know, the problem that Sonia had on Sunday. When she texted you?"

I didn't blink when I said, "Oh, we handled that right away. There're no problems now. I just wanna check out things and get myself acclimated to hit the ground on Monday."

He nodded and I did everything that I could not to break eye contact, the sure sign of a liar. When he leaned over and kissed my forehead, I exhaled, though I didn't feel relief. I didn't think that would come until I had this thing with Trey truly worked out in my mind.

"Okay." He gave instructions to Magic (who he called his number one boy Friday) to take me to the spa first. Then to me he said, "I'm gonna run by my office, too. So, we'll meet up at home. You want me to send Magic back for you?"

I shook my head. "Nah, I'll Uber home."

"Just don't be too late, okay?"

His mood was still somber when we stopped in front of the spa and I kissed him. "I'm going to miss you."

I expected Damon to come back with one of his make-me-swoon lines, but all he did was kiss me. Grabbing my purse, I stood on the curb and waved until the car rolled away, then turned to the spa. Thank God it was Saturday. If it had been a weekday and Sonia had been here, Damon would have wanted to come in and talk to Sonia himself. I was going to have to come up with a lie, to cover up the lie. I sighed—that was the problem with lying.

I walked up the steps, but before I could get the key in the door, it swung open.

"Surprise!" Sonia stood with her hands in the air. *"Bienvenido a casa, mi amiga."*

"Thank you." I pulled her into a hug. "How did you know I'd be here?"

"I had your flight information, remember? You said you were coming back this morning."

"Yeah, flying back, but I hadn't planned to come into the office, and didn't expect to find you here on a Saturday."

"First of all, you may not have had plans to come into the office, but I know you, *chica*, I suspected that you wouldn't be able to resist. Seems like I was right."

My grin told her that she was.

"And secondly, I had some of the workers come in this morning to clear out the back so that we can finally get working on those rooms." She waved her hand in the air. "But I don't want to talk business. Tell me everything." She pulled me all the way inside. "How was your honeymoon?"

But the only answer I could give her was, "Uh, Sonia." I stopped and did a slow three-sixty swirl.

"Oh, yeah." She paused and raised her hands in the air again. "Surprise."

"Well, that's one way to put it." When I'd left, the reception area looked like a construction site. Now it looked like— Utopia, right in the middle of DC.

The sketches that the designer had drawn for us had come to life. Right away, my cheeks slackened, my shoulders relaxed as I took in the space. It was the aura—from the rich copper-colored tiled walls to the stone fountains (with streaming water) in all four corners to the magnificence of the copper, rust, and brown marble tiles beneath our feet. This was the manifestation of peace and calm.

"How did you get all of this done so quickly?"

"What are you talking about?" she asked as if she didn't understand my question. "You were gone for a whole week."

"But this wasn't supposed to be done for another two weeks."

She waved her hand, her way of saying that exceeding expectations was her expectation; just something that she always did. "Don't get too impressed. I only did this front part and . . ." She took my hand and dragged me down the hallway. She was right; it seemed like nothing else had been touched and we had to step over wood planks and paint cans and boxes containing more floor tiles. But then we walked into my new office.

"Oh, my God," I whispered.

Just like in the front, Sonia had waved her magic wand here and created peace and harmony. My office was the color of serenity, different shades of soft blues. Even the desk was a royal color, and somehow Sonia had purchased a chair the exact shade. But the carpet was the best part. Not only because of its gradations of blue, making it look like the sky, but because with each step, I felt like I was walking on air.

She gave me a tour of my space: built-in shelves already filled with books, mini fountains that matched the ones out front, my collection of elephants. I hardly moved from my spot as Sonia chatted. All I did was turn and turn and turn, taking in every inch of this incredible transformation.

"Oh, and you have to come over here." She took my hand and led me to the full bathroom. "The shower's not working yet, but all the rest of it, knock yourself out." Looking back at the office, she said, "So all you have to do is unpack the stuff that you had in my office." She pointed to the boxes in the corner.

"I don't know what to say."

She grinned.

"Thank you so much for this."

*"Para eso están los amigos."*

"Yeah, that's what friends are for, but you've gone way beyond friendship."

"That, *chica,* is called a paycheck. Your man pays me well, and speaking of your man . . ." She sat down on my sofa as if she planned to stay awhile. "Tell me about the honeymoon."

But the moment I sat down next to her, she jumped up. "Oh, my God. I almost forgot about Allen."

"What?"

"He rode in with me so that he could get to the barbershop over on Fourteenth before the Saturday-afternoon rush. I promised him that I'd get the men started and wouldn't make him wait, and he promised me a fabulous brunch over at Georgia's."

"Sounds like a fair exchange to me," I said, following her back down the hall toward her office. But after just a couple of steps, she stopped, almost making me bump into her. "The guys. Out back. Are you gonna be here for a minute?" She didn't give me a chance to answer before she said, "They've been work-ing for a couple of hours. I can let them go."

"No, don't let them go. I'm gonna be here for a little while. I wanted to check out my calendar, look at the financial spread-sheets, get everything in order so that I can jump back in, since you carried everything for the last week. Even before that, really."

"No problem." She waved my words away. "So you can lock up when the guys leave." She glanced at her watch. "They should be done within the next hour or so."

She grabbed her purse. "Where's Damon?"

"He went into his office. He'll be there for a while, so I have time before I meet him at home."

She nodded. "The two of you—workaholics. In my lan-guage, you're . . ."

"*¡Adictos al trabajo!*"

She raised an eyebrow. "Impressive."

I shrugged. "I picked up a few things. Now go." I shooed her away. "Go take care of your husband."

"You do the same, chica. *Te amo.*"

"Love you, too."

I locked the door after her, then stood in the foyer, taking in all that Sonia had done. It really was amazing how something I'd imagined was coming to life. Walking back down the hall, I didn't stop at my office. Instead, I peeked out the back door at the three men who were filling a truck with debris.

"Can you let me know when you're done?" I shouted out to them.

All three turned, all three grinned and waved. I waved back, then shook my head. In any language, men were men.

Back in my office, I lifted one of the boxes to the top of

my desk and searched until I found my calendar. I really needed to get into the habit of keeping my calendar on my phone. It was hard, though; this was the only paper that I didn't want to give up.

Sitting at the desk, I checked and rechecked the timeline Sonia had given me with all the delivery and installation dates and when the final inspections would be. There were several agencies we had to deal with and I added each one to the timeline. We were just a little more than thirty days out, so staying with this schedule was crucial.

Sonia had left the budget folder on my desk, and when I was done with the calendar, I switched to the numbers, studied each line, then prepared a new budget, P&L statement, and balance sheet. I smiled when I looked at the numbers. I'd be able to give Damon a good report—we'd be on time, on budget, and in the black within the first few months, I believed.

Next, I made a list of the things I wanted to discuss with the publicist, deciding that an email wasn't enough. A face-to-face meeting was necessary.

Just as I reached for my phone, I heard, "Miss?"

My head snapped up and I saw one of the men I'd spoken to earlier out back.

"I'm sorry," he said, dipping his head. "I just wanted to tell you that we're finished."

Had that much time passed? I glanced at my watch. It had! I'd been working for hours; it was already after two.

"Okay, thank you," I said.

He nodded before he turned away. I listened for the back door, then I leaned back in my chair and closed my eyes. It felt good to be back working, even though I could say that I missed

Dubai already. It was the best honeymoon ever, especially after last night.

All I could do was sigh as I thought back to that moment, though I didn't remember a lot of it. Except for when it happened, that moment when Damon finally took me to heaven and I didn't have to fake the trip.

It was all kind of a dream. Literally. I'd returned from the spa feeling like a noodle with a brain. There wasn't much I could do except lie down. It wasn't that I was tired, but having three masseuses working on me at the same time—one on my head, one on my body, one on my feet—it was a wonder I didn't have to be wheeled back to our room.

So, I'd lain down, closed my eyes, and dreamt. I dreamed about that feeling. I kept having it, over and over. And then I felt it. Like it was *really* happening.

And then it was. It was so bizarre when I opened my eyes—and looked into Damon's. For a moment, I wasn't sure which part was the dream and which was reality, because Damon was not the man who'd been in my mind. But he *was* the one who'd delivered. Finally! If I'd had any kind of energy after that, I would have jumped up and done a hallelujah dance.

But even though I was thrilled about last night, I did wonder—had it really been Damon who made me feel that way when it was Trey who was in my dreams?

"That doesn't matter," I told myself. And it didn't. Because men fantasized all the time, right? Even if Trey were in my head, he'd never make his way into my heart. That place was only for Damon. And now I was sure that Damon and I would be fine, because if he'd done it for me once, he could do it for me again and again.

"Just like Trey," I whispered.

"Excuse me."

My eyes snapped open and the chair jerked forward so far I almost fell out. *Just blink.* That's what I told myself, because like last night, I was having one of those dreams. I probably wasn't even at Utopia. I could've still been back in Dubai.

So, I blinked. That is, I closed my eyes, squeezed the lids together, then opened them slowly.

Trey was still there.

The entire time I was in Dubai, that center part of my body had pulsed, a constant reminder of him. Now that pulsing turned to throbbing and I could feel the heat building.

"How did you get in here?"

"Well, first, hello. And I came in just as those guys were going out."

Dang! I hadn't even thought about getting up and locking the back door. "What are you doing here?"

"So, you're not even going to say hello?"

"What are you doing here, Trey?" I repeated. It probably would have been better for me to jump up, get in his face with all kinds of indignation. But there was no way I could do that. Because I needed every part of my body to help in my fight to keep that mental flash out of my mind.

"I came by to see you guys," he said, stepping all the way into my office.

"You have no need to see me, and *Damon* isn't here."

My hope was that the mention of my husband's name would change the energy and shift both of us.

"I was talking about you and Sonia."

My eyes thinned. "What do you want with her?"

"You jealous?" He grinned.

"No. I just know my best friend doesn't like you."

He chuckled and had the audacity to sit down in the chair on the other side of my desk. He leaned back as if he'd been invited into my space. "Now, how can she not like me when she doesn't know me?"

"What do you want with her?" I asked. Ignoring his question made me feel like I had a little bit of control.

"Is she here?"

"She will be."

"Oh." He sounded like he was disappointed, then he laughed. "You're not even a good liar."

"What are you doing here?" That time, my voice quivered a bit, and I prayed that I sounded steadier to him than I sounded to myself.

"I knew you'd be back today and I wanted to stop by to see you."

I pressed my lips together, knowing that what I needed to do was push this man out the door and run the other way. But I knew what would happen if I got anywhere near him. I'd been dreaming about it.

"How was your honeymoon?" He kept his eyes on me, never blinking.

"I don't want you here." I kept my eyes on him and I couldn't stop blinking.

Then he asked, "Did you get my texts?"

I tried to keep my body as still and as steady as possible. But my legs were forsaking me. I thanked God that my trembling was hidden beneath my desk. After I moment I responded, "When are you leaving for Atlanta?"

He laughed again, like he was at some comedy show. "We have two separate conversations going on."

I needed him to stop talking, because then I wouldn't have to watch his lips. And if I didn't watch his lips, then I wouldn't want his lips all over me.

"You need to leave."

He raised an eyebrow. "Is that any way to treat a friend?"

"I'm not your friend." That part was true. As much as I wanted him, I hated him.

He stood. I exhaled with relief. But he didn't walk toward the door. Instead, he took slow steps toward me.

No!

He rounded the corner of my desk until he was right over me. "I missed you, Tiff."

I shook my head, more to get air than anything else.

"We never finished what we started."

Flash:

Me.

And now I wanted him to finish it.

When he leaned down and kissed me, there was nothing I could do. Just his being stole every bit of resolve from me and I became nothing more than a ball of lust.

One second his lips were on mine, the next second my lips parted, and the third second, we were devouring each other as passion overcame me and I just could not get enough.

Our lips stayed locked, even as he pulled me from my chair, and when one of his hands snaked inside the waistband of my skirt, I gasped. And he hadn't even gotten to the good part.

His hand moved lower and lower, and with each inch, I lost another piece of my mind. By the time he got to my center, I was done. I shuddered and shuddered and shuddered. But that done part? That was a lie. Because I wanted more and more and more.

He pulled away, just for a moment. Just so he could look into my eyes. And laugh.

I didn't care that he teased me; it was that feeling that I craved from deep inside my DNA, that feeling that I had to have, that feeling that only he could give me.

So, even as he laughed, I forced his mouth back to mine and gripped his neck like I had no plans to let him go. Then, the same way he'd caressed me, I fondled him. He may have laughed at me, but when I touched him? All laughter stopped.

We kissed, we fondled, and I was once again filled with that feeling.

Until.

My mind filled with questions: What was I doing? And right after my honeymoon? What kind of woman did this?

With the palms of my hands, I pushed him away. "No!"

He looked at me and I yearned for him.

He took two steps back and I ached for him.

When he nodded, wiped his mouth with the back of his hand, and turned away, panic attacked me. My voice betrayed my hunger when I asked, "Where are you going?"

He paused, right at the threshold. His eyes, still dark, still seductive, held me. "You said no." He paused, letting the words hang in the air for a couple of seconds. "And when a woman says no to me, I understand what no means." And he turned again to the door.

I did mean no. I really did. Because I couldn't do this, not to Damon, and not with Trey. I hated this man. But in the next second, I said, "I don't mean no," because my hunger was much stronger than my horror.

He turned back and, giving me his cocky smile, he asked, "What did you say?"

I hated him. "I mean yes." I hated myself.

"You mean yes?" He repeated my words in a whisper.

I swallowed. I nodded.

"Say it out loud so that there's no confusion."

I tried to keep it inside, because maybe if I didn't say it, he would leave. But I spoke because I had no control. "Yes."

"You want me, don't you?"

A tear squeezed from my eye as the word came out of my mouth again. "Yes."

He spoke slowly when he said, "You should learn to say what you mean."

Then, before I could blink or think, he wiped my desk clean with one swipe, making the box I'd been unpacking tumble off and crash onto the floor. In the next second, I was up and in his arms before he laid me back on the desk and pushed my skirt up, up, up until it was above my waist.

I was already reeling, but when he lowered his head, I was once again done, before he even got started.

This was a death wish, that was the only thought I had when Trey pushed my panties aside. But then, Trey's tongue was a magic eraser as he cleared all thoughts from my mind. I was empty of everything, except for that feeling that was better than anything I'd ever felt before, and that feeling became me.

I screamed and screamed and screamed. And shuddered and shuddered and shuddered. It may have been minutes, it may have been hours, or it could have been days. When his face came back into my view, I was still panting, in the glow of the aftermath. But that glow dimmed when Trey looked at me. His victory smirk made me shrink beneath the weight of my guilt. Yet that guilt wasn't enough to make me stop. I wanted more, I wanted him.

He licked his lips, and this time he moaned as if he loved the taste of me. With a chuckle, he turned around . . . and walked out the door.

Like the night before my wedding, I lay there even after I heard the front door open, then close.

That was it?

What was I thinking asking myself that?

That was enough!

My back began to ache from pressing against the hardness of the desk, but then when I rose, what I still felt between my legs was like a balm for my back pain. That ache was gone. But the throbbing remained. Even as I rolled my skirt down, even as I slipped off the desk, I throbbed. And that throbbing made me wonder, who was Trey? What was he doing to me?

The bigger question, though, was who was I? Who had I become? And who was I going to be now?

# 29

# Damon

Those three hours in my office did my mind good. Sitting behind that desk, where I'd made all kinds of decisions, helped me to see my situation with more clarity.

There was nothing nefarious going on with my wife. What could have been going down, anyway? Basically, deceit fell into three categories: money, drugs, and sex. Well, she had all my money, so I knew she wasn't out there caught up in some kind of scam or scheme. Drugs? Nah, not the way my girl hated my past; that's why she was still so leery of Trey. Finally, there was sex— that one almost made me laugh out loud. Tiffanie involved with someone else? My wife had been a virgin when I got with her. She wasn't going anywhere.

The bottom line was, my wife wasn't like all those females I'd dealt with in the past; she wasn't scandalous, she wasn't gold-digging . . . she was just Tiffanie. All the things that I'd conjured up in my mind, all the things that had me twisted had no basis. I was trippin' over a text and an orgasm. And not every situation had an explanation.

I had it together now that I'd had time to work it through

logically. Yeah, my gut was still trying to talk to me, but I'd figured that out, too—it was all because of the years I'd spent in the streets. My gut kicked in no matter what, but I was gonna ride on intelligence and common sense on this one.

"Something's got you all happy." Magic, the key man in my crew, looked at me sideways from where he sat behind the wheel. "You over there practically singing."

"I'm supposed to be happy, son. I just got married."

He shook his head. "Yeah, all right. If that's what it takes to be happy, then I'm gonna be one sad cat 'cause I ain't trying to be hooked up like that anytime soon."

"Oh, you will when you meet the right one." I nodded. "'Cause when she's right, there won't be anything that you can do about it."

"Trust me, I can't afford to take that plunge."

We laughed together, but what he said was true. There were a couple of guys who rolled with me from the old days, and Magic was one of them. I didn't even know his real name; he was always known only as Magic, and it had nothing to do with his basketball skills. It was more about his life skills, what he could do on the streets. And what he'd done in his past made him wary of getting too close with anyone.

He brought the SUV to a stop in my driveway and then both of us hopped out and got a bag out of the back. I almost trotted to the front door, anxious to see if Tiffanie was here.

When I stepped inside our house, I called out, "Yo, Tiff, you home yet?"

There was nothing and that made me smile. Because once I'd gotten my head clear, I remembered that I had to carry my wife over the threshold the first time she stepped back into our home. Not that I was superstitious, but I wanted to have it all covered.

"Thanks, Magic," I said to my boy when he brought the other bag and my golf clubs inside.

"Yo, no problem. You need me for the rest of the night?"

"Nah, I'll be good. The first night back with the wifey; we're just gonna stay in."

He grinned, gave me dab, and then said, "I'm just a phone call away."

I locked the door behind him, then clicked on my cell and pressed the last number called.

"Hello, Mr. King," the voice said.

"Are you close?" I asked.

"Open your door."

I took two steps, did as I was told, and there was Glory, the proprietor of one of the catering companies I worked with, who made a dish that was one of Tiffanie's favorites.

"Wow, that was quick." I grabbed one of the shopping bags from Glory and the other lady with her.

"I had all the ingredients I needed and with your offering to triple my fee, I couldn't get here fast enough."

I laughed with her as I led her into the kitchen, then left Glory and her helper to take care of their business. Just as I was heading upstairs to get ready for my wife, the doorbell rang. Trotting back down, I opened the door, and then my day got better.

"Son, what are you doing here?"

Trey laughed. "Everybody is asking me that today." When I frowned, he added, "I just came by to see you."

"Well, I'm glad you did." I pulled him into one of our

brother hugs. "So what's been good?" I asked as I led him into the living room.

He didn't answer me, though. His eyes scoped the place, the massive ceiling, the crystal chandelier that hung in the center of the foyer, the furniture that had been purchased and arranged by one of California's top designers, whom I'd flown in to take care of our home.

I said, "Oh, that's right, you haven't been here."

"Nah, bruh." Trey's eyes still weren't on me when he said, "You came up."

He was right about that. Even though we had been stackin' back in the day, what we'd had was new money and new money often had no class. But I'd changed all that when I started hanging out with a different crowd of achievers and shakers who never tried to impress anyone but themselves. I was new money with an old attitude.

"I have to say, this place is fresh."

I thanked Trey, but I wasn't into showboating anymore, so I changed the subject. "I'm glad to see that you're still here."

"I told you I would be."

I nodded but kept my thoughts to myself. He didn't need to know that I was still bothered by the fact that he wouldn't talk to me. Wouldn't tell me what was going on with him. But instead of asking him more questions that he didn't want to answer, I asked, "How's Ms. Irene?"

He leaned back on the couch and paused. I knew what that was about. The chesterfield-style sofa was upholstered in cashmere, which felt as good to sit on as it did to wear. Finally, he said, "She's good."

"So, did she talk you into moving back home yet?"

"Nah, but I'm giving it serious consideration because of you." I raised an eyebrow but said nothing as he continued. "I thought about what you said, about us partnering up again. And like you said, we're boys. Always have been. So I want to get down to the business of taking care of business."

That made me grin big-time. "So you're really considering my offer?"

He nodded. "Enough to wanna sit down and talk it all out, you know, figure out what my role will be." He paused. "But yeah, I'm thinking about staying 'cause there's a lot of good stuff going down here."

I was going to ask him about that other business he'd talked about on my wedding day, but I got a bit distracted by the look on his face. "A female," I said. "You met someone."

His side-smirk was the only answer he gave me.

I chuckled. "Is it the girl you met at the Willard?" Again he said nothing and that made me laugh more. "She must be serious if she's got you mute."

His smirk became wider, but he answered my question with a question. "How's married life?"

Now I gave him my own wide grin. "It's everything."

"Really?" He seemed surprised. But I guessed a man who'd never been in a committed relationship had no way of knowing what it was like to have that one girl love you.

So I schooled him. "Son, at the risk of sounding too sensitive, I can say that this is the way life is supposed to be."

He shook his head like I'd gone down in defeat or something.

"I'm serious." I laughed. "All you cats still out there, going from one chick to another, you don't know the real deal. What I have with Tiff, this is the way God planned it."

He gave me a long look, like he was studying me and my words. "I don't know. I've never met a female that I could trust. Not one. Not yet."

That made me remember. "Is that why you said what you did? Right after Reverend Cooper came and talked to me?"

He frowned like he didn't know what I was talking about, but I didn't know why he was playing possum like that. Trey remembered, he always remembered everything. That was one of his problems; his memory was too long. He held grudges that in the past had led to wars.

But for some reason, now he was pretending like he didn't remember anything. So I let him and I took on the role of reminding him. "You told me that you hoped Tiffanie didn't hurt me."

"When did I say that?" The way he asked that question made me wonder—maybe he really didn't recall his words, and that made me feel a little bit better.

I reminded him of where we'd been minutes before my wedding, but inside, I gave my own self dap, because that was another point where those doubts in my head hadn't made any sense. Trey hadn't really been talking about Tiffanie; he had just been talking off the top of his head about his own experiences.

He said, "Well, I don't remember that, but it makes sense that I would say it."

That took my grin away.

He finished with, "I just know that females . . . are females."

I shook my head. "Not Tiffanie."

He shrugged. "I hope you're right."

"No hope here, son. It's all knowledge. I know who I married."

For some reason, my words seemed to crack Trey up, but before I could ask him what was up with that, I heard Tiffanie's key in the lock. That made me forget all about Trey, and I jumped up and dashed to the door like a sprinter. Before Tiffanie could push it open, I was there, making sure she didn't step a foot inside.

She looked confused and I grinned. "Welcome home, bae." I stepped outside and swooped her into my arms. Her purse dropped, but that didn't matter to me. "I wanted to carry you over the threshold."

The look on her face turned into a soft smile, a loving smile. "Didn't we already do this?"

"But that was at the hotel. This is our home. Welcome home." I kissed her, and with our lips still together, I stepped into our house.

# 30

# Tiffanie

The guilt had felt like a heavy overcoat that was too heavy to wear. But then Damon rescued me, meeting me at the door and taking that coat of guilt off me. Did I still have regret? Was I filled with remorse? Yes, and I would probably feel that way for the rest of my life.

But as I'd sat in my office and gone over it all in my mind, I resolved that nothing would happen with Trey again. I just had to find a way to stay away from him until he returned to Atlanta. And if I were ever alone with him, I made a vow that I'd get out of there.

Now, as Damon kissed me, I was so grateful for the bath-room in my office, where I'd stripped and washed up (all water, no soap) and rinsed my mouth over and over. At least he wouldn't smell Trey, even if I could still feel him.

Our lips were still together when Damon carried me inside. Then I slid down his body and opened my eyes.

Trey!

If I'd been any kind of woman, I would've fainted right then. Because there was no way that I could stand here and take the humiliation, since I didn't have an explanation for what I'd done.

I trembled as I looked from Trey to Damon, back to Trey, and finally settled on my husband. How was I going to explain what had happened this afternoon? And the night before our wedding?

But I corralled my thoughts. If Trey had told Damon what happened, my husband wouldn't have greeted me the way he did. Still, I stood there, as frozen as an ice sculpture, and watched Trey step out the door. I wanted to kick it shut, then pray that somehow the door had hit him, hurt him, killed him.

But in seconds, Trey was back and handed me my purse that I'd dropped outside.

"Welcome home, Tiffanie." He leaned in and kissed my cheek. I squeezed my legs together before my body betrayed me.

It took everything inside me not to snatch the purse, but I had no gratitude to give him, so I said nothing and stepped away.

"Did you get a lot of work done at the spa?" Damon asked me.

Without looking at Trey, I nodded, then said, "I'm going to go upstairs and leave you and Trey—"

"Don't leave on my account," Trey said.

I had to force my head to turn, then force myself to speak. "I'm not doing this on your account. Everything I do is for my husband."

He smirked. "Everything?"

I wanted to die a couple of deaths. It felt like I was cheating on Damon right in front of him. Trey and I were having this conversation and Damon had no idea what was going on.

Leaning forward, I kissed Damon. "I'll be upstairs."

He grabbed me before I could turn around. "No, really. Trey is leaving." There was a smile on Damon's face, but there was an edge in his tone.

"Yeah, yeah," Trey piped in. "I wanna leave you lovebirds to do whatever it is that lovebirds do."

He gave Damon dap and then, when he looked my way, I stepped back and swore that if he came near me, I would hit him upside his head with my purse and just explain it to Damon later.

He must've read my mind because all he did was chuckle, fist-bump Damon again, and walk out the door.

When we were alone, Damon gave me one of those looks that studied me, penetrated me, and made me grateful that he wasn't a mind reader. "Are you okay?"

I nodded. "I am."

His glance moved to the closed door, then came back to me. "Seems like something's going on between you and Trey."

I shook. I swallowed.

He said, "I know you don't like him, bae."

"I don't."

"I think it would be better if you got to know him."

"It won't."

"Well, we're going to have to figure this out because he's staying."

I frowned. "Staying where?" That was a stupid question, because of course I knew the answer. But my prayer was that Damon was just telling me that Trey planned to stay on earth instead of going to hell where he belonged.

"Here in DC." As he told me what I already knew, he wrapped his arms around my waist. "But I don't want to talk about my best friend."

If only Damon knew.

"I want to talk about this surprise I have for you."

I didn't think I could take any more surprises, but when I followed Damon into the dining room and saw the table already set, complete with candlelight (even though there was still some sunlight at five o'clock), my heart fluttered with love and my stomach rippled with shame.

"Welcome to your first night in our home," he said.

I wasn't going to mention all the times I had stayed here before because I knew what he meant. When he pulled out the chair for me, I sat down, even though all I wanted to do was go upstairs, get out of these clothes, and burn them. Damon sat at the head of the table and held my hand, until Glory came out.

When she served the Brazilian fish stew (my favorite), I couldn't even smile. And after Damon blessed the food and then chatted about the guest list for Jaleesa Stone's event, I couldn't even talk.

"It's going to be a zoo, but if her people don't mind paying this kind of money, who am I not to take it? And they know that whatever I put together will be poppin'."

I nodded, because that was all that I could give him.

It took him a while to realize that I hadn't said a word, and he frowned. "What's wrong? You're not hungry?"

Looking down, I realized that it wasn't just my silence that was giving me away. My bowl, filled with cod and tilapia and shrimp and some of my favorite vegetables, was still filled to the brim. Putting down my spoon, I just said, "I'm tired. It must be the time change."

He glanced at his watch. "Yeah, what time is it in Dubai?" He paused for just a second. "It's between one and two in the morning. We've had a long day."

I nodded.

"So, what's going on over at Utopia? What did you work on today?"

Even though I wanted to squeeze my eyes shut because I could feel the memory of that feeling coming on, I looked straight at Damon. I wanted to tell him about Sonia's surprise, I wanted to tell him all that Sonia had done, but my lips began to tremble.

The legs of his chair scraped against the floor as he pushed it back and then hunched down beside me.

"Bae, what's wrong?" His voice was no more than a whisper.

I bit my lip. "I'm tired, I guess." I swallowed, I blinked, and none of it worked. That first tear fell, so now I had to add another lie to my list. "And, I'm happy. So happy."

His lips curled up a little. "I have got to stop making you so happy."

"No." Now I pushed my chair back. "Don't ever stop. Please." I stood up and when he stood with me, I laid my head on his chest and cried.

Gently, he pushed my head back and once again tried to kiss my tears away. But this time they overflowed like a faucet, just running, never stopping.

As I sobbed, Damon lifted me into his arms, and for a moment, I had another flash—of Trey doing the same just a few hours before. That made me hold Damon tighter, made me sob even harder.

He cradled me as if I were his baby and carried me up the stairs. Now I trembled more. Because I was so scared.

Damon was taking me to our bedroom, to our bed for the first night in our home as husband and wife. But, I couldn't do this. I couldn't sleep with Damon, not after what happened with

Trey today. We hadn't had intercourse, but what we'd done . . . it was sexual; some might say it was more intimate than intercourse. So I couldn't be intimate with Damon now.

That made me cry even more. When Damon laid me on the bed, that made me bawl. It wasn't a trick, though it did the trick. It did keep Damon away, because I really couldn't stop crying.

And Damon, he was always such a gentle man; he understood. Not my tears; I knew he didn't understand that. But somehow he knew that we wouldn't be able to make love tonight.

So instead, he just held me and kissed me, until I cried myself to sleep.

# 31

# Tiffanie

awakened to darkness. Not literally, because the morning sun was already rising above the horizon and brightening our bedroom. Still, to me, it felt like midnight.

I wanted to pull the covers over my head when the alarm sang out. But instead, I rolled out of bed. Not because I wanted to; I had to. I had to get up for church like I'd done on the hundreds of other Sundays since I'd met Damon. I had to, or else this morning would be like last night—another moment of our life that was out of order. I couldn't allow another situation that I couldn't explain. Another raised flag would move Damon from curious to confused and all the way to suspicious. I had to find a way to be normal, even though I was not.

As I sat on the edge of our bed, his soft voice came over my shoulder. "Good morning."

I returned his morning greeting, though I didn't turn and kiss him. Because if I did that, I would've had to look into his eyes. And if he looked into mine, he'd have questions. And if he asked me a question, I'd have to come up with more new lies to explain my breakdown last night.

I rushed into the bathroom and into the shower. Under the spray of the warm water, I was grateful that I had made the effort to get up for church. Being in the house of God was what I needed. Maybe He could fix me, because surely, I was broken. Just thinking about being in church made me feel a bit of relief . . . which dissipated the moment I stepped from the shower. Damon stood right outside, waiting, with a warmed towel.

"Thank you," I whispered as he wrapped it around me, though my glance kept shifting so it wouldn't meet his.

He paused, as if he were waiting for more from me, then he kissed my forehead. My heart ached because I loved this man so much, but my betrayal kept my lips sealed.

Inside our bedroom, I shimmied into my red sheath, keeping my eyes on the floor. I slipped into my black pumps, and as I brushed my hair back into a ponytail, I didn't even look in the mirror, afraid to see his reflection.

It was painful, but it worked. Damon didn't say another word, didn't ask a single question. From the corner of my eye, I watched him, and saw that his glance never broke away. We were so connected, I could feel him studying me like I was a science project, a dead rat under a microscope.

In our relationship, I was always the one who took at least an hour to get dressed, wanting perfection every time I walked out the door. Today, though, I was dressed in just a bit over ten minutes and for makeup, I only brushed on a thin layer of foundation and left my eyelashes and lips naked. Then I scurried out of our bedroom before Damon had even chosen what suit to wear.

Downstairs, after I popped two pieces of bread into the

toaster and poured two glasses of orange juice, I leaned back against the counter and let my mind wander. Upstairs, it had been easy to keep my thoughts in check since all of my focus was on dodging Damon.

But now I was free to think. And that freedom took me to yesterday.

And Trey.

And that feeling.

I squeezed my legs together and blinked back tears. How many more tears could I shed? And what would crying do anyway, besides make Damon more suspicious?

I had to keep myself together. But how? How could I do that when all I could think about was what Trey had made me feel?

When I heard Damon's steps on the stairs, I grabbed my iPad, sat down at the counter, opened Safari, and by the time Damon walked into the kitchen, I looked like I was scanning the Sunday papers.

Damon stood just a few feet from me, studying me as he ate his toast in a couple of bites and drank his juice in a couple of gulps. I just waited it out until he broke our silence.

"You ready to go?"

I nodded and pretended that I didn't hear the confusion, sprinkled with a bit of hurt, in his voice. I wanted to reach out and hug him, assure him that I was all right, he was all right, we were all right. But how could I give him any assurances when I felt no surety (of anything) myself?

The best moment of the morning came when Damon held my hand as we walked into the garage and he led me to the passenger side of the Bentley. I was so grateful for his touch, though still, the sounds of silence continued. As he drove, I searched my mind for something to say, and when I couldn't find anything, I stayed mute. I guess Damon was feeling the same way.

I was filled with gratitude when we pulled into the church's parking lot and Damon parked next to my grandfather in the space that had been reserved for us since we'd started coming to church together. It felt so normal when he jumped out of the car, came to my side, and opened my door.

He held my hand again as we walked across the lot to the church. It seemed impossible that just nine days ago, I'd made this same trek up the steps to get married. And now, here I was returning and that one mistake I made had turned into two.

As soon as we entered the church, thoughts of my personal failings as a wife were swept away in a barrage of greetings that stopped all of my thinking.

"Welcome home, newlyweds."

A female usher kissed our cheeks.

"Congratulations."

A deacon hugged us.

Every few steps, we were told how good we looked together, how wonderful it was that we'd found each other, how God had been so good.

I did my best to find my smile, but like at home, my words were missing in action, so my husband stepped up and spoke for both of us. As we walked down the center aisle, I hated that we kept getting stopped, because this aisle just reminded me of the vows that I'd taken and hadn't been able to keep. It felt like a special kind of torture, and I found no relief until we took our seats in the second pew, right behind where my grandmother would sit. If nothing else about this morning was right, our timing was, because just as we got settled, the praise team entered the sanctuary.

> *I want to praise you, forever, and ever, and ever . . .*
> *For all you've done for me . . .*

Damon and I stood, and I pushed enthusiasm into my swaying and clapping. My grandparents marched in, swaying, singing, stepping with the choir. Even though my grandmother never considered herself a preacher and never sat up on the altar, she always walked into the sanctuary with my grandfather. I was about twelve when I asked her why she did that.

"I'm not a preacher, but I walk alongside your granddaddy because I'm his crown."

When I asked her what she meant, she told me to look it up in Proverbs.

That memory brought a small smile and also tears, because I'd wanted so much for Damon and me to be like my grandparents. It was only after I was sure that I didn't carry my mother's curse that I'd agreed to marry Damon, and I'd wanted to be his crown.

But his crown was tilted and he didn't even know it.

My eyes were on my grandparents and I watched my grandfather lead my grandmother to her seat and kiss her cheek, and then, like always, he acknowledged me with a wink.

Even though the choir was still rocking, my grandmother turned to hug me, but then she paused, and she stared. That was when I knew I should have stayed in bed this morning. Damon . . . he only had suspicions. But my grandmother? That line to God told her the truth. It was only because of where we were that she stayed silent, even as she hugged me and then turned her embrace to Damon.

She gave me one last frown, but still spoke no words, and once again I was grateful for being in church. I gave her a smile, but it was as fake as I felt, though it was enough to get her to turn back around to face the altar.

The music director raised her fist in the air, ending the song for the choir, but not for the worshippers, who continued their praise. Usually I stood, like everyone else in the church, raising my hands to the Lord (though I never danced in the aisles). But today I sat down and bowed my head, praying that God would fix this, would fix me.

When the church settled enough for the service to continue, the visitors were greeted, the announcements were made, another song was sung, and then my grandfather stood up.

"Let the church say Amen!"

The church did as my grandfather asked.

"Amen," he said. "Well, you know I have a Word from the Lord after that amazing singing."

More Amens rang throughout.

"Before I begin to share the church, I want to first give thanks. We always give thanks, Amen!"

"Amen!"

"My thanks is personal today. I want to welcome home the second love of my life." He winked at my grandmother. "My granddaughter and her new husband, who is now officially my grandson. Greater First AME, let us all welcome Mr. and Mrs. King home from their honeymoon."

The people stood and applauded as if we'd accomplished

something good. While Damon stood and gave a one-eighty wave, I wanted to shrink. Of course, I should have been standing proud with my husband, but I had no strength of character, so how could I stand next to a man whose character could never be impugned?

But when Damon took my hand and pulled me up, I was forced to do what I didn't want to do. I stood by his side, without turning to the left or the right, just kept focused on my grandfather, because I was afraid that anyone closer would be able to see the truth in my eyes.

Even though the applause stopped, the congregation remained on their feet as my grandfather spoke. "This young couple right there, this is a union that the Lord intended."

With those words, his smile, I had to look away from him, and I made my glance rise to the cross behind him.

"For this reason," my grandfather continued, "a man shall leave his father and his mother and be joined to his wife; and they shall become one flesh."

My grandmother twisted in her seat to look up at me. I kept my eyes on the cross.

"I am proud of these two young people and I am looking forward to all the plans that God has for both of you."

I wasn't sure if Damon was ready, but I couldn't stand any longer and as the applause began and the ovation continued, I shrank back into my seat.

It was probably just a few seconds, but hearing all the undeserved accolades and adoration made it feel so much longer. When the congregation finally sat, Damon also sat down, took my hand, and squeezed it.

Meanwhile, I kept my eyes on the cross.

"Now that I've taken care of my personal business, let's get to God's business. Amen!"

Amens resounded.

"Today, church, I come to you with this message, a message that is for everyone. The title of this message: When Temptation Comes."

My eyes widened, my mouth opened; I was having one of those moments—you know, when you're sitting in church and the pastor zeroes in on your sin? The fact that the pastor was my grandfather made this moment even worse.

"Notice that I said *when* and not *if*, because, you see, this is what I know . . . Temptation *will* come. Do you know how I know?"

There were rumblings inside the sanctuary, though no one answered.

"Because the Bible says so." He held the book above his head. "If Jesus was tempted, what would make you think that you'll be exempt?"

I closed my eyes and thought about all the temptation that had come my way in just the two weeks since Trey had come to DC.

"Over and over, we're told to pray so that we will not fall into temptation. The Lord's Prayer says 'Lead us not into temptation.' So, it's gonna come. But what is so interesting about temptation is how we all, each one of us, will react to it."

I held my breath.

"Now, I know some of you sitting in this sanctuary are saying that even if temptation came your way, you would *never* fall. I can hear you now. 'Oh, that would *never* have happened to me. And even if it did, I would have done this or I would have done that.'" He paused and shook his head. "Let me tell you some-thing. In any given situation, you don't know what you would do until you are faced with it."

"Amen!" This time the chorus was louder.

I breathed. My grandfather wasn't talking about me.

"Now, let me go to the other side. To those falling prey to temptation, neither should *you* say that this is the norm, that ev-eryone is going through this. Here's the thing—yes, temptation will come, but the Word of God is clear on what you should do: Resist the devil and he will flee!" His voice boomed.

"Amen!"

"Preach, Preacher!"

"But here's the thing about temptation." He paused and low-ered his voice a bit. "You have to resist it . . . first. Hear that word, *first*. You have to resist that devil when he *first* comes to you."

The devil. Trey Taylor.

"You have to stop the devil before you open the door to him."

"Tell it!"

"Because once you open the door and the devil walks in . . ." My grandfather didn't finish the thought, but he didn't have to.

"Fighting temptation is never easy, because it's a spiritual battle and most of us don't know the difference. Most of us try to fight temptation with our weak flesh. But you see, you have to fight it with that willing spirit that is within you. You have to dig deep to get to that place, but it is easier to get there when you battle temptation . . . first. When you fight before the devil walks in."

The devil. Trey Taylor. He'd walked into the elevator at the Willard.

"Don't let him inside your house. Because once he's in there . . ." There was another pause, as if my grandfather was giving everyone time to consider his words, and I remembered how I'd let Trey into the bridal suite. I'd given him the key . . .

"Think about what happens if you let the devil in your house. Have you ever had someone come to visit and he just won't leave?"

There were mumbles of agreement throughout the church.

"You're ready to go to sleep so that you can get up for work the next day, but that person just stays and talks and talks and talks."

Now there was laughter, though I didn't join in. I thought about yesterday. How Trey had come into my office and stayed, even when I asked him to leave.

"The devil is the same way. Don't let him in, because it will be hard to get him out. Now, he won't stay forever! He'll leave after he's killed you, or stolen from you, and definitely destroyed you."

The congregation stood, waving their hands and Bibles.

I wanted to stand up, too, but not to shout out praise. I wanted to scream a thousand questions at my grandfather. I'd let the devil in, what was going to happen to me? Was it too late? Would Trey destroy me?

When Damon rose to his feet and shouted, I had a new question—would Trey destroy him?

"This is what I can tell you," my grandfather continued. "God is faithful and He will be right there in that fight with you. Because whether the devil is outside or whether he has wormed his way inside, he is defeated. And notice that I said he *is* defeated. I didn't say he *will be*."

"Amen!"

"You have the victory, Saints. All you have to do is claim it. It's yours!" he shouted, and the congregation shouted back more amens.

"God will not allow you to be tempted beyond what you can bear. And if you can bear it, you can get out of it."

Those were the first words of hope that I heard.

There was a long pause and my grandfather closed his eyes for a moment. "I feel like I'm speaking to someone in this sanctuary."

I lowered my head, making sure that my grandfather didn't look at me, because while my grandmother may have had a telephone line to God, my grandfather sat down in meetings with Him, I was sure of that. If given the chance, God would tell my grandfather that this entire sermon had been preached for his harlot granddaughter.

"All I can tell you is that God has your back." I tilted my head and peeked at the altar. When I saw that my grandfather wasn't looking at me, I sat a little straighter.

He said, "God wants to provide a way out for you. All you have to do is ask Him."

I felt more than hope now, I felt a certainty. Because if there was one thing I'd always been taught, it was that God would do what He said He would do!

So, once again, I lowered my head and I prayed from my heart.

*Lord, help me. I need that way out.*

Around me the service continued, but I kept my eyes closed and my heart open.

*Lord, help me. I need that way out.*

My eyes were still closed when I sent the request to God for the third time, and then I felt a knowing, a confidence that this would be solved. Still, I sat for a moment, wanting to absorb everything until I was sure of what I'd heard, and understood the plan that God had etched onto my heart. It seemed so simple, just a little different from what I'd done before my wedding. But since it had been given to me by God, I knew that it would work.

*Thank you, Lord.*

I opened my eyes and was drawn right to Damon, who was staring at me. His frown was deep, but my prayer had given me fortitude and I was the one who reached for his hand this time.

But, though I held him, his frown remained. Even when we stood for the benediction, even as we greeted members of the congregation after the services, even as we spoke to my grandfather in his office and told him and my grandmother about Dubai, his frown stayed in place. While I amped up my gaiety to rid any concerns that my grandmother had about me, Damon was sullen, bordering on angry.

Gram finally asked him, "Damon, are you all right?"

He nodded, though that frown stayed like it might become his permanent expression. "I am. A little jet-lagged, I suppose."

"Oh, yeah, that makes sense." Her smile was back when she said, "So y'all wanna come by the house for dinner?"

"Sure," I said, but the word was barely out of my mouth when Damon declined.

"I'd love to, but I have to get home and finish up some details for this big event I have next week."

My grandparents accepted his explanation, but I didn't. Something had set Damon off, and I felt his suspicion.

He said, "But Tiffanie, you can go on with your grandparents. You're free to do whatever you want to, right?"

Before I could answer, Gram said, "No, she's not. She's married now and y'all should do things together."

"That's right." I nodded and tried to make my smile bigger. "If you're going home, I'm going with you."

He shrugged as if he didn't care and fear washed over me. What had happened?

We kissed my grandparents good-bye, and when Damon put his arm around my waist and led me from the church, I pushed away all negative thoughts. I didn't need to focus on what had happened, I only needed to look forward with the plan that God had given me. I could never erase what I'd done, but I could make up for the two mistakes I'd made and put them so far behind me that I'd never think of them again. The silence that had accompanied us to church remained as Damon drove, but it gave me time to focus on what I had to do. My plan that I would begin as soon as we got home.

# 32

# Damon

It was as if the life I was living didn't belong to me and the wife in my bed wasn't the one I'd married. Anybody else would have been happy with what had gone down in my home this past week, and I should've been, too. It was just that Tiffanie was so . . . different.

This journey into the life that was not mine began on Sunday, in church, where Tiffanie was praying. Her head was bowed, and so, I bowed my head in solidarity with my wife. I didn't know what she was praying for, but whatever it was, as her husband, I wanted God to give her the desires of her heart.

But her prayer, which began in silence, came out of her in a whisper.

*Lord, help me. I need that way out.*

At first I wasn't sure that I'd heard her right, until she repeated it.

*Lord, help me. I need that way out.*

Even now, as I repeated her words in my head, my eyes squinted with my thoughts. What kind of out did she need? Her grandfather had been preaching about temptation; what kind of temptation did she have?

That question troubled me all the way through the rest of the service, and even afterward, when we visited with her grandparents. By the time we got in the car, I was looking at her sideways.

*Lord, help me. I need that way out.*

I couldn't figure out her prayer and planned on asking her about it, but I didn't get a chance. The moment we got home, right after we took two steps into our house, my wife attacked me like some kind of starving beast. Before I could even figure out what was going on, she had me pressed against the wall, kissing me like I was the oxygen she needed to live.

And she kissed my questions right out of me. After the first couple of seconds, all I wanted to do was take my wife up to our bedroom. But then she began to strip me, even as we walked, with lips locked, toward the stairs. I was down to my briefs and socks when we got to the staircase, where she stopped and pushed me down. A moment later, only my socks were left. She didn't take off her clothes; she just pushed up her dress, mounted me, and then rode like she was trying to win the Kentucky Derby.

Now, I wasn't no stiff, I was the kind of guy who loved to get my freak on, and I could prove it by the fact that I'd had sex everywhere, in all kinds of positions, with females doing all kinds of things to me and each other. But all those females? They'd been nothing more than random chicks, strippers without a pole.

My wife was better than that. And that's why, with Tiffanie, I liked it straight, missionary-style mostly, and in our bedroom always. That's why I bought that big ole bed. Because that's what my wife deserved—she was classy and I treated her with respect, especially in bed.

But there was nothing I could do to stop her on Sunday, and while the sex left me spent, her aggression left me more confused. Now I had her prayer and her behavior to figure out.

I might have been able to put some kind of spin on Sunday until Monday rolled around. First, Tiffanie was up, out of bed, and dressed before I turned over to hit the alarm at seven.

*"What are you doing up so early?"*

*"I wanted to get to the office." Her voice was chipper, as if she'd been awake for hours.*

*I pushed myself up to get a closer look. "This early? What's going on?"*

*"Nothing. I've been away for a week and want to get back into the swing of things. We have the opening coming up, remember?" Then she kissed me and, I'm telling you, she skipped out of the room.*

It took me a couple of hours to add that morning to the day before and make it equal something that made sense. Then, about twelve hours later, I came home to find my wife wearing an apron and standing next to Glory.

*"Hey!" She greeted me with a kiss when I stepped into the kitchen. "I'm learning to make that beef stew."*

*"And a whole lotta other things," Glory added, shaking her head and giving me a side-eye. "I can't believe you're trying to domesticate this career woman."*

*"That's not what I'm trying to do," I said.*

*Tiffanie was all smiles when she said, "I told you, Glory, this is all my idea. I want to learn to cook for my man. I'm gonna be taking lessons for a week."*

After that, every night, I came home to a meal fit for Thanksgiving. And over the three or four courses, she told me all that was going on with the spa:

"I had to have the windows redone, the tinting was off, but I handled it without a hit to the budget."

Then, "There was a problem with the plumbing today and before the plumbers even got there, I had it figured out."

And "I decided to go ahead and have Utopia wired for Wi-Fi. I want women to come there and relax, but in reality, if someone can't check their email or Twitter . . ."

Every night I listened to her in amazement. She was holding it down at the spa, even with this Susie Homemaker routine. Then every night, after all of that, Tiffanie took to our bed like she was trying to make those dozen babies that I wanted.

It was all good.

But it was all different.

And I didn't know what had changed my wife so suddenly.

I sighed. Why was I trying to figure it out? Having a woman who worked hard, cooked well, and could bring it in bed *every day*? Who wouldn't want that?

I would . . . if it weren't for my gut.

"Knock, knock!" Trey's voice broke through my thoughts. When I looked up, he added, "Is it okay if I come in?"

I nodded. "Sure." When Trey stepped into the VIP office, I asked, "How did you know I was here?"

"I went to your place on U Street, and your assistant told me. I wanted to know if you could hang out for a couple of hours."

I shook my head. "Sorry, son, I got lots of work to do."

"It's all good." He paused and looked around at the space, which was darkened by the two black walls, but then lightened by the other two walls, which were all glass and looked down onto the club's floor below. "This place is the truth. DC After Dark? I like the name."

I nodded. "It's only been open for a few months; this is their first big event."

"Cool. They've really done something over here, haven't they? I remember when you came to this part of DC at your own risk."

As he stood at one of the windows looking down, I answered, "They're trying to turn all these old warehouses into something. All part of the gentrification of Southeast."

"I see. When Hillary first gave me the address and told me it was over by the Navy Yards, I thought she was kidding. I didn't know what kind of event you'd be having down here." He shook his head. "But, man, did you see all of those restaurants on the Potomac?"

Watching Trey rediscover DC would've been something I would've enjoyed if I didn't have so much work on my plate and so many thoughts on my mind. "Yeah, come back tonight and it'll be packed down here. Even I'm trying to figure out how to capitalize on it. I bought a couple of the warehouses next door a few years ago, though I haven't done anything with them yet."

"For real?"

"Yeah. I've been holding on to the property, trying to figure out the best way to monetize the spaces. After Tiffanie opens her spa, I'll makes some decisions."

His head bobbed as he took a seat in the chair in front of the desk. "You're really making moves."

I shrugged. "I do what I do."

"I guess so." He grinned. "And now, you're putting together this thing for that phine Jaleesa Stone. You think you can hook a brutha up?"

For the first time in the hours since I'd been sitting at this desk, I smiled. "I can if I can get you past her bodyguard-fiancé."

Trey leaned back in the chair. "You know me. There ain't a dude on earth who scares me. I fear no man."

I swallowed the words that I wanted to say; I wanted to tell him that his lack of fear would one day be noted on his tombstone. But I said nothing because I'd given him a lifetime of lectures. This time around, when we partnered up, I was gonna let Trey be the man he needed to be. I'd be fair, I'd give him a warning or two, and after that, I'd have to cut him loose.

"So, when are we gonna hook up and talk more about us working together?"

"Yeah, yeah. I really want us to do that, for sure. Maybe we can figure out what to do with these warehouses. Just let me get through this event and we'll sit down. We can do it on Monday if you're free; you'll still be here, right?" I didn't give him a chance to respond. "You're not making moves back to the ATL, are you?"

"Nah, at least not yet. I've been waiting on you to see what you wanna do. So, we'll talk on Monday and then I'll make some decisions."

I felt my eyebrows bunching together. I'd been so self-absorbed this week that I hadn't made any real contact with Trey. Except for his text letting me know that he was checking out of the Willard, I had no idea how he was spending his time. Yeah, he was grown, but he was still Trey Taylor. Free time wasn't a good look for him.

"So what have you been up to?" I asked, my way of doing a brother-brother check on him.

His shoulders hardly moved when he shrugged. "A little bit of this, a little bit of that."

His words made me uneasy, because if he was already involved in something shady, I wouldn't bring him into the fold. "You still with Ms. Irene or have you hooked up with a shorty?"

"Nah. I'm using this time to reconnect with my grandma."

"I know Ms. Irene is glad about that."

"And that shorty?" he said, making a left turn back to the second part of my question. "I'm still working on that."

"The one you met over at the Willard?" I asked.

"Yeah. We've hooked up a couple of times." He paused. "And it's all good. She might be a keeper."

"Really?" I still found it unbelievable that Trey was ready to settle down with any female. "Well, you'll have to bring her around. Tiff and I would love to meet her."

For some reason that made him laugh. "Yeah, well, we'll see about that. Anyway . . ." He stopped for a moment and looked around the office once more. "Is there anything I can do to help you with this rollout?"

"Nah, I got it together."

After giving me a long stare, Trey said, "Okay, bruh. Talk to me. What's going on with you?"

I frowned.

He leaned forward, resting his arms on his knees. "I can see it all over you. We've known each other too long for me not to know when something's got you worked up. You wanna talk about it?"

In the next seconds that passed, I sifted through all the things in my head from the past week. And, added to that, all the things that Trey'd said all along. "Can't say that anything's wrong. Just got a lot on my mind; in particular, what we talked about when I first got back from Dubai." His frown told me that he had no idea what I was talking about. "How you don't trust women."

"Oh, that." He leaned back and shrugged. "Just my rule of

life. I told you, I've never met one who wasn't in it for herself."
He paused and gave me a stare that made his next words sound
cold and hard. "I would even doubt your wife."

I returned his stare and told him the truth. "Tiffanie's not
like that."

"She got a vagina?"

That muscle in my jaw starting pulsing, and right away, Trey
backed up. He raised his hands in police surrender mode.

"Look, you asked the question and I'm telling you how I
live. You know this, you used to be the same way."

Maybe that was true. But that was before.

He continued, "The way I see it, all females are the same.
Now, some are classy with it and maybe that's how Tiffanie is . . ."

"My wife ain't like all those other females!"

"Whoa . . . okay." He paused. "I thought you wanted to have
a discussion, but you're protesting kinda hard." Then he chuckled a little. "What? You figured out something already?"

Even though Trey was my boy, I'd never been one to talk to
him or anyone else. I handled my own business, never bringing
anybody else into it. It wasn't necessary, since I wasn't usually
the emotional type and always handled situations on facts. But
this . . . this *was* emotional because I had no facts.

So, if there were ever a time to talk to someone else, this was
it. And if there was ever a person, Trey was the one. He knew
me; he could be trusted.

"What's up?" Trey pushed. After another moment's pause,
he added, "Ah, hell nah! Don't tell me you found out she's cheating on you already!"

"Nah!" I shook my head. "That's not it at all. It's just
that . . . I don't know . . ."

He gave me a second to provide a better explanation before he asked, "So you don't think she's screwing around on you?"

"Nah, nah. It can't be that. We just got married and I'm holding it down." I thought about our honeymoon, I thought about our week since we'd been home, and all of that made me shake my head even more. "It's not that, I'm sure of it. But something's off."

"What?"

I had to ask myself, did I really want to go there with him? Especially since I was missing facts. "I don't know. She just switched up."

At first I thought he was just studying me. Then he cracked up. "Oh. She's not letting you hit it?" He laughed even harder now. "I heard how women change up after they get married."

"She's changed, but not in that way." I left out the personal details, that was none of Trey's business and that wasn't my purpose for having this talk. I just wanted to hear my words out loud, see if I could make what I was thinking make sense.

Trey said, "Well, if she's acting differently, maybe she's pregnant."

That made me pause. That would be a great excuse for what had been going on.

He asked, "Have you talked to her about it?"

I shook my head. I did have lots of questions, but I didn't know what I was supposed to ask. Why do you go to work so early? Why are you cooking every night? How come you're sexing me like you can't get enough?

I said, "I haven't said anything, because there's really nothing to ask. It's just something that's going on in my gut."

He nodded, leaned forward. Even though we were alone, he

lowered his voice. "Listen, bruh, I know you love your woman and I pray that there's nothing going on, but just make sure you watch her. Because what I know . . ."

This time I was the one to hold up my hands. "You already said it."

"I'm just telling you. They're all scandalous. So if you want to make sure, you need to ask her straight out. Ask her if she's hittin' anybody else, if she wants to hit anybody else, if there is anybody else."

Even though I was still shaking my head, I asked, "So you think my gut . . . you think this is about another man?"

He shrugged. "It always is . . . another man . . . for sex, drugs, or money."

Trey really was my brother; I'd had the same thoughts.

He kept on. "She doesn't seem like the drugs type and you got plenty of money, so unless she's looking at God Himself, it ain't that."

He chuckled; I didn't.

He said, "So, what's left?" He stayed quiet, leaving me to answer his question. Then he hit it home: "Since I've known you, your gut has never been wrong. You've never been wrong."

He stood, gave me a fist bump, then walked out of the room as if he had just dropped the mic.

Trey was right. I had never been wrong. And my gut was talking. The problem was, I had no idea what my gut was saying.

# 33

# Tiffanie

Our honeymoon was a faraway memory, but that wasn't a bad thing. Damon and I were back on the grind, only now, husband-and-wife was added to our list, and for me that came with many more responsibilities. I was doing everything I could to handle the candle on both ends, working all day, working all night, taking care of the spa, taking care of my man.

I'd been handling it for the last two weeks, even though I have to say all of that had left me beyond exhausted. I was so tired that my bones ached, but at the same time, exhilaration flowed through me.

I was winning.

In truth, I loved taking care of Damon and, with the way he was responding, it was just like grandmother had promised, I really was the great wife that she told me I'd be. But the first chance I got, probably right after my spa opened, I was going to turn into Rip Van Winkle. Well, maybe I wouldn't sleep for twenty years, but I was looking forward to being in bed for seven days straight.

I chuckled at that thought, but then got serious real quick. Because sleeping was the only challenge in my life. Those were the hours when I couldn't keep Trey away. When my eyes were open, I could fight.

*Resist the devil and he will flee!*

The words from my grandfather's sermon became my mantra, and the mantra was working. I'd kept my mind and my time filled with so many tasks, so much cooking, so much attention to my husband, there was little room for Trey to slither into my thoughts. Trey crept into my unconscious, though, and took over that time and space, invading my dreams, forcing me to relive and remember.

But even though every morning I awakened feeling as if I'd spent the night with Trey, I was sure those dreams would go away. Especially if I never saw Trey again. Never saw him, never talked to him.

I didn't even know if he was still in DC, though I assumed that he was not. It had been more than a week since . . . I sighed. But Damon hadn't mentioned him. And I certainly wasn't going to ask. I didn't want my husband to mistake my question for an invitation to set up a lunch or dinner with the three of us.

But they were best friends, and surely, if Trey were still in the city, Damon would have said something, would have made some kind of arrangements to get together with his boy. So my assumption, which was really more of a hope, was that he was gone. And if he was gone, then my temptation was gone, too.

"Hey," Damon said as he palmed my butt through my satin cover-up.

As gently as I could, I laid aside the eyelashes I was just about to apply, then turned around, making sure that the beltless robe I wore was all the way open (on purpose) before I wrapped my arms around my husband's neck. I didn't blink when I said, "You want some more of this?"

His eyes settled on my blush-colored push-up bra and barely-there thong. "Why are you doing this to me, woman?" he moaned.

"What?"

He shook his head. "You're incorrigible and you're insatiable."

"Only for you." With my teeth, I nibbled on his bottom lip and as he moaned, in my mind I replayed my half-lie, though I preferred to think of what I'd said as almost-the-truth. I *was* insatiable and it *was* because of him. Because all of my efforts and all of my hope were wrapped up in my expectation and my anticipation that there would be one time when Damon could make me feel the way Trey did. Every time I got close to my husband, I was in search of that moment. It hadn't happened yet, but my hope stayed alive.

After a few more moans, Damon stepped away, though I could tell he didn't want to. "Okay, bae. We've gotta get out of here." Glancing down at his watch, he added, "I'm ready to leave now, I can give you fifteen minutes."

I shook my head. "There's no way. I won't be ready." Right before he released a sigh, I added, "I need a little more time to be fabulous."

Even though he shook his head, I could tell he wasn't really all that annoyed. "I told you what time we had to be there."

"I know." I turned back to the mirror. "But I got home later than I wanted to. Remember . . . the windows at the spa. Remember . . . they came in today."

"Oh yeah, right. Did they replace them all?"

I secured one of the eyelashes and said, "Every single one. And, like I promised, without a dollar added to our budget."

His lips twitched into a slow grin. "Well, I guess I can't be mad at my baby for taking care of business like that."

Turning around, I looked up at my husband through the eyelashes I'd just applied. "No, you can't be."

"Okay," he said with a sigh. "I'll send Magic back for you."

I shook my head. "That's crazy. You need all hands on deck at the club; I know it'll be a madhouse. I can Uber over, and then tonight"—I encircled him again, this time wrapping my arms around his waist—"you can send Magic on his way, and as you drive us home, I'll do all kinds of freaky things to you right there in the car."

He agreed with a kiss that was filled with a moan and I laughed as he walked backward away from me. "Okay, I'm outta here."

I blew him a kiss, then turned back to the vanity. I heard Damon trotting down the stairs as I applied foundation, and as I brushed on the finishing powder, I heard the chug of the garage door lifting and then, a few moments later, closing.

Not even a minute passed before I heard the doorbell. I frowned, then sighed. What in the world had Damon forgotten?

I dashed down the stairs, swung open the door, began with, "What did—" and finished by taking two steps back. It was reflex that made me do that, because if I'd had a single wit about me, I would have moved forward and slammed the door closed.

But the shock of seeing Trey made me back up. "What . . . what are you doing here?"

He gave me a half-shrug, stepped over the threshold, and closed the door behind him. "What do you think I'm doing here?" In the moment when he paused, his eyes took a slow stroll up, then down my body, and even as I clutched my robe to close it with my hands, I felt myself warm. He did that lip-licking thing that made my heart stop mid-beat before he said, "I'm looking for Damon. Is he here?"

I only had a moment, but all kinds of lies passed through my mind. I could say that Damon was upstairs . . . in the shower. But I decided on "He just called. He's on his way home. He'll be here any minute."

Trey didn't even give me time to finish before he chuckled. "Is that why I just saw him driving away?"

My eyes narrowed, even as I gripped my robe tighter. "You're stalking us?"

He shook his head. "Nope, I just happened to be coming down the street while Damon was going the other way. I really did come here to see him, but now . . ." More staring, more lip-licking. "It's good to see you, Tiff."

My legs trembled, my heart banged, and I remembered. That was the worst part. Remembering made me feel, and my body was ready for him again. It was like I had no control over the wanting, it was like I was drowning in the yearning that took over every time I was around him. But I kept my voice as steady as I could when I said, "You need to leave."

He took a step forward. "I can't because I've missed you." Another step forward.

I matched his forward steps with my own moving the other way. I trembled, though I wasn't convinced that it was out of fear; I shook because I remembered the last time. "No." I closed my eyes as if that would make him disappear.

"What do you mean no?"

My eyes were still closed, even as I backed up, even as I felt him moving closer. "No."

He said, "I can't figure out why you keep saying that. What are you denying me?"

I stopped moving, but only because my back was against the wall. Now I had to open my eyes, and he was right there. His eyes, dark, seductive. But though it was his eyes that had first captured me, at this moment it was those lips that took every bit of my sense away.

He leaned in so close there was no room for air between us. "I want you." With just a shift of his head, his lips grazed my ears. "I want you the way I had you the other day."

Oh, God!

"I loved the way you trembled beneath me. I want to do that to you again."

Oh, God!

"And I want you to do it to me. Can you make me do that, Tiff? Can you make me tremble that way?"

My eyes were open but lowered. I didn't have enough courage to look at him, but I had enough strength to say, "Please just leave; I need you to leave."

"And what I need is to finally have you. It's my turn, Tiff. That's what you want, right? That's what you've wanted all along."

His words, his scent, the memory of his lips . . . I wanted him. God help me, but he was right. From the moment I'd met him . . . he was right.

His eyes were on mine as he peeled my fingers from my robe. When it fell open, we both gasped.

I watched him study me. I saw him appreciate me. "You're so fine."

Just the way he looked at me took me to the edge, but I didn't stay there. I fell off when he pressed his lips against mine. And then when he traced his finger down the center of my chest down to my belly, I started falling, falling further, and I knew then that no one and nothing would ever bring me back.

I was trying to think about what I was doing, the mistake that I was making, but it was hard to focus on anything beyond the single objective that clogged my mind—I wanted this man. All of him. I had no other purpose in life.

I'd fought the fight, but I'd lost. And now I was a willing loser, who could wait no longer. I parted my lips and welcomed his tongue inside. And the moment our tongues connected, the air filled with moans that blended into a lustful fusion of melody and harmony. He raised my arms above my head and pinned me against the wall. I felt helpless and hopeful.

And then a thought pierced through my lust.

*Resist the devil and he will flee.*

My eyelids fluttered at the mantra that had been saving me, but as quickly as the mantra came, it was gone. Because I couldn't hold on to it, not with the way Trey's hand caressed my skin, setting every inch of me on fire.

*Resist the devil and he will flee.*

I wanted to conjure up more of my grandfather's words so that I could do the right thing, but I couldn't remember anything.

Except.

Me.

Spread-eagle.

Waiting.

Wanting.

The anticipation.

The expectation.

That.

Feeling.

Trey pulled me away from the wall, swung me around, and slipped the robe from my body. By the time he pushed me down on the stairs, he'd unhooked my bra and was moaning as my breasts filled his hands. I was the one who moaned when he pressed his body on top of mine. And then I had new thoughts.

These stairs.

With Damon.

Damon.

My husband.

No!

Beneath Trey's kisses and caresses, I heard my mantra again. Only this time, it wasn't my voice . . . it was Damon's.

*Resist the devil and he will flee.*

I raised my hands and with my full force, I pushed Trey away. He stumbled backward and stared down at me.

Trey's breath was as heavy as mine; he wiped his mouth with the back of his hand. But his lips spread into a grin as he took in the sight of me. I imagined how I looked: breathing as if I'd been drowning and was just getting my first gasps of air . . . and naked except for a few inches of satin thong.

I sat and he stood. All I could think about was how much I wanted this man. But there was something that I wanted even more.

Damon.

Trey took a step toward me.

I said, "I need you to leave."

His grin told me no.

Jumping up, I only had to take about four steps to the console table and grab the phone. Holding up the landline, I said to Trey, "Leave now."

His eyes narrowed as he studied the phone . . . and then turned his gaze to my body. I prayed that he couldn't see the heat that rose within me. After a few seconds, he said, "You don't want me to go."

My body trembled. "Yes, I do."

He chuckled. "You know you want this; you know you want what I'm about to give you."

*Resist the devil and he will flee.*

It was Damon's voice again.

I said, "I want you to go."

I understood why he took the next step toward me, I understood why he didn't believe me. That's why I pressed *9* on the phone, making sure he saw me.

He paused. "Tiff?" Now there was more confusion than certainty in his tone.

"Leave," I said. Now there was more determination in mine.

This time he didn't take another step; this time he unbuckled his belt, and my eyes went to the bulge between his legs, the bulge that could be between mine. That was his point, I guess.

*Lord, you have to deliver me from this evil.*

This time it was my voice and my prayer. I pressed *1* on the number pad.

I said, "If you don't leave now, the police will be on their way." I added, for both Trey and myself, "I mean it. One more step and I'll finish the call."

It still took him a few moments, but he backed up as if he

finally believed me. He squinted as he fastened his belt, frowning, even though his eyes still scanned my body. I wanted to run to my robe, to cover up. But I had to stay still and focus on only one move. The next move had to be making this call—or else my marriage, my life as I knew it would be over.

As he stared, I glared, even more determined now than before—if he took a step or a thought toward me, I was going to press the last number.

After a few more moments of this standoff, Trey backed up all the way up. His eyes stayed on mine until he reached the door. Then he spun around and, without a word, stepped outside.

It was only a few steps, but I ran like a track star, slammed my body against the door, then clicked both locks before I turned around and leaned against it. My heart was racing as if I'd just been in a battle and my body was weary as if I'd fought hard. When my legs could no longer hold me, I slid against the door until my butt hit the floor and pulled my legs to my chest.

"Oh, my God." I was filled with such a jumble of emotions: fear, longing, shock, determination. The important thing was, though, I hadn't succumbed to the temptation. For the first time, I hadn't given in.

But there was the shame of it, too. I'd wanted it and had come so close to having sex with Trey. Damon's best friend. In our house. Disrespecting my husband in a trio of ways.

But I hadn't. I resisted the devil and he'd fled.

When the phone rang, it startled me so much I dropped it, forgetting that I still held it. Picking the receiver up, I glanced at the caller ID and closed my eyes. I didn't want to answer. But I had to.

I inhaled the deepest of breaths and then exhaled. "Damon."

"Bae. Where are you? I've been calling your cell."

"I was . . . I was . . ."

"Come on, Tiff. You're not ready yet?"

"I'm ready, Damon," I said, even as I sat on the floor just about naked. "I will be there really soon."

"Okay," he said. I could hear the disappointment in his tone. "It's already started and I'd wanted to walk the red carpet with you."

"Soon, I promise," I said. "And Damon." After a pause, I added, "I love you so much."

When he said, "I love you, bae," I heard the smile in his voice. And all I could do was pray that when I got to the club, there'd be no tears in my eyes.

# 34

# Tiffanie

wanted to focus on my victory, but the guilt was like a five-hundred-pound boulder anchored to my heart. And the guilt was heavier when partnered with thoughts of Trey, making me wonder if he would be here tonight.

I hadn't considered that before, having talked myself into believing that he was back in Atlanta. But since he was still in DC, that meant he could very well show up tonight. I kept trying to tell myself no, he wouldn't do that. He wouldn't come to Damon's event, not after what he'd tried to do with Damon's wife. But that was the kind of thinking that was not only wishful but stupid. When had hooking up with his boy's wife ever stopped Trey? The last time, he'd left me withering on my desk and had gone straight to our home to hang out with Damon.

So I braced myself for seeing him, but I was putting every precaution in place. I had to make sure that Trey couldn't get close to me. I didn't want him in the same zip code, but while I couldn't control that, I would be able to keep him out of my personal space. I wasn't going to give that devil a single chance.

Checking my location on the Uber app, I texted Damon:

**I'm about 3 minutes away.**

A second later, his text came back:

**Magic's on his way out.**

I knew that would be his response and I sighed with relief; I was safe, at least from Trey. I couldn't tell from his text if Damon was annoyed. He probably was; I was arriving almost ninety minutes after his call. I couldn't help it, though—that's how long it had taken me to try to wash my sins away. I had planted myself inside the shower, scrubbing away the dirt deep inside my pores. What I hadn't known was that there wasn't a body scrub strong enough to get rid of the stench of shame.

*It was a mistake, Tiffanie.*

That's what I told myself then, and that's what I kept telling myself now. It was hard to convince myself, though. How many times was I going to call it a mistake? The first time, yes. The second time, maybe. But the third time? What was that cliché about three strikes?

As the driver slowed in front of DC After Dark, I closed my eyes and prayed once again for God's forgiveness and for Him to save me from the churning in my stomach that filled me with such foreboding. When I opened my eyes, I wanted to tell the driver to take me home. I'd make up some lie to tell Damon. But before I could figure it out, Magic was at the car's door, opening it, then reaching inside for my hand.

He was here to take me to my man.

Though the event had started almost two hours ago, the crowd hanging outside behind the red velvet ropes was thick with people holding up cell phones poised and ready to capture pictures of any late-arriving celebrities. There was still a long line to enter the club, but the sea of people parted as Magic walked through and led me inside to dim lights and music bumping off the walls.

Now, Damon and I were old-school connoisseurs, but we could get down to today's beats, too, and so could the folks on the dance floor. There in the center was my girl, Sonia. A small group had formed around her and her husband, Allen, but Sonia wouldn't have noticed because her eyes were closed as her arms were raised high above her head. She gyrated to the music and sang along with Kent Jones:

> *She said, "Hola. ¿Cómo estás?" She said, "Konnichiwa."*
> *She said, "Pardon my French," I said, "Bonjour, madame."*

Watching her for a moment made me smile and though it didn't make me forget, my guilt eased up a little more. I hadn't done anything with Trey—not really. And the most important thing that *had* happened was that I'd fought and won.

I had to find a way to let it go. Repent and move on. That would be my new mantra.

Strolling behind Magic, I took in the celebs sprinkled throughout, as they were at any star-studded King Commotions event. From the Democratic senator to the son of the former Republican president, the Washington journalists and TV pundits—I was used to all of them. But it was nice to see a few Hollywood types, and I waved to Will and Jada, whom I'd met a few times before.

Then I spotted Damon. I'd expected to become tense and tight seeing him, fearful that my husband would be able to sense my sin. But what happened instead was that I relaxed. Just seeing that man calmed me.

He stood in the center of a semicircle of men all dressed in suits, though he was the only one without a tie; what he wore instead was influence. It was the way the men stood with their attention on Damon, listening, as if they were being given the keys to the secret of life. Watching him for a moment made me even prouder to be his wife.

As if he felt me, he paused. Then he turned, and he captivated me with that smile.

I paused, too . . . just stopped moving and stared at him from where I stood. I could have cried because I loved him so much.

"There's my beautiful wife."

I guess because I'd stopped, Damon came to me. He kissed my cheek. "Mmmmm . . . you smell so good."

I said nothing.

He added, "I guess that's what happens when you take a shower." His laugh let me release more guilt. Taking my hand, he led me back to where he'd been standing. I greeted those of his friends whom I knew, and he introduced me to the others. From that moment, I was my husband's wife, standing tall by his side as we moved through the crowd together, chatting with each guest. We spent the most time with Jaleesa Stone, who'd come to the party with her mother, her aunt, and her bodyguard, whom she introduced as her fiancé. For more than an hour we roamed through the people maze, even stopping for a moment to hang with Sonia and Allen. Right then we heard a salsa beat, and Damon spun me around to the center of the dance floor.

We shook our shoulders, shifted our feet to the three beats, and turnt up with our favorite rapper and our absolute favorite song: *I thank God you came / How many more days could I wait? . . . / I think I'd lie for you / I think I'd die for you . . .*

This was the best moment of the night. I leaned my arms on Damon's shoulders and his hands rested on my hips as we rocked to Drake's words and swayed to the beat. When the song ended, I wanted to tell the DJ to play it again.

But Damon said, "I need a break." He took my hand and led me upstairs. Even though the DJ and the crowd had moved on to the next song, Damon and I were still singing softly, "I think I'd lie for you, I think I'd die for you . . ."

That stopped, though, once we stepped into the VIP office, because I was stunned by the expansive space, especially the gigantic windows. "This is amazing," I said, looking down at the crowd on the dance floor. "You can see everything from here."

"And the best part is, no one can see you." Damon grabbed a bottle of water from a small refrigerator in the corner, took a sip, and handed it to me.

I shook my head. "I'm good."

Taking my hand, he moved me away from the windows and perched himself on the desk, bringing me to stand between his legs. "Are you good?"

I tilted my head. "What do you mean?"

He shrugged. "I dunno. You don't seem like yourself."

The strength of our connection frightened me right now, but I kept my calm. "I'm fine," I said, then rested my head against his shoulder. "I may be a little tired," I began, thinking that would be a great excuse to cover up anything he saw, "but that's only because I've been working so hard."

I felt him nod. "You have. You've been doing so much, and I've wondered why?"

Raising my head, I said, "Why?"

"Yeah. You work for hours at the spa, then come home to your second job—taking care of me."

"That's not a job," I protested with a pout. "I love taking care of my husband. That seems strange to you?"

I expected him to back up his words, maybe even apologize and tell me that's not what he meant. But he just gave me another shrug. "Nah, not strange, but different. It's different from before, before we were married."

"Well, Mr. King"—I wrapped my arms around his neck—"I would think that would be a good thing."

He gave me a long stare, and I fought hard to keep eye contact. I couldn't blink, because if I blinked, I might confess. So I kept my eyes on him and my arms around him. And I did my best not to tremble. When he blinked first, closed his eyes, and kissed my nose, I almost collapsed with relief.

"Okay, bae. I'm just gonna take this and take you for the blessing that you are to me."

"I bet you that you're a bigger blessing."

He gave me a dimpled grin. "Let's see who's the bigger blessing later. Right now, let's get back to the party."

I laughed. "Okay. Is there a bathroom up here?"

"Yeah, over there." He pointed to a door on the left. "I'll meet you downstairs when you're done."

"Cool." I nodded.

In the bathroom, I took care of my business, then paused to give thanks once again to God. Damon suspected something, of course he would. Our connection was too strong for him to be completely blind. But God was keeping me. Keeping the scales over his eyes, keeping my secret in the dark.

I paused for a second, remembering something I'd heard about everything always coming to light, but I felt like this was God's protection. And as long as I kept the vow never to be in that position again with Trey, God would be my shield.

For the first time all night, really for the first time in weeks, I felt free. But then I stepped out of the bathroom. And froze. Again.

I was living in a horror movie—the devil kept coming back.

"What . . ."

Before I could finish, Trey said, "I was looking for you."

"For what?" I moaned.

He crept toward me like a snake. "Because . . . you know why."

For every step he took forward, I took three back.

"What happened today, Tiff? Why'd you turn me away?"

"Because I'm married . . . to your best friend." I wondered if he heard the emotions in my voice. Of course he heard the trembling, but did he hear my fear? Or worse, did he feel my longing, the stirring between my legs?

If he heard or felt any of it, he didn't care. All he did was shrug at what I'd just told him. He brushed off my words as if my being Damon's wife meant nothing. And then he crushed my heart when he said, "Married to my best friend? That hasn't stopped you before."

His truth made me want to cry. "But it should have. Because I love my husband. And that love is what's stopping me now." I raised my chin and my shoulders.

*Resist the devil and he will flee.*

"Tiffanie."

It was slow and sexy, the way he said my name. He sang it as if it were the last note in a song. A love song . . . no, a lust song.

He still had a pull on me, I couldn't deny that. But what I had now was a push, and that's what I did: held my breath, lowered my eyes, and moved to push past him. He stepped in front of me, blocking my path.

I inhaled his scent—a mistake, because the fragrance of this man took me back. He leaned toward me the way he always did, his lips aimed for mine. He wasn't even an inch away from touching me when I took the strength that could only have come from God and slapped him so hard I knew my hand would sting for a week.

At first I was too stunned to move. So was he. But I found my good sense before he found his, and this time I was the one who fled.

# 35

# Damon

My gut had been talking, but I hadn't been listening. Now that my ears were open, it made so much sense.

"You sure you okay?"

I shifted my glance from the window to Magic in the driver's seat. His eyes were on the road and that made me glad. Because while I could lie with my words, there were times when I wasn't such a good liar with my body. And I had no doubt that this was one of those times, since my rage was rising in direct proportion to the number of hours that passed.

"Yeah. I'm good." My teeth were clenched as I leaned back and closed my eyes, replaying the truth that played out in front of me tonight.

I might have missed it all if it hadn't been for April Ryan. The White House correspondent was far away from her regular gig, but she'd recently started hosting a popular YouTube show, *DMV Happenings,* and she'd interviewed me a few times. So I wasn't really surprised when she rolled up with her crew tonight wanting to talk to me about this star-studded event.

I'd told April that I wanted Tiffanie by my side and she'd

be right down. April had been graceful enough to give me five minutes, but when she couldn't wait any longer, she turned on the lights, the cameras, and got to the action.


Three hours earlier . . .


THE INTERVIEW HAD gone quickly, with just a few questions about Jaleesa and tonight's event, but then April got to the crux of the news that she really wanted to break.

"You are certainly making your mark on the District," she said. "What's this about you buying the two warehouses down here next to DC After Dark?"

"Now, April, you know I never tell my business."

She laughed. "Oh, come on, you can give me just a little piece of news here."

I was just about to give her my answer when, from the corner of my eye, I saw Tiffanie rush from the hallway. Even when she stepped into the main part of the club, she kept moving, her eyes lowered. She had to see the bright lights of the camera just a few feet from where she passed; she had to see me. But she didn't stop, she didn't look at me, and it didn't even seem like she was looking for me.

What was going on?

"Mr. King?"

"Ah, yes," I said, trying to return my glance and attention to April. "There are so many . . ."

And then I saw Trey. I hadn't even noticed him come into the club tonight, but there he was. Coming from the same hall-way. Following Tiffanie, moving just as fast. He called out to her, but then he paused, turned, and zoned in on me. My frown was deep when our eyes locked and his smile got wider and wider. But it wasn't just that his lips had curled into a grin of pure pleasure. It was his eyes that really spoke, glaring at me with a look of . . . what was that? Triumph?

He gave me a single nod and disappeared through the front door.

"I'm sorry, April . . ." My eyes were still on the door. "I'm sorry. I can't do this right now."

"Okay," she said, signaling to the cameraman, and the lights dimmed right away. "I think we have enough. Thanks for letting me do this at the last minute."

I didn't acknowledge her gratitude because I was in the hunt. Dashing outside, I looked to the left, I looked to the right. Trey was nowhere to be seen.

Damn.

And where was Tiffanie?

Pulling my phone from my pocket, I pressed her name on the screen. After four rings, my call went straight to voice mail. I waited a second before I rushed back inside, where the music met me and people called out to me. I saw no one and heard nothing as I ran toward the stairs. So many thoughts spun through my head that I felt like I had vertigo and slowed down a bit. Once inside the office, I pressed against the window, looking down onto the floor below, and scanned the bodies. It was approaching midnight, but the crowd had yet to thin, so it took me a moment. Still, I spotted her by the bar, having what I assumed was a glass of wine. She stood alone at the far end, and I watched her, drinking one glass like it was water, then ordering another.

The impulse of any other man would have been to rush down and start asking questions. But I rarely acted on impulse, especially since I knew that answers often came without a single question being asked. That's why I pulled out my cell and called Tiffanie again. As I heard the ringing in my ear, I watched her pull her phone from her purse, glance at the screen, then drop her cell back into her bag.

The muscle in my jaw twitched.

For a moment, I thought about calling Trey, but I had what I needed. What just went down with Tiffanie sealed it for me.

I watched my wife for a few minutes more before I trotted down the steps and made my way back into the party. Midnight must have been the bewitching hour, because I was able to move through more easily now. I said my good-byes to Jaleesa and her family, then Will and Jada and others who were leaving. I strolled through with no intention of looking for Tiffanie. I wanted to see how long it would be before she searched for me. I finally felt that tap on my shoulder.

Turning around, I saw my wife smiling up at me. "I was looking for you, babe."

I clenched my teeth, needing a moment so that I spoke the right words. "You were looking for me? For what?"

My question didn't even make her flinch. She went right into her role. "To give you one of these."

Her lips felt soft and I tasted the white wine as her kiss lingered. For a moment, I wondered if I'd been just plain wrong. And then in the next moment, I wondered where her lips had been. That made me pull back.

I was never one to pull away from affection, so I knew that would make Tiffanie wonder. After a short frown, she leaned in and asked, "So, how much longer are you going to be here? It looks like it's winding down."

"You ready to go?"

Her smile widened as she nodded.

I raised my hand in the air just as Magic walked by.

"What's up?" he asked.

"Take my wife . . . take Tiffanie home."

"What?" She blinked as if my words confused her. "No. I want to go home with you. I'll wait. I don't mind waiting."

"Nah, I know you're tired. Just go on home."

"No . . . I want . . ." It must have been the look on my face that made her ask, "Are you sure?"

My words were as hard as my stare. "I've never been more sure of anything in my life."

Deep lines dented her forehead. "Oh . . . kay." She kissed me good-bye; I didn't respond in any way. She leaned back with questions in her eyes, but she asked nothing and I said nothing.

I watched as she followed Magic to the door, and right before she stepped outside, she turned to look at me.

I didn't blink, I didn't smile, I just turned my back to her.

EVEN THOUGH MANY hours had passed, I was still turning it all over in my head. There were so many parts and they all fit together. Or did they? It was a big leap thinking that my boy was bangin' my girl.

"Boss."

Magic's voice cut through my misery.

"We're here."

My eyes opened, though I kept them squinted to relieve the pain of the throbbing in my temples. I looked up at my home and thought back to the day that I'd brought Tiffanie here.

*I love you so much, Damon.*

That was what she'd said then, that was what she always said. It was hard to remember each time she'd spoken those words to me, but what I did remember was the sincerity with which she'd said it every single time. Had I been tricked?

Now I had to go inside this house that I shared with the woman I loved. What I really wanted to do was go to a hotel, stay there a few days, and figure out my next moves. But I'd learned never to tip my hand, never to let the enemy know what you knew.

The enemy.

I shook my head. It was crazy that I was thinking about my wife this way. But if she had betrayed me . . .

"What you wanna do, boss?"

"You head on home and I'll call you in the morning." I gave him dap, then slipped out of the car. My steps were slow and my thoughts were heavy as I walked to the front door.

It was time to face my wife.

# 36

# Tiffanie

I hadn't expected to come home early or to come home alone, but as I snuggled in between the sheets and the duvet, I felt such peace. For hours I enjoyed the tranquility that came with rest, and just lay there drifting in and out of consciousness, dreaming about how I'd fought and won. Twice.

It was over. Whatever hold Trey had over me, whatever curse had attached itself to my DNA—it was broken.

Still, I prayed that Trey would be leaving DC soon; that was the extra assurance I needed, because the feelings I had weren't gone. I wasn't even going to lie to myself about that. The truth was, if I'd given in to what I felt, I'd be laid up in some bed with Trey at this moment. Because I wanted that feeling . . . again. I would never stop wanting that. I'd just have to find a way to get it with Damon.

Damon.

The thought of my husband made me roll over so that I was facing our bedroom door. After my encounter with Trey, I'd needed a couple of moments and a couple of drinks to get myself together. But once I'd done that and hooked up with Damon again, he was . . . different. Something had changed.

I was trying to convince myself that Damon's actions had nothing to do with me, had nothing to do with Trey. He couldn't have known, I knew that. But something was bothering him. Maybe it was just exhaustion—he'd worked hard for the success of this event, and for my husband, it wouldn't be over until the last person walked out of DC After Dark.

Still, he was more than distracted, he was distant. Like he wanted to put as much space between us as possible. Maybe that was why he'd sent me home, why so many hours had passed and he was still not home.

I raised my head again to glance at the clock; it was after three. Damon never stayed this late after an event. Usually he had his crew handle cleanup and closing. But I guessed tonight he wanted to take care of that himself.

Why?

I wondered . . .

The beep of the alarm system brought me out of those thoughts. The front door had been opened, and that meant, if Damon wasn't coming in through the garage, he was so tired he'd had Magic drive him home.

Even though I was as exhausted as my husband had to be, I pushed myself up, wanting him to know that I'd been waiting. I'd give him a massage, if he wanted. That would help him wind down, fall asleep, and get the rest he needed. Maybe tomorrow he wouldn't go in to his office. Maybe I would stay home, too, just to take care of him.

When he walked into the bedroom, he stopped and stared, as if seeing me was the last thing he expected.

"Hey," I said.

"I'm surprised you're awake."

His words felt cold, surprised me. But I told him, "I waited up for you."

"I thought you were tired."

"I was, but never too tired for you." I reached for him, but he didn't return the gesture, and when he left my hand hanging in the air, I finally dropped my arm.

Damon slipped out of his jacket, tossed it onto the chaise, then strolled into our bathroom. My eyes followed him the entire time he moved, and now, as I stared at the closed bathroom door, I pressed my hand against my chest, trying to catch my breath. Did my husband know? About me and Trey?

The answer came back the same as when I asked that question earlier—no! If he did, the way he was acting now, as curious as it was, wouldn't have been his reaction.

I rolled over the evening in my head, wondering what else could have happened, but I came up with nothing. So I sat. And waited. I stared at the bathroom door. When he came out, I was still in the same position and my eyes followed his movements again, even when he went into his closet. My question was waiting for him, but then, when he came out wearing nothing but his briefs, I got a bit distracted. "Uh," I began, raising my eyes to meet his, "are you upset about something?"

Standing there, all muscles and bulges, he said, "Why would you ask me that?"

I shrugged. "You seem different," I said, repeating the words he'd said about me earlier. "Like something happened."

I thought his stare was hard, until I heard his question. "Did something happen that you want to tell me about?"

I swallowed and again asked myself the question. But no! There was no way. "If you're upset with me, I wish you would just say what's wrong."

After a moment, he said, "It's not you." Then, another pause as if he was trying to figure out what to say next. "It's Trey."

I blinked, though I didn't breathe.

He let Trey's name hang in the air for way too long before he continued. "It's just . . . I thought . . ." He paused like he wanted me to say something.

That was the only reason why I asked, "What did he do?"

He looked away from me as he shook his head. "I'd wanted him to go into business with me."

I didn't mean to, but I sucked in air.

"But he doesn't want to; says he's going back to Atlanta. And I guess I'm a little disappointed by that."

For the first time since my husband came home, I smiled. This was what had my husband off-kilter tonight. But while I never wanted him to feel bad, his pain was my salvation; still, I wanted to be thoughtful and careful. "I know you want to do right by him, Damon, but I really think his leaving is for the best."

He looked right at me. "You do?"

I nodded. "I don't want him pulling you back into anything."

"He could never do that."

"He might try."

A couple of beats, then, "There're lots of things he might try, but trying to pull *me* into something wouldn't be one of them."

That sent me right back to wondering . . .

After a long moment, Damon turned his back and began walking toward the bedroom door.

"Where are you going?"

He paused and faced me. "I need to get a little bit of work done."

"Now? It's after three. Aren't you tired?"

He nodded, though he didn't have to do that. I could see the exhaustion all over him. Especially in his eyes—exhaustion and sadness. "I am," he finally said. "But there are a few things I have to work out."

"Damon . . ." I said, even as he moved away from me.

He stopped once again. "I know you're tired," he said. "With all that you've been doing. So you get some rest."

It was only because he crossed the bedroom, leaned over, and kissed my forehead that I accepted his explanation. And while I wanted more, while I wanted him to get between these sheets and hold me, I would be fine now. I could sleep knowing that he didn't know anything about me and Trey.

I slipped back down on the bed and he turned off the light on my nightstand. Then, in the darkness, I watched his form leave me alone in the room.

I may have been tired, but my eyes stayed wide open. The conversation had me on high alert. I should have been rejoicing . . . Trey was leaving DC and Damon hadn't found out!

But my stomach was churning, even as I gave thanks and praise to God. After a while, the only thing I could do was close my eyes. Yet, while my flesh rested, I knew that all was not well with my soul.

# 37

# Damon

Even though I was desperate to know the truth, it had taken me four days to pull this together. But my success had always come from patience and planning, and this was a two-part plan for me. First was my mission to secure the truth. And the results of part one would determine what would happen in the second phase.

But now that part one was in place and I was ready to roll, I was doing something that was foreign to me—I was hesitating. Did I really want to move forward with this? Because knowing for sure meant that I had to do something for sure. Knowing for sure meant that my life would never be the same.

Since Thursday, I'd been working hard to steady my emotions, even though I was drowning in the suspicion that my boy had slept with my wife. It was hard to look at Tiffanie, even harder to talk to her—and sleeping next to her? Impossible! But because I wasn't ready to show my cards, I'd had to fake not feeling well, and that was my answer to everything.

When she asked, "What's wrong, Damon?" my reply was "I'm not feeling well."

When she asked, "Why are you so quiet?" my reply was "I'm not feeling well."

And when she reached out and touched me in bed, my words were the same, accompanied with a move that took me to the edge of my side.

We wouldn't be able to live our lives this way much longer. I was bursting, ready to tell Tiffanie what I knew. The challenge was, I didn't know enough. And that's what this plan was about.

So why was I hesitating?

I guess I wasn't really ready to lose Tiffanie forever.

I stood at the window, staring out into the bleakness of the day and the gray sky that promised a coming storm. But finally, I turned and did what I'd always done—I made the decision. I was ready to make this move.

Hitting the intercom, I said, "Hillary, send her in."

I'd never met the woman who was about to enter my office and my life. I'd called Hillary first thing Friday morning and she'd done the interviewing and then the hiring after I'd given her the two requirements. The first was that I wanted a professional actor.

There was a single knock, then, "Damon?" The blond, blue-eyed woman peeked into my office and the first thing I noticed was that she was the color of paste.

That had been the second requirement. I wanted a white woman, making the bet that her voice would give what I was about to do some legitimacy.

"I'm Liz," she said, shaking my hand.

I didn't exchange any pleasantries; I didn't say how nice it was to meet her or ask if her day was going well. This was all about business and I wanted to get down to it.

"You read the script" were my first words to her.

"I did."

I motioned toward one of the chairs in front of my desk and then sat beside her. "You don't need to stick to those words," I began, as she unbuttoned the jacket to her suit, which was the same color as this day. She opened the document I'd sent on her tablet. "I just wanted to give you an idea of what to say, how to proceed, how to get . . ." I paused; I was talking too much. "You know what I'm looking for."

She nodded.

"You ready?"

Another nod.

The number to my office was always blocked, so all I had to do was turn the phone toward us and press the number that had been saved. My heart sped up, the way it did back in the day when a life-changing deal was about to go down. I guess this was the same.

The phone rang only twice before my wife answered her cell phone.

I nodded to Liz, then sat back down in the chair beside her.

She began, "May I speak to Tiffanie King, please?"

"This is Tiffanie speaking."

Liz gave a slight cough before she went into the script. "You don't know me, but I know you . . . very well." She paused. "I'm going to get right to the point. I know what you did."

"Who is this?" My wife sounded annoyed, like she didn't have time for anyone who was playing on the phone.

"I know about you and Trey."

The pause that followed made air catch in my throat. I had to stand to keep breathing because the truth was in her silence.

Still, I hoped. I hoped as I paced.

"Trey who?" my wife asked.

Liz sighed. "We both know who I'm talking about, but if you want to play games . . . Trey Taylor. I know what you did with Trey Taylor."

In the next pause, my heart dropped to my knees and I stopped moving. I stared at the phone, wondering for a moment if Tiffanie had hung up. But then I heard her voice, her question, "Why are you calling me? What kind of game are you playing?"

Liz chuckled all the way into her role. "I'm not playing any game," she said. "And I'm calling you because if you don't want your husband to find out what I know, then you'll do what I ask."

Another pause and my heart continued its free fall, going all the way to my ankles. "Who is this?" she asked again.

"My name's not important," Liz said, as if she made this kind of call all the time.

"It is if you expect to get anything from me."

The tremble of Tiffanie's voice was more evidence for me.

"So, you're saying you want me to give these pictures to your husband?"

The sucking in of air made my own heart stop.

"Pictures?" Tiffanie whispered.

"Yeah. And I'm sure Damon King will pay a lot for what I have. He wouldn't want *these* pictures to end up in one of the tabloid papers." Then Liz dug the knife in deeper, for both of us. "With all that your husband has going on, he won't want, and he can't afford, any kind of scandal." More guilt from my wife in the form of her pause. "So, like I said, money is what I want. Either I'll get it from you or from Mr. King. It doesn't matter to me."

"What? What kind of pictures are you talking about?"

"The pictures of you and Trey Taylor," Liz said, as if Tiffanie should know. "Doing . . . what would you call it?"

In our email exchange, I'd told the woman not to be specific in this part of the conversation because, of course, there were no pictures. I didn't want her to claim that there were pictures at Tiffanie's office or in a hotel lobby, since I didn't know any details, and I didn't know anything for sure . . . at least not until now.

"I really don't know what you're talking about." Her protest was much softer, made weaker by the tears in her voice.

I made a gesture for the actor to wrap it up. I had enough.

Liz said, "I'm not going to play this back-and-forth with you. Do you want these pictures or not? You can have them all for fifty thousand dollars."

I'd given her the blackmail amount. Something that my wife would feel that she could afford to pay without having to come to me.

Tiffanie said, "I'm not giving you any money."

Her words gave me a split second of hope. If Tiffanie wasn't willing to pay . . .

My wife said, "I need to see the pictures first."

My fingers curled into the tightest of fists, and if Liz hadn't been in my office, if Tiffanie hadn't been on the phone, I would have punched something—a wall, a window, anything. But I had to press my lips together so that I wouldn't shout out and call my wife a lying whore.

"All right. I'll call you back with a time and a place where we can meet." She leaned forward and disconnected the phone herself. As she leaned back and closed her tablet, she kept her eyes away from mine. But she couldn't look away forever, and when she glanced up, her gaze held such sadness.

I'd given Liz no information about my personal life, but she didn't need to be a genius to figure this out.

"Do you need me for anything else?" she asked, in a tone thick with pity.

I shook my head as I reached across the desk for an envelope with the rest of the cash I owed her. She took it without even glancing inside.

Standing, she said, "I'm . . ." She paused and held back her apology. "Thank you, Damon. If . . ." Then she turned and scurried out of the room.

I waited until I was alone before I stumbled to my desk and fell into the chair. I'd been in all kinds of fights with all kinds of weapons. Though I'd come out the victor in most, I didn't win them all. But there had never been a time when I felt more defeated.

Tiffanie had given herself away, not only by keeping the conversation going but when she asked for proof of the pictures . . .

I closed my eyes and massaged my temples, needing to get rid of all the mental pictures I now had of my wife and Trey.

Trey.

My boy.

My brother.

My fam.

My fam who was bangin' my wife!

Pushing myself back, I kinda walked, kinda stumbled to the rain-streaked window. The storm had come, bringing puddles that covered the streets where my brother and I used to roam.

*"To my man, and his bride, may she bring you all that you deserve."*

*"I just hope you'll be able to handle it . . . when she hurts you."*

*"I've never met one who wasn't in it for herself . . . I would even doubt your wife."*

Trey's words were on a fast-forward reel in my mind, striking me in my gut the same way they had when he'd spoken them. I didn't know what he'd meant then; I knew now.

This is why I'd never wanted to be attached, especially not to a woman. I'd never wanted to let anyone get close enough to hurt me. To hurt me just like this.

Tears tried to well up in my eyes, but I blinked them back. I wasn't no punk. I wasn't gonna cry. I'd let the sky do that for me. Maybe this was God crying, I didn't know. All I knew was that I now had business to handle. Phase two.

Trey had been sending me a message and I needed to let *my boy* know that his message had been received.

Turning back to my desk, I reached for the bottom drawer with one hand and with the other, I pressed a single number on my cell phone and put it on speaker. I checked my Glock, and when Magic picked up, I said, "I need your help. The old-school kinda help."

There wasn't a hint of hesitation. All Magic asked was, "Where? When?"

And I told him.

# 38

# Tiffanie

Tiffanie, we need to handle . . ." When I looked up, Sonia stopped walking and stopped talking. She stared at me for a moment, then took a few slow steps toward me. "*Chica*," she began, perching herself on my desk right next to where I sat. "*¿Que pasa?*"

Even if I'd wanted to tell her that nothing was wrong, that I was okay, the tears streaking my face and my trembling hands would be signs that I was lying. And not only that, I wanted to talk, I had to tell somebody what had just happened.

So I said, straight out, "I'm being blackmailed."

Sonia covered her mouth with her fist. "Oh my God! Oh my God!" she shrieked. But then my words must've started to make sense—or not—because she asked, "Wait. What? Blackmailed? By who? And for what? What could anyone have on you?"

Shaking my head, I said, "I can't answer the who." The next part was going to be easier for me to say than it was going to be to hear Sonia's disappointment. "I'm being blackmailed because of me and Trey."

"You and Trey?" Her face contorted in complete confusion.

"How can anyone blackmail"—her cadence slowed—"you . . . about . . . Trey?" It was a question that she didn't give me a chance to answer. "Oh my God, Tiffanie! You're sleeping with Trey?" If the look on her face had been a word, it would've been *Ewwww*. But I couldn't tell if her disgust was for me or Trey or the two of us together.

"No! I'm not sleeping with him." When Sonia tilted her head, I added, "I mean, not exactly. Not sex. Not really?"

I noticed the deep creases in her forehead as she walked to my door, closed it, I guess, to keep out the listening ears of any contractors, then stood with her arms folded. "Okay, you're gonna have to start explaining this one, because right now, *chica*, you sound like William Jefferson Clinton."

That would've been funny, except that it wasn't. I did sound like the former president.

"You'd better start talking," she demanded.

So I did. I told her everything, skipping, of course, the night before the wedding, because she knew that part. But I told her about Trey texting me on our honeymoon, and then meeting me here in my office. As she heard the story, all that happened that morning after she'd left me alone, she sank into the chair with her mouth open.

"Damn!" she said.

"But it was only that one time," I whined, needing Sonia to know that I wasn't a serial cheater.

"Damn!" Then she added, "Right here?"

I nodded. "On my desk."

Both of our glances dipped, taking in the desk, and Sonia pushed her chair back just a little.

Since I was telling her everything, I wanted her to know that

I hadn't taken that risk for nothing. "Sonia, I have never felt the way Trey made me feel."

She shook her head. "And so for a feeling you're willing to throw away your marriage?"

"No! I love Damon. And that's why I knew I had to stop Trey. Somehow. And I did." I finished the story, telling her about the last two incidents on Thursday and how I'd won them both. "I resisted, that's all that matters. Even though I wanted Trey with my body, I wanted Damon with my heart." I paused; telling that story had left me feeling spent. "But that feeling . . ."

She gave me one of those eyebrow-raised-girlfriend-please looks. "Just remember it's *that feeling* that has you in this predicament."

"I know," I moaned. "And she wants fifty thousand dollars for the pictures."

"You took pictures?" she shouted. Now the look on her face was one of those who-are-you-and-what-have-you-done-with-my-friend glares.

"No! I wouldn't take any pictures!" I hissed. "And keep your voice down."

"Then what is she talking about?"

"I don't know. She said she has pictures."

She let out a sigh and shook her head. "You are so green. Suppose she doesn't? Suppose she doesn't have a single picture and is just playin' you?"

"I thought of that," I said, with an attitude, even though I hadn't. "But the question remains, suppose she does?"

For a moment, Sonia didn't say anything, but I could tell she was studying me and the situation. "I don't know, *chica*. I have a bad feeling about this. Like she'll get this money from you and never stop. Or she'll get the money and the pictures will show up anyway."

"Oh, I'm gonna get the pictures. If I give her money, I'll get the pictures."

Now, her look said *yeah, right!* "But even if she gives you every picture that she allegedly has, that won't do anything. It's not like photos have negatives anymore. Everything is digital. With one hand she can be depositing your money, and with the other hand she could be pressing a button to post the photos on every social media site known."

Another thing that I hadn't thought about.

"Wait, was she black or white?"

I shrugged. "I dunno. How am I supposed to know that? She called on the phone, she didn't come to meet me."

"Oh, come on." Sonia bounced back in her chair. "You can tell what most people are even over the phone. Was she black or white?"

I squinted, trying to remember the voice. "She sounded white . . . I guess. But you never know. Why? What difference does that make?"

Sonia leaned forward; she glanced at the desk before she laid her arms on the edge. "'Cause I would've been suspicious of a black girl. We don't blackmail. We're too emotional, we're into instant gratification. So if we know information like this, we don't think about monetizing it. We go for the gusto and tell all that we know to everyone that we know. It's all about the gossip for us." Now Sonia stood and paced beside the chair. "But a white woman"—she shook her head—"white people are all about money. They have the patience for blackmailing." She spoke as if she were stating scientific facts.

"Well, while my life is falling apart, thank you for that lesson on the blackmailing skills of the races."

She stopped moving. "You might not appreciate it, but I'm telling you what I know. And that means that if a white girl called, it *could be* legitimate. I'm not saying that it is, but there's a better chance."

"Well, that doesn't make me feel better."

Sonia gave me a long look before she came around the side of the desk and perched herself next to me once again. "And what I'm about to tell you is not going to make you feel better either." She took my hand. "This blackmail . . . if it's real, it may never end." Another breath as she reached for my other hand. "You're going to have to tell Damon."

I snatched my hands away, opened my drawer, pulled out a bottle of aspirin, and handed it to her.

With the deepest of frowns, she asked, "What do you want me to do with this?"

I folded my arms before I said, "Count the number of pills, because I'm about to swallow them all, and then you'll be able to give everyone the cause of my death, right down to the number of pills they won't need to pump from my body."

She glared at me and I gave her a hard stare right back. "That's not even funny."

"And I'm not trying to be funny. Because for the first time . . ." I paused and swallowed so that I could speak through the lump in my throat, but my words only came out in a whisper. "For the first time, I completely understand what my mother did . . . and why she did it."

Sonia hunched down and looked at me. "It's not that serious."

"Yes, it is. Things haven't been good with me and Damon."

"What do you mean?"

"I don't know. He says that he hasn't been feeling well, but I think it's more than that." I stopped for a moment, remembering just how distant Damon remained. "He hasn't touched me, he hasn't kissed me, he hardly talks to me."

She frowned. "That doesn't sound like Damon."

"I know. And so, if he's acting like that now and were to find out about this . . ." I shook my head, not even wanting to imagine his pain. "I couldn't do this to him."

She nodded during her pause before she said, "Think about it this way. You're not doing anything to him, you're informing him so that he can help you." She held up her hand as if she anticipated me speaking, but I didn't have any words. "I think you should tell him everything, like you told me. How Trey targeted you from the moment he met you at the airport. Tell Damon that Trey came to your wedding just to do this to you, just to humiliate Damon. He'll believe you because, remember, it was Trey's idea to come."

I thought about what she'd said. "You really think this is just about Damon?"

She nodded. "I do. For whatever reason, he hates Damon and this is the way he proved it." After a moment of thought, she added, "You know what? He could be the one behind the call."

"What?"

She stood and began to do that pacing thing again; apparently that was how she did her best thinking. "Now that I think about it, suppose Trey put someone up to call you. Yeah, that makes sense. Suppose he's just trying to get money out of you." She stopped moving. "Oh my God! I think it's Trey."

"You think?"

"I do." Sitting back down, she said, "Maybe you should call him. Maybe he'll tell you that he did it or at least give himself away with something he says."

Even though I didn't want to speak to Trey, that was a good idea. Not that I had a plan for what I would do if he admitted he'd called, but at least I'd know something for sure. "I don't have his number, though."

"Dang." She blinked a couple of times. "Wait. He texted you. Give me your phone."

I did as she demanded.

"Do you remember the area code of the number he texted you from?"

I shook my head and shrugged at the same time. "I didn't lock him in. I wasn't trying to keep anything going with him. I told you—"

She interrupted me. "Would you just focus? Try to remember. Did he call from an Atlanta area code?"

With a nod, I said, "I think so, try 404."

It only took her a few seconds to search, only a few moments to scan through the texts she found and then only a single moment to read one of them and shake her head. "Here." She pushed the phone back to me. "There's his number. Call him. Put it on speaker."

I glanced down at the phone and the text that she'd found:

**I can't wait to see you, I can't wait to have you. I can't wait to screw the hell out of you.**

As happened every time I had some kind of encounter with Trey, I had to squeeze my legs together, and I kept my eyes down and away from Sonia's. I pressed the icon to dial the number.

"Don't tell him that you're on to him," Sonia whispered. "Just tell him that you got the call and see what he says."

I nodded and as the phone rang, my heart ached. Had all of this been just a way to get back at Damon? Had I been the most naïve pawn ever used in a game?

"Tiffanie."

I might have not known his number, but he seemed to know mine. That wasn't what had my attention, though. I zoomed in on the way he said my name. The way he drew that longing out of me, even while I was in the midst of this misery.

He said, "I didn't expect to hear from you, not with the way you treated me last week."

Sonia mouthed: *Just get to the point.*

I said, "I got a call . . . from a woman . . . she's blackmailing me."

"Really? I'm sorry to hear that."

"She said she has pictures of you and me."

"Wow."

The word was one of surprise, but not his tone.

He added, "I wonder if I can see those pictures." There was laughter in his voice.

My eyes narrowed. Trey was behind this! "So . . . you took pictures of us?"

"Now, Tiffanie." He slow-jammed my name again. "When would I have had time to do that? My eyes, my hands, my mouth were always focused only on you."

Trey wasn't standing right in front of me, but I still felt like I was in a battle. Not with his person but with the memories. It was probably only because Sonia was sitting there that I was able to keep my focus. "Trey, do you know about these pictures or not?"

He chuckled. "Look, this is your drama, don't bring it into my life."

Sonia mouthed: *Damon.*

My best friend wanted me to threaten my almost-lover with my husband. But I hated saying my husband's name to him. "She said that she's going to tell Damon."

"And . . . like I said"—he brought his cadence to half speed as if he thought if he slowed down, I might understand him better—"this is your personal problem. You're on your own."

"So, you don't care if Damon finds out?"

His laugh was filled with contempt. "I don't give a fuck about your husband. And really, Tiffanie, I don't give a fuck about you." His laugh continued, and when I heard the wickedness inside that sound, I finally got it. It was his laugh, even more than his despicable words.

He kept on laughing and my tears were already falling when I pressed End. Sonia rushed around the desk, leaned over, and held me in her arms.

"*Chica, lo siento.* I'm just so sorry."

I didn't allow myself too many sobs. This was the bed I'd made and if I didn't take control, I'd never be able to save my marriage.

Leaning away from me, Sonia said, "You know what you have to do, right?"

I nodded.

"Do you want me to go with you?"

That would've been perfect. But when Damon heard this news, when Damon reacted, when Damon blew up, I didn't want Sonia in the crossfire. "No."

"Are you sure? Do you think you can do it?"

"No." I shook my head. "I don't know how I can tell Damon, but I don't have a choice. Because you're right. Trey's behind the blackmailing and that means this is all a game to him. At any time, he could go to Damon and tell him." I inhaled. "It will be better coming from me."

With a tissue, Sonia wiped my tears away, then leaned over and kissed my cheek. "I'm praying for you, Tiffanie. I just have a feeling it will work out fine."

I nodded. "Give me just a minute to get myself together. And then I'll go."

"Okay. You're gonna go to his office?"

I shook my head. "I'm gonna go home. Wait for him at home. Tell him at home."

"That's best. I know it's scary."

"It is."

"I know he loves you."

"He did."

"He will continue to love you."

"I pray."

She pulled me up from the chair, hugged me, and when she turned away, I could have sworn there were tears in her eyes. Maybe the ones I'd had transferred to her some way. Because I wasn't going to cry. Not anymore. I was finally going to do what I hadn't done since I'd met Trey. I was going to be honest with my husband.

My hands trembled as I reached for my purse. My hands trembled as I checked for my keys. My hands trembled and trembled all the way home.

# 39

# Damon

I pressed the button for Bluetooth, dialed the number, and when he answered, I said, "What's up, son?"

Trey said, "Just you."

My hands squeezed the steering wheel. "Where you at? Ms. Irene's?" The mention of his grandmother's name made me pause, made me think, made me wonder.

"Nah, I'm just out and about. I rented a car to get around a little easier. So, I'm roaming the earth, looking to see what I can get into."

If I wasn't in this mental space, I might have chuckled, might have backed up and told Trey to change up his words since they were so similar to what the devil had said to God. But I didn't say anything. Because what he'd said was the truth.

He added, "I wasn't sure if I'd hear from you."

The muscle in my jaw twitched, but I did my best to lie with not only my words but with my tone, too. "What're you talking about? I told you I'd give you a call today."

"Yeah, you did."

"I said we'd get together and talk about how we would partner up. You remember, as brothers."

"Yeah, you said that."

"So, why're you surprised?"

In the silence that followed, I wondered what he knew, or what he even suspected. Did he realize that I'd seen him chasing my wife at the club? Had he seen the look in my eyes when he faced me? Did he know that I knew?

But he didn't answer my question. All he said was, "So what time do you wanna do this?"

I squeezed the steering wheel, then relaxed my hands. "What you got going on now? I was thinking we could meet down at one of my warehouses. The one right next to DC After Dark."

"That's cool. I wanted to check out that neighborhood some more. Didn't Tiff . . . I mean, Tiffanie, didn't your girl use to live down there?"

Tiffanie wasn't my girl, she was my wife. Maybe that was the problem. Maybe that was why this cat had disrespected me in this way. Maybe he didn't realize that this was far more than disrespect alone. Maybe he didn't realize that he'd played with my heart. "Yeah, *my wife* used to live down there before we got married." Then I remembered that Tiffanie was the one who had found the warehouses for me. How apropos for what was about to go down. "She tell you that?" I asked. "She tell you that she used to live down there?" Before he answered, I was filling in the answers for myself. Maybe they'd met down there, near her old apartment. Maybe that's where they'd hung out, had dinner, made love.

Even though I was driving down Connecticut Avenue, I closed my eyes for a moment, not even caring if I crashed this car. It was a sad realization for me that I was hurt like this. Hurt by my girl, hurt by my boy.

But then he said, "Nah, it wasn't Tiffanie who told me that; I can't remember how I knew, but it definitely wasn't your girl."

There it was again—*your girl.* More disrespect, and I made the move back to mad from sad.

I asked, "So can you hook up now?"

"Yeah, bruh. I'm not far from there."

Even though I was alone, I nodded. That move was for me. That nod was my signal that I was ready. "Okay, son. See you in ten."

"Bet."

I clicked off the Bluetooth, waited a second, then picked up the throwaway phone on the passenger's seat.

I made the call, and when Magic answered, said, "It's on."

All he said was, "Bet," and then the phone went dead.

✦

I'D BEEN HERE before, so I knew how to park legally (no tickets) blocks away from the warehouse, I knew what to wear (clothing that wouldn't bring any attention to me, along with rubber-soled shoes), I knew how to act (walking, not too fast, not too slow, no movements that made me stand out or that anyone would remember).

Navigating through the streets, I blended in with the end-of-lunch crowd, making sure to walk the route that Magic had laid out, a route that avoided the stores with outdoor cameras. About two blocks away, I dropped the now-crushed throwaway phone down a street drain, then continued to P Street. Right

outside the back door to the warehouse, my glance was quick—
to the left and to the right—before I slipped behind one of the
two heavy doors.

Like Magic had texted me, Trey was there, standing in the
center of the 25,000-square-foot space. The door creaked as it
closed and Trey turned, facing me with a grin. I didn't bother to
adjust the temperature of my stare. I kept it cold, I kept it real.
There was no need to tell any kinds of lies now. This was going
to be straight business.

My steps were silent as I approached, and as I got closer, the
ends of Trey's lips dipped a bit, his smile no longer so wide. I
wondered what it was that he noticed. He'd been in enough situations with me, was it my clothing? Or the fact that he couldn't
hear me approaching? That there was not any semblance of a
greeting on my face?

"What's up, bruh?" Not giving me a chance to respond, Trey
said, "This is some space here." He looked around at the brick
walls of the old building. "I can think of a lot of things we can
do with this, together." He faced me again. "Together . . . as
brothers. That's what you said, right?"

My stare didn't make him back up or back down. Not that I
expected he would. He just gave me that hard stare back.

I spoke my first words. "You fucking my wife?" I was never a
man who wavered, who changed my mind. So, there was no need
to spend any time, play any games.

For a moment, there was no smile on his face. But what was
so surprising to me was that he didn't seem pressed by my words.
Like he'd almost . . . expected me to ask him this question.

He shrugged. "So you know about that, huh? Who told
you? The blackmailer?"

Now I was the one who *was* pressed. Because that did shock me on so many levels—the most important one . . . if he knew about the blackmailer, he'd spoken to Tiffanie. Within the last few hours. That meant they were still hooking up. That meant more hurt. From both of them.

But I wasn't going to answer any of his questions. And I told him that by asking my question again.

"Not yet," he said, and I knew he was telling me the truth. Because if he were hittin' my wife, he would have definitely wanted me to know. His words gave me a moment of reprieve, and took a little bit of my hurt away. But he gave it all right back to me. "But, I know this"—he didn't pause, he didn't stutter—"I can have her any time I want."

I was ready to end this now, but I swallowed my rage for the greater good. There were still a few facts I needed to know. I needed information, but I stayed silent, because Trey would tell me more on his own than with his answers to any questions I could ask.

When I didn't say anything, he chuckled. "Don't you want to know what this is about?"

I kept my stare steady and my mouth closed.

Like I expected, Trey did just the opposite. With a shrug, he said, "You screwed me and I wanted to screw you." He chuckled and held up his hands. "Well, not screw you, but your girl."

"Yo, son. She's not my girl. She's my wife."

Now he laughed right in my face. "So that's all you have to say?"

"Just want to remind you of the difference. Just want you to understand why this is on a whole 'nother level."

He said, "Maybe it is, maybe it isn't, but I can tell you this.

If I'd gotten here a few weeks earlier, your girl would've never been your wife." He spat those last words at me. I shook my head; it was a signal. I was trying to help Trey out. Let him know that he needed to shut up. But Trey only knew one way; Trey only knew how to be Trey.

So he kept talking, "Your *girl* is so green, it was like plucking a new flower." He laughed again. "Was she a virgin or something when you hit her?"

My lips pressed together, my fingers curled into a fist. In that statement he revealed so much. Told me what and how it had gone down.

Trey's glance lowered to my hands, then he lifted his eyes to mine once again. "What? You wanna hit me?" He did a little bouncing move with his shoulders like he was giving me a dare. "You mad? You wanna fight?" Then he stopped moving, hardened his face and his words. "Well, now you know how I felt. Now you know how it was for me when you left me in that prison to rot!" His eyes glared and his nostrils flared. His breaths were rapid and shallow. And now *his* hands formed fists.

"Do you know what it was like in there? All that time?" he shouted. "You left me alone in there!" His voice kept rising. "No calls, no visits, no nothing!"

Over the last few days, as I'd tried to figure out the reason for Trey's betrayal, my thoughts kept returning to his time in prison and how he got there. I'd kept rolling it over, going over our conversations in my mind, but had pushed aside thoughts of this being his reason, because I had explained it all to him . . . how many times? I just couldn't believe this was something as simple as a grudge. That was the problem, though . . . Trey was simple.

"I was abandoned by the man who had always called me"—he paused long enough to shift his tone from anger to sarcasm—"*brother.*"

I wondered what would happen now if Trey learned the truth? About the money on his books or about the attorney who worked all seven of those years to get him out. Not that it mattered, because how could he take back the ultimate betrayal? How could he take back what he did to my wife? And the truth shouldn't have been what mattered. What should have mattered was that we *were* brothers, we *were* fam.

"So now you know how it feels to be tossed aside like trash by someone who was always supposed to have your back."

Any issues between us could have been worked out . . . except for this.

I said, "You know that's not how it was, right?"

"What?" he growled. "You talking about my grandmother? Because you took care of her?" He swatted the air as if to push his questions aside. "You were *supposed* to do that, bruh, 'cause she took care of you as much as she took care of me. If it wasn't for her, there would've been days when you wouldn't have had anything to eat and no place to sleep. So don't give me that bull about you had my back with my grandma."

His words about Ms. Irene were the truth. Which was why, no matter what went down in this warehouse, I was always going to take care of her.

"So," Trey began, "what happens now?" Then, with a smirk, he asked, "You want details?"

He had long ago entered the danger zone, and my only explanation was that the seven years he'd been away must've erased his memories. He'd forgotten that I was Damon King. It was that or he was counting on our connection. I wondered if he realized yet that our connection had been completely violated and our bond totally broken.

"No details needed, son. You answered the most important question I needed to know."

He smirked. "And what question was that?"

I only answered him inside my head: *Now I know you hit on Tiffanie, not the other way around.*

When I said nothing, he shrugged. "Whatever." Then he added, "So what do we do now? Where do we go from here?"

I kept my stance and my silence.

He said, "I'm thinking that now that everything is out in the open . . . I don't want her anymore. You can have her . . . back."

I growled.

"And maybe, one day, we can get back, too. 'Cause this loyalty thing is supposed to work both ways. Maybe that's a lesson that your father should have taught you."

I didn't even try to stop that muscle in my jaw from dancing.

"So we good?" It only took him two seconds to raise his fist to give me dap; but I moved faster. By the time his fist was chest level, my Glock was pointed at my target—his heart.

He blinked more than a few times, and his eyes got wide. He took a step back, but that was only reflex. If he'd had time to think, he would've been dumb enough to take a step toward me.

Then, with a smile and a little shake of his head, he said, "So what? You gonna shoot me now?"

I didn't say a word.

"Over a female?" he asked with incredulity.

I didn't move a muscle.

"I can't believe you gonna go out like this over some chick."

I pressed my lips together. Now I needed to calm my jumping jaw. I needed every part of me steady.

"She doesn't care anything about you."

I wasn't sure if that was another taunt or something he believed as fact. Either way, now I had to speak. He wasn't going to his grave thinking that. "You're wrong. She loves me."

He shook his head. "Then why was she so easy?" He paused. "You wanna know how easy she was?"

That was confirmation, on top of what I already knew. I raised my Glock just a fraction higher. And for as long as it takes for an eye to blink, Trey's eyes flooded with fear. But the problem was, his fear didn't stay. Maybe if he was afraid, maybe if he'd begged for his life, this wouldn't have been so easy for me.

"So what? You gonna kill me. Just 'cause I took your girl?"

I gave him a slow nod.

He released a roar in my face, laughter that didn't seem to stop, and I let him have those moments. When he finally got control, he held his arms all the way out, making a T with his body, making my mind focus on that for a moment. His voice brought me back to my purpose.

"Go ahead, shoot." He said it as if he didn't think I ever would. "If you want to choose a ho over a bro, do what you gotta do! 'Cause you know"—he brought his arms down and with one fist pounded his chest—"I fear no man!"

"Then you's a fool!"

And I pulled the trigger.

A single shot, that's all I needed.

I was that cat. I was that onetime gangsta.

It was quick, the way Trey's eyes showed shock in the instant that he stayed standing, and then he dropped, first to his knees, before toppling onto the floor.

My hands were still raised, my finger still on the trigger, and when he was completely motionless, laid out on the concrete, I lowered my gun. By the time I knelt over him, his eyes were closed. By the time I pressed my fingers against his neck, his breathing had stopped.

I didn't hear Magic approach, but I felt his presence when he stood over me. I lifted myself from the floor and gave him a nod. "Do what you do best, Magic. Make this disappear." He reached for my gun and I gave it to him, knowing he'd take care of that, too.

Then, without even glancing back at the man who, for more than thirty years, I'd considered my brother, I walked out of the warehouse. Now I had business to take care of at home.

# 40

# Tiffanie

had been on my knees, hunched over the edge of the sofa, for hours, or so it seemed. I was praying and praying, though my petition to God didn't have anything to do with me. This was my fault, so I expected no mercy. My prayers were for Damon instead. I prayed that God would lessen his pain, reduce it to almost nothing, and heal Damon's heart so that one day he wouldn't even remember this, maybe wouldn't even remember me.

The thought of that, the thought of no longer even being in Damon's memory, made my heart grieve, but this is what I wanted for the man that I loved so much. This is what I wanted because I'd taken so much from him.

Now I had to take steps forward, positive ones for Damon. The first step was to pack my bags; I'd done that as soon as I came home—went straight into our bedroom and, with my hands still trembling, gathered as much as I could. I might as well have been packing with my eyes closed, too, as I went to the dresser, flung drawers open, and tossed items into the suitcase. I only packed a few things; I'd need time and help to get all of my clothes. But I had enough so that I could leave tonight and not have to bother Damon with anything more than arranging a time to get the rest.

Once my bag was packed, I was tempted to do what I'd almost done the morning of my wedding, when I wanted to take the coward's way out and get on the first plane to anywhere. But that was my head. My heart told me that I had to complete this second step. I had to face Damon; I owed him that, and he deserved that.

There was no way I could sit around and wait, though. The silence alone would drive me to take that coward's way. So, instead of running, I knelt. And instead of worrying, I prayed.

"Dear God," I whispered over and over. I wasn't sure what else to say, so I just closed my eyes and reminisced. About the years I'd had with Damon. About how he'd loved me before I'd loved him. Of how his love was sincere and complete.

I thought of all he'd given me beyond his love and of what a gift he'd been to me. And I thought about what I'd done to curse the blessing that was my husband, and those thoughts of Damon made my mind drift to that night before and the morning of my wedding. And then to that dream I'd had of Damon. With his gun. Raised and centered on me.

My eyes popped open.

"Oh my God!"

I was still on my knees as the dream replayed, though, this time my eyes were wide open. I remembered running, screaming, certain that I was about to die.

"I have to get out of here!"

I couldn't stay and face Damon. I couldn't tell him what I'd done. The man I'd married was a good man, but he'd come from someplace dark. He'd never told me all that he'd done, but I had no doubt of what he could do. Yes, he'd changed, but had he changed in his core?

I jumped up. Reaching for my suitcase and purse, I paused and wondered if I should leave him some kind of note. No! I'd send a text or an email later, explaining everything. By then I'd at least know where I was going. But right now, I had to get out of this house.

With a breath of determination, I stepped forward, looked up, and froze. My heart went straight into heart-attack mode.

"Damon," I whispered.

How had he come into the house without my hearing him? It was like he'd snuck up on me. I didn't hear the garage open, the house door, his footsteps.

In my head, the dream played again.

All I could say was his name, as tears burned my eyes. Slowly, I set my roller bag aside and watched his glance shift from me to my suitcase.

I expected that when he brought his eyes back to me, his face would be scrunched in a frown. But there were no lines of confusion anywhere on him. It was as if he had no questions.

Did he know? Had the blackmailer contacted him? Had Trey?

"I . . ." I had to pause, because there was no way he could understand my words with the way my lips were quivering. "I . . . have . . . something . . . to tell you," I stated with a courage that I didn't really feel.

He shook his head, and I didn't know what he meant by that. I didn't have time to ask him, though, because suddenly he moved, in quick steps that shocked me, scared me, and brought him into my personal space before I had a chance to blink twice.

I wanted to back up, because there was no way to tell Damon

what I needed to say when he was standing so close. It was bad enough that I was going to break his heart; I didn't want to be near enough to hear it cracking. And I certainly didn't want to be so close that in his anger he would do to me what I'd seen in that dream.

But the backs of my legs were already pressed against the edge of the sofa and I had nowhere to go. I tried to find my voice to do what I had to do anyway. God would just have to take care of this.

Before I could speak, he said, "I have something to ask you."

His voice was softer than a whisper, but his tone? That was hard. And that was when I knew for sure. *He knew!* He had to know. And now he wanted me to tell him.

I was scared, but I felt ready. I formed my lips to speak.

He asked, "Do you love me?"

I blinked. And blinked. Blinked again.

"What?"

That wasn't the question he was supposed to ask. But he repeated it.

"Yes!" I didn't hesitate this time. "Yes. I love you so much. I have loved you for so long and for so many reasons. I love you in . . ."

He interrupted my words, pressing his lips against mine, and for a moment, I stood there with my hands at my side, with my eyes open.

What was going on?

There were so many questions going through my mind and so many answers that I wanted to give him. But right now all I could do was close my eyes and open my mouth and let my husband in.

It was long, it was sweet, it was the best kiss I'd ever had.

When Damon stepped back, I felt a bit dizzy. But once my legs steadied, my thoughts did, too, and I went back to wondering. What had just happened? Had that been a real kiss or was it a kiss good-bye? And there was still the question of all questions: Had Damon found out?

I took a deep breath. "There's something I have to tell you, something you need to know."

He shook his head. "I know all that I need to know."

I tilted my head, confused.

He said, "I asked you what was most important to me. And you said you loved me."

"I do, Damon." My lips went back to quivering. "I really do."

He shrugged. "That's all I need to know. And all you need to know is that my love for you is unconditional. As long . . . as you . . . love me, it's always unconditional."

I mashed my hand over my mouth to hold back my sobs. But it didn't work, not when Damon pulled me toward his chest. What was he trying to tell me? That he knew and he forgave me?

No, it couldn't be that. No man would forgive what I'd done. Especially not that easily. No man would forgive without someone paying a price.

A whole bunch of minutes passed before I stepped back, finally somewhat composed, ready to ask my husband all the questions that were swirling around in my head.

But, as my lips parted, he held me close and placed his finger over them. He nodded toward my suitcase. "That's a good idea. We need another vacation."

I didn't bother to remind him that we'd just returned from Dubai. And when he took my hand and led me upstairs to our bedroom, I didn't bother to tell him that the sun still hung high in the sky. None of that mattered.

All that mattered was that I loved Damon King, and though I couldn't explain what had happened, I knew this: Damon King loved me, too.

When my husband laid me on the bed, undressed me, connected with me, I was dizzy with love. I wasn't able to think about it then, but later, when I looked back, Damon still didn't make me feel the way that Trey had; Damon made me feel *better* than that. It was deeper than a feeling. Damon's heart reached into my head, into my soul; Damon's heart touched mine.

In those hours spent loving my husband and he loving me, I knew that no one would ever come between us again. Because I realized then that it was true. That what God truly brought together, no man, no woman, no affair, and definitely not the devil could take it apart. It could only be destroyed if you allowed it to be.

So from that day forward, I honored every vow I'd made before God. I was able to forsake all others. Forever. And ever.

# Epilogue

Mamacita, look at you!"

Sonia stood up at the little round table where she and Allen sat. Damon took my hand and spun me around. I did one of those Simone Biles spins, like I was a top gymnast, but when I stopped after just two revolutions, Damon had to hold my hand to steady me and keep me upright.

We all laughed as I smoothed down the gold bustier mini that Damon had paid a couple of thousand dollars to have an upcoming fashion designer make for me.

"You look fabulous anyway," Sonia shrieked over the music.

I hugged Allen first, then Sonia. "You act like you haven't seen me. I've been looking fabulous for weeks."

"Yeah, but you're always wearing one of those muumuus. Or a smock at the spa."

I waved my hand, scooting next to her in the booth. "I haven't worn a muumuu since DJ was born."

She held her hand over her heart. "And how is my godson?" She swooned every time she heard my son's name.

"Perfect." I posed my hand over my chest the same way, since I always swooned, too, whenever I looked at or heard or thought about the six-pound, two-ounce baby God felt that Damon and I were worthy to have.

"Bae, you want something to drink?" Damon shouted.

"Just a glass of wine," I said.

He nodded, leaned over, and kissed me and then he and Allen did one of those strut-strolls that men always do when they know women, especially their women, are watching.

I sighed and my eyes followed him until he disappeared through the crowd. "I love that man."

"I know." She shook her head. "Who would've thought after . . ."

I turned and held up my hand up right in front of her face. "Let's not go there."

She nodded as if she accepted my words, but now that she'd brought it up, I couldn't do anything but think about it. Especially since we were back here at DC After Dark, the place where I'd had my last encounter with Trey Taylor.

I'd hardly thought of that man, and it always surprised me whenever he come into my mind. It was as if God had blotted him from my memory and the earth at the same time.

Sonia must've heard my thoughts because she said, "It's hard to believe that Trey hasn't shown his face back here."

I shrugged. "I think you called it. This was all about Damon, this was all about hurting him. I still think he was behind the blackmail and I still think he told Damon something."

Sonia waved her finger in the air. "Trust me, your husband doesn't know anything, because he's still your husband and you should be glad about that."

"I am," I said, even though I didn't entirely agree with her. Though Damon would never talk about it, I was sure that he knew *something*. That had to be the reason why the blackmailer never called me again and it had to be the reason why he and Trey were no longer friends. Trey had disappeared, probably returning to the underbelly of life that he loved. I wouldn't have been surprised if he'd been picked up and convicted again, and if that was the case, I hoped this time he'd serve his twenty years. "The only thing that I will always regret is that whether Damon knows or not, Trey knows. And I let him use me to get to my husband."

"Really, *chica*?" She did one of those gangsta leans away from me. "You're still saying that? When someone comes after you like that, when you're at the top of someone's revenge agenda . . . how many times have I told you that it wasn't totally your fault?"

Sonia had said that a million times in the months that had passed. But, while it was good to hear, it was hard to believe. I just couldn't get myself to understand how I'd gotten so caught up with that man. Sitting here right now, I couldn't even remember what it was about Trey that had me coming so close to paying such a high price, and I wasn't sure if I just had a bad memory or that my life with Damon was so good it had wiped away all thoughts of Trey.

"Well, whatever," Sonia spoke through what I was thinking, "you're living a good life."

Now I leaned away from her. "Stop reading my mind."

"I'm just sayin', this could have gone a whole 'nother way if Damon had ever found out. Trey is one lucky dude."

"I don't know how lucky he is, but I know how blessed I am."

"Well, if he wants to stay lucky . . ."

"You know what?" I said. "Let's talk about something else. Like my wonderful son?"

Sonia pressed her hand against her chest once again. "Is Ms. Irene with him tonight?"

I nodded. "My grandmother is there with her, too, you know. Because we don't like leaving Ms. Irene alone with DJ. He can be too much for her."

"But she loves him. I see it every time I see her with him."

I nodded and once again was grateful that Ms. Irene was in our lives, and so happy that she'd moved in with us. She'd been heartbroken when Trey left DC without even calling her. But Damon told me that was Trey's MO. He'd done it before and this time, Damon wanted to step up even more than he'd done before.

"She's getting too old to leave alone," Damon had explained when he asked me what I thought about having her live with us.

I'd agreed right away, feeling in some way that being able to live with her and love her was a kind of penance. And by having her there, Damon Jr. made her wake up with a smile every day, even when her biological grandson had deserted her.

"Well, I haven't seen DJ in, like, forty-eight hours," Sonia said. "So that means . . ."

"You'll see him tomorrow. I'm bringing him to church."

"Nah, nah, nah."

We glanced up and Allen was shaking his head as he and Damon approached our table, each carrying two drinks.

Allen said, "We're gonna break this up."

"What?" Sonia and I said together.

"No talking shop." He sat down next to Sonia and kissed her cheek. "That's what you were talking about the whole time we were gone, right?" He laughed, looking from Sonia to me, and then back to his wife.

"¡Absolutamente!" With that, she gave her husband a kiss. A real kiss, one of those tongue-on-tongue kisses as if no one else was around.

"Ah, son, get a room." Damon chuckled and took my hand. "Well, since they're gonna make out, let's get our dance on."

As if on cue, the salsa beat filled the room. We were still on the edge of the dance floor, shimmying our shoulders and shuffling our feet, when Drake began to sing, and we joined him: *I thank God you came / How many more days could I wait? . . . / I think I'd lie for you / I think I'd die for you . . .*

Damon put his hands on my hips and pulled me close. As I swayed to the beat, my husband's lips grazed my ear and I sighed.

He whisper-sang in my ear. "I'd make a deal for you, I'm sure I'd kill for you . . ."

Laughing, I leaned back. "Has it been so long since you've heard the song that you've forgotten the words?"

"What?" He frowned. "Those ain't the words?"

"No." The music changed to a slow jam and we slowed our roll. I leaned in against my husband. "And I like Drake's words better."

"Okay."

"'Cause I don't want you killing anyone for me."

He sighed. "Okay. I won't."

I laughed at his feigned reluctance. "Mr. King, do you know how much I love you?"

He nodded. "I do. And do you . . ."

I kissed my husband before he finished. Because if there was one thing I was sure of, it was that he loved me. He didn't have to tell me. He always showed me. In ways known and unknown.

# LUST

## Victoria Christopher Murray

# For Discussion

1. What are the various ways that lust drives a wedge between people in *Lust*? Do you think it's the most dangerous of the seven deadly sins?

2. Tiffanie is so scared of turning out like her mother. Do you think lust is stronger in some people than in others? Do you think it runs in families as Tiffanie fears?

3. Respect is very important to Damon. Why do you think that is? Do you agree that Trey should show him and Tiffanie more respect when they're first reunited? What does Damon's emphasis on respect tell you about his character?

4. History and loyalty are also very important to Damon. Why do you think that is? Do you agree with him that you should always try to help those you've known for a long time?

5. Trey's intent to use Tiffanie as a pawn makes him seem like the actual devil. Do you agree with that characterization? Why do you think Trey seduces Tiffanie? Is this temptation really from Satan?

6. What does Tiffanie's orgasm represent to her? Why does she risk so much for "that feeling"? Do you think she even-

tually finds sexual satisfaction with Damon? Are there connections in life that are more important than a sexual one?

7. How does Sonia's marriage align with what Tiffanie wants for herself? These two women have been through so much together. Why do you think Tiffanie doesn't always listen to Sonia's wisdom, even though it's offered with love?

8. There are three people in the older generation that are important in the book: Reverend Cooper, Tiffanie's grandmother, and Ms. Irene. How do they guide Tiffanie, Damon, and Trey and influence the younger generation's decision-making?

9. Trey ends his toast, "I wish you two all the happiness that you deserve." Why is this wish a double-edged sword? Have you ever made a statement to someone that seemed kind but implied your true feelings?

10. Tiffanie prays for the strength to resist the devil. Has there ever been a time in your life when you've called on God to help you resist temptation, whether in the form of lustful thoughts or other seven deadly sins?

11. The shifting urban landscape of Washington, DC, plays a major part in Damon's business and in *Lust.* How have you seen your own city or town change over time as new developments come in and old businesses leave?

12. How did you react to Damon's attempt to get the truth? Would you have done the same or confronted Tiffanie directly? Do you think what he did was right?

# A Discussion with
# Victoria Christopher Murray

**You've written more than twenty books. Do you learn new things every time you write a new book? How is each book a distinct experience for you?**

This is a really good question because I do learn something every single time I write. You would think that with all of these books if I don't know everything, I know a lot. But each time, my agent, Liza Dawson, and my editor, Lauren Spiegel, challenge me with questions I never thought about. I continuously learn to layer my story, to have multiple issues going on with the characters at the same time. The learning process is what I love best about writing.

**What made the DC area the perfect place to set *Lust*? Why did you choose Dubai for Tiffanie and Damon's honeymoon? Have you been to Dubai?**

I chose DC because I'm living there now and this is only my second book to take place there. So, I knew that I could "flavor" the book with the music of the District of Columbia. I enjoyed that part. As far as choosing Dubai, I had to find a place where someone like Damon would have taken Tiffanie on their honeymoon. He was a rich young man, so he wouldn't have taken a domestic trip, and there's no place more exotic than Dubai. I did think about Hawaii, but with Dubai, I felt that I could take the readers on a trip to someplace they'd never been. I haven't been to Dubai, but I'm planning a trip in the next two years.

**Where did the idea for *Lust* come from originally? What drew you to the challenges of fidelity as a theme for the characters?**

Actually, the idea for this series came from another author, Vickie Stringer, who told me that I needed to write the seven deadly sins. She told me she thought this was a topic that I could grapple with and turn into an interesting story. That was back in 2011, and though I did try to write it, the book never moved from being half finished. Then, this year, my agent said this was the time. And I'm glad she pushed me.

**You write in both Damon's and Tiffanie's voices. Which was harder to get right? What were the rewards of switching between the POVs of your two main characters? What were the challenges?**

It was definitely more difficult to write in Damon's voice. Not because it was a male voice—I've written in male voices before. The challenge was Damon's character. He was from the streets and I can't even lie—the only thing I've ever done is cross a street. So, I had to find a way to find his voice. ReShonda Tate Billingsley suggested that I watch a couple of TV shows. That helped a bit. And then speaking with male friends helped as well.

**The book ends very happily and several years after the conclusion of the action. Why did you choose to end the book on such a happy note after having put Tiffanie and Damon through such struggles to get to the ending?**

Well, that's interesting. I'm not sure that the book ends all that happily, especially since I'm not known for happy endings. And, I'm not sure how much time has passed in the epilogue, but if I had to guess, it's only about a year and a half or two. But, I ended the book the way I did to wrap up the story. I'm hoping that there are no holes for readers so that I won't hear screams for a sequel . . .

**Who are some ladies in your life who serve the purpose that Ms. Irene and Gram do in the book? Do you have older women in your life who have guided you?**

Well . . . at my age, I'm the older woman. LOL. But of course, I have my mom and my mother-in-law is amazing, too. My pastor, Beverly "BAM" Crawford has been a wonderful example for me as well.

**What's your favorite passage from the Bible? What was the most influential to you in writing this book, if they're not the same passage?**

My favorite scripture is Jeremiah 29:11 and interestingly enough, I don't think I used it in this story, though I've used it often before. As far as scriptures for this book, I can't say that there was one that influenced me because though people believe this, the seven deadly sins are not in the Bible. I think many will be surprised to hear that. So, there wasn't a scripture as much as there were some of the tenets of the Christian faith for me. Like, how when God really brings a couple together, nothing can tear them apart. Those two people are the ones who decide to break apart. Also, how God does give us a way to escape temptation. It's difficult, but we can do it. So I relied more on what I know as a Christian rather than specific scriptures in this book.

**Do you identify more closely with Tiffanie or her best friend, Sonia?**

Hmmm . . . probably her best friend, Sonia. For many of my friends, I serve as the one who gives advice. And I have my friend's backs—don't come for them . . . I'll always protect them if I can.

**Who would make up your dream cast for the book? Alternatively, who did you have in mind as inspiration for Damon and Trey?**

This is always such a difficult question because I use pictures of every day people from magazines when I'm writing. So, I have no idea who would be good for these roles.

**You're a prolific author across both adult and YA genres. What are you working on next?**

I'm working on three things right now: another YA book—I haven't written one in a while, but it will be based on my second novel, *Joy*; then, I'm working on the second deadly sin, envy, which will feature Sonia and her husband, Allen; and finally, I'm working on a book with ReShonda Tate Billingsley, *If Only for One Night*. So, I'm spending a lot of time writing right now. And that always makes me happy!

# Enhance Your Book Club

1. Play the songs from Tiffanie and Damon's wedding, "The Most Beautiful Girl in the World" and "Adore." Why do you think Murray chose these songs for this couple?

2. Read another Victoria Christopher Murray book and compare it to *Lust*. Her most recent titles include *Stand Your Ground* and *Forever an Ex*. Or, create a joint book club with young people who have read one of Victoria Christopher Murray's YA books.

3. Schedule a book club for the same weekend that you attend church and/or a club, two of the major settings in *Lust*. Discuss the different aspects of each experience and how they relate to the book.